Praise for Molly O'Keefe

"If there is one contemporary romance novel you must read in 2013, this is it . . . this book, *this book* . . . I could go on and on . . . but I will just end with this: not only was the plot beautiful but the writing was as well."
—*Love's a State of Mind*

"One of my favorite things about [O'Keefe's] books is the way they refuse to shy away from messy, complicated characters and relationships. *Wild Child* is no different in that regard. . . . It is a testament to O'Keefe's skill as a writer and a storyteller that she imbues Jackson and Monica's stories (as a fledgling couple and as individuals) with a tremendous amount of emotional depth and sensitivity. . . . O'Keefe can bring characters . . . into vivid and compelling life as they stumble, sometimes joyously, often painfully, always passionately, toward love and mutual happiness."
—*Dear Author*

"I fell in love with this book from the very beginning. . . . It has the right amount of romance. . . . And the sex scenes were hot, too."
—*Night Owl Reviews,* 4 stars

"As I have come to expect from Molly O'Keefe, *Wild Child* is a deliciously steamy romance that has plenty of substance. . . . Another fabulous book by a very gifted author that I highly recommend to anyone who enjoys contemporary romances."
—*Book Reviews and More by Kathy*

"Molly O'Keefe is one of my favorite writers. You can count on her to create characters that will test you and take your emotions for a spin, one moment loving them the next wanting to give them a good shake. Well, she didn't let me down with this story! . . . The writing is spectacular and meaningful, the story has depth and the characters are *extremely* interesting and true to their designed nature. I make no bones about O'Keefe being one of my favorite writers and, even though I was prepared for a good book, I was blown away by this one."

—*The Book Nympho*

"Super hot scenes, funny moments and some of the most romantic gestures I have ever read. . . . Happy reading!"

—*The Reading Café*

"It's no secret that Molly O'Keefe's novels are my favorites in the very crowded contemporary romance genre. Her books . . . are brilliantly subversive. All of the novels I've read by this author riff on romance archetypes and conventions in a deliciously satisfying manner. . . . When it comes down to it, if you're looking for an authentically complex romance narrative . . . read *Wild Child*."

—*Clear Eyes Full Shelves*

Crooked Creek Novels

Crazy Thing Called Love

"There is no stopping the roller coaster of emotion, sexual tension and belly laughs. O'Keefe excels in creating flawed characters who readers will root for on every page. Despite very serious subjects and tear-worthy emotion, the tone of the novel is a perfect balance of fun and heart."
—*RT Book Reviews,* 4½ stars

"O'Keefe's newest romance hits the high notes with a storyline that tugs on the heartstrings, maintains a sizzling degree of sexual tension, and plays on realistic, authentic conflicts that keep the audience emotionally invested from start to finish. Gripping storytelling and convincing character-building allow the story to unfold in the present and in the past, offering windows into the psyches of a damaged hero and his restyled first love. An intense, heartwarming winner."
—*Kirkus Reviews*

"*Crazy Thing Called Love* has become my all-time favorite contemporary romance! . . . Don't miss out on O'Keefe's Crooked Creek series! These are the books you will still be talking about in twenty years!"
—*Joyfully Reviewed*

"There is nothing lacking in Molly O'Keefe's *Crazy Thing Called Love.* I am glad to say that it has every possible thing a woman could want in a good romance story. The Crooked Creek series is something that you will definitely want to get your hands on."
—*Guilty Pleasures Book Reviews*

"Wonderful story . . . unlike anything I have read before. . . . Highly addictive."
—*Single Titles*

"This was an absolute joy to read. . . . Definitely a book worth picking up."
—*Cocktails and Books*

"O'Keefe keeps the momentum of the present story going at a breathtaking pace with well placed visits back to the past, providing insight into these characters."
—*Fresh Fiction*

Can't Buy Me Love

"Readers should clear their schedules before they pick up O'Keefe's latest—a fast-paced, funny and touching book that is 'unputdownable.' Her story is a roller-coaster ride of tragedy and comedy that is matched in power by believable and sympathetic characters who leap off the pages. Best of all, this is just the beginning of a new series."
—*RT Book Reviews*

"From the beginning we see Tara's stainless steel loyalty and her capacity for caring, as well as Luc's overweening sense of responsibility and punishing self-discipline. . . . Watching them fall for each other is excruciatingly enjoyable. . . . *Can't Buy Me Love* is the rare kind of book that both challenges the genre's limits and reaffirms its most fundamental appeal."
—*Dear Author*

Can't Hurry Love

"Using humor and heartrending emotion, O'Keefe writes characters who leap off the page. Their flaws and foibles make for an emotional story filled with tension, redemption and laughter. While this novel is not a direct continuation of the first in the series, it makes the reading richer and more interesting to devour the books in order. Readers should keep their eyes peeled for the third book and make room on their keeper shelves for this sparkling fresh series."
—*RT Book Reviews*

"Have you ever read a book that seeped into your soul while you read it, leaving you feeling both destroyed and elated when you finished? *Can't Hurry Love* was that book for me."
—*Reader, I Created Him*

"*Can't Hurry Love* is special. It's that book that ten years from now you will still be recommending to everyone because it is undeniably great!"
—*Joyfully Reviewed*

"An emotion-packed read, *Can't Hurry Love* . . . is a witty, passionate contemporary romance that will capture your interest from the very beginning."
—*Romance Junkies*

Between the Sheets

Between the Sheets

MOLLY O'KEEFE

BANTAM BOOKS • NEW YORK

A Bantam Books Mass Market Original

Copyright © 2014 by Molly Fader
Excerpt from *Indecent Proposal* by Molly O'Keefe copyright © 2014 by Molly Fader

Published in the United States by Bantam Books, an imprint of Random House, a division of Random House LLC, a Penguin Random House Company, New York.

BANTAM BOOKS and the HOUSE colophon are registered trademarks of Random House LLC.

This book contains an excerpt from the forthcoming book *Indecent Proposal* by Molly O'Keefe. This excerpt has been set for this edition only and may not reflect the final content of the forthcoming edition.

ISBN 978-0-345-54903-7
eBook ISBN 978-0-345-54904-4

Cover design: Lynn Andreozzi
Cover photograph: Claudio Marinesco

Printed in the United States of America

www.bantamdell.com

9 8 7 6 5 4 3 2 1

Bantam Books mass market edition: August 2014

To Geoff and Regan Koski,
the laid-back activists changing the world
one craft beer festival at a time.
Your partnership and outlook are an inspiration.
Thank you for answering all my questions
about politics and Atlanta (any errors
are my own) and for being such a big part
of so many of our favorite memories.

Between the Sheets

Chapter 1

Shelby Monroe was not having a very good morning.

Last night, her new neighbor—a motorcycle enthusiast apparently with insomnia and a hearing problem—didn't stop revving his engine until nearly dawn. Then Mom put the coffeepot on the stove thinking it was the kettle and it shattered when it got too hot.

So here she was for her first day of classes after the Christmas break at Bishop Elementary, frazzled and without coffee.

Which was no way to deal with Colleen.

"Welcome back!" Colleen, the school secretary, stood up from behind her desk and for a moment seemed as if, in the three-week break, she'd forgotten that Shelby wasn't a hugger.

Thank God it came back to her at the last moment and instead of throwing her arms around Shelby like they were old friends, she turned to the bottom drawer of her filing cabinet and yanked it open. Shelby dropped her phone and purse in it. There was no office for the part-time staff, so she made do with Colleen's bottom drawer. She shrugged out of her winter jacket and hung it on the coat hook with her scarf, then tucked her gloves in her coat sleeves.

"How are you doing?" Colleen asked.

"First day back. It's always a good day."

"You must be the only teacher in the world who thinks that."

Shelby laughed. That was probably true. Her first days back in the school after winter break were her favorite of the whole year. All the hard work of getting to know the kids, understanding them, and getting their attention and respect was done. And now they were recharged. The next two months would undoubtedly be her most productive with the kids, before spring fever hit.

She just needed to shake off this bad morning she'd had.

"Coffee's fresh."

"You're a saint." She grabbed a mug from the cupboard above the coffee area and waited for the machine to belch and steam before she poured herself a cup. Colleen went nuts if you robbed the pot, and no one wanted to get on Colleen's bad side.

In her years as a part-time employee for the school district, Shelby had come to know one thing for certain: principals did not run schools; the secretaries did. And Colleen's desk was like the bridge of a giant spaceship. A phone system with a gazillion lights and buttons. Color-coded Post-its. The sign-in book, which she guarded like the Holy Grail. The first-aid kit, the small fridge with ice packs. Printer, computer, jars with pens. One drawer had hard candy, the other a box of Triscuits. There was a heat lamp at her feet. A fan at her back. Two different sweaters over her chair and a small hot plate for her coffee cup.

Colleen could survive the zombie apocalypse at her desk.

"How is your mom doing?" Colleen asked.

"Fine," Shelby said, because she had to say something and that was the sort of answer people expected. Colleen didn't want to hear how her mom had spent the night pacing the hallway looking for her mother's old cookbooks.

"It's nice to see her at church again."

Why was everyone so scared of silence? Shelby wondered, contemplating the drip of the coffee machine.

Shelby loved silence. And everyone from the woman behind the cash register at the grocery store to Colleen wanted to force her into conversation because her silence made them uncomfortable.

"Shelby?"

"I'm sorry, what did you say?" She poured coffee into one of the spare mugs; this one had a sleeping cat on it. There were a thousand cat mugs on that shelf.

"I said it's real nice to see you both in church again. It's been a long time."

"Well, it's a comfort," she lied, glancing at the big clock over the door. She had five minutes before the bell. "I'm starting in Mrs. Jordal's class?"

Colleen swiveled in her chair to face Shelby. "There's a new student in there," she said. "He's a handful."

Shelby smiled. Perhaps she was in the minority, or maybe it was only because she was part-time and in the classes she taught out in the Art Barn in the summer and after school the kids wanted to be there, but she would take a kid who was a handful every day of the week.

The quiet, studious boys and the girls who were so eager to please all too clearly reminded her of herself and she wanted to scream at them to get a backbone, to stand up for themselves. To take a lesson from the kids who caused problems, whom no one could overlook. Because waiting to be seen, to be noticed, only led to midlife crises and psychotic breaks that tore apart your world.

At least that was her experience.

But that was probably a little heavy for an elementary school art class.

"We've been back for a week and he's been in the office almost every day," Colleen said, lifting her own mug—no cats to be seen—from the hot plate. "Fighting, mouthy, stealing from classmates." She turned her giant chair back around to face the door and the computer, her kingdom. "And his father is a piece of work, clearly the apple doesn't fall far from that particular tree. Mark my words: that boy is nothing but trouble."

Mrs. Jordal taught fifth grade and had for about a hundred years. There wasn't a problem or a type of kid she hadn't seen a dozen times before. And Shelby really liked the fact that her class, no matter how many handful kids she had, was always calm. The kids were respectful.

It was tough at the beginning of every new year because something happened to kids between fourth and fifth grade. Some hormonal surge that made them all short-circuit. But by Thanksgiving, Mrs. Jordal had those kids in line.

Christmas break, however, caused some regression.

Shelby took a deep breath, girding her loins, before she walked in.

"Hello, class," she said as she entered the room. All the kids looked up from the free reading they'd been doing and some of them answered her. Some waved. Scott and John whispered behind their hands. One boy in the back with shaggy red hair blinked, owly and worried-seeming.

Oh no, his expression said, before he schooled it into a predictable but ill-fitting sneer, *not another new thing.*

His whole vibe screamed "new kid."

Mrs. Jordal stood from behind her desk and walked

over, limped actually. She needed hip replacement surgery but was being stubborn about it. "Hello, Ms. Monroe," she said. "Welcome back."

"Thank you, Mrs. Jordal. Anything exciting in the fifth grade in the new year?"

"We have a new student."

"That's what I heard."

"Casey?"

The redhead waved with one flip of his hand. Funny, that hormonal surge inspired all of the kids to walk that line between being respectful and being sent to the principal's office to varying degrees. Even the good kids started fifth grade with a little attitude.

This kid was really trying hard to seem like a badass.

"Nice to meet you, Casey." Shelby set down her coffee and bag beside Mrs. Jordal's desk, in front of the Regions of America bulletin board. "I thought, in honor of our new student . . ." Every eye in the classroom went to Casey and he shrank down in his seat, glowering.

"We're going to start on a new project today and it's going to last for the next three weeks. It's called Things About Me." From her bag she took the stapled packets of paper and began to hand them out. "You get three images, but no words, to convey what you know to be true about yourself."

"About anything?" Jessica Adams asked. She honestly looked terrified at the idea. Jessica was a girl who needed to be told what to draw. Most of the kids did, but that was the fun part of fifth grade—they were just beginning to realize they had ideas of their own. Largely inappropriate, but the ideas were tied more to identity than ever before.

"Anything."

"Like I know this is lame?" Scott Maxwell said, and John James high-fived him.

"If you think that's true, sure." She gave Scott the

packet of papers and then stood next to him for a moment, her hand on his shoulder. Scott had been in her summer art camp for three years in a row and was doing an after-school class on Thursdays, working in clay. He was a good kid and she liked him as much as she imagined he liked her. The poor kid was just short-circuiting. "But you have to figure out how to draw it. How to convey it without using any words."

A couple of the kids started to groan, realizing how hard this was going to be.

She took out two examples and taped them to the blackboard with masking tape.

"What do you think these mean?" she asked.

One was a picture she'd drawn in the manner of Van Gogh's *Starry Night*. She stood in a field surrounded by beautiful swirls and explosions of color and texture. The other was a picture of her Art Barn, filled with kids who were part human, part foxes, all mischief.

"Is that me?" Scott asked, pointing to one of the kids in her picture.

She squinted at the picture. "You know, I do see a resemblance."

"Are you saying we're all animals?"

"Not exactly."

"She's saying you're all foxes," Casey said.

She smiled at Casey, who beamed at her attention before he remembered he had a sneer he was trying to make stick.

I'm on to you, she thought, and felt that surge of affection she always felt when she saw past the too big veneer of the "problem kids."

"Why do you think I picked foxes?"

"Why do *you* think you picked foxes?"

Shelby blinked, not at his tone, but the way he'd rephrased the question. She wondered if Casey with the shaggy red hair and freckles, slouching in his chair as if at the advanced age of eleven he'd seen it all, had spent some time with a psychiatrist.

"Because you're all sly and mischievous and looking for trouble," she answered. "But you're still cute."

"What about the other one?" Jessica asked.

The room was silent and Shelby turned to look at the picture again. The figure in the middle was clearly her, even though she'd drawn herself from the back. The blue tee shirt she wore said Art Barn across the shoulders, and any kid who took a class out at the barn got the exact same shirt.

"Art is everywhere?" Jessica asked, giving it her best shot.

"You need to get your eyes checked?" Scott said.

She bent forward, to look him in the eye. "Do we need to have a conversation in the hallway?" she whispered, and he blanched, shaking his head.

"Beauty is everywhere," she said. Though she'd drawn that picture perhaps more in hope than as proof of anything.

"So, you've got three pages there. Take your time and think of three images that convey something to me about who you are. Or what you feel. Or know. Or believe."

A dozen desktops were lifted and pencil boxes were pulled out. "Don't just draw the very first thing that comes to mind. Think about how you're going to surprise me. Or make me work to figure it out. For instance," she turned and found Jeremy in the corner. Sweet Jeremy who grinned up at her, blinking through his thick glasses. "Jeremy, perhaps you could consider not drawing dinosaurs."

"But . . . I love dinosaurs."

"I know that. We've all known that. Since you were in kindergarten there has not been a child on the planet who has loved dinosaurs more than you. Try to think of something else."

"What if I can't?"

"Then at least draw me a very good dinosaur."

He beamed at her. Just beamed, and all the black soot that lingered on her heart from her late night and frazzled morning was gone.

Children and art were simply the best medicine. The very best.

Heads were bent over work and the room was silent but for the scratch of pencil and crayon over paper. She walked up and down the aisles until she got to the far corner where Casey, who was bent so far over his desk she couldn't see his paper, sketched furiously. His pencil was a short, bitten-off thing, probably salvaged from the broken pencil bin Mrs. Jordal had for kids who kept forgetting pencils.

"Do you want some colored pencils?" she asked. "Or crayons? I have some."

"I'm fine," he said without looking up, without taking a break. Without giving her a chance to see what he was working on.

A couple more kids raised their hands to ask questions, and she had to finally move Scott to the far side of the room because he wouldn't stop talking to his friend John. Casey didn't look up. She set a sharp pencil down on the edge of his desk but he ignored it.

"You have five minutes left," she said at almost the exact moment Mrs. Jordal came back in. Shelby took her own pictures down and tucked them back in the bag. In the kindergarten class after this they were going to start a finding-shapes-in-nature exercise, which was basically just an excuse to get them outside and moving around.

"Time's up," she said. "Hand in your pages. I'll see you next Wednesday and we'll keep working on this."

Students flooded up from their desks, a giant wave of kids who smelled like graphite and wax crayon. Casey didn't meet her eyes and handed her his page facedown. "It's nice to meet you, Casey," she said, and he shook his hair out of his eyes in that weird, totally practiced and ineffective Justin Bieber way.

"Yeah," he said and shuffled back to his desk. He was tall, really tall. The tallest kid in the class by at least a few inches. She hadn't noticed that when he was slouching at his desk.

She gathered up the pages and grabbed her bag and empty cat coffee cup and went back to the office for another cup of coffee before heading to kindergarten.

The new kid forgotten for the moment.

Chapter 2

Shelby stared up at the ceiling of her bedroom and contemplated the many circles of hell she called home. Her mother's Alzheimer's, that was a circle. What happened to her on national television the past summer, the details of her sad sex life broadcast to the world, that was a doozy of a circle. Her childhood—another one.

But this! Listening to her jerk new neighbor rev motorcycle engines at midnight, for the third straight night in a row—this was a whole new world of torture.

The engine cut off into silence and she held her breath, waiting for the next grinding, squealing roar to begin, but the silence stretched on. Nice . . . thick . . . deep silence.

Her eyelids fluttered shut.

Vroooaaaaam, vrooooaaaaam, vrraaaa vrraaaa vraaaaooooom.

"Shelby!" Her bedroom door swung open and there was her mother in her long pink-and-white nightgown, her gray hair falling down around the marching-into-battle set of her shoulders. But her hands, like tiny nervous white birds, picked at the buttons at the front of her gown.

"Who is doing that?" Evie asked. "Who is cutting down all the trees?"

That's it, jackass. You're freaking out my mom.

Shelby kicked off her sheets and grabbed her robe from where it hung over the rocking chair that no one ever rocked in. "He's not cutting down trees, Mom." She tied the sash of the robe nice and tight over her tee shirt and sweatpants. If she could find herself a breast-plate and helmet she'd put that on, too. She shoved her feet into her thick winter slippers. "It's our neighbor."

"Phil is cutting down the trees?"

Oh, Mom.

"Tell your father to go tell Phil to stop it."

"It's not Phil. Phil died years ago. It's our *new* neighbor."

"Well, tell your father to make him stop."

"Don't worry. I'll handle it." She curved an arm over her mother's shoulders and tenderly led her into the hallway. "You go on back to bed."

But in the hours since Shelby had kissed her mother good night, Mom had been busy. Evie's room was a mess; it was as if the clothes from her double closet had been belched onto the bed and across the floor. "What . . ." All of Mom's shoes, the years-out-of-date heels and boots and summer sandals, were tucked, toe first, under the bed skirt. They formed a moat of shoes around her bed.

"Mom," she breathed. "What are you doing?"

"I was going to sleep, but then I remembered that I need my coat with the trim?" Mom started back into the closet. "I could swear it was back here. Do you know where it is?"

"I don't know where your coat is. But you can't even get into your bed." She lifted her mother's old church dresses and the rare business suit off the bed, but Evie grabbed the hangers from her hands.

"Don't. Shelby. Don't touch it."

"You need to sleep."

"I'll sleep after I finish this."

But she wouldn't. The whole house was filled with

projects Evie started and never finished. Messes created and never cleaned up. A thousand thoughts and plans unfinished. There were times, like right now, it took every single bit of power and energy and strength Shelby had not to scream. Not to tear her hair out and fall on the floor and yell *what do I do? How can I help her?*

Vroooaaaa, Vrooooaaaaaaam.

That was something she could do. Take apart her neighbor!

She turned, her robe sailing out behind her as she raced down the stairs and out the front door. Not even the cold night air of January cooled her off. The silvery moonlight cast white light across the grass; it turned the shadows of the house and the garage into long dragons that she stomped across. Steam billowed out of her mouth. Her feet, in her old moccasin slippers, didn't feel the cold or the gravel of the road that separated her from her neighbor.

She was furious. And righteous. And she felt no pain.

The new motorcycle-loving jackass had moved into the old O'Halloran farm. The door to his garage was open, throwing out a wide square of yellow light accompanied by the faint bass line of a rock song.

On one side of the garage there was an older-model red pickup, and what looked like a repair shop filled the other half. She tilted her head, considering the man currently destroying her sleep. He was much older than she'd thought. For some reason she'd expected a kid. Because kids were often insensitive and didn't think about their neighbors. Full-grown adults knew better.

Or should.

He had blond hair pulled back into a short, stubby ponytail at his neck. As he stood up from his crouch beside the offending motorcycle (which was surprisingly small considering the amount of noise it made), she slowed to a stop beside a big crack that bisected the driveway.

Not a boy. At all.

He was a man. Tall. Wide. Really . . . very wide. He wore a black short-sleeved tee shirt over a white waffle Henley. The tight sleeves of his shirt revealed arms thick with muscles that bunched and shifted as he put his hands on his waist, staring down at that bike as though it had disappointed him for the very last time. Dark leather cuffs circled both wrists.

A man in jewelry of any kind was exotic in Bishop, Arkansas. But those bands . . . there was something overtly—flagrantly—erotic about them.

Ridiculous, she thought, tearing her eyes from his bracelets.

His black tee shirt had some faded, worn lettering on the back that she couldn't read, but she could imagine it once said *badass.* Or *warrior,* or some other self-fetishizing nonsense.

The bike.

The body.

The ponytail.

What a cliché.

He leaned over the tall red toolbox and set down the wrench in his hand only to select a new one. Then he crouched again, his worn jeans pulling taut across his legs and . . .

"Excuse me," she spoke up, making sure the belt to her robe was good and tight.

He spun toward her, the wrench lifted like a weapon. Gasping, she took a step back, even though she was a good fifteen feet away from the threat of that wrench. Immediately he dropped his arm and smiled, sheepishly. It was a disarming smile on a man so big. Gave his fearsome size a softness.

"Sorry." His voice was low and deep. Gravelly, like

he'd just woken up or hadn't been speaking for a while. It was an intimate voice. Private. "You scared me."

He was over six feet tall, packed with muscles and power, wearing a tee shirt that probably said *I've done five years for assault.*

Scaring him seemed ludicrous.

"Yes, well, you've been scaring *us* for the last three nights."

"I'm sorry?"

"I live across the street." He glanced over her shoulder at her big white farmhouse as if it had just magically appeared for the first time.

"Hey, we're neighbors. Nice to meet you," he said. He put the wrench in his pocket and stepped out of the garage, across the driveway toward her with his hand out. "My name is Ty. Short for Wyatt. Wyatt Svenson. People just always call me Ty."

"I'm . . . Shelby. Shelby Monroe." She shook his hand, looking into his face for any reaction from him. Any recognition of her name or what had happened to her on national television six months ago. But his expression was blank, genial. As if it were noon instead of midnight, and neighborly small talk at this hour made sense.

"Can I get you something?" He jerked his thumb back at the garage. "A beer? Never had a house with a garage before, much less a garage with a beer fridge, and I had no idea what I was missing."

"It's midnight, Wyatt," she said. She wouldn't use his nickname. Ty. And even his full name felt too familiar, but this man with the grease stains on his hands was hardly a Mr. Svenson. "I don't want a beer."

"It's midnight?" A furrow appeared between his wide blue eyes. "You've got to be kidding. I thought it was ten."

"Maybe you should put a clock over your beer fridge."

"I suppose you can hear the bike, huh?" He rubbed his hand across the back of his neck and smiled at her, looking at her through his eyelashes. Like every high school sophomore who didn't do his art assignment and came looking for a pass.

"Yes. I can hear the bike. I have heard the bike. Last night until three in the morning. And it's a weeknight. Some of us have to work."

"I'm sorry." His wide mouth kicked up in a crooked, boyish grin. At some point someone must have told him he was charming, because he was waving that grin around like it was a get-out-of-jail-free card. "I am. I lost track of time. I found this old Velocette and the carburetor—"

"I don't particularly care. Please." She gave him a raking look. From his blond hair to the frayed cuffs of his jeans, just so he knew she wasn't scared of him or charmed or impressed by his muscles and frankly . . . she just wanted to be awful. It went against everything she was taught, all the things she believed, but at the moment, she was flat out of grace. The pressure valve on her life hadn't been loosened in a very long time. And being awful to this guy . . . for very little reason, it let off some of that steam. She wasn't proud of it, but for the moment it felt good. Like eating cheap chocolate.

She crossed her arms over her chest and backed out of the light into the shadows toward her house. "Just keep it down."

Blank-faced, he nodded, and she turned, walking home.

She was nearly at the road, acutely aware that her baby toe had gone numb in her slipper, when he spoke again.

"Pleasure meeting you, neighbor." He wasn't so charming now, and the next word was not a surprise.

She'd heard it more times than she could count, from older students she wouldn't let charm her into a better grade. From strangers who didn't see past her prickly and cold surface.

From her father, once he gave up the ruse of loving her.

She'd heard it so much, with far more venom than this man could muster, that it didn't come close to piercing that cold and prickly surface.

"Bitch."

It wasn't until lunch on Thursday that Shelby had a chance to look at the identity projects the fifth-grade class had made. Sitting in the Bishop Elementary teachers' lounge with another cup of coffee and a terribly unsatisfying salad that she'd given up on, she pulled the packets from her bag.

Jeremy had drawn a very, very good stegosaurus. His detail, particularly with the colored pencils, was really improving. Jessica had drawn a picture of herself praying and what she hoped was Jesus standing over her shoulder.

"Oh, hey, it's Art day."

Oh God, it's Joe.

Sixth-grade teacher Joe Phillips stepped into the small lounge and it got even smaller. It seemed to shrink to the head of a pin, and she didn't know what to do with her arms and legs. It felt like she had extra, as if she'd turned into an octopus upon his arrival. She sat up, crossed her legs, and then uncrossed them and when he wasn't looking, made sure all her hair was back in its ponytail and she didn't have any food on the front of her sweater.

She was worse than a teenage girl. And utterly powerless to help herself.

Other women knew how to do this. How to like a man, how to know if he liked her. And then, in some kind of magical alchemy, take all that interest and turn it into something. A date. A passionate make-out session in a broom closet. Anything.

But somehow, she had missed those lessons. When other girls were pulled aside and taught how to put on mascara, or figured out how to flirt, or how to be confident around a man she wanted to like her, she'd been busy praying.

Busy begging forgiveness for sins she didn't even know how to commit.

There'd been a man at her Teachers of Arts and Sciences Conference last summer—an Ag teacher from the other side of the state whom she thought she'd been flirting with at the conference for two years. For two years she'd been drinking white wine spritzers in the hotel bar with other teachers, waiting, hoping for him to make a move. Any kind of move.

But he never did.

So last summer she'd worked up the courage to take matters into her own hands and when the moment arose, she planned to ask him up to her room—she'd even brought a thong! A *thong*.

He brought pictures of his new wife. Their wedding in the Ozarks.

Oh, how foolish she'd felt in that thong. How stupid. And how furious.

As a child, in the face of her father's violent disapproval, she'd created this identity, this cold distance between herself and other people's opinions, in an act of defiant self-protection. Dad couldn't hurt her if she pretended not to care. Pretended she didn't need affection or approval.

And then no one could hurt her if she pretended she was above the messy needs and wants of the human heart if she just buried what she wanted so deep they couldn't see it—so deep that she even forgot it.

It had been an abused and scared kid's way of coping.

And as a woman, she didn't know how to change it.

She'd smiled at the conference bar, toasted the newly-weds, all while tucking away those things she wanted, cramming them into an already full box buried deep inside of her.

Driving home from that conference in an uncomfortable thong, she'd stopped to help a man on the side of the highway whose car had broken down. And that man, in the five-minute encounter, had said something sleazy, something about how good she looked bent over a car, and that overfull box of thwarted desires cracked right open. So she kissed him, let him put his hand up her skirt.

That man ended up being Dean Jennings, the CEO of the Maybream Cracker Company, who was coming to town for a contest being run by the *America Today* morning show, and when she saw him again a few days later Shelby lost her mind. That was all she could attribute it to; she flat out had a mental breakdown, because she jeopardized everything so she could engage in one of the worst affairs in human history.

And when he left after three weeks of strange unsatisfying, increasingly mean sex, she said good riddance.

But Dean must have been engaged in his own mental breakdown, because he wanted more from her and he wouldn't take no for an answer. So much so that on the morning of *America Today*'s live taping he'd ambushed her, telling the world about their affair. The things she let him do to her.

Why don't you tell them all what you said while I was fucking you like an animal. While you were sucking my dick.

The memory of the words while sitting in the teachers'

lounge, Joe behind her at the fridge, made her skin quake. Bile rise in her throat.

"How was Christmas?" Joe asked.

She pushed it all away—the shame, the longing, the strange secret wish that Joe Phillips would believe what Dean had said about her and look at her, really look at her as a woman, as a possibility.

"Good," she said after clearing her throat. Mom's mind had been pretty clear on Christmas and they'd lain around watching kids' movies on TV. Eating pizza. No salads. "Yours?"

"My brother had the whole family at his house in Little Rock. My parents, brother, and sister. Ten kids."

"That's a lot of kids."

"Made me happy I don't live in Little Rock." He shot her a smile over his shoulder and her stomach fluttered.

"You're in my class this afternoon?"

"I am," she said. "We're working on some identity projects."

"You're a masochist," he said, walking back toward the door with his lunch in a plastic bag and his bottle of Coke. "It's a crisis of identity in the sixth grade every day. Half the girls will probably start crying. See you later."

She laughed and with a wave he was out the door, taking all the air in the room with him.

After a long moment feeling like the world's worst coward, she bent back down over her students' work.

"Hey Shelby?"

Joe was half in, half out the door. He was so handsome, not in any outrageous way, but in a regular guy way. A man who would probably lose his hair at some point and get a paunch, but his kindness and sense of humor made all of that unimportant. His hands were wide, his fingers long. Handsome hands. And he wore glasses, sometimes cockeyed. Which was silly but en-dearing.

He was *exactly* the kind of man she'd pictured herself with. Exactly.

He held his Coke bottle between his fingers and pressed it against the doorjamb.

"Yeah?" Her heart kicked in her throat.

"I . . . I ah . . ." He blew out a breath and laughed awkwardly. "I've always wanted to say that what that guy said last summer? The cookie guy?"

The winter she was ten there'd been one of those freakish Arkansas storms that shrouded the world in ice. Trees, blades of grass, and toys left in yards were totally encased in ice. Daddy made her walk out to the church with him, a mile down the highway, and she'd been mad and spiteful and wouldn't put on her boots or mittens like Mom told her to. She'd gotten frostbite on her fingers and ankles, and when the blood returned to that white, numb skin it caused an icy-hot pain, tingly and cold and swollen and awful.

This moment felt like that.

"What about him?" She stared at the blue-green foot of Jeremy's stegosaurus, unable to look at Joe's hand-some face, those well-meaning eyes.

"No one . . . no one believed him. I just want you to know that. Everyone knows he was lying."

Right. Lying.

Her reputation was exactly like that ice storm, keep-ing her precisely as the town saw her. Encapsulated. Un-touchable. Unfeeling. Undesirable.

This was it, a moment when she could open up that box where she had all those things she desired and pull out something she wanted. She could say, *Joe, I sucked his dick. I let him fuck me like an animal. I did those things. And I like those things. Perhaps not so much with Dean Jennings the horrible cookie guy. But in general, in theory, those are things I like.* And should she be so brave, she could look right into his lovely, kind brown eyes and say, *I'd like to do those things with you. Now, what do you say?*

But instead, she said, "Thank you, Joe."

He nodded, his lips pursed in that way that said, *It sucks, but I'm on your side insofar as your side does not require any more from me than this.*

And then he was gone. She waited a few more moments in case he decided to come back and further grind her second day back after the break into dust, but the doorway stayed empty.

In the heavy, dark silence he left behind, she stacked and put away those small desires to be someone else, to want more than she had, and she got back to the business of being Shelby Monroe, Art Teacher. It was enough. And if sometimes she wanted to scream, or cry, or find some stranger to prove to her that she wasn't totally dead inside or invisible to the world, it was an urge she could easily overcome.

She had overcome worse.

Shelby stretched her legs out, crossing them at the ankle, and spread out the student assignments until they covered the whole table again.

Scott had drawn himself with wings, flying over what looked like the school. Interesting.

One picture, without a name, probably John's . . . she tilted the page, trying to make sense of the dark charcoal line drawing. It was very detailed. Very creepy. It looked like it was from inside a fence . . . but the fence posts were far apart and vertical, not horizontal, and on the other side of the fence there were a man and a woman with terrifying round eyes and their mouths were open, revealing sharp teeth.

That wasn't John's usual thing.

At the bottom of the drawing, clutching one of the metal rungs of the vertical fence, were hands. And at the top of the drawing there was hair and . . . *oh dear God*. She sat up. That wasn't a fence.

It was a cage.

Chapter 3

Ty put his cell phone back in his pocket and climbed down off the ladder. He was installing a retractable awning over what—if the permits ever came in—was going to be the front patio area of Sean Baxter's bar and barbecue joint, The Pour House. And Ty had installed the unit into the brick building, but the thing wasn't working. The tracks guided by carriers kept jamming and the awning wouldn't unroll out of the metal box.

Ty was pretty sure he could fix it once he took the mechanism apart, but he had to go.

God, it was just past noon. He'd had this job for less than a month and already he had to bail early. It was a good thing Brody Baxter, despite his serious badass vibe, was a cool guy.

"Hey, boss," Ty approached Brody where he was measuring the paved area for a fence. The sun hit the asphalt so hard the two of them had taken off their coats, working in long-sleeved tee shirts and old leather gloves. Brody's shirt said USMC, which wasn't a shocker. The guy seemed pretty Marine Corps to Ty.

"Didn't I tell you not to call me that?"

"You did." Ty smiled and Brody shook his head.

"How is it going on the awning?"

"It's up, but the mechanism isn't working. I know we've got to be back at Cora's the rest of this week to work on the patio, so I figured I could come back this weekend."

"You don't have to work on the weekends," Brody

said. "You're already working overtime during the week."

"I like to work."

"And I like that attitude. But still, a day off won't kill you."

"Hey!" It was Sean coming out of the bar. Ty liked Brody a lot. They worked well together. Brody didn't ask questions, he paid on time, and the work was steady. Sean, on the other hand, was a nosy pain in the butt and rubbed Ty the wrong way in every way. "How is the awning coming?"

"The mechanism doesn't work," Brody said.

"Bummer." And the guy said "bummer" without any irony. He meant it. That the awning wasn't done simply bummed Sean out.

Ty never asked, but obviously one of the brothers had been adopted. Brody was tall, dark, and powerful. Sean was shorter, wiry, and had pale freckled skin and red hair. Brody matched his USMC tee shirt. Sean wore one of the shirts from the café that his girlfriend, Cora, ran that said "Real Men Eat Pie."

It was as if a Maori warrior were brothers with a leprechaun.

But there was no time to stand around wondering about the blood ties between the Baxter brothers. He had his own family problems to deal with.

"Actually, I could use some time right now. I . . . I need to go grab my son from school. The principal wants to meet with me."

Sean's blue eyes went wide and Brody pushed his glasses up onto his forehead.

"You have a kid?" Sean asked.

Ty nodded, but he didn't brag or pull out his phone to show him pictures. He didn't have any. Well, that wasn't true; he had a few from last weekend when they'd gone fishing at the river. Casey had caught a fish the size of a whale, but then he'd dropped it on the bank and it flopped back into the river. Casey had looked so heartbroken, so totally destroyed, Ty had waded into the river to grab the fish with his hands, but he'd slipped in the silty mud and nearly fallen on his face in the cold water.

Casey had laughed so hard he'd had to sit down.

The picture on his phone was of Casey eating the fish fry they'd gotten from a roadside stand outside Marietta. The first really good memory the two of them had and Ty wasn't ready to share it.

Truthfully, he didn't know how to share it. The words "my kid" still got hung up on his tongue.

"Holy shit, man, you've been in Bishop for how long?"

"A month."

"And you never told anyone you have a family?"

"It's just me and Casey. And I figure it's no one's business." That was as pointed as he could get, but Sean still didn't take the hint to back off.

"How old is he?" Sean asked.

"Eleven. Well, twelve in a few weeks."

"Is he in trouble?"

Ty sighed. "It's what he seems to do best."

"Go ahead, take whatever time you need," Brody said. "And no working this weekend to make up for it."

But Sean elbowed his brother as if suddenly realizing something. "Unless . . . I guess unless you need money. I mean, we could float you some if—"

"I don't need money." Ty didn't like it, but he understood why Sean had asked. Why else would a single dad work on the weekend instead of spending time with his kid?

Ty didn't need the money.

He just didn't know what the hell to do with his kid.

Ty locked up his tools and grabbed his helmet. In front of the bar his 1947 Indian Chief gleamed in the sunlight. He'd put a good year in on that bike, finding the original parts, including the skirted fenders and fringed saddle. He'd rebuilt the 1200cc V-twin engine practically from scratch, nearly tearing out his hair at least twice in the process.

But it was worth it. She crouched at the curb, all tarted up in her cherry-red paint with the gold trim, the silver chrome. Flashy, but elegant.

Show-off, he thought with fondness.

"That's quite a bike," a man said as he walked by, holding a toddler's hand. He grabbed a cell phone out of his back pocket. "You mind if I . . . ?"

"No. Go right ahead." Ty stepped away and let the man take a few pictures.

"Thanks. No, buddy, don't touch." The man grabbed his toddler's hands just before he made contact with the fresh paint job.

"It's okay," Ty said. "He can touch it."

The man let his son run his fingers through the fringe and Ty thought of his grandfather. Pop, the big, gruff biker who always let Ty touch the fringe.

Ty blinked and glanced away.

"My dad used to have a bike like that—he'll love the pictures," the man said, picking up his son. "Is it for sale?"

"Not . . . ah . . . not yet." Ty smiled. He wasn't quite ready to let her go. Largely because the Velocette was being more difficult than it needed to be.

The guy took off with his kid and his phone, and Ty slipped on his helmet, even though the law didn't require it. An unintentional part of Pop's legacy.

The Chief started with a roar and flattened out to a nice loud purr as he pulled away from the curb and headed to school to bail his son out of the principal's office.

* * *

Bishop Elementary was like a school in a movie, with all the artwork and gym shoes lining the hallways. He liked places where kids were taken care of, where the sunlight created no shadowy corners. It even smelled the way a school should—like tomato soup and industrial-strength cleaner. In the front foyer a big banner welcomed visitors to the home of the Bishop Bulldogs, and in the glass cabinet there were trophies and pictures kids had drawn of bulldogs.

He smiled, happy that he'd brought his kid here. Whatever happened, this was a good place. Miles better than the school in Memphis that Casey had been attending.

At least I've done one thing right.

There was commotion down the hallway and a woman came walking around the corner with a long line of very young kids behind her. She stopped and turned, her finger to her lips, but half the kids weren't paying attention. They were twirling and poking their friends. One boy was practicing his ninja kicks.

Just the sound of those voices created a ball—a spiky, painful ball—in his throat. The awareness of every single moment with Casey—ten years of them—that he'd missed made physical in the base of his throat, across his chest.

The ninja kicks, he'd like to have seen those.

"Excuse me?" A woman stood in the doorway to the office. Colleen, he remembered from their brief meeting when he'd enrolled Casey in the school. She was terrifying. "Mr. Svenson?"

"Call me Ty." He had it on good authority that his smile was charming. Women of all ages—even women who hated his guts—agreed he had a good smile.

She didn't respond in any way to his smile. Not unlike Shelby the Ice Queen last night. *What's with the women in this town?* "Follow me—Principal Root and our art teacher are waiting for you."

They walked through a small, crowded office, and outside a closed door sat Casey. Ty's heart kicked into his chest at the utter surprise of him. The sight of the boy with Vanessa's hair and sneer, but his own eyes and height, was still a shock to the system.

"Casey," he said, coming to stand in front of the kid, who didn't look up. Instead, Casey crossed his arms over his thin, bony chest and sneered a little harder at his shoes. "Is this meeting going to be what I think it is?"

Casey looked up through the stupid flop of hair he liked to have in his eyes all the time but he got one look at Ty's pissed-off face and had the good sense to swallow his grin.

"It's just a picture," he said.

It was never just anything with this kid. It was always something surrounded by a bunch of drama or attitude or outright lies—like a bullshit candy coating he had to dig through to get to the kid underneath.

"The principal is waiting," Colleen said, giving Ty and Casey a stern up-and-down.

The way the woman looked at them made him bristle. Her eyes were narrowed with the same disdain Shelby Monroe had had in her eyes last night. He'd called her a bitch—not the kindest thing he'd ever done and he didn't do it because she'd come over and asked him in a prissy, unfriendly way to stop working on the bike. She had every right to do that. In fact, he was glad she did. Nana would have killed him for being so insensitive.

Ty called Shelby a bitch because she took one look at him and decided she knew everything about him.

And all of it—all of *him*—was beneath her.

Colleen was doing the same thing, and he wanted to grab his kid and tell her to fuck off. The principal and art teacher on the other side of that door, too.

The urge to grab his kid, get on a bike, and get gone

was powerful, like a rolling blast of heat up from his feet. It made his skin tight and his head hurt. Because leaving was something he was real good at. And he needed to figure out how to stay, for Casey's sake.

"Let's go, then," he said, and Colleen opened the door.

Inside there was a thin man behind a desk wearing glasses and a red polo shirt, and when Ty walked in he stood up. "Mr. Svenson," he said, but there was no smile, no good to see you again.

Oh, man. Casey must have really screwed up.

"Principal Root, good to see you." He shook the guy's hand.

"This is our art teacher, Shelby Monroe."

It was like getting hit in the stomach. Not enough to put you down, but still a good, hard shock to the system that took a few seconds to recover from.

Of course. Of course it's her. Because God hates me, he really does.

He turned to see the tall blonde staring, open-mouthed, at him.

"You," she said. It was a relief to know that she was shocked, too.

"Yeah. Me. Someone want to tell me what's happened?"

"Have a seat." Mr. Root pointed to the other chair across from his desk, and Ty sat down, burningly aware of Shelby watching him.

She looked almost exactly the same as she had last night, as though even in the middle of the night, pulled from her bed, she didn't dare go out in the world looking messy. Her blond hair was pulled back in a sleek, tight ponytail and she didn't seem to wear a whole lot of makeup. Not that she needed it. Her skin was all pink and white.

For a second last night, before he realized she was

there to give him hell, before he realized what time it was and that she was in her robe, he'd been happy to see her. Happy for company.

Ty wasn't used to being lonely and last night his loneliness had come up out of nowhere, and she'd been, for one second, a welcome surprise.

And then the whole thing went really wrong.

"Ms. Monroe teaches art in your son's class, and Casey drew something that we thought was worth discussing with you."

"Where's the picture?" He glanced over at Shelby.

"It was an identity project." She had a piece of white paper flipped over on her lap. "They had to draw three images that would tell me about them without words."

"Is that the picture?" He pointed to her lap.

"Yes." She put her hands over the paper like she wasn't going to give it to him yet.

"You calling in all the parents?" he asked. "Or just the new kid's?"

"Normally, we wouldn't have a meeting over one drawing, but it's graphic and, frankly, disturbing," Mr. Root said.

"He's a fifth-grade boy. They're kind of graphic and disturbing by nature, aren't they?"

Shelby blinked her big brown eyes at him. Brown eyes and blond hair—you didn't see that very much. And her eyebrows were dark. Stern. It seemed impossible, but there it was: she had stern eyebrows.

He held out his hand, and after a moment she put the picture in it. Even before he flipped it, he had a pretty good idea that it was going to be one of three drawings.

He glanced down. *Right*. Casey had gone with the cage again.

"You think Casey's drawing you a picture of what his life is like?" He focused on Shelby as if Mr. Root weren't even in the room.

His grandmother had this cat, a huge, fat black and white cat, who hated everything on the planet but Nana. In fact, Sweetie (a ridiculous joke of a name) sat on top of Nana's chair and judged everyone as a subspecies.

Shelby was exactly like Sweetie. He couldn't tell exactly what she thought when she looked at him, but it wasn't good.

"It was an identity exercise."

"And you think this is me." He pointed to the snarling man in the picture. Actually, this one looked more like him than it ever had. Casey had finally got the nose and hair right, which only made this little stunt worse. Because he'd been practicing it. The woman in the picture was Vanessa. Right down to the avarice in her eyes. "And this is his mom, and we put him in a cage and bark and snarl at him?"

"It's a violent picture that even if not true needs to be discussed." Shelby was getting up on some kind of high horse. Her back going even straighter, her full lips going thin and flat.

Discussed. Right. He rubbed his forehead. They'd been discussing this for months; every time Casey drew one of these pictures in counseling or group therapy, it had to get discussed.

"I don't put him in a cage," he said. "And his mom . . . his mom isn't around right now. He does this kind of shit. Sorry—*stuff.* All the time. It's either him in a cage, or him sleeping outside because I locked him out, or me forcing him to eat dog food." Shelby and Mr. Root stared at him with open mouths. "Here. Watch."

Ty opened the door and gave Casey a hard look. "You want to come in here and talk to these people?"

Casey stood, his white tee shirt hanging down to his knees. Ty shut the door behind them and crossed his arms over his chest. Casey studied the floor.

"Casey." The one word had enough warning in it that Casey took notice.

"I made it up," he finally said. "He doesn't lock me in a cage or make me eat dog food or anything like that."

"Why did you draw the picture?" Shelby asked.

Casey shrugged. *Oh, God, those fucking shrugs.* Ty put a heavy hand on Casey's shoulder, a cut-the-crap gesture. Casey twitched away and sighed. "Because it was a stupid assignment. Because I'm bored. Because . . . I don't know. It's more fun than my real life?"

"Getting locked up in a cage is more fun than your real life?" Mr. Root asked.

"No," Casey muttered.

"But getting me pulled out of work is," Ty said, staring hard at his kid. "Being the badass kid sent to the principal's office on, what . . . the second week at a new school? . . . is more fun than actually sitting in class, right?"

Casey sent him a fleeting smile and Ty wanted to pull out his hair. *I know my kid,* he thought. *I was this kid, with the attitude and the smile and the stupid need to be noticed. To be bad. Because the places we're from and the people who raised us put more stock in being bad than being smart. It's better to be tough than to fit in.*

And Ty was trying—with both goddamn hands, with all his strength—to change that.

"This isn't funny, Casey," he said.

"Casey," Mr. Root said, "can you please wait outside?"

Casey shuffled out and Ty shut the door behind him, fighting the urge to slam it.

"Clearly we're dealing with a behavior disorder," Mr. Root said.

Ty whirled away from the door. "Wait . . . what? Behavior disorder?"

"This isn't the first time he's been in my office. It's been once or twice a day every day."

"Why is this the first time I've heard of it?" he demanded.

"Because a certain period of settling in is to be expected. And if your son isn't telling you what's happening, that, too, is part of the problem." Mr. Root pulled open a drawer in his desk and pulled out a file an inch thick.

"This is your son's file from his school in Memphis. This behavior is nothing new. He was suspended three times last year for fighting, in the fourth grade. He was moved to two different foster homes—"

"Because one of those homes had ten kids." Ty's skin, his blood, everything burned and itched because he knew what was in that file. He knew every detail of how Vanessa had screwed around with this boy's life, and by not once being mentioned it was clear that he wasn't around to try to stop it. "And he's not there anymore. He's with me. We moved here so he could have a fresh start."

Mr. Root crossed his hands over the file and sighed as if this were something he'd known all along. "That's a laudable idea, Mr. Svenson. But for a true fresh start I think a psychologist should test him—"

"He's just a smart-ass kid," Ty said, "going through some shit. Sorry. *Stuff*. Why do you have to go slapping labels on him? You barely know him!"

"Because that's how we can best help him." Mr. Root crossed his arms over his chest. "We get him assessed, identified, perhaps medicated—"

"You've got to be kidding me." Ty couldn't sit for this. He stood up but there was no room to pace. He felt like the kid in the cage in Casey's picture.

"Let's not get ahead of ourselves." Shelby finally spoke up. "Mrs. Jordal says he's a very bright kid, a smart aleck but for the most part engaged in the class."

"He's not stupid," Ty said. "Don't you have to be smart to be a smart-ass?"

"Yes. But . . . there's something wrong right now, isn't there, Mr. Svenson?" she asked.

He nearly laughed. *Something wrong? Try every-thing. Every damn thing.*

"Perhaps if he saw the school counselor?" she asked.

"We've done that." For three months they did that. A month of weekly counseling meetings. All part of getting custody. Of getting Casey out of the foster system.

"We can get a state psychologist here to test him," Mr. Root continued and opened a calendar. "Next month, probably."

Ty sat back down, bracing his head in his hands. He didn't know much, he was totally new at this, but his gut was telling him that what was wrong with Casey wasn't chemical. It was partly Vanessa's fault, partly Ty's fault. Once the kid had something steady in his life, things would get better for Casey. "He doesn't need testing. He doesn't need medicine. He doesn't need a label."

He needed a swift kick in the pants, but Ty had far too much experience being on the other end of that particular parenting tactic and had no interest in visiting that on his son.

"Do you have any other ideas?" Mr. Root asked.

Staring at his shoes, he shook his head. "I kind of hoped that was your job," he said.

"You've heard my recommendation."

He swiveled to look at Shelby. "What about you?"

"My ideas?"

"I'm guessing you probably have a few."

"I do," Shelby said. She folded her hands in her lap and lifted her chin. "Casey's been in counseling before, hasn't he?"

"Yes. A lot of it." He sat back in his chair, his legs out

in front of him. He was aware that he was taking up all the space, crowding her into a corner, and he was okay with that. Even took a little vindictive glee in it. "We talked to a very nice overworked woman once a week for months."

"You just talked."

"Well, *I* talked. Casey didn't say a whole lot."

"Traditional talk therapy isn't always effective for kids. They don't know how to process what they're feeling, much less tell someone. And if it seems like punishment or something scary, they're even less likely to talk."

Ty remembered those weekly appointments in the Department of Child and Family Services building in West Memphis all too clearly. There had been a grief counseling session for women who had lost babies in the room next door and they could hear the crying through the walls. Casey had stared at the wall, the watercolor paintings of boats on their side, as though he could see through it to the weeping women. "The counseling we went to was pretty scary."

"I think you should try art therapy."

Mr. Root made a throttled laughing sound in his throat, which made Shelby bristle up like a hedgehog.

"It's a pretty good tool to get kids to open up. Especially if he's already done traditional therapy."

This was a turn Ty never would have expected. That Shelby Monroe would be going out on a limb for his sake. After last night, he would have guessed that they would be in a standoff for however long they lived across the street from each other.

But now she was offering him a huge olive branch.

"Okay. Let's give it a try."

She smiled as if she were relieved, and he wanted to tell her that he wasn't setting out to fuck up his kid, he was trying to make things right. Ashamed, he pulled his legs back toward his chair.

"The art therapy isn't run through the school, Mr. Svenson," Mr. Root said. "It's not a state program."

"So?"

"So, the costs will come out of pocket. Yours." Again, Ty had that sense of being judged on one glance, a glance that included his jeans and frayed denim jacket with the shearling collar.

"That's fine." He chewed on the words as they came out.

"I'll leave it to you to sort out the particulars." Mr. Root looked like a man who'd just sucked on a lemon. He stood up, spreading his hands across his desk. "But I can't keep having your son in my office. Next time he's going to be suspended."

Ty stood up. "You don't think this will work?"

"For your sake and for Casey's, I hope it does."

"I'll handle Casey. He won't be back in your office."

"Good luck with that," Mr. Root said, and Ty turned back around ready to satisfy the sudden urge to tell this guy exactly where he could shove his smarmy condescension and bullshit medical solutions.

"Let's go outside and talk about this," Shelby said, crowding him toward the door. There was a time in his life when he'd never let himself get herded. There was a time he would have knocked to the ground anyone who tried.

But he turned, feeling this woman at his back like a grease fire. His skin prickled and stung. Outside the door Casey was slouched in the chair, and it was all Ty could do not to grab him by the scruff of the neck.

"Let's go," he said as he walked past, and he was relieved to hear the slap of Casey's sneakers on the linoleum behind him.

He headed past the secretary out toward the sunlit

entrance, with the pictures and the trophies and all things bright and innocent—every single thing he wanted for his son and the boy was throwing aside like it all meant nothing.

Art therapy. It sounded ridiculous even to him. Looking at Casey, at that chip on his shoulder, and knowing all the pain that had been heaped on his back, he couldn't help but doubt how much drawing was really going to help.

He turned on Shelby. "You really think this can work?"

"I think it's better to exhaust all options before turning to medication."

"Who is getting medication?" Casey asked.

"You," Ty said.

"For what?"

"Behavior disorder."

"That's bullshit!" Casey cried. Ty looked over at Shelby to see if she was still so sure about this art therapy idea, but she was glaring at him.

"What?" Ty asked, not sure why he was getting the hairy eyeball.

"No one is putting you on medication," she told Casey, her eyes far kinder when she looked at his son than when she looked at him. "We just want to help you adjust."

She'd stood up for his kid in that office. Against the drugging, labeling principal. Just like she'd stood up for herself last night when he'd been revving that engine.

He saw her fierceness as something of its own—instead of just something standing in his way. And it was disarming to see her that way. Disorienting.

"When can you start with him?" Ty asked.

She blinked at Ty; her mouth opened and then shut. "I'm . . . I think you've misunderstood me. I don't do the art therapy."

"What?"

"I'm sorry if I gave you that impression. I'm just the art teacher. Not a therapist."

Of course not. Because that would just be too easy. He felt once again the sudden weight of caring for someone else. And not just feeding or clothing him, but making decisions on his behalf. And then worrying if every single decision was wrong or right.

"What's going on?" Casey asked.

"Let's go, man," Ty said. "You're not going back to class. And apparently I need to spend some time on Google."

"I can help you find a therapist," Shelby said, her hand stretched out as if to stop him. She had long fingers. The nails, though, were chewed down to nothing.

What, he wondered, stressed the implacable Ms. Monroe out so bad she had to gnaw on her fingernails.

"I have information on plenty of local counselors who might work."

"Really?" Well, that was a relief. A big one.

"Really. Come by the Art Barn tonight after dinner. We can talk then."

He felt the back of his neck getting hot, belated embarrassment for the way he'd talked to her last night. "Ms. Monroe—"

Her smile was a flash and then gone, like a fish underwater, flipping into the sunlight only to retreat to the cool depths. "You can call me Shelby."

"Shelby," he said, tasting her name, the sweet round sounds of it, no hard edges, so unlike the person. "Thank you. Very much."

"You're welcome," she said without a smile and walked away, deeper into the school.

He hit the release bar to head out the door, Casey beside him.

"Do you have a date with Ms. Monroe?" Casey asked.

"No."

"Do I?"

The hope in his voice, it was ridiculous. What was the deal with this kid? One minute Ty wanted to shake him, the next he wanted to laugh.

They stopped next to his beautiful Indian, and he unclipped his helmet from the handlebars and handed it to Casey.

"Come on," the boy moaned. "Helmets are lame."

Ty's patience was so far past thin that he put the helmet over Casey's head himself and pressed it down, mashing all that red hair farther into his eyes. "Why didn't you bring the truck?" Casey moaned.

"Because I didn't know I was breaking my son out of school."

"This is lame."

"Whine one more time, Casey, and I swear to God you can find your own way home." Ty swung his leg over the bike and slid forward, making room for Casey on the back.

Casey didn't say anything, he just got on the bike behind him, but instead of wrapping his hands around Ty's waist, he held onto the back of his jacket. Ty wanted to tell his son to get a firmer grip, but it was all just a fight with Casey, and he was done for the moment.

A cold wind blew down the street as Ty took off, turning toward home, and he felt his son behind him like a kite in danger of being blown away.

Chapter 4

At home, Shelby parked her car in front of the garage and gave herself a second before going inside. The roses beside the house swaying in the cold January wind looked like skeletons, still covered in the last blooms' dead heads. They should have been trimmed back, maybe covered in burlap, but she'd never gotten around to it and probably never would. It would be nice to just yank them out so she could stop feeling guilty about them, but she'd just find something else to feel guilty about.

Like, for instance, not being an art therapist just to make Wyatt Svenson's life a little easier. She was wholly aware of the power of incremental relief. The small things that, when everything was going to shit, made the difference between surviving a day and giving up. And Ty seemed like a guy in serious survival mode.

She caught herself chewing on her thumbnail and pulled it out of her mouth.

Another wind blew up and the roses rattled against the aluminum siding on the garage. They had planted the roses after Dad died, the summer of her freshman year in college. The morning of the funeral, Mom woke her up at dawn and they'd planted the rosebushes—red, pink, and white—in their pajamas.

That had been an act of celebration. Shelby wasn't sure if Mom understood that at the time, she'd probably done it out of survival. Out of a need to be busy, to try to make right something very wrong. But Shelby had planted those roses with joy.

The back door of the house opened and Cathy stepped out onto the porch. She crossed her arms over her mountainous chest and frowned. The universal sign that it had not been a good day.

Right. Here we go. I can't sit in the car forever.

She popped open her door. "How was your day, Cathy?" she asked needlessly.

"You don't pay me enough for this, Shelby," Cathy yelled, no doubt to be heard over the wind and perhaps just to yell. A day requiring never-ending patience with Mom sometimes needed to end with a little yelling off the back porch.

"What happened?" She crossed the gravel to the cracked cement steps. Another thing that needed to be fixed.

Cathy had control over her eyebrows in a way that could baffle and amaze. And wither. And when they arched like that, Shelby withered.

"I'm not a nurse. And that's what you need. I'm a cleaning lady you pay to stick around to make sure she's not burning the place down."

"And she hasn't. You've done a great job."

Cathy came down the steps and flipped her long black braids over her shoulder. Once, Shelby got in the way of those braids and they'd smacked her face and stung, but not nearly as much as the pity in Cathy's face at the moment. "Honey, I was happy to help out. But you need a nurse. A real one. Not a babysitter. She's confused, angry. Secretive. I'm trying not to get offended every time she calls me 'girl,' because I know she doesn't mean it, but . . ." She shrugged. "You don't pay me enough for this."

"I could pay you more."

"It wouldn't be enough." Cathy's eyebrows melted

back down to their regular place and her big brown eyes were sympathetic. "My sister's been telling you about Glen Home."

"I'm not putting her in a nursing home. We're not there yet." Cathy's eyebrows were telling her she was wrong and Shelby bristled. Cathy's sister Deena was a nurse who had a lot of experience in geriatric care, and she said Glen Home was a nice place. But it was still a nursing home. And she and her mother had made a promise to each other—they stuck together. "We're *not*," she reiterated, and Cathy threw up her hands.

"You're more stubborn than your mother. And I don't think that's good for either of you."

Stubbornness was really all they had going for them, so she'd stick with it.

"Is she awake?" Shelby asked. Mom had started taking a nap in the afternoon. Passing out between cleaning closets and searching for photographs long ago thrown out. She woke up around dinner refueled for her midnight campaigns of pudding making and searching for the keys to the garage.

The online support chat rooms called it sundowning. And Mom had started doing it about a year ago. That was about the last time Shelby had a full night's sleep.

"Been asleep for a half hour. I made you some squash soup; it's on the stove."

Cathy grabbed her big quilted bag with the knitting needles sticking out of the top and endless little bags of grapes and cut-up carrots because she was always on a diet. "I'll give you two weeks."

"Wait, what?"

"What did you think I was talking about?"

"I thought you were complaining. Asking for a raise."

"I'm quitting, honey. Two weeks. You need someone like Deena now, not me."

If Shelby were the kind of person to just melt into the ground, like the Wicked Witch of the West under that water, she'd do it. Right now. But Mom had raised her to be made of sterner stuff.

"Thank you, Cathy." There seemed to be more she could say, but she didn't really know how. So, she repeated herself. "Thank you."

Cathy got in the little sports car that Shelby envied with all her heart, and Shelby watched her drive away until the plumes of dust kicked up by her leaving vanished.

Inside the house it was quiet and still. Dim late afternoon sunlight filtered through the rose curtains of the living room, and the hallway and kitchen all seemed to glow pink. It hid the shabbiness of the house, the fact that it needed massive renovation and a serious cleaning behind its rosy blush.

The house without Cathy would have been a disaster zone. Last year, Shelby had never known what she was walking into when she came home from work, but now that Cathy spent a few hours here every day, the chaos was organized into stacks. A thousand little stacks all over the house.

On the kitchen counter there was a pile of photographs. In a glance she realized they were all of her. An infant buried in pink blankets, a child in her Sunday best. A painfully awkward and serious adolescent at Bible camp.

A furious teenager in acid wash and a Shaker sweater, hiding all her anger behind good grades and Student Council.

Bored, she shoved the pictures away.

Identity projects didn't work in retrospect.

Not for her.

* * *

"I'm sick of hamburgers," Casey said as he took his plate to the sink.

"Doesn't seem to slow you down any." Ty sat back with his milk and shoved his plate over to Casey so he could take it to the sink, too.

"I'm hungry. It would just be nice to eat something besides hamburger."

"Like what?"

"I don't know, man, you're the adult." The plate clattered into the sink and Casey got ready to huff off to his room to slam the door, which was how a lot of conversations between them ended. It had been radio silence since leaving the school. Once they got home Casey had gone to his room and Ty had gone to the garage, to stare at the carburetor in pieces on his workbench and try to think of what to say to his kid.

He still didn't know what to say, but he knew he had to say something.

"We need to talk about school."

Casey gave it his entire repertoire. Eye-rolling and sighing, then a giant slouch against the counter, as if every single vertebra had just given up, all at the same time.

"If you get in trouble again, you're going to get suspended."

"So?"

"So. You can't."

"That school is lame, Ty. Everyone here is a hick." Ty put up his hand, but Casey kept going. "They're rednecks. They are. And I don't know why we had to come out here."

"Because you needed a fresh start, Casey. You . . . your mom, you burned every bridge you had in Memphis. Don't you get that?"

Casey's silence said it all. He rubbed his thumb along the grout around the sink.

"You're beginning to burn those bridges here," Ty said.

"Mr. Root is a dick."

"That's it. We're getting a swear jar."

Ty tended to agree about Mr. Root, but if he said that to Casey it would be like giving the kid permission to be even more disrespectful and they needed Mr. Root, they needed that school, they needed to make all those things work.

"He is!" Casey protested. "He took one look at me and hated me."

"He doesn't—"

"Yeah, he does."

"Then give him a reason not to!"

Ty rolled his shoulders against the hard-backed chair. He'd rented this house unseen and furnished, and it looked like a house in a catalog. A fussy one. The white table and chairs had that fake worn-in look. The couches looked comfortable but weren't. The refrigerator door was built to look like the cabinets. Who the hell wanted that? A camouflage fridge.

Every single part of his life was unrecognizable. It was disorienting. He didn't know whose life this was.

"Don't you want to be more than the kid who always gets in trouble?" he asked.

Casey stared out the window over the sink toward the backyard, which looked at this point, in his total neglect of it, more like an overgrown field.

"That dog's back," Casey said.

"Casey?"

"That skinny stray. He's back in the garbage."

There were a ton of strays out here. People dropped dogs along this highway like they were black bags of trash. "I'll handle him."

"He looks hungry."

"Casey!"

"What?"

"Don't . . . don't you have anything to say?"

Casey looked back over at him and smiled, but it was mean. Calculating. A chilling smile on an eleven-year-old.

Ty tried so hard to give Vanessa the benefit of the doubt and he did his best not to bad-mouth her in front of Casey, but when he smiled like that—like he was small and vicious, and just looking for someone to hurt—he was the spitting image of Vanessa. "Mom always said that about you. You were the guy in trouble."

Vanessa had told Casey more lies than truth about Ty, but this particular thing was plenty true. There was nothing that Casey had done or was contemplating doing that Ty had not already done and been kicked out of school for. But again, he didn't know how to tell that to his kid without making it sound like permission.

"We're not talking about me," he said, and Casey looked away. The "bullshit" he was thinking, though, was loud and clear.

"This is a new school, Casey; no one knows you here. No one knows anything you've done. You get to be someone totally different—"

"I'm *not* different!" he cried. "I'm me."

"I know, but there's more to you than what Mr. Root thinks. Isn't there?"

More to you than this troublemaking, sullen kid you're showing me. Please. Please. Let there be more.

"Come on, Ty, that picture was just a joke—"

"I'm not laughing!" He turned on Casey. "Don't you get that? I'm not laughing."

Casey had these big blue eyes. His Svenson grandparents' genes showing up. But those blue eyes, sometimes they seemed like they hid deep waters and dark, scary fish, while other times they were as shallow as a puddle. This was one of those puddle times, and Ty worried that he was never going to understand this kid. Or maybe . . . maybe Casey was just too far gone to reach. The foster mother that Casey had been placed with had told Ty that the most important years for a kid's development were between the ages of birth and six—that's when they learned how to live in this world.

If that was true, maybe the kid was screwed. Vanessa's influence was just too imprinted.

But then he remembered Casey in the garage four months ago. Dirty. Skinny. Scared and angry.

"I think you're my dad."

That kid wasn't too far gone. That kid was brave and tough and smart. Ty would bet his life on that kid if only he could find him again.

"Jesus Christ, Casey. Isn't this hard enough for us without you pulling this shit?"

Casey looked at him for a long time and Ty held his breath, wondering if maybe they were really going to talk. And if they were, what would he say? He wasn't too proud to admit that he was terrified of the prospect.

"Can I go to my room?" Casey asked.

"Yeah," Ty answered, embarrassed to be so relieved.

It was dark and cold when Ty crossed the street to Shelby's house. Every light was on in the white farmhouse, but he passed it as she'd instructed, and was surprised to see behind it a series of dark buildings. A big barn and two smaller outbuildings.

It reminded him of Nana and Pop's place in the country outside of Ellicott City. And how, when he was thirteen and forced to live there, it had seemed like the worst place on the planet.

Why did so many of the great things—the best things—disguise themselves at first, he wondered. Or why was he always so blind to their goodness?

His breath steamed in the cold air, and the grass covered in frost crunched under his boots. There was a musical bass line thudding through the crystalline night, coming from the largest of the buildings. He grabbed the big iron handle and pulled open the heavy door. It was like opening the door to some kind of kid wonderland. Wires crisscrossed the ceiling with dozens of pictures clipped to them. Christmas lights surrounded bulletin boards covered in more pictures. Giant tissue-paper flowers blanketed one whole wall; next to that wall were two couches and a lamp. There were some of those pottery wheels in the corner and a bunch of easels facing a table with a wilting bouquet of flowers on it.

On one of the three low circular tables was a chandelier in pieces.

Art Barn indeed.

Jack White was playing not so quietly in the background. And the heavy, dirty guitar riffs were a total surprise.

I want love to change my friends to enemies.

He'd had that kind of love and there was nothing, absolutely nothing, to recommend it.

"Hello!" he yelled over the music.

"Hey!" Her voice came from down the hallway to the left. "Just a second."

The music was turned down and Shelby walked out of the shadows into the glitter-and-construction-paper palace she'd created.

"I'm sorry," he said, right away, because it needed to be said. "I'm sorry for calling you names the other night. It was crappy of me."

She stopped next to the table with the chandelier and put down a small stack of folders.

"Thank you." Her pink lips curved into a smile. She still wore her green sweater and the pink shirt underneath it, but instead of khaki pants she had on a pair of stretchy sweatpants and running shoes. Those pants showed off the long lines of her body. The strength in her legs. The muscle and meat of her.

He sucked in a quick breath, stunned and embarrassed by his thoughts.

"I'm sorry, too," she said. "I was ruder than I needed to be."

"Sometimes rude is all I understand." He tried to joke, not expecting her in any way to respond. She'd proven herself pretty impervious to his charms, which made her smile in response to his joke all the sweeter.

"Isn't Casey ever bothered by the noise?"

"Once he's asleep, nothing wakes him up. I've never seen someone sleep so hard."

"Well, I hope we can put all of that behind us in an effort to help Casey."

"Absolutely," he said and clapped his hands together. "Happy to." If only it were always so easy to put the worst of his actions behind him. He'd spent a good part of the last ten years running from his mistakes.

"Have a seat." She pointed to one of the low tables without the chandelier. "And we can talk."

"Are you an art teacher *and* an electrician?" he asked, looking down at the chandelier guts.

"Sadly, no. I can't figure it out."

He almost offered to look at it while they talked, because it would be great to have something to do with his hands, but he didn't want to give her the impression that he wasn't totally involved in the conversation.

"Can I get you something to drink?" she asked and he shook his head.

They both settled into the hilariously small chairs. His knees came up nearly to his chin, and she smiled.

"Sorry," she said. "I think you get used to it."

"It's fine," he lied, hoping that in time it would be,

because right now he felt stupid. "Hey, before we get started I've got to tell you, this place is awesome."

She glanced around, her face giving away none of her feelings. "You know, I've kind of stopped seeing it."

"I lived in St. Louis for a while," he said. "And at first I couldn't believe that arch—it was like every time I looked up it smacked me in the face with how freaking amazing it was. As wide as it was tall and all that. But then, after a while, you get used to it."

"Well, the Art Barn is no St. Louis arch."

"Don't sell it short," he said, looking at that flower wall. "It's beautiful."

Her gaze touched his face, left, and came back and after a long moment, as if she wasn't sure if he was lying or about to trick her, she smiled. "Thank you."

He nodded and tried to shift on the miniature chair, but his butt was going numb.

"I don't have access to Casey's school file," she said. "So, perhaps you'd like to fill me in on some of the more pertinent issues he's faced."

"Ahhh . . ." It wasn't that he drew a blank; it was that he didn't know where to start.

"You've had some counseling?" she asked, giving him a toehold in the story.

"A few months ago," he said. "It was part of my getting custody."

"You are divorced?"

"Is this relevant?"

She blinked, her eyes suddenly wide. "You don't think it is?"

He hung his head. Christ, those eyes—they were like a judge and jury all in one. "Sorry, let me try again." He shrugged off his coat and pulled the elastic from the ponytail at his neck. He gathered his hair back up and put the rubber band back in, pulling it tighter.

"Okay. The story is, I didn't know about Casey until

four months ago, when he showed up on my doorstep in West Memphis and told me he thought I was his dad."

Her mouth fell open. "You didn't know . . ."

"About Casey?" He shook his head. "Nope. His mom, Vanessa, and I dated twelve years ago, back when I was pretty young and stupid. We broke up and I didn't hear from her again. But about six months ago, Casey'd been put into the foster system because Vanessa had been convicted of possession with intent and sent to jail."

"Marijuana?"

"Meth. She . . . she ran with a pretty bad crowd."

"Bad crowd" was putting it mildly. The Outlaws were the kind of motorcycle club the uninitiated thought about when they thought of motorcycle clubs. The kind of club that gave them all a bad name.

Not every club was like *Sons of Anarchy*. Most of them, actually, weren't.

But Outlaws was. Meth. Guns. Prostitutes. They had dirty thumbs in all of it.

"When she was sent to jail she still didn't try to contact you?"

He'd gotten over his anger at Vanessa, or at least he thought he had. But every once in a while, he found a vine of it that he hadn't chopped down, or poisoned with forgiveness. That she would have her kid dragged into the foster system rather than contact him and ask for help was a pretty shitty thing for a mom to do to her kid.

But when he was truthful with himself, he knew he hadn't given Vanessa much to recommend him as a father.

"She had her reasons for not wanting me around Casey; it's not like we brought out the best in each other."

"So, she was arrested. Casey was put into a foster home."

"Two. Two different foster homes. The first one was too crowded."

"They moved him to a second one and he ran away and found you?"

It was like one of those stories about dogs that got moved to the other side of the country, but ran back thousands of miles and found their old home—except Casey's story was way more sad and terrifying. He'd crossed state lines, from Memphis to West Memphis; he'd crossed the damn river, walking for hours with nothing but an address in his pocket. The thought of it could still wake him up out of a deep sleep with nightmares.

"She'd told Casey enough about me that he found my grandfather's repair shop and then found me." She stared at him slack-jawed and he laughed. "Sounds unbelievable, I know."

"It *is* unbelievable! It is amazing. Casey—"

"Bravest kid I know. Bravest person." It felt good to say it out loud, as it reminded him that there were other sides to Casey than what he was seeing on a day-to-day basis.

"You were able to just take custody?"

He shook his head, trying to get comfortable in the tiny chair. "There was no 'just' about it. I took him back to the foster home; we called his case worker and started the process."

"Blood tests, court dates, counseling . . ."

"All of it."

"And then you moved to Bishop?"

"Fresh start. For both of us." He didn't want to talk about all the trouble Vanessa had gotten into, or the things Casey had seen. That was all shit he wanted whitewashed. He wanted it painted over with good memories. Safe memories. Normal childhood stuff. "I thought it was a good idea. We both needed a clean slate."

"And this was all four months ago?"

Ty wasn't sure why he remembered, but when Casey had walked into Pop's old shop the boy's shoes had been untied.

Tall and gangly, he'd walked in the first bay and had stood in the shadows until Ty noticed him. And the second Ty got a look at Casey, with his chin up like he was daring the whole world to take a swing, something cold pierced his snake brain. Something knowing.

"Do you know Vanessa Ponchet?" the boy had asked.

"I did. Long time ago." Ty wiped his hands off on a rag, fixing his feet to the ground to absorb the hit he'd somehow known was coming.

"I'm her kid," Casey said. "And I think you're my dad."

He'd stepped back, putting his weight against the red tool cart behind him, because his knees had buckled.

"What makes you think that?"

"She told me. Like a million times."

"A million times," he'd said, because his mind was blown blank. Funny. She hadn't told Ty, once.

"Hey, you got a bathroom around here I can use?" Casey had asked, and Ty, on legs that did not feel the ground, walked the boy through the shop to the can in the back.

Casey had gone in and shut the door, and Ty stood outside listening to the kid vomit his guts out and felt his life irrevocably change.

That day seemed like it was both yesterday and a hundred years ago.

"Yep," he told Shelby. "Four months." He stretched his arms out wide because he felt the need to move. It was a current under his skin that he didn't know what to do with. The current came and went, part stress, part anxiety, part guilt, and the knife's edge of failure he felt against his neck. Part wanting to get the hell away from the constant, grinding fear that he was screwing things up for Casey. The current made him want to drink until he forgot everything. Or find a soft, willing woman to make him feel good.

It made him want to leave.

"So, as you can see, we've got some issues."

He tried to make it a joke, but Shelby wasn't laughing.

"That's a lot of change in a short time. It must be so difficult," she said.

He didn't like pity. There was nothing about his life that was pitiful. Pops taught him that; *as long as you were trying, as long as you were fighting, no one should pity you*.

But it wasn't pity on her face and fuck if he didn't wish it was, because compassion just wrecked him.

He folded his hands together, turning his knuckles white. When he'd moved in with Nana and Pop after his parents' accident, Nana had made him hot chocolate. The real kind, on the stove with milk and melted chocolate—he'd only ever had the powdered stuff. And that only once or twice. Nana put in a whole bunch of marshmallows and she hummed while she did it. Didn't make conversation, didn't try to pretend that everything was great. She just let everything suck, because she knew nothing she said could change it.

But she put that mug in front of him, looked him right in the eye, and cupped the back of his head in her hand and he'd fallen apart. Bawled like a baby.

Shelby's level eyes had the same effect.

So he looked down at his blistered and callused hands. At the grease stains caught in the ridges of his thumb that never came out. Would never come out.

"It hasn't been easy," was all he said. "I had just moved back to West Memphis, too. Like a year and a half before he came and found me, and some nights I can't sleep thinking—what if Vanessa had been busted earlier, and I missed him? What if he walked all that way and I wasn't even there?"

"But you were," she said, emphatically. Still, nightmares were nightmares and not so easily banished.

"Mrs. Jordal says Casey is a good kid," she told him as if she knew he still didn't have any clue what kind of kid he was.

He pressed the pad of his grease-stained thumb against the edge of the table, hard enough that his finger went white. "That's great."

Again, he was bitten by this terrible loneliness and it seemed she was the perfect antidote for it. Before in his life, moving around so much, when he was lonely, he went to a bar. Met a girl. Met a group of guys watching whatever game was on TV. Ty had taken his easy way with people for granted. The way he made friends everywhere he went. Until moving to Bishop, where he didn't know anyone and he was so deeply off balance, so terribly raw and irritated, he couldn't seem to remember how to talk to people.

But somehow this woman, the contained universe of her with her stern eyebrows and deep, unruffled quiet— she seemed like the kind of friend he needed right now. Or if not a friend, a surprising ally. An intriguing confidante.

"Thank you," he said.

"For what?"

He shrugged. "Listening."

"Well." Her pale skin glowed pinker and he loved it. Loved that reaction. Loved that he'd somehow caused a ripple across her calm surface. "It's . . . it's no problem." She opened the yellow file and took out a business card. "These are the therapists that I've worked with in the past. Dr. Osmond is my favorite. Kids respond very well to her, but I'm sure she'll put Casey on a waiting list. In fact, most of these counselors are going to put you on a waiting list. No one, unless it comes with a court order, is going to see you right away."

"Waiting list?" *Damn it!* He was drowning, and every single piece of floating wood that drifted by sank when he grabbed it.

"Probably a month."

Ty wasn't sure Casey had a month. Not at this rate. Suspension from school loomed and Ty didn't have any tools to make sure it didn't happen.

Frustration boiled through him.

But he said, "Thank you." She handed him one of each of the cards from the files.

"Please use my name when you call them," she said. "I don't know if it will help, but I doubt it would hurt."

She had this habit of catching the corner of her lower lip under her tooth. Just a little, just enough that she seemed somehow less . . . removed. Less cold. It made her seem doubtful or worried. Human. And he liked that. He liked it a lot.

Because all of his wires were crossed these days, because nothing was as it had been or what he was used to, the sight of that full, pink lip caught under the edge of a perfect white tooth turned him on.

She was a hot mix of stern and tolerant. Reserved and open. The humanity of her: of her tennis shoes and ponytail. The color-coded folders, that flower wall behind her that was somehow the prettiest thing he'd ever seen. The cling of her pants on her long legs, the way he had to work for her smiles but never had to work for her attention—it all joined forces against him and made him think of sex. With her.

"I wish there were more I could do for you."

What he'd told her, he'd only told a few people. Counselors. A few friends. And suddenly this barn was the

most intimate place he'd ever been. Which said probably way more about how sad his life was than the everyday magic of this barn.

He was attracted to her because she was decent.
Because she'd listened to him.

Because the way she bit her lip made him think about
sex.

Because he was so damn frustrated with his life, he
needed a release or someone was going to get hurt.

He imagined her letting him in. All the way in. Opening her arms, kissing the anxiety from his head. The
doubt and worry and fear. He imagined her letting him
work out all his aggression inside of her willing body.
He thought of causing more than just a ripple across her
calm surface. He thought of her screaming under him.
Sweaty and undone.

The thought spread like spilled motor oil; thick and
viscous, it covered everything in his brain. And he
couldn't think about anything but her.

You could do that for me, he thought. *You could help
me forget just for a little bit that so much is at stake.*

That electrical current that traveled through his body,
making him crazy, making him want to leap out of his
skin half the time, it lit him up from the inside. Focused
and hot, vicious and violent, it roared through him. He
wanted to fuck all the ice from her, sort through all the
different and surprising pieces, the sharp edges and hidden softness, until he got to the heart of her. The animal
of her.

He shifted in his chair, hiding his hard-on.

"Mrs. Jordal says he doesn't have many friends." She
pushed the edges of the blue file in front of her, to match
up with the yellow file. Perfectly straight. He wondered
what she would do if he pushed all those files to the
floor and laid her out on that table. Pulled down those
yoga pants and fucked her with his tongue, his fingers.

Messy and hot and wild.

"Wyatt?"

"Hmmm?" He jerked himself away from the porn running in his head. Stoic and silent, she blinked at him, and his filthy thoughts shamed him, utterly shamed him. She was lovely and smart and kind and . . . serious. The opposite of every single woman he'd ever dated or fucked or looked twice at. He pulled the reins on his thoughts, his animal lust.

"Does Casey have any friends?"

"Not that I know of. Not that he talks about." He'd been so worried about school and houses and counseling and court dates and starting fresh he didn't think about friends. Another check under the total fail column.

"Does he like sports or anything?"

Ty shifted again in the chair. His butt was now totally numb, which combined with the semi hard-on was a deeply uncomfortable feeling. "I . . . I don't really know."

"Well, I run some after-school and evening classes here for all different ages and there are a few of his classmates that come. Most of the other kids go to his school, too, so there would be some familiar faces."

"You're talking about art classes?"

She nodded. "If you're interested."

"Yes." *God, yes.* "Sign him up. When is it?"

There were plenty of women who were prettier when they smiled. His last girlfriend . . . Christ, a year ago? She'd had a smile that loosened his knees. Shelby didn't just get prettier . . . she changed. Her face, her whole vibe; it was as if a door opened and he got to see inside for just a second.

And inside, Shelby Monroe was radiant.

"Well, there's one tomorrow after school."

"He'll be here. What's the cost?"

"Let's see if he likes it first," she said and stood up. He was being dismissed, and that was okay. He stood up, too, blood flow returning to his ass with a hot rush.

"I don't know what to say." It was unusual for him to be at a loss. Casey got his mouth from him and there was no such thing as speechless for either of them. "The way we started out, I never would have expected you to stick out your neck for us this way."

"It's a small town, Wyatt."

"Please, call me Ty. My grandfather was Wyatt. It's weird to hear that name." Sad, was what it was.

"Okay. Ty, it's a small town. Sooner or later we're all sticking our necks out for each other."

He shrugged into his coat and Shelby picked up her folders.

"You're working with Brody Baxter?" she asked.

"Yeah. We're working on Cora's back deck, plus doing some stuff for The Pour House."

"That's gotta be dangerous," she said. "Spending your day at Cora's."

Ty laughed, tucking the cards in his back pocket. "It's torture when she makes those fritters."

"I have to walk on the other side of the street when she makes them. I usually go in on Sunday mornings with my mom."

It wasn't surprising she had a mom; everyone did. But it struck him that he'd told her so much about himself and he knew nothing about her. It was awkward, as if she was fully dressed in a snowsuit and he was totally naked.

He had never let a person like Shelby into his life, never wanted someone like her in his life before. His past was littered with drama queens and women of a certain *what you see is what you get, asshole* mentality. It wasn't just the obvious good girl, bad girl nonsense, though she was very clearly a good girl. It was the containment of her; she was a universe unto herself. A mystery.

"You want to go out for dinner?" he asked.

"Dinner?"

He nodded, very aware that as much as he liked the idea of a woman like her in his life, she probably had zero interest in stepping any further into his chaos. He had an image of him and Casey clinging to her boots like mud as she tried to figure out how to shake them off.

"Never mind."

"Okay," she said at the same time. She had that corner of her lower lip caught under her tooth and his blood sizzled at the sight.

"Okay never mind? Or okay let's have dinner?"

"Let's have dinner."

Well, holy shit. Look at that. He grinned at her. "Great. Saturday night?"

"Saturday night is perfect. I'll meet you at your house. Seven thirty?"

He nodded, wondering how he was going to handle Casey. Did he need a babysitter? It was already weird leaving him alone in the house to come over here for ten minutes. Dating was complicated all of a sudden.

At the door, he turned back to wave at her and wondered how a guy dated a woman like Shelby Monroe.

Chapter 5

Friday morning, Ty put down the drill and stood, twisting to get rid of the kinks in his back.

Half of the deck was framed and it wasn't even noon. He'd spent an hour in the morning getting Sean's awning to work and then he'd hightailed it over here to put up the posts and start framing. He could keep going and knock out most of the rest of it before quitting time, but inside Cora was frying chicken. And if there was a better, more distracting smell in the world, Ty couldn't think of it.

"Going to lunch?" Brody asked.

Ty rolled his eyes. "I can't take it anymore, man."

Brody's lip lifted, about as much expression as Ty could get out of him.

"All I've been thinking about is chicken for the last half hour," Brody said. "I'm waiting for—"

"Brody!" a woman called, and Ty didn't have to turn around to see that it was Ashley Montgomery. Brody, that silent, serious former Marine, just relaxed. It was as though he carried a load every minute of every day that he was away from that woman. And then at the sight of her, he was finally able to put it down.

The only other time Ty ever saw that version of love was with his grandparents. And they'd been so rare, so outrageously out of his ordinary, that he never imagined other people had a shot at that. But here it was again. He wasn't sure if that gave him hope or depressed the hell out of him.

"I thought you could break for lunch," Ashley said.

"You smelled the chicken?" When Brody smiled at his girlfriend, Ty had to look away, because there was a world revealed in that smile. A secret, warm, loving, sexy world.

"The wind shifted and now the smell is all over town. This place is about to get packed, so we'd better get some now," Ashley said.

She hooked her arm around Brody's waist and gave Ty a big grin. She was pretty in a seriously wholesome way. Like she should be on a box of breakfast cereal. "Hey, Ty! Great job on the deck."

"Thanks."

"You want to have lunch with us?"

"You guys go on in—I'll clean up here." He didn't like being with both of them. No matter how nice Ashley was, or how cool Brody was, he couldn't help but feel like an intruder. He felt like an intruder with everyone, unable to get comfortable with himself, much less anyone else.

Instead of arguing, Brody just started picking up tools and putting them in the lock box. Ashley helped and it was done before Ty even bent over to pick up his drill.

"Let's go," Ashley said at the door, her cheeks pink in the cold, her eyes glowing when she smiled at Brody.

"Seriously, you guys go ahead. I don't want to be a third wheel . . ."

Ashley leaned forward, grabbed his jacket, and pulled him into Cora's behind her.

Behind him, Brody laughed. "Ashley kind of gets what she wants, Ty. No use arguing."

The café was beginning to fill up. In the far corner, Sean waved them over and Ashley made a beeline for the booth.

Ty followed behind, somehow a little grateful that he'd

been forced to come in here. Forced to be social. He'd been a hermit in his garage for too long.

You want friends, he told himself, *this is how you make friends.*

Brody slid into the bench across from his brother. Ashley slid in after him, and Ty and Sean exchanged nods before he sat down.

The bell over the door rang and in walked a teenage girl with long blond hair. The way she walked and the look on her face indicated her youth was a lie. She carried herself like an adult.

"Gwen!" Sean yelled, lifting his hand to wave the girl over. Ty shrugged out of the way.

Christ, this was turning into a homecoming party.

She smiled and crossed over to the table. Gwen hugged Ashley and exchanged elaborate hand slaps with Sean. Brody just nodded and smiled.

"I'm Ty," he said, giving the girl a little salute.

"Gwen." She nodded as if they were meeting at City Hall or something.

"You meeting Jackson here?" Sean asked.

"Monica." She glanced around. "This place is packed."

"Sit." Ashley scooted over and made room for the girl, who shrugged out of her jacket and sat. All five of them crowded into a booth meant for four.

Ty was ready to be social, but this was a little ridiculous.

"How long you home for?" Brody asked Gwen.

"Jackson's law school stuff starts earlier than mine, so Monica and I thought we'd hang out here for a few days."

"How is school going?" Sean asked.

"It's good. I really like my teachers. My roommate is way better since she broke up with her boyfriend, who was a jerk." Ty admired how this girl talked to adults. She looked so young, but she met everyone's eyes instead of staring at her shoes, mumbling her answers down at her lap.

I wonder if Casey will ever be able to do this. If he'd ever be able to sit at a table full of adults and just talk. Not sneer or slouch in the corner like he was being tortured. Was it something kids learned? He didn't remember from his own childhood; it had been torn so badly down the middle that a lot of the little memories had slipped away. But one thing was sure: Casey needed to be around people like Gwen.

"You looking for work for a few days?" Ashley asked, wiggling her eyebrows.

Gwen laughed. "No, I'm doing some stuff with Shelby out at the Art Barn."

Ashley snapped her fingers. "Rats."

"You babysit?" Ty's voice cut through their chatter.

Gwen blinked and looked quickly over at Brody, who nodded as if giving the girl permission to answer Ty truthfully. All up and down Ty's neck his skin got hot. He totally understood why she would look to Brody for some kind of affirmation of his character, but it still rankled.

"I do," she said. "Do you need some help?"

"Tomorrow night, actually. I got a fifth-grade boy who isn't quite ready to be left alone, even though he might think otherwise. It's just a few hours. I live across the street from the Art Barn."

"Yeah, actually, that would be great." Her smile was so composed. She reminded him of Shelby—a little self-contained universe.

"You got a hot date?" Sean asked.

His instinct was to tell Sean to fuck off, but everyone else was staring at him.

"I guess you could say that," he answered.

"Where are you going to go?" Gwen asked.

"The Pour House?" Sean said, quickly.

"Not if I want the night to go well," Ty joked. But not really.

"Who is your date?" Ashley asked, all wide-eyed. Ashley was not a self-contained universe. She was a sponge, soaking up everything.

"Shelby Monroe," he said.

It was as if he'd detonated a bomb at the table. Everyone jerked back. And then they all started looking at one another, having little silent, meaningful conversations about his taking Shelby out for dinner.

The surprise was palpable and the judgment rolling off Sean was suffocating.

And that was the end of lunch with these people. Maybe they were good people, maybe in a few more months he'd be on the inside and this shit wouldn't bother the fuck out of him like it did, but right now he just needed to go.

He gave Gwen a smile, because he needed a babysitter and he didn't need her scared off. "Tomorrow at seven," he said. "I'll order a bunch of pizza and pay you whatever babysitters get paid. Feel free to take me to the cleaners." He grabbed his gloves off the bench and took off without a backward glance.

Art class. With Ms. Monroe.

Casey crossed the road up to the Art Barn on Friday after school, feeling, he didn't mind saying, like a stud.

An art class stud.

"I," he whispered, liking the way his breath poured out of his mouth like he'd just smoked a cigarette, "am an art class stud."

Ty didn't want him to walk over here by himself, because Ty had been a freak-out just waiting to happen ever since the meeting at school. But Casey managed to convince him not to walk him over to Ms. Monroe's barn like he was a baby.

Hard to be an art class stud when your dad-type person was dropping you off.

At the door, there was a sign made out of wood and sparkles and feathers and paint. It said "Open for Art." It didn't look like the kind of thing that should be outside; it was really fancy. He touched one of the blue feathers and it fell off the sign onto the ground.

Shit. Shit. He grabbed the feather and tried to stick it back on, but instead he knocked another feather off. And then a big, shiny fake pink gem fell off.

Casey grabbed all the stuff and took a big step away from the barn so that nothing he did would ruin the sign any more. He shoved the feathers and the gem in his pocket and pulled open the door.

Inside it was like that Willy Wonka chocolate factory movie, but for art instead of candy. Art was everywhere; it hung from the ceiling and on the walls. There was one whole wall of paper flowers. Even that was cool, and he hated flowers. There were shelves of paper and trays of markers. Tinfoil and feathers and gems and sparkles and scissors. Glue. Paint. Big, fat blobs of clay in a whole bunch of colors.

And in the middle of it all was Ms. Monroe.

Polishing diamonds.

"Whoa," he breathed.

"Hey!" she said with a nice smile. It wasn't really big, that smile, like those of a lot of teachers and counselors and social workers who thought that if they smiled big enough, he wouldn't notice how shitty his life was. Or how they were making it even shittier. Ms. Monroe's smile just made him feel like she'd been waiting for him and she was super glad he was there.

She glanced over at the clock on the wall. "You're early."

His stomach fell into his shoes. *Early*. That was impossibly lame. He didn't want to go home; he supposed he could go outside and sit for a while. He took a shuffling step backward. "I can come back."

"No. It's awesome you're early. I need some help." She held up the diamond in her hand; it was huge.

"Where'd you get that?" he asked.

She pointed to the metal light sitting in the middle of the table. It was one of those things that hung from the ceiling.

"It's a chandelier. I'm just polishing the crystals."

"Crystals?" He stepped closer, and next to her in a faded blue towel on the table were a bunch of those diamond crystal things. "They're not diamonds?"

"No." Again she smiled, and he didn't feel like a bonehead for thinking they were. "I wish they were. Here." She handed him a cloth and kicked out one of the tiny chairs across from her. "I could use your help."

He sat down and took one of the heavy crystals from the blue towel. Sucked that it wasn't a real diamond.

"How was school?" She held her crystal up to the light.

"Fine."

"Fine good or fine bad?"

"Fine fine." He watched her hands on the crystal and copied what she did, running the cloth over the sharp edge. She hummed and picked up another crystal.

"Where are you going to put this thing?" he asked. The metal looked like a plant with leaves and stuff, and he guessed when these crystals were put on it, they would look like the flowers.

He liked this light.

She pointed up. There were about four other lights like this one hanging from the rafters.

"You barely see them up there."

"That's all right."

"But if you bought it—"

"I didn't buy it. Someone just dropped it off. People leave stuff out here all the time. Stuff they don't want."

"You use it all?"

"I try to. Rugs. Butcher paper. Chandeliers. I have a piano back there." She pointed into the shadows over his shoulder. "And couches over there."

Over her shoulder next to the wall of flowers were two couches.

"That's cool," he said.

"I think so, too." She put the crystal she'd been polishing in a row with a few other ones. He put his down next to hers.

There were ten of them all lined up, shooting rainbows around the barn.

A long time ago, his mom had these earrings some guy gave to her and they were a lot like these crystal things. Shiny and sparkly. Fancy. She used to put her hair up in a ponytail and wear those earrings. When she would lean over and kiss him good night, they were so long they brushed his cheek. One night she came home messed up with a split lip and only one of those earrings. Pissed off, she threw the other one in the garbage under the sink.

When she'd passed out on the couch, he grabbed it from under the sink and hid it on his bookshelf. But a few nights later, she woke him up in the middle of the night, shoved all his clothes in a garbage bag, and skipped out on rent.

The earring had been left behind.

"Have you seen the dogs?" he asked.

"The strays?" She pursed her lips. "People drop their dogs out here. I try to call the shelter in Masonville, but it seems like there are more every day."

"We've got this stray that eats our garbage."

"You should tell your dad to call the shelter. They can be dangerous."

Casey was never going to tell Ty to call the shelter. Ever.

"Casey," she said with a little laugh, as if she'd read his mind. "Some of those dogs are really sick with rabies, or they've been trained to fight. You shouldn't try to make friends with them."

"I won't." She narrowed her eyes at him as though she knew he was lying and he laughed. "I promise. I won't."

"Do you like Mrs. Jordal?" she asked, after they both went back to polishing crystals.

"Yep," he said. "She's nice."

"Nice?" She laughed. "I don't think she's ever been called nice."

"She's nice to me," he said with some pride. Because Mrs. Jordal wasn't nice to everyone; that was totally obvious.

"Then how come you're in so much trouble all the time?" She watched him out of the corner of her eyes.

He shrugged. He got in trouble on the playground and in the lunchroom, and sometimes in the computer lab. But never in Mrs. Jordal's class.

The crystal was hard under his fingers; he could feel its sharp edges even through the cloth and he wondered if he could break it. And as soon as he thought it, he wanted to break it. That's how his brain worked sometimes. As soon as a bad idea got in there, he wanted to see it done. He wanted to see what would happen.

Carefully, he set the crystal down.

He didn't want to talk about why he got in trouble. He didn't want to talk about why he was so angry and how sometimes he couldn't control it and how sometimes when the world seemed so unfair and like it just wanted him to die, all he could do was fight back.

He hated talking about that.

One of his counselors told him that when things got bad, he had to pull up all the bridges around himself. That he couldn't let the things he saw, or the stuff Mom did, or the way that they lived get inside his head. He had to pull up the bridges, close his eyes, and be an island.

Sometimes he was amazing at that. Sometimes he was the best island in the world—nothing got to him. But sometimes he was too late with those bridges and he was totally swamped by not just bad stuff but good stuff, too. And what was weird was that the good stuff was worse than the bad stuff.

Like the other day, when Ty took him fishing. Even though they didn't catch any fish, it had been the best day in his whole life and he'd tried not to show Ty how happy he was. How close he was to bawling like a baby. So, at the restaurant they went to after fishing, when no one was looking, he took a pack of cigarettes out of a woman's purse when she went to the bathroom.

After that he didn't feel like crying anymore.

"What . . . what sort of stuff do we do in the class?"

"Scott from your class is working on some miniature sculptures."

Scott was a pretty cool guy. He had been in Casey's group for the medieval castle project at school and he'd made this really awesome tiny throne and some soldiers and horses for the castle.

"Look over there," she said, pointing to a low shelf in the middle of the room. The top of it was covered in tiny clay figures. He recognized half the figures from the Skylanders video game.

Ty got him that game. And the second one. Ty had bought him like a gazillion video games when they moved here and he'd put them all in Casey's bedroom. Which had been awesome for a while; Casey had played video games all night, but now he'd totally figured out that Ty did that so he wouldn't actually have to look at Casey. Or talk to him.

"These are cool," he murmured, picking up a little elf character with a flaming arrow notched to a tiny bow. "Really cool." This was where Scott must have done the work for the castle project. He imagined Ms. Monroe helping him, and his skin itched he was so jealous.

"Well, if you'd like, I'll give you some clay and you can work with that today."

He bent down, peering closer at the tiny flames eating up that arrow. They looked so real.

"That would be all right, I guess," he said.

She started to gather up the crystals and cloths. "I'd better get ready." She picked up the metal chandelier and the towel of dirty crystals and headed down the hallway on the other side of the barn.

He looked down at the crystal in his hand. It caught the light, and a bright little circle showed up on the clay figures in front of him. He moved the crystal in his hand and the circle shifted from figure to figure, like a little spotlight.

He put the crystal in his pocket, where it sat heavy and hot.

And then he picked up that elf with the flaming arrow and he put it in his pocket, too.

Chapter 6

"I don't need a babysitter." Casey was picking the pepperoni off the pizza Ty had ordered. The kid, as far as Ty could tell, had a pizza eating system. Eat all the pepperoni, eat the cheese, eat the crust. Repeat.

"So you've said."

"I'll just watch video games in my room. It's not like I'm going to burn the house down."

"I'm pretty much done talking about this." Ty stood at the front windows, looking for any sign of Gwen. It was nothing but dark out there, the lights of Shelby's house set back from the road the only break in the thick blackness.

All the lights were on in that house, again. Which was weird. Even the little window up in the eaves.

I wonder what's going on.

"Can I have another piece of pizza?" Casey asked.

"How many have you had?"

"Five," Casey burped the answer.

Ty winced and turned on his kid, who was beaming as if he'd won the talent show. "I'm going to give you a little advice, buddy. This girl that's coming over? She's pretty. Really pretty. And that garbage, that won't impress her."

"Is she as pretty as the girl you're going out with?" Casey asked, angling for information. Ty hadn't told him who he was dating because he worried his dad dating his teacher might be weird for Casey. When he was Casey's age, if his dad had done that he would have died a thousand horrible humiliated deaths. Not that his dad would have ever had a chance with one of his teachers, and not that Mom, no matter what phase of broken up or together she and Dad were in, would have ever let that happen.

"Save Gwen some pizza," Ty said.

"Gwen," Casey muttered. "What kind of name is Gwen? Is she like a hobbit?"

Ty smiled and went back to looking out the window. Casey was going to eat those words when the pretty blonde showed up.

Finally, some headlights slid through the night and pulled into his driveway. The headlights went dark and two people stepped out of the car. Two women.

The motion sensor lights over the garage clicked on as they walked past and he recognized Gwen, but the other woman, dark-haired and tall, wasn't familiar. She was drop-dead gorgeous in black jeans and tall black boots.

But not anyone he'd met yet.

There was a knock at the front door, and much to his surprise Casey jumped and tore down the hallway to open it. Ty followed at a cooler pace.

"You must be Casey?" he heard Gwen say. "I'm Gwen."

Ty stepped into the hallway just as Gwen was coming in.

"And I'm Monica," the other woman said, stepping in behind Gwen.

In every single way the woman was stunning. Dark, nearly blue-black hair. Red lips. Honest-to-God purple eyes.

Wonder Woman, he thought. Wonder Woman was the first woman he'd ever had the hots for. And Monica was a dead ringer.

"Hi, Monica," Ty said, stepping into the mix. "I'm Casey's dad, Ty."

Monica's smile was not the most welcoming and he realized she was here to suss out the situation; he supposed if he'd been in her spot, he'd do the same.

"Nice to meet you," Monica said and they shook hands. She had a firm, no-nonsense grip just like, he imagined, Wonder Woman. "I'm Gwen's sister."

Gwen had a little smile about that.

"Come on in," Ty said, trying to be welcoming when he wasn't totally sure what the protocol was here. Did she need a urine test? A blood oath that there were no bodies in the basement? "There's pizza."

They walked down the small hallway toward the kitchen with its camouflage fridge and fake old table. In front of him, Monica put a hand to the hallway wall, as if feeling for something under the surface of the wood.

"You haven't changed it much," she said, glancing over her shoulder at him. "My mom lived here before you."

"Your mom is that reality show star?" he asked. The guy he'd rented the house from had told him all about the television star who had remodeled and lived in this very house, disguised that very fridge, for nearly six months.

"Simone Appleby," she said.

"I've seen that show," Casey said, watching Gwen from the corner of his eye.

"You are not alone," Monica laughed, looking around the kitchen with its pizza boxes and the carburetor parts on the counter.

"Then that makes you . . ." Ty said, connecting all his pop culture dots.

"Monica Appleby," Gwen said, beaming with pride.

And that hero worship was very sweet, but it did nothing to dispel the insanity of having Monica Appleby in his house.

Monica and her mother had been on a reality show,

years and years ago, at the birth of the craze. Monica had been a teenager—and a full-throttle rebel, too. One could say that the terrible trend of teenage movie stars and celebrities behaving badly started with the woman who was now standing in his kitchen, making sure *he* wasn't going to corrupt Gwen.

Hilarious.

At some point in that show with her mom, Monica had run away to become a sort of glorified music groupie. She'd resurfaced a few years back, with a cool book about growing up backstage in the music industry.

"I liked your book," he said. "The Wild Child one."

"Thank you," she said, and he imagined her having this exact exchange a million times in the past.

"Her new book is going to be even better," Gwen said, shrugging off her jacket. "It's for teenagers."

"Can't wait to read it," Ty said.

Monica put her hand on Gwen's head. "Gwen is going to be my publicist."

The conversation stalled out and Ty glanced at his watch. It was after seven thirty.

"We've got Netflix," Casey said to Gwen. "We can watch like every movie."

"Not *every* movie," Ty said. "Remember, when I come home I can see what you watched. So, nothing R-rated, and none of that creepy violent anime stuff you watched last time. Don't think you're getting away with anything."

Casey shot him a humiliated angry look.

"Come on," Gwen said, grabbing a plate and piece of pizza, "let's see what our options are."

Casey led Gwen into the living room, where the flat screen and couches were, leaving Ty alone with the Wild Child.

In an instant of stifling silence he decided not to wait

for Shelby here. He'd head over to her house to pick her up.

"I've never had a babysitter before, so I don't know what . . . ?" he asked.

"I'm doing here?" Monica supplied, staring at him from the corner of her purple eyes.

"I guess it's to see if you can find the bodies, but really, I just needed a babysitter. Gwen came along at the right time."

Monica laughed, thank God. "Jackson, Gwen's brother, has grown a little protective, so I thought I'd just come and check things out. I'll just stick around long enough to eat a piece of pizza and see them settled."

Ty wasn't sure if he should be grateful or offended.

"That's fine . . . but I need to go." He grabbed his coat from the pegs by the back door.

"Right!" Monica waved her hands. "You've got a date with Shelby."

He stopped halfway into his jacket. "How did you know?"

"Small town," she said with a shrug. "Gossip is part of the deal."

He pulled his jacket all the way on and took his keys out of his pocket.

"How do you know Shelby?" she asked.

"She's Casey's art teacher. She helped us out of a bind."

Monica flipped open the pizza box and made a big show out of studying the selection. Which was pepperoni and more pepperoni. "And that's the only way you know her?"

"No," he snapped, tired of everyone's sideways glances and roundabout questions. "We were spies together."

"Shelby's a friend," she said, as if that justified the way everyone looked at him when he said her name. "To all of us. We're just looking out for her."

"That's nice and all, but this is just a date. And unless you want your friend stood up, I need to go."

"You're right," she said, smiling as if that would fix it all. She was hot, he'd give her that, but she was no Shelby. "I'm sorry. Have a great time."

He walked away from the kitchen toward the front door. "All my valuables are upstairs in my dresser. The sock drawer."

"Good to know."

He opened the door and stepped out only to turn and see Monica standing there as if it were her house.

"This is weird, you get that, right?" he asked.

"Welcome to Bishop."

Up?

Shelby pulled her hair back into its standard ponytail. But that just looked so . . . standard.

Down?

She let it go and it rained down over her shoulders, halfway down her back. It had been so long since she'd worn it down, the length really surprised her. It felt oddly . . . decadent. Like she was Lady Godiva. Or a woman in a Sir Frederic Leighton painting.

Down wins.

She put on some lipstick, wiped it off, and tried another shade. The brighter of the two she owned. A little mascara and she stepped back, trying to see as much of herself as she could in the mirror over the bathroom sink. The black wrap dress had a deep V-neck. For her anyway; for the rest of the world it was downright demure. The underwear she'd bought last summer in an effort to seduce the man at a conference, made the most of her figure, and the small mounds of her breasts, rising up from the neckline, looked pretty. Sexy.

She looked very much not like herself. Which was awesome.

The thong was still as uncomfortable as it had been the first time she'd worn it. But in for penny, in for a pound.

She blew out a long breath and gave herself a good, long look in the eye.

"You're fine," she whispered. "Totally fine."

A glance at her watch confirmed she was late. And Deena, Cathy's sister, who was coming over to be with Evie, was late, too.

She opened the bathroom door only to collide with Mom, standing in the hallway in her high-necked nightgown.

"Hey, Mom, what are you up to?"

Her mother's eyes traveled over Shelby's dress. The hemline that flirted with her knees. The low-heeled boots that she'd polished. The neckline and the pearl-drop necklace Mom had given her upon her confirmation in the church.

Then she saw Shelby's hair.

Mom's face hardened, became a mask of sour anger. Shelby didn't have time to process the change, to see what was happening before it actually happened.

"Look at you," Mom spat. Cold dread slid down Shelby's spine. Mom had drifted away from herself again and that was never good. Shelby took a half-step back hoping to get out of arm's reach, but she was too late and her mother reached out and grabbed a handful of her hair. Yanking it so hard Shelby's head turned sideways. Tears stung her eyes.

"Mom!" She tried to pull herself away, but her mother only yanked harder.

"You need to pray," Mom said. "Your father is waiting for you at the church."

She eased Mom's fingers, trying not to hurt her, away

from her hair and leapt out of reach. "Daddy's dead. The church is gone. There's no—"

Mom's gray eyes raked her and she felt the overwhelming need to hide her chest, the length of her legs under her skirt. Mom hadn't had one of these episodes—where she seemed to take over Daddy's old place in this world—in weeks.

Shelby had locked down the routine, made sure everything was the same in their world so that nothing would set her off. And it had helped.

This is what happens when you change the routine.

When Daddy had been alive and preaching, Mom had been the roadblock between Shelby and his zealousness. She hadn't been perfect, Shelby still spent more than her share of time begging forgiveness for sins that had never been committed, but Mom had tried. Mom had kept her safe as possible.

Which made these moments when she adopted Dad's religious fervor and censure all the more terrifying.

"All dressed up like this. Like a slut. You need to repent. Repent your deeds. Your filthy thoughts."

"Mom—"

Fast as lightning, Mom smacked her across the face, and before Shelby could recover, Mom got ahold of her wrist, a bone-and-steel manacle forcing her to her knees.

Mom came down with her, clenching their hands together, bending her head over their clasped hands, her lips moving in prayer. "Forgive us, Father," she nearly moaned, rocking back and forth. "Forgive us for our sins. Our sinful thoughts. Our sinful bodies."

Shelby tried to pull herself away, to get to her feet, to get her distance. But Mom yanked her closer, spittle flying from her lips as she prayed with anguish. With more devotion than she'd ever exhibited.

Shelby felt panicked tears burn behind her eyes. Her chest was so tight she could barely breathe.

"Hello?" a cheerful voice cried out. Shelby collapsed forward, her chest nearly on her knees. It was Deena.

"Mom," she whispered, trying to pull her mother back from the wilderness she was lost in. "Mom. Deena's here. Remember Deena? She's helping you sort the photographs. The pictures."

"You're a liar!" she spat, her fingernails digging into Shelby's hand.

"Mom." She swallowed a pained gasp and tried to smile. "Deena from church is here." Deena wasn't from church. She was a nurse with a daughter in her second year of college and she made extra money sometimes doing this kind of work. Reverse babysitting.

Mom glanced up, some of the fervent light draining from her eyes. Her mother was more child than adult sometimes. And nothing could pierce Shelby, nothing could destroy her, more than that lost, scared look in her mother's eyes. Because behind the fear was knowledge. Understanding.

She knew.

Mom knew that she was drifting away from what was real. All of her anchors were uncertain.

"Deena?" she asked.

Shelby nodded, biting her lip. "She's helping you go through the photographs."

That wasn't true, but Mom had an ongoing project with the photographs; it changed in nature and focus, but it was a constant.

"The pictures of the church."

Shelby closed her eyes against the bitter ache in her chest.

"Yes. The pictures of the church."

Carefully, she began to stand, not sure if her mother

was with her or would suddenly pull her back down again. But Mom got to her feet, their hands still clenched.

"Hello?" It was Deena again, now at the bottom of the stairs.

"We'll be down in a second, Deena," she called. Mom dropped her hands and looked around the hallway, lined with piles of books and stacks of sewing projects. Boxes of yarn that she had ordered from a shopping network before Shelby cancelled the credit card she'd been using.

Do you see? Shelby wanted to ask. *Do you see this or not? Are you here?*

"What happened to you?" Mom asked. She reached up and touched Shelby's hair where it was messed up from her yanking on it.

"Nothing," she breathed, trying to smile through the squeeze of the vise around her heart.

"You look so pretty," Evie said, stroking down her hair. "Your makeup is running."

Shelby nodded and felt hot tears fall from her eyes.

There wasn't going to be a date. She couldn't do it. Couldn't sit across from Ty in some bar or restaurant and make small talk after her mother had called her a slut, smacked her face. Logically, she understood that Evie didn't mean it. That it was the disease. Dr. Lohmann said the days would come when her mother no longer recognized her, when the care Shelby gave her would not be enough, when the disease already swallowing Mom's life would start to swallow hers and she would need help. More help.

It was inevitable.

But in her heart there was no way she could reconcile everything; she didn't have the personality, the wherewithal to bridge the gap between coping day to day with her mother's Alzheimer's and going out on a date with a man who wore leather bracelets.

A date. Who was she kidding? Shelby didn't date. She pined after men who didn't want her. She made terrible sexual mistakes. Dating was for regular women. Normal women.

She was devastated inside and she could not pretend otherwise.

"Let's go downstairs," Shelby said, leading her down the steps to where Deena was waiting. There was no fooling Deena, who knew every inch of the Alzheimer's battlefield, and when they came down the stairs she felt Deena's sharp eyes taking in the messed-up hair, the tears, the despair Shelby could not hide.

Deena's smile was a tight, knowing knot, and Shelby had to look away, uncomfortable with pity and compassion.

"Hello, Evie," Deena said, quietly, but kindly. "How are you tonight?"

"I'm fine," she said, though it was obvious she was confused. Scared.

"Mom's ready to look through those photographs with you," Shelby said meaningfully, but Deena needed very little prompting.

"Looking forward to it. Why don't you get settled, Evie, and I'll get us something to drink."

Evie shuffled off into the living room, where all the boxes of loose photographs and the albums were stacked.

"Are you all right?" Deena asked.

"Is it that bad?" She smoothed down her hair, wiped her thumbs under her eyes only to pull them back covered in black mascara.

"You just look like you've been smacked around some."

"Some," she breathed, but it rattled in her chest. Through her body, as if it were made of tin cans and string. "I can't leave . . ."

Deena shook her head and grabbed her hands. "Nonsense. We're fine. Your mom is calm now. She'll have forgotten about it already."

"I can't."

"You can and more importantly, you should."

"How do I—?" She stopped, swallowing the words and the tears.

Deena took a deep breath. "You need to think about care, honey."

The tears again, and she had to look away or fall to pieces in Deena's soft, strong arms. "She hasn't had an episode like that in a long time. I think . . . I think it's just because I'm dressed this way."

"So you should never dress up again?"

Shelby shot her an arch look, because Deena knew it was more than that. It wasn't anything that could be simplified into a question of either/or.

"You look beautiful, honey. Just beautiful." She smoothed Shelby's hair down and handed her a Kleenex to clean up her mascara.

"Thank you," she said, gathering up the edges of herself, but they were jagged and sharp and she felt herself shifting under her skin. Writhing and squirming. Distressed and out of sorts. "But I really don't think I can—"

A loud knock at the door interrupted her. "Damn it," she muttered. It had to be Ty. It was seven forty-five and he must have crossed the street to get her. She ran to the front door before he knocked again, setting Mom off.

She took a deep breath at the door, formulating a lie about a stomachache or a sudden migraine, anything that would keep her from having to sit at a table with him and pretend everything was okay.

Hoping her smile didn't look as bad as it felt, she pulled open the door.

It was Ty. Ty in a denim and shearling coat over a

light blue sweater that made his eyes look like the sky in August. His breath steamed in the cold air, small puffs from his beautiful lips. Sudden, sharp, and unpredictable lust lit a dangerous spark and the combustible emotions in her chest, her heart—they went up in flames.

"Wow," he breathed, taking her in. "You . . . you look great."

"Thank you," she managed to say, past the sudden horrible raging heat in her blood. "You, too."

"You ready? I don't mean to rush you or—" He tilted his head, the smile draining from his face. Those blue eyes, they turned cold. The color of ice. "Are you okay?"

He lifted a hand, as if to touch her cheek, where perhaps there was a pink mark from her mother's hand, but she shifted away, unable to be touched like that by him.

With compassion. With kindness. She would shatter like glass under his kind touch.

She swallowed down a thousand responses. The truth, versions of the truth, outright lies. She swallowed down all of them. Where they boiled and burned in her stomach. She felt her own break with reality coming and she needed to change her clothes, put her hair back up in a ponytail. Remind herself who she was. *I am my mother's daughter. Her caregiver. Everything else has to slide in around that.*

"I'm sorry, Ty," she said, closing a door between them, one she never should have opened. "I don't think—"

Suddenly, she was pushed from behind out onto the porch. She turned, only to have her coat thrown over her head. She yanked it off to see Deena grinning in the doorway.

"Go," Deena said. "Get drunk. Don't come back for at least two hours."

And then the door slammed behind her. Ty and Shelby

stared at each other under the porch light. Which then blinked out.

Ty's laughter rumbled through the partial darkness.

And she couldn't help it—she just gave up holding onto who she was. She just dropped every jagged edge she'd been clinging to and she let her world fall away. All of her pretenses.

This is Dean all over again, she thought, panicked. *This is some kind of awful self-destructive behavior. I use sex with inappropriate men as a coping mechanism. How can this be okay?*

But she knew in her gut that Ty wasn't Dean. Ty wasn't going to hurt her, not the way Dean had.

"I don't want to go on a date," she whispered, staring down at her boots.

"Oh." He sounded surprised. Hurt even. "Well, then—"

She was past worrying about whether or not this would work. Whether it would turn around and ruin her life in a few months. The pressure release valve was in danger of breaking right off, her whole life about to implode.

And she had to do something.

"Follow me," she breathed and stepped off the porch toward the barn.

Chapter 7

Ty had been around the block a time or two, and if it were any other woman leading him across the silver-tipped grass to a dark barn, he'd think he was about to get lucky. But this was Shelby, and she'd answered that door looking both gorgeous and like she was about to twitch right out of her skin.

I'm either going to get laid or she's going to take an ax to my head.

She pulled open the door and turned on a few of the lights. The chandelier she'd been fixing now hung above the small gathering of couches near the flower wall and created a gold pool of light.

"Would you like a drink?" she asked.

"Sure."

"All I have is bourbon."

"Bourbon is fine."

She threw her coat down on the low table where they'd sat the other day and he followed suit. The barn wasn't freezing. She must have had it insulated at some point. He contemplated his couch choice: a blue velvet thing that looked like women used to faint on it or a big, fat leather couch with some of the stuffing coming out. He chose the leather and sat in the corner of it, one arm along the back, the other along the armrest, and waited to see what was going to happen next.

Who knew a date with Shelby would feel . . . dangerous.

It was a good sign when she came down the small,

dark hallway with a bottle of bourbon and not an ax. He noticed the bottle was the good stuff, too. And she had two mugs.

Volatile energy poured off her and he was surprised the lightbulbs overhead didn't shatter as she walked under them. As she got closer, her energy, like a virus, spread to him and he felt the hot coil of need in his belly.

Need. And want.

She sat across from him on the blue velvet couch. With her hair down like that and the flowers behind her, she looked like a woman from a different era. A different time. A pristine, beautiful lady in an ivory tower somewhere.

He wanted to get her messy. Dirty.

She put the mugs down on the floor and poured a hefty double shot in each mug.

"We're getting drunk?" he asked.

"That's my plan."

He nodded and accepted the mug. She lifted hers in cheers and then shot it down.

"You . . . okay?" he asked. She leaned back over to pour more bourbon in her mug and her hair fell down over her face, over her arms. So much hair, a golden curtain.

He liked it. Imagined it against her bare chest, that golden hair obscuring her pale skin. Her pink nipples. He imagined it in his fist. The silk of it caught in his fingers as he pulled it, making her cry out.

A deep breath shuddered and shook in his lungs and he took a big sip of the bourbon.

The need and want she inspired in him scrubbed away at the polite veneer he was determined to hold onto.

"Not really," she said. She drank another ounce and took a hissing breath. "I am not really okay."

That she wasn't all right wasn't a surprise. It was all

over her face. But that she was being honest and telling him that—that was a surprise. And, kind of an honor. "Can I help?"

She laughed, glancing at him through her hair. "Probably." She downed what was left in her mug.

"I feel like we should get some food in you if you're going to drink like that," he told her, putting down his mug. One of them needed to have a clear head.

"I don't want to go out to eat." Those level brown eyes saw right through him. Past skin, past muscle and bone. She looked right at his heart, beating hard with anger and lust and frustration.

Anticipation sizzled through him. It had been a very long time since he'd anticipated this. And never with a woman like her. Someone so far out of his realm of experience. The whole act felt new.

"What do you want?" His voice was low. Hot. Loaded.

"I want to fuck you."

Hard. His cock was hard as stone in a heartbeat. The world swam for a second and he didn't fully grasp the implication of her getting to her feet and crossing the small, worn rug to stand between his legs.

And then she sank to her knees.

"Shelby," he breathed, part prayer. Part *are you sure you want to be doing this*?

"Do you want this?" she asked. Again, straight to the point. No bullshit.

He nodded, speechless.

"Me, too. I just . . . I just want to forget for a little bit."

It took him a second, because he didn't intend this. He'd expected a dinner date, some small talk. He'd even been polishing up his bad first date stories to tell her over the appetizer. But at the root of his attraction to Shelby, at the base of it, was *this*.

He wanted to forget for a little bit, too.

She tucked her hair behind her ears and when she looked at him she was steadfast. Rock solid. Whatever had driven her here, between his legs, she was making this choice. She wanted to be down on her knees in front of him.

He stretched his arms back out and shifted his hips forward slightly on the couch and she took him up on the subtle invitation. Her fingers moved over his belt, the buttoned fly of his jeans. On fire, he pulled his sweater over his head and she glanced up, her eyes running over his chest like fingers. She shifted on her knees, her lips falling open, her brown eyes dilating, and he felt stupid hot pride swell through him. He liked the way this woman looked at him. He liked *her,* but suddenly, the way this was playing out was totally wrong. It was hot that she planned to kneel between his legs and suck his dick. But he hadn't even kissed her. And a woman like Shelby, she should be kissed.

He grabbed her waist, feeling the tension of her muscles and the soft give of flesh, and pulled her up into his lap, shifting so her legs were split over his, her butt against his knees. She tried to shift closer, but he kept her there. Someone had to slow this shit down.

"I haven't even kissed you," he whispered.

She blinked at him as if considering his proposal. "Okay."

He cupped her face in his hands, his fingertips pulling on the thin strands of hair by her ears. "You're beautiful."

She flinched. "Don't—"

He sat up, stopping her words, sealing her lips with his. Softly at first, because she was that kind of lady. Because whatever sexual instinct he had, he had the good sense to do the opposite with her. Instead of feasting on her, opening her mouth with his tongue, sucking on her lips, he pressed his closed mouth against hers. A little respect, because she was something to revere.

The heat of her sigh against his cheek inflamed him but he kept it slow. Gentle. She put her hands against his shoulders, the fingers curling over the muscles to bite into the skin on his back. He hissed against her lips; he loved that touch. The sharp pain of a woman's nails against his back. Nothing threw gasoline on the fire better than that.

Slow, he told himself. *Slow.*

She leveraged herself against him, crawling upward on his knees until she was fully in his lap. The heat of her pussy hard against his dick. He recited the parts of the Velocette carburetor in his head.

She licked at his lips, merciless and driven. He stopped trying to resist it and let her in. The kiss he wanted, she gave him. And then some. Hot and wet, sucking at his lips, his tongue, she raked her teeth over the inside of his lip. Her hands left his shoulders and cupped his head, yanking out the ponytail until his hair filled her hands. She gathered it up and *pulled.*

He yanked his mouth away, more turned on than he could handle. "Slow down—"

Her eyes were wild and she pressed herself hard against the erection in his jeans. "I don't want slow." Her hands dropped his hair and ran down his chest, her fingers trailing across the muscles of his stomach down to his belt. He didn't stop her this time. He was powerless to stop her, and her fingers slipped in the gap of his open jeans and grabbed him through his boxers.

"Fuck," he breathed, the word nearly soundless. He arched his head back and she leaned forward, licking his throat, biting at the soft skin under his chin. He jerked in her hands.

"I don't want gentle," she whispered into his ear. And

then she sucked the lobe into her mouth, bit at the tender flesh with her front teeth, and he nearly twitched right out of his skin. His hands grabbed her hips, his fingers curving over her ass, and she moaned into his ear.

The walls could have come down around them. The place could have been on fire and it didn't matter. Nothing mattered but this sudden surprising heat that melted them together.

"Honey," he breathed, lifting a hand to stroke her hair, but she dodged it. Instead, she gripped his hair in her hands, fists of it like she didn't care if she hurt him, like she *wanted* to hurt him. He hissed and arched against her, unable to stop himself, unable to curb this wild violence humming between them, a motor running at full throttle. She pulled his head back until he met her eyes. "I. Do. Not. Want. Kind."

She was the fiercest animal on the planet; he'd never seen anything like it.

He shed any idea of the way he should be with her and gave in to the animal living in his skin. The animal that had been working really hard to play by the rules, to do the right thing, to be a father and an employee and part of this town. He gave the animal—who remembered selfish, wild pleasure—free rein.

He pulled her harder against him, so his cock nudged up right to her, separated only by the fabric of their underwear. And then he took that long blond hair of hers in his fists and pulled her down for a kiss. His kind of kiss. Raw and wild. He fucked her mouth with his tongue, and layers fell off of them. Civility. Manners. Courtesy.

They were animals against each other. Hair and teeth, tongues and lips. He curled a hand over her shoulder, holding her hard against him while he ravaged her mouth and pushed himself between her legs. He felt her muscles shaking, her throat working as she groaned into his mouth.

Fuck, he thought and stood, pulling her with him, her legs around his waist.

"What—" she panted, pulling her mouth away as he walked over to his coat. "What are you doing?"

"Getting a condom," he said, walking over to his coat, wallet, and the small silver packet of wishful thinking he'd slipped in there earlier tonight.

"I'm . . . heavy." Her muscles, so loose a second ago, were now tight and she was pushing against him. He made a pit stop at the low bookshelf and shoved art projects out of the way so he could set her down there and kiss her back into agreement. Into soft muscles and small groans against his mouth. He slipped his hand from the top of her boot up her thigh, under her dress.

Her ass was bare, the muscles twitching under his palm.

"Oh," he whispered against her lips, smiling as his fingers found the small bit of silk between her legs, running through that dark valley between her cheeks. She twitched away and he stopped, not wanting to force anything on this woman. But then she pressed back against him.

"Yeah?" he whispered against her lips, wanting permission to be clear.

"Yeah."

"So hot," he breathed, tracing the edge of her thong down between her legs to where she was wet and hot and perfect. He pushed the silk against her. Against her clit. And she dropped her head back, crying out. He followed that silk back down to the hot, sweet entrance of her body and then back farther, all the way up to her waist. He did it three times, until her hips were arching against his fingers like she wanted all the touches. All the places.

"You are so hot," he whispered into her ear, pressing kisses against her cheek. The corner of her mouth. She made a groaning, laughing noise as if her hotness were all news to her and he hated that that might be the truth for her. He circled her clit again through the silk and she started to grind against him.

He stepped back.

"Show me."

"What?" Her lips were swollen, her eyes unfocused. The neckline of her dress had been pulled aside to reveal the black lace edge of a bra. Oh, fuck, he was going to strip her down to that underwear and make a feast of her.

"Show me," he said but she didn't move, so he turned her around so that her hands were braced against the bookshelf and lifted the back of her dress, revealing her strong white thighs, the perfection of her round ass, bisected by the black silk.

He groaned, palming her in his wide, rough hands, and she pushed back against him, arching against his touch. He bent and kissed her there, once on the top of each cheek, and then bit her. Her hands splayed out, her fingers curling around the edges of the bookshelf.

"You are gorgeous," he said, running his hand up over her ass, over her dress to the back of her neck. He lifted her, held her back to his front, the hard length of his cock pressed right against that thong. He didn't have to turn her face; she was right there kissing him so hard he saw stars. She turned around, pushing herself up onto the bookshelf, wrapping her legs around his hips. Her lips still fused with his, she dropped her hands back between his legs and he shifted his legs wider, giving her room to do whatever she wanted. Whatever. She. Wanted.

She broke the kiss and looked down, her hair falling

over her face so he couldn't see her eyes, her expression, anything. But he hissed when she pulled him free of his boxers, her hands tracing the hard length of the veins that pounded against the thin skin. Her finger touched the head, the slit, and he bit his lip as she swirled the liquid she found there against him. He held onto her shoulder, careful not to grab too hard when she circled her hand around him and jacked him, once. Twice. Down to the sac, up to the head.

Unable to bear it anymore, he gathered her hair up in his fist and held it away from her face so he could see her watching him. But she was focused on what she was doing. Her eyes locked on her own hands, the hard length of his dick.

"Your hands look so good on me," he whispered.

Her sigh was a rush of breath against his chest.

He reached down and pulled the dress out of the way so he could see her breast in that black lace bra. God, she was stunning. He cupped her in his palm, his thumb against the hard ridge of her nipple. She jerked against him, soft wild sounds coming out of her mouth. Her hands squeezed him so hard he had to bite his lip against the feral groan reaching up out of his chest.

The orgasm was right there. Barreling down on him from way up high.

With shaking hands she pushed him back and jumped down off the bookshelf.

She took the three steps toward the small table and grabbed his coat.

"It's in my wallet." He stood where she'd left him because he was scared that the way the fabric of his jeans would rub him if he moved, he might just come. That's where he was at. That's where she'd pushed him.

She pulled out his wallet and grabbed the condom he'd put there.

"Back to the couches," she said. It was the same woman with the level eyes from Mr. Root's office, but he barely recognized her with the flushed skin and the wide eyes. The swollen lips. Her dress was still pulled aside and he was mesmerized by the sight of that ivory flesh through black lace. Like he'd never seen a woman in a sexy bra before. Somehow she redefined all of it.

"Go," she said, unsmiling.

He walked back to the couches and toed off his beat-up cowboy boots and shucked off his pants.

"Sit down," she breathed, pointing to the corner of the leather couch where he'd started the night. He sat and she went back to her knees in front of him, but this time he didn't fight it. Had no power to. She braced her elbows on his knees and bent toward him, but he stopped her.

"Take off your dress."

She shook her head.

"Take it off. I want to see your body while you suck my dick."

She turned away, resting her cheek against his thigh as if gathering her strength. "No. I want to do this my way." When her eyes met his, he realized she was serious. It wasn't a game. And that her unwillingness to be naked in front of him had nothing to do with a few extra pounds or this idea she had in her head about what was supposed to be sexy. It wasn't even about the illicit thrill of having him naked, while she was fully dressed.

It was way colder than that.

She might fuck him. She might let him put his finger and his tongue and his cock inside of her, but she was not going to show him any piece of herself that she didn't want to expose.

This was what she meant by her way.

Fair enough, he thought and nodded.

She came up between his spread legs and wrapped one arm around his waist, while the other pulled his hard dick away from his belly and right into her mouth. He hissed, arching against her, involuntarily shoving himself farther into her mouth.

"Sorry—"

She took him deeper. Deeper still. He looked up at the ceiling, unable to watch, though it killed him not to. It was liquid and silk. Firm and soft touches, the feathering of her tongue, the suction of her mouth. She worked him hard, only to slow down and gently take him. She swirled her tongue over the head, the cupped palm of her hand following. A one-two punch that killed him.

"Fuck," he groaned. He gathered her hair in his fist, too rough, he knew he was being too rough, but she pushed into the vee of his legs harder, took him deeper.

Rough was apparently good. Rough was apparently her way.

"Yeah. Look at you."

She moaned in her throat and pulled away. "Now," she said. She took the condom and handed it to him with shaking fingers. He stood up, ripping the wrapper open with his teeth, and she leaned back against the rug, slipping her hands up under her dress to pull off the thong.

"Stop," he told her. He knelt down between her legs, unzipped her boots, and pulled them off. The short white socks she wore under them nearly wrecked him, they were so sweet. He scooted her back against the rug to give them some room to move and then reached under her dress himself, pulling the silk away from her hips and down her legs. He put her underwear over by the white socks.

"I want to taste you," he said.

She started to shake her head but he reached under her dress anyway, his fingers sliding between her legs right into the wet and the hot of her. He found her clit and she jerked away at the touch.

"Too much?"

"I'm so . . ." Her breath shuddered and she stared up at the ceiling.

"Beautiful? Sexy? Wet?"

She shot him a look under an arched brow that nearly made him laugh. "Close," she said. "I'm really close."

"So what if I do this?" He pressed the callused edge of his thumb against her clit, and she moaned, sucking that bottom lip into her mouth, holding it in place with her teeth.

"Just . . . come on." She moaned, rolling her head on the floor. She braced her foot on his knee and her dress rolled up her legs, revealing his hand buried in the light brown curls between her legs.

"I want to watch you come," he whispered, compelled by the need to see her undone. To see her falling apart under his touch.

But she took the decision right out of his hands. She tangled his hair in one hand and pulled him down to her, and he had to put his hands out to stop himself or he'd fall with all his weight against her. With her other hand she found his cock, shifted and arched, and then he was slipping into her.

It was incendiary.

Why had he been fighting this? He pumped against her, slow and steady, easing his way, because while she was hot and wet, she was tight and he didn't want to hurt her.

She arched against him, but he held her hips down.

"Ahhhh," she cried, her eyes going wide. Her hands fell from between them to the floor at her side. He thrust into her, high and hard, and she closed her eyes, a red flush building from her chest to her throat. His hands left her hips and her eyes popped back open, as if she were startled. When she looked up at him, he read a question in her eyes. One she wasn't quite ready to say out loud.

Oh, this woman, he thought, speeding up his thrusts, feeling the power of his orgasm like a roar in his head. This woman who wanted to be held down but didn't have the guts to say it. Who would fuck him, but only with her clothes on. Would suck his dick but share almost nothing of herself.

If she wanted more from him, she was going to have to ask.

Instead of grabbing her wrists and holding them over her head, instead of whispering some choice filth in her ear, which she would undoubtedly like, he sat back on his heels, pulling halfway out of her, and then slid her legs over his. He spread his hand over her tummy and put his thumb right against her clit.

But he didn't move.

She arched against him, fucking herself against him, sliding over him, forcing his thumb against her clit. It was raunchy, lewd. Watching this woman use him. Her eyes were closed, her hands in fists at her side, and for a second he wondered if she even cared that it was him she was fucking. Or if he was just something hard between her legs.

The thought sent him hurtling and he braced himself over her, pounding into her. Her eyes opened wide and the soft gasps and groans turned to full-throated cries. They shifted across the carpet, their heads nearly hitting the blue couch. She braced her hands against it and when he thrust as hard as he could into her, she pushed down.

"Ah, fuck," he breathed, his head bowed over her chest, and as the orgasm became unavoidable, as he felt her building and tightening, her legs squeezing his hips, he leaned down and took her nipple between his teeth.

And bit.

She exploded against him. One giant contraction squeezing him and he gave in to the orgasms, roaring into the empty barn.

Eyes watering, head spinning, he pulled out of her and collapsed onto his back against the rug. She put her arms over her face, panting as though she'd run a marathon.

"Are you okay?" he asked, when he got his breath back. He lifted his hand and rested it on her tummy, the best he could manage until movement returned to his limbs.

"Fine," she said. Her voice muffled through her arms.

"That was kind of—"

"Good?"

He laughed. "I was going to say intense."

She sat up, his hand fell from her tummy, and he started to feel the temperature in the barn. Or maybe it was the temperature coming from her. She didn't look at him. Didn't smile. She sat there and ran her hands over her hair and then down her face.

"Are you sure you're okay?" he asked, sitting up next to her.

"Fine." She started to fix her dress, pull up the part under her bra, wincing slightly when her hand brushed her nipple.

"Oh God." He reached for her. "I was too rough—"

She stood up, looking down at him, her face totally composed. She was completely dressed.

He'd never felt so naked.

"That was just what I wanted." There was a ghost of a smile on her face. "Every part of it. You have nothing to feel bad about."

She put on her thong, the little white socks, and then zipped up her boots.

He stood and began to put on his jeans, trying to get

some kind of read on her, but it was impossible. If he hadn't just been balls deep in her, he never would have suspected she'd just been having screaming sex. With him.

"Would you like to go get dinner?" he asked. "I mean . . . we should maybe . . ."

She seemed to be considering it, as if dinner with him had some serious weighty implications that needed to be measured before an answer could be given.

"No, thank you," she finally said and a soft sigh of air left his body. The sound that usually accompanied a fist to the gut. "I need to get back."

She gathered up the mugs and the bottle of bourbon and took them down the dark hallway. While she was gone, he put on the rest of his clothes. Tucked the used condom back in its wrapper and decided he'd throw it away at home. He didn't want any kids to see it in a garbage can.

When she came back into the room he didn't feel quite so naked, but he still didn't know what was going on.

She needed to get back? Back to what?

She was pulling her hair back into a ponytail. Once the elastic was in, she pulled the hair tight, and he winced on behalf of her scalp.

"Shelby," he said. "I don't know what to say . . ."

"Good night, I suppose."

"Good night? Just like that?"

"What do you want?" She asked him as if she really didn't know. As if she was totally clueless to how dates normally went.

"Well, I wanted to take you out for dinner." He hadn't expected to be dismissed like this. Didn't want to be dismissed. But his sarcasm had the likely result and she boarded herself up tight against him.

Shit.

"I'm sorry I forced you into having sex instead."

"Shelby—"

"You had a condom, Ty. You must have at least thought the night might end this way, so we just cut out the boring dinner."

"Boring?" Now he was offended. "Right. Well, thank God we didn't have to bother with getting to know each other before you put my dick in your mouth."

She flinched, and his anger popped like a balloon.

"I'm sorry," he said. He reached for her, thinking maybe if they were touching they wouldn't get their wires crossed so badly. But she stepped out of reach.

"I think maybe we should just say good night." When she said it like that, there was no arguing. It was as if she'd pushed him right out of the room. But then, that ghostly smile showed up again and he was totally off balance. "But . . . thank you . . . for this. I really did enjoy it."

This. Some of the most intense, conflicted sex of his life and she called it "this."

"Glad to be of service," he said flinging sarcasm around without care.

Again he was met with that brown level stare and he refused to be cowed. She was the one treating him like a piece of meat. "I would appreciate it," she whispered, attempting to sound strong and tough but failing miserably, and something pinged in his chest. A small warning bell that said, *pay attention. Pay attention right now.* "I would appreciate it if you didn't tell anyone about this."

Just when he thought he couldn't be more offended. "Who do you think I am, Shelby? Of course I won't tell anyone."

She nodded once and then grabbed their coats from the low table. His wallet slipped to the floor and they both reached for it, nearly bumping heads. He stood back and then she did and he leaned forward, only to nearly get clobbered in the head as she did, too.

"Oh, for fuck's sake," he muttered and grabbed his wallet. "It's been just about the weirdest date ever. And that's saying something for me. Good night."

He stormed out of the barn, but at the door he heard her say, "Good night, Wyatt."

Chapter 8

The door clicked closed behind Ty, and Shelby sagged against the couch, a sobbing breath tearing out of her throat.

Oh, that had been a mistake. A terrible amazing mistake.

Her fingers shook as she touched her lips, then the hollow of her throat where her heart still pounded. If she ran her hands down her body, she worried there would be parts of her missing. Her hips, her breast, the back of her leg. Giant chunks of her gone, or rearranged, because there was not a single bit of her that didn't feel touched and different.

The sex had worked, the pressure in her life was now under control, but something else had shifted. Something that seemed important and worrisome.

Panic flooded her and she couldn't pinpoint the cause, as if the source of the river was deep underground and grown over with vines and trees.

Go to dinner? She nearly laughed at the thought. She wasn't sure she could get back to her house without falling apart. Without falling down. And she'd been cruel, she knew she had been, but it seemed the only way to get him to leave, to get him to stop being polite or interested.

So she could get on with the business of putting herself back together.

Only now, the silence she usually loved . . . felt very lonely.

As composed as she could manage to be, she locked up the barn, walked across the moonlit backyard, and let herself in the back door of her house, hoping that Mom and Deena would be in the living room, giving her a few more moments to find the pieces of herself that had gone missing.

"Well, hello, Shelby," Deena said from the kitchen table. Her smile was carefully knowing and Shelby could not look at it. "What have you been up to?"

"A few drinks, that's all." She looked instead at Mom, wearing a purple sweatshirt over her nightgown.

Evie was smiling at her, present inside herself. "You should go out more," Evie said. "You look like you had a good time."

Carefully, feeling as if she'd been scattered on some hard wind, she put her fingers against the counter to keep herself upright.

This. This was the underground source of the tears. The things she could not look at too long or too carefully.

She'd been told when Mom was first diagnosed that routine was key. Any changes in environment or schedule could disorient her, cause an episode. And Shelby had embraced that particular prescription. Routine allowed her to lock herself away from the world; it gave her reasons to turn down drinks with co-workers, book club invitations, lunch with girlfriends. What a relief it was not to *try*.

And now, here she was, her body sore and somehow totally liberated, and she felt guilty. She felt awful.

For everything.

For treating Ty like that.

For not knowing how to say *thank you, but this is all I have for right now. This is all I can spare.*

For not taking better care of her mom. For the way her own life had shrunk down to this house and the

barn behind it. Which she knew was totally unfair because she'd agreed to it. She'd signed up; she—most of
the time—relished their solitude. Their routine.

Quickly, she got herself a glass of water with shaking
hands.

This is the reason not to see Ty again, she thought. *I
cannot process all of this. My life has no room for this
version of me in it.*

Even as a voice in her head whispered that was un-
true, that believing it was simply easier than trying to
change her life.

But the beautiful sex and the terrible way she'd ended
it was all so fresh—a wound the blood from which she
could not stanch.

"Shelby?" Deena asked, and Shelby gulped down the
water so fast it spilled out the sides of her mouth.

Too much. That was the problem with Ty. He was too
much. The sex, the way she felt, all of it. Too much. She
felt better at the thought. She knew what to do with too
much—reject it. Deny it. Trim it back to nothing.

"Thanks, Deena," she said, wiping her mouth and
turning to smile at her friend. "Thanks for making
me go."

"Well, he was too good-looking to leave standing
on your porch." Deena began to gather her things. "I'll
see you next time, Evie, and we'll get to work on that
album of yours."

"That would be fine, Deena. Thank you." Evie said
it with such grace, totally aware that she needed care. It
was such a shocking moment of clarity that Deena and
Shelby shared a look.

"She was calm the rest of the night?" Shelby asked as
they walked to the front door.

"I wouldn't say calm, but the last twenty minutes she
was doing just fine. Real clear." Deena put her hand on
Shelby's arm and as electrified and out of sorts as she

was, she fought the urge to shrug it off. "Honey, you've got to think about a consistent system of care. You can't keep cobbling things together and hoping for the best."

"It's working—"

"Barely. You look worn down to the bone."

Shelby bit her tongue and smiled. "We'll go see Dr. Lohmann next week."

Deena nodded. "And look, if you need any more help in the evenings . . ." Her big brown eyes twinkled in a way that made Shelby incredibly uncomfortable. "You let me know."

"Thanks, Deena."

Shelby showed her out before going back into the kitchen with Mom, who was poring over her old Kodachrome photos. Behind Mom the windows were black with night. Her silver hair was matte in the stark light from the overhead lamp, her face was washed out, her purple sweatshirt the saturated color of a bruise.

She looks like a picture. A moment in the past already gone.

She leaned forward and pressed a kiss to her mother's head.

"What is that for?" Evie asked, laughing, cupping her hand over Shelby's cheek.

"Because I love you."

"I love you, too, Shelb."

"I'm going to go change my clothes," Shelby said.

Upstairs she quickly got out of the uncomfortable underwear and washed the makeup off her face. Her lips were swollen and she had beard burn across her neck, the tops of her breasts. She turned sideways and saw the red mark on her ass where Ty had grabbed her.

With the tip of her finger she touched the edge of that red mark; it was her imagination, she knew that, but where he'd touched her, her skin was hot. Where he hadn't, cold.

Ridiculous, she thought and pulled on her thin sweatpants, a tee shirt, and her robe.

In the hallway she heard her mother in her own bedroom.

"Mom?" She leaned against the doorway, watching her mother curled up on the bed with more photos.

Her father had been the one obsessed with the camera. With cataloging every moment, as if without proof people wouldn't believe they were a happy family. Or they themselves might forget the story they were supposed to be telling.

Shelby hated the pictures. Hated Mom's fascination with them. The smiling father with his mouth full of nonsense and hate. The scared but dutiful mother. The seething girl. That was all she saw behind the first-day-of-school shots and Christmas portraits.

She had no idea what her mother saw.

"Shove over," Shelby said, moving aside the pictures to sit down beside her against the headboard.

Mom smelled of roses and bedsheets. Good smells. And when she looked up at Shelby, recognition was bright and comforting in her eyes. Mom forgot more things than she remembered, but she always knew Shelby. Perhaps that's why she felt that no matter how bad things seemed, or how cluttered the house, or how little sleep she had, they were okay. Because it was still the two of them against the world.

She knew the day would come when she didn't recognize her. Didn't remember who they were to each other. When Evie would look at Shelby with that blank face. She didn't know what would happen when that foundation collapsed.

There is enough trouble today, she told herself. *You don't need to borrow tomorrow's.*

"Thomas after they built the church." Evie held up a grainy picture from the early eighties. It was Dad's brief mustache phase, which, she supposed, made him look a little like Tom Selleck. Without the short shorts.

"He was very happy," Evie said. Her hair had come slightly loose from the bun and a thick curl rested against the pillow.

"What are you looking for in the pictures?" Shelby whispered as she twined the curl through her fingers.

"What do you mean?" Evie was distracted by another stack. "Oh, here's one!" Evie held up a picture of the two of them, just after Shelby's junior high graduation. Mom, in a halo perm and a green polka-dot dress, was beaming hard at the camera with such pride she glowed. Shelby, wearing a blue cap and gown, looked at her mom as if the sun were rising upon her face.

It was the two of them together, in a perfect bubble of time and happiness that excluded anyone but them. That was the way they had been for as long as Shelby could remember.

But the day after that picture had been taken, Dad preached from the pulpit the sins of pride. How it distracted people from truly understanding God. How those with too much pride would never know love. In a twenty-minute sermon he crushed Mom from his position, crushed the two of them and their happiness that had not welcomed him.

And that was only a minor trick of Dad's.

Anything Mom accomplished—her promotion to manager of the plant, her raises—he had to diminish. He had to make her smaller and smaller until she disappeared.

Shelby was seven when she realized that no matter what she did, how hard she prayed, how good she was, it wouldn't matter, because her father would never love her. Not really. From that moment he no longer had any power over her; he could beat her until she bled but he couldn't touch her. Not where it mattered.

So he turned his attention to his best audience, the person he could reduce to rubble with only a glance.

Evie.

This is your fault, he'd say to Shelby while Mom scurried across the floor to clean up broken dishes. To wipe up blood, holding closed the torn sleeve of her dress. *All your fault*.

But instead of giving him what he wanted and drawing his disastrous attention away from Mom, Shelby withdrew even further and became a knowing, willing accomplice to the systematic abuse her father heaped upon her mother.

The thought of it—the memory of it—made her sick and she closed her eyes, pressing her face against her mother's hair.

If I could change the way I was, Mom, I would do it. I would do anything to change the past.

"I look at these photos and keep thinking I'll see what I saw," Evie whispered. "I'll see why I married him. Why I felt like he was all I deserved."

"You deserved more than him," Shelby whispered, but Evie shook her head.

"I was older, and I wanted a family and then . . . then there he was. So handsome and charming . . ." Her voice faded to dust. "I'm sorry I was too scared to take you and leave. I'm sorry I made you stay."

"I stayed with you. Wherever you were was where I was going to be."

Evie's grip on her hand was cold iron. "No," she whispered. "No. That's not the way it should be. None of this is the way it should be."

"Mom." Evie was growing agitated. Restless. Shelby put her hand around her mom's shoulder, holding her close. "It's us, Mom. It's us together and it's going to be okay. It's all going to be okay."

* * *

Ty's involvement with the Outlaws had happened slowly. Or at least that was the way it seemed. There was of course the good chance that Ty had just been too drunk to notice.

When Ty was twenty-five, Pop, his grandfather, died in a motorcycle accident. It had been raining and Highway 12 was slick, and Pop had been staunchly anti-helmet. He'd died instantly, which wasn't a whole lot of comfort when it could have been prevented.

After the funeral, Ty went off the deep end. For a while it was just too much partying. He never met a bottle of Jack he didn't want to get to the bottom of, and then he met Vanessa, whose brother, Chad, was a sergeant-at-arms with the Outlaws, and before he knew it he was partying with her brother and his club, some of whom he'd known from working off and on at Pop's shop.

Nana kicked him out of the house. Said he was a disgrace to Pop's memory. It still stung when he remembered the cold, calm way she'd said it. The tears in her eyes that she would not let fall.

It must have just killed her to do that. Just gutted her. And he hated that he'd put her through that.

After being kicked out, he moved into the apartment above Pop's shop even though at the time he'd barely been showing up to work. Ed, the manager, had threatened to fire him a million times. He told Ty the only reason he was still around was because Pop would have wanted Ed to keep an eye on him.

If he started to wonder what the hell he was doing, Vanessa would give him another bottle, another joint, let him fuck her in the bathroom of the Outlaws' compound, go down on another girl so he could watch.

Would start a fight so he could whale the shit out of some guy.

But nine months after he fell in with the club he woke up in the shitty trailer outside the compound with Vanessa passed out beside him, a roll of cash in his pocket, and a gun on the bedside table.

A gun.

He'd sunk in way too deep. Rock-bottom too deep.

He packed up his shit, then woke up Vanessa to get her to come with him. He even proposed to her. But she'd refused, laughed in his face. Told him to go to hell. And then when he walked out of that trailer she'd chased after him, in a shirt and panties, crying, begging him to come back.

And threw rocks at his bike when he rode off.

He'd said goodbye to Nana, promised to turn his life around, and went to St. Louis, where he didn't know anyone and no one knew him and he could figure out who he was without Pop, without Vanessa, without the bullshit drinking and fighting he'd been doing.

To his huge surprise, the first thing he realized about himself was that he really liked church. He'd suffered through his share of Sunday services with Nana and Pop, but once he was on his own, he sought out a church and found the perfect one—a weird little Unitarian down on the south side off Kings highway, with a good choir and a black female minister who preached such kindness that he felt bathed in goodness just being in her presence.

For the next seven years he'd traveled around the states, working odd jobs, making friends, leaving whenever the impulse struck. But the first thing he did when he pulled into a fresh city was find a church. Find some goodness.

And now he was trying to get Casey to do the same.

"No way!" Casey cried, slouching in his seat at the table, a spoonful of Cheerios dripping its way to his mouth.

"I told you that was part of the deal," Ty said, trying to put a shine on his boots. They were mostly a lost cause, but he remembered Pop shining up his boots every Sunday, so he figured he'd do what he could to follow tradition.

"The deal sucks."

"I think the swear jar is going to start including the word *sucks*."

"That sucks."

"That's it. You owe a quarter."

"You can't just change the rules like that!"

"I can. I'm the dad. Now go. Finish your cereal and go get dressed. That green polo I bought you that you never wear and your khaki pants."

Casey made a big show of stomping back to his room, and Ty finished the last of Casey's cereal and put the bowl in the sink.

His cell phone rang and he shoved his feet into his boots as he answered.

"Hello."

"Someone from Mark H. Luttrell Correctional Facility is trying to get in touch with you. Do you accept this call?" It was a recording and it took him a second to figure out what it meant.

He jerked the phone away from his ear and looked at the screen. *Mark H. Luttrell Correctional Facility.* Jesus Christ.

"I accept," he said.

"Ty?"

"What are you doing, Vanessa? We agreed you wouldn't call for six months." To give the kid a chance to settle in. To give him a chance to forget and maybe forgive. Though, frankly, Ty hadn't been working too hard on the forgiving part.

"I just wanted to talk to Casey."

"That's not going to happen."

"Ty. I'm his mom. You can't pretend I don't exist."

"I'm not pretending you don't exist! But you can't call

out of the blue and expect to talk to him. He needs a chance to be prepared."

There was a long silence and he expected a swearing diatribe to erupt, but instead she only sighed, a shuddering, audible sigh. "That's fair, I guess."

It was a Sunday miracle.

"Will you tell him I called?"

"Yeah, and if he wants to talk to you, we'll call you."

"How is he doing?"

Ty leaned against the counter and rubbed at his forehead. He was going to break the skin one of these days. "He's good. I mean we've had some problems, but he's a good kid."

"He always was. He was the best kid and I . . ." He heard her muffled sob and would have given anything in the world to be able to hang up the phone.

"You threw it away, Vanessa. And I can't let you back into his life unless I know you won't hurt him like that again."

There was a loud sniff and a husky laugh. Not quite as mean as it had been in the past, but still tinged with the old Vanessa awfulness. "Look at you. I never would have guessed you'd be such a good dad."

"Good" was a mighty stretch, but considering how badly she had done, he looked like a saint.

"Yeah, well, me neither. I gotta go, Vanessa."

"Tell him . . . tell him I miss him."

"I will," he said, unsure if he would.

He hung up and tossed the phone onto the counter. When was it too early on a Sunday to drink?

"Was that my mom?"

Ty whirled at the sound of Casey's voice at the doorway. *Shit. Shit. Shit. Shit.*

He couldn't change this for his kid. He couldn't make his mom go away. But it didn't stop him from trying.

"Don't worry about it." He got really busy with his keys and his wallet.

"You're kidding, right?" Casey asked, his voice all high and broken. "My mom called you from jail and I'm not supposed to worry about it."

Ty ran his hands through his hair. "Yeah . . . that's probably not possible, huh?"

Casey stood in the doorway, in the green polo and the khaki pants and without his armor. Without his attitude. A boy. Just a boy.

Ty took a deep breath. "She wanted to talk to you but I said I had to discuss it with you, and if you wanted to talk to her, we'd call her. She says she misses you."

Casey flinched, his hands reaching down to tug at the hem of his shirt. He stared at a spot three feet in front of him and Ty had this weird instinct to go and stand in that spot, to give the kid something to look at. To see.

I'm here.

I'm not going anywhere.

You are not alone.

But in the end he didn't do it. He stood where he stood. Casey stood in the doorway, and the distance between them seemed like a foreign country with armed guards and a language he could not begin to understand.

"I don't miss her," Casey whispered.

Good, he wanted to say; *she's not worth missing.* But there had been a time in his life when he hadn't been worth missing either and he'd turned his shit around and . . . ah, hell, he had no freaking clue what he was doing.

"You don't have to talk to her if you don't want to," he said.

Casey shrugged as if it didn't matter, but Ty was no fool. He was just clueless.

"Let's go, Casey—we're late," he said.

For one long second Casey stared at him. Right at him.

Ty couldn't handle it, couldn't handle the pain and anger and confusion in his son's eyes, and like a coward he looked away. He grabbed his keys from the counter and headed out to the garage, to the truck and across town toward salvation.

Chapter 9

Sunday was one of those strange Arkansas winter days when a warm wind blew up from the gulf and it felt like spring had arrived, months early, a totally welcome surprise visitor. Outside the church, mothers gave up the fight to keep their kids in jackets and let them run around in shirtsleeves. Everyone was caught at one time or another lifting their faces to the honeyed sunlight only to close their eyes and breathe deep.

But Evie had on her winter coat and leather gloves. Her steel-gray hair pulled back in the bun she wore every day. Her face folded into familiar lines of worry.

"These kids will catch cold," she said with a sniff.

"It's nearly sixty degrees." Shelby ran her hand over the worn nap of Mom's coat. It was ancient, something that should have been given to some charity years ago, but somehow the ugly afghan coat survived every purge. "Aren't you hot?"

"I'm fine. I wish someone would put a coat on those boys. They'll catch cold."

Evie watched the closed front doors of the church, waiting for them to be thrown open. They could go around to the back, where the doors had been open since seven, but Mom wouldn't have it.

She came at God head-on.

"Good morning, Shelby!" It was Colleen, the school secretary. "God's grace is shining on us today, isn't it?"

It's a Gulf Stream thing. She didn't say it, because no one outside the Methodist church wanted to hear that.

Beside her, Mom beamed and said, "Amen." She and Colleen clasped hands.

"Those your boys?" Mom asked.

"The Billings boys? No. And thank the Lord."

"Someone should get them jackets."

The church doors were thrown open and the greeters, Mr. and Mrs. Gingerich, got down to the business of handing out the programs and special earpieces for the hard of hearing.

Back when Daddy was preaching, Shelby and Mom used to sit in the front row. They were human props, part of Daddy's spectacle: the devout wife, the faithful daughter. Their heads bowed, eyes squeezed shut, lips moving in prayer. Mom at times would actually weep and Shelby had stared at her, aghast and amazed, that she could muster up that kind of emotion to share with Daddy's congregation.

The more Daddy wanted Shelby to show, the less she gave him. Everything he wanted to pull and drag out of her to hold up in front of that group of strangers as proof of his ability to care for their souls, to shepherd them into God's holy light, she denied him.

The only thing she'd ever known about that congregation at the old church down the road was that they believed in Daddy. Which was nothing to recommend them.

Now that her faith wasn't part of a spectacle, Shelby took Mom to sit up in the balcony, behind Fred, who ran the sound and took care of the feed into the radio station down in Marietta.

Mom sat and got out her hymnal, looking in the program and then finding the first hymn and then the second, marking them with her fingers. It was a little trick she used to keep herself rooted.

The sight of her mother's small but strong fingers

wedged into the pages of that hymnal made Shelby both impossibly sad and proud at the same time.

Mom had run the sixth biggest Del Monte plant in the state at a time when women didn't do that. Not at all. She taught Shelby to change tires and her oil. Fix leaky faucets. Mend and re-mend, hem and re-hem. Mom taught her to be endlessly useful to herself. And even though so much of her was eroding from beneath, creating giant sinkholes of memory and personality, Evie was still able to be useful to herself.

Shelby settled into the pew beside her mother and crossed her legs, promising herself she would only look at her watch twice in the next hour. Twice. That was all she got.

Pastor Mike began his welcome.

There were a few whispers and mutters behind her as a latecomer came up to the balcony and the floorboards at the top of the steps creaked. She turned just in time to see Casey sliding into the pew beside her, his face lighting up when he realized who he was sitting next to.

Beside him, his mouth wide with surprise, until he seemed to realize it and schooled his face into an expressionless mask, was Wyatt.

She'd put last night behind her. Shoved all those details, those feelings, the shocking way her body had unraveled and imploded under his touch, down deep into some secure safe in her memory.

But at the sight of him, in the same blue sweater he'd worn to her house, those memories staged a jailbreak and wreaked mayhem in her mind.

Yeah. Look at you.

She tore her eyes away from his surprised face and stared blindly at the front of the church.

"Hey, Ms. Monroe," Casey whispered, but before Shelby could say anything, Mom leaned over and shushed him.

Shelby gave him a wink and then tried very hard to pay attention to the church service.

But painfully, as if her whole left side were sitting far too close to a fire, she was aware of Wyatt sitting there two feet from her. Her cheeks were hot, her neck, her breasts. Every single place he touched Friday night suddenly lit a spark and she couldn't stand her own skin. Her own body. She wanted to shed herself like a coat and run out of there.

"Sit still," Wyatt muttered, and she turned toward him, astounded that he would attempt to chastise her, only to find him giving his son a pretty good death stare.

Beside her, Casey managed to sit still for about thirty seconds before he started squirming again.

"Casey," Wyatt whispered. "I'm serious. You made me a promise."

"I said I would try," Casey whispered back. "But it's so boring."

Inspired by her own boredom, she grabbed the pencil from the guest register and flipped her bulletin over to a blank page. She drew a tic-tac-toe board in the corner and pushed it toward Casey.

"Tic-tac-toe?" he whispered. "Am I six?"

A laugh bubbled out of her and now her own mom was giving her the death stare. She composed herself and drew a hangman and the spaces for a ten-letter word.

"Hangman," he whispered. "I like it."

She pointed to a blank spot where he could write down his guesses and handed him the stubby pencil. Over the top of Casey's bright head, Wyatt was watching her, and despite her years of experience ignoring things, she could ignore him for only so long. Almost as if her eyes were magnetized and he was true north, she could not help but look at him.

Only to find him staring at her, specifically her neck revealed by her ponytail, his eyes hot, his face set in hard lines.

Burning. Agitated. She turned away, focused on the game she was playing with Casey. The *Hallelujah* he seemed to be in no hurry to guess.

Did Wyatt show up at her church on purpose? she wondered. Was this some kind of weird stalker thing after Saturday night, after she'd asked him to leave?

Was it Dean Jennings all over again?

Her body went cold in a heartbeat.

"Sorry," she muttered, and let Casey grab the pencil she'd dropped. Over the boy's bent back she met Wyatt's eyes and stared back at him.

Pastor Mike told them to all rise and slowly everyone around them stood, leaving them caught in a terrible world of her own making.

As a rule, women kind of made sense to Ty. With some women the drama got intense and he quickly found a way to bail. But for the most part he understood women. He liked them. They liked him. Some of them were better matches than others, but he had a pretty good sense that he knew what made each of the women he'd ever been involved with tick.

But Shelby Monroe was like no woman he'd ever known. Ever. Certainly not like any woman he'd been involved with. Though he wasn't sure what he'd had with Shelby—fucking the shit out of each other and then being kicked to the curb—could be considered "involved."

And after she'd caught him staring at her neck and remembering how she'd shuddered, trapped between his body and the hard floor, she'd been glaring at him. The small tension of familiarity and kindness between them had been severed by her icy indifference.

Man, she had that indifference shit down pat, and it was withering. Confusing.

As soon as the benediction was over, he got Casey and hightailed it out of the pew and the balcony.

"Coffee hour," Casey protested, pulling away from the heavy hand Ty had on the kid's shoulder.

"Case—"

"You promised."

Yes, he did. He'd promised all the donuts the boy could stuff in his pockets, because it was the only way to get him to go to church without literally dragging his feet.

It would be nice if they could find the right church, but so far they'd had two big strikeouts. He'd had high hopes for the Baptist church, he'd had luck with Baptist churches in other towns, but the minister started talking about the sins of homosexuality and he'd gotten Casey out of there pretty fast. He didn't like churches that preached hate.

This laid-back Methodist church had been nice. So far no hate, lots of kids.

Shelby, however, might be a problem.

"Go," he said, lifting his hand off his son's shoulder, and the kid took off like a rocket toward the banquet hall in the church basement.

"Wyatt?" His name—his grandfather's name—in Shelby's no-nonsense voice had the ability to stop the blood in his veins. Perhaps it was the phone call from Vanessa, but he felt utterly incapable of handling Shelby at the moment.

So he kept walking, pretending he hadn't heard her.

The church basement was filled with people drinking coffee out of little Styrofoam cups and he caught sight of Casey, waiting his turn in line for the Sara Lee coffee cake and donuts.

After the phone call from Vanessa, Casey had been nearly electric with his anxiety and Ty had thought for a few minutes in the church parking lot that the boy would run. Just take off.

The more Ty tried to talk to him about anything *but* his mother, the worse it had gotten.

But as soon as they sat down next to Shelby, it had vanished.

Which, because he was pissed off and miserly, bugged the shit out of him.

He watched as one of the older women in charge of the spread put a hand on Casey's shoulder and asked what he would like. Casey shrugged away from her touch and filled up the plate by himself. Over his son's bent head, the woman shared a knowing glance with the woman filling up coffee cups.

Trouble, that look said. *This one is nothing but trouble.*

Ty had to keep himself from tearing over there and explaining that the kid's life, fragile and barely stable, had just been torn apart by a phone call from his mother in jail so a little fucking Christian kindness from the coffee-hour crowd wouldn't go unappreciated!

"Wyatt?"

Shelby. Now he felt so on the edge of himself, he knew it would be impossible to deal with her in any reasonable way.

"I know you can hear me," she said.

Not smiling, he turned to face her. "Shelby," he said. He took her in with one quick glance. The dark skirt and the boots she wore last night. The thin red sweater over the white tank top.

"What are you doing here?" She wrapped her arms over her chest. He very painfully remembered how naked he'd been in front of her—in so many ways. And how she'd been dressed and armored and locked away someplace inside her body. At the time, when it was all happening, it had been hotter than hell, biting her nipple through her clothing, the sight of his hand between her legs under the hem of that dress.

Now it just made him feel like a fool.

"It's church, Shelby. What do you think I'm doing here?"

"Are you following me?" she whispered, not quite able to look him in the eyes, which was weird. She'd looked him right in the eye last night when she'd all but told him not to let the door hit him on the ass.

"What . . . following . . . ?" He laughed. "Watch yourself, Shelby. Your crazy is showing."

She lifted her eyes to his and he saw the absence of crazy. He saw something very nervous. Very honest. It was the most naked he'd ever seen her.

"Casey and I are looking around for a church that fits. This week just happened to be the Methodist church's turn to feed Casey all the donuts he could eat."

She glanced over at Casey crossing the room toward them with a paper plate piled high with Danish and donuts. A small flicker of a smile illuminated her face, which he wasn't going to be moved by.

She owed him an apology for all but accusing him of stalking her.

Following her? To church? What the hell?

His past was checkered with women who wore so much of their damage like clothing. Like accessories. He was beginning to understand that Shelby's was deep and there was a good chance she had buckets of it, hidden under those still waters of hers.

Run, man, run while you can, said the cynic in him, who'd had more than his share of relationships implode. *You clearly dodged a bullet.*

"Hey, Ms. Monroe," Casey said, giving her one of his rare smiles.

"Hey, Casey," she said. "You leave any Danish for me?"

"There's something with apricots in it. You can have that." Casey shuddered. Ty leaned over and swiped one of the chocolate mini-donuts that tasted so comfortingly like church coffee hour, no matter the church. Or state. Or decade.

Casey gave him a dirty look and then started gobbling things down as though Ty had designs on the whole plate.

"You're like a feral badger, Casey," he laughed. "We'd better get going before they ask us to leave."

Anxious to leave Shelby and the way she made him feel insufficient and at the same time outrageously horny, he turned away only to nearly run into a small older woman with steel-gray hair pulled back into a tight bun. Her unsmiling mouth was thin and while not stern, neither was it very kind. Everything about her seemed to scream *unforgiving*.

"Mom," Shelby said. "This is our new neighbor. Wyatt Svenson and his son, Casey."

Brown eyes very much like Shelby's looked him over top to bottom and then did the same with Casey. It was so bold, so strange, that Casey stepped closer to Ty. Though he'd never done it, Ty put his hand on Casey's shoulder and pulled him a little closer still.

"How do you do, ma'am," Ty said, polishing up his church manners. Under his hand he could feel Casey laughing. He gave him a little of the Dr. Spock squeeze and the boy stepped away.

"You moved into the O'Halloran place?" she asked.

"Ah, the farmhouse, across the street from you? It was Simone Appleby's before it was mine."

"Before that it was the O'Halloran place," Mrs. Monroe said. She wore a thick coat, and he wondered if she was hot with all the sunlight coming through the basement's high windows.

"All right, then yes, I'm in the old O'Halloran place."

"You're the one chopping down trees all the time?"

"What trees?" Casey asked.

"Who are you?" the woman turned glittering brown eyes back to Casey. Ty gave Casey a nudge.

"I'm Casey Svenson," he said slowly and loudly.

"I'm not deaf. You don't need to shout," Mrs. Monroe said. "The O'Hallorans didn't have kids."

"Mom, these aren't the O'Hallorans," Shelby explained.

"I know. They didn't have kids. You must be the people chopping down trees all the time."

"We're not chopping down trees." Ty shared a startled look with Casey.

"My husband is going to walk across the street next time you do that and give you a piece of his mind. It's disrespectful cutting down those trees all hours of the night and my husband doesn't like it."

"Mom." Shelby's voice was a hard, sharp crack and Mrs. Monroe looked up. Slowly, that pinched look relaxed from her face. She was younger than he'd thought. Prettier. Her daughter's lush lips were revealed without the stern hold she'd had on them.

Shelby shook her head, her eyes absolutely full to the brim with a resigned kind of grief. A silent and thorny conversation was had in the silence between the two women.

Ty felt one of those lightning strikes of empathy, deep right into the heart of him.

Whatever this situation was between Shelby and her mother, it wasn't easy. And he could so relate to that.

"We should go, Mom," Shelby said.

Shelby's mother blinked and looked around, suddenly older. Suddenly ancient and sad. Out of the corner of his eye he saw Shelby put a hand to her stomach, as if putting back together pieces of herself that had fallen apart.

"Have we had cake?" Mrs. Monroe asked, confused.

"Here." Casey handed Mrs. Monroe his plate, still full of fruit Danish and coffee cake.

"Is this yours?" She looked down at Casey as if he'd just arrived.

"Nope," he said. "It's yours."

Mrs. Monroe smiled and she had her daughter's smile. That revealed a side of her unseen before. A hidden gracious warmth. "You should wear a coat, son," she said. "You're going to catch a cold."

"Let's go, Mom," Shelby said, holding out her arm, herding her mother into motion. Casey and Ty watched them cross the room toward the big double doors that opened onto the stairs leading up to the parking lot.

Shelby turned around at the last minute and looked right at Ty.

She didn't smile and neither did he. But when she lifted her hand in a strange little wave, he lifted his, too. And he realized he'd seen more of her right now, in this church basement, than she'd let him see while fucking him in the Art Barn.

"What's the deal with her?" Casey asked.

"Shelby's mom?"

"Yeah. That was weird, right?"

Ty didn't say anything for a long time and Casey turned to look up at him. Ty, since the moment Casey stepped into his shop, had been braced for disaster. Diligent against the constant, numbing sense of his failure with this kid. And he'd been so scared. So worried he realized he'd never taken the time to show him the kindness that Casey had shown that total stranger.

"I'm proud of you," Ty said, and Casey's big blue eyes opened wide, confirming the worst of his suspicions. He'd been stern. Unforgiving. Dismissive. Exasperated.

But never very kind. "You handled all of that really well."

Under his freckles his pale skin turned pink. "Does that mean I can go get some more donuts?"

"Nope, let's go get something better," he said.

"Nothing's better than donuts."

"Have I taken you to Cora's for breakfast?"

"What's Cora's?"

Oh, man. "Brace yourself, kid. Your life is about to change."

Chapter 10

At lunch recess, Casey sat with his back against the school's brick wall. He'd found himself a little corner between the entrance to the gym and the second-grade classrooms. The wind wasn't bad and no one bothered him here. A couple of the second-grade girls came over, but after a few rounds of him pretending to be a monster who tried to grab them without ever moving and them shrieking and running away, they got bored and left.

From his coat pocket he grabbed the little bit of clay he'd swiped from Ms. Monroe's Art Barn last week. He told himself that if he'd asked, she would have let him have it, but he was just so used to not asking. And she never would have let him have Scott's elf, which he'd also taken, and the diamond/crystal chandelier thing.

He'd taken the red and white clay and he was trying to make a miniature version of the Indian Chief motorcycle Ty had just finished refurbishing.

Ty said he was going to sell it soon, and Casey thought it would be cool to give him a miniature version. But only if he could figure out how to make the handlebars.

"Hey!"

Casey tried to put the clay back in his pocket, but it was too late. Scott and John were already around the corner.

"Hey guys," he said, jumping to his feet.

"You working on something for Ms. Monroe?" John

asked. No matter what John said, his tone of voice always said "you're a total pussy."

"No." There was no way he was talking about Ms. Monroe with John. No. Way.

"No?" John looked back at Scott like he was confused. "Scott said you were in his little art class after school."

Casey didn't say anything, but his hands curled into fists. John was such a jerk.

"You like Ms. Monroe?" John asked, stepping closer. He shoved his hands deeper into the pockets of his camouflage hoodie. John went hunting every weekend with his dad and he bragged about it every Monday. Casey didn't want to admit it, but that sounded pretty cool. Cooler than church, that was for sure.

"She's cool," Casey said.

John grinned, showing off his two big front teeth that were probably going to need braces real soon, and Casey couldn't wait for that day. "Yeah, but do you like her?"

"What do you mean?"

"Do you think she's pretty?"

Casey thought Ms. Monroe was the most beautiful woman on the planet, but he wasn't going to breathe a word of that to John.

Pull up the bridges, he heard that counselor's voice in his head. *Become an island; do not let these guys get to you.*

But it was too late. They were here and they were getting to him, and the counselor had never told him how to get all the bad thoughts and all the people who wanted to do him harm off the island once they were on.

"Come on, man, this is stupid," Scott said, still standing at the corner, close to the tether balls that the second graders were using as Tarzan ropes.

John ignored Scott and pulled an iPhone from his pocket.

"You aren't supposed to have that on school grounds," Casey said, because he was getting kind of scared and because he was totally jealous that his own iPod had been confiscated practically his first day at school.

"The teachers don't care, not if you don't use it in class," he said and turned it on. "So what's Ms. Monroe like at the Art Barn? Scott won't tell me anything."

Casey blinked and stepped back as John stepped forward. "She's just like she is in class. Cool. Nice."

"Has she sucked your dick?"

Blood roared through his ears and he felt himself go super hot and then freezing cold. "What!" he cried, too loud, probably.

"Has she sucked your dick?" John shrugged, his arms out wide. "You know what sucking dick is, don't you?"

"Why do you let him talk like this about her?" Casey yelled to Scott.

Scott shook his head and looked away.

"Hey, hey," John said, playing around with his phone. Casey could barely hear him because his heart was pounding so hard. "Let me show you something, it's on YouTube. There was a TV show this summer and Ms. Monroe totally sucked this guy's—"

"Shut up, John!" Casey didn't want to see anything like that. He didn't want to hear any more about it. He felt like crying. He felt so angry and so scared and so freaked out by all this bullshit that he just wanted to go into the boy's bathroom and hide until it was time to go home. And then he wanted to hide at home.

But Mom had called. Mom had called and now that house with the weird fridge and the overgrown weeds and the stray dog—that house wasn't safe anymore because she had gotten in.

He turned to run, but John grabbed the pocket of his hoodie.

"She's a slut—"

Casey jerked away and his pocket ripped, and the sound of the heavy cotton tearing away at the seams ripped away something in him.

Casey punched John. It only got him in the arm and shoulder, but John dropped the phone and lurched back and sideways.

"Shut up about Ms. Monroe!" Casey could feel himself spit as he yelled, but he didn't care.

"Look on YouTube, Casey. Everyone in town knows what she's like." John's face screwed up good and ugly and he opened his mouth to let more of his filthy garbage out into the world.

Casey pushed John against the wall, where he punched him again and again. Hitting John's face, his chest. He felt the cut of John's teeth across his knuckles. John was yelling and crying a little and Casey felt like there might be blood on his hand somewhere and he knew this was bad, all of this was really, really bad, but he couldn't stop.

Mom had found him.

"Casey!" Scott yelled. "Casey, stop!"

Casey took a deep breath, so deep he nearly fell backward.

Suddenly Scott was there, pulling Casey back, holding onto his arms. Casey felt like there was a swarm of bees in his head. His hands hurt, the knuckles stung. His palms where his fingernails had been digging into the skin throbbed with his heartbeat.

John stood up and faced him. He was bleeding from his lip and his eye looked red and puffy. He was rubbing his shoulder where he'd landed when Casey shoved him to the ground. "What the hell is wrong with you, Casey? You're a freak. You get that, right? A total freak. Everyone knows your mom is in jail. Ms. Monroe is only nice to you because she feels bad for you."

John bent over and reached down for his phone.

Casey knew better, knew he should just stop, but he couldn't. He kicked John in the chest, knocking him over. It took him a second but John stood up, his face full of hate.

Uh-oh, Casey thought, *this is going to be bad.*

Casey tried to brace himself, but it wasn't enough.

John when nuts on him. While Scott held Casey's arms, John totally beat the crap out of him. One of his punches got him square in the nose and something popped and there was a gush of blood.

He heard the scream of one of the second graders and he wanted to tell John to stop, that he was scaring that kid, that they were all going to get in trouble, but there was so much blood.

And then Mr. Phillips, the sixth-grade teacher, was yanking John away. Someone was pulling Scott away, and Casey spun around, not sure what he was going to do but still feeling like he needed to do something. Needed to hurt someone. Needed to apologize or scream or find out if that second grader was okay. He was torn in a thousand different directions at once. None of this was right. None of it.

And he wanted to make it worse just as badly as he wanted to try to figure out how to make it better.

Ms. Monroe was there. She wore silver earrings, long leaves that brushed her cheeks.

There was blood on her white sweater.

"Casey?" she breathed and he could see the tears in her eyes, and when she held out her arms as if to touch him or hug him, he dodged out of the way. She dropped her arms, but didn't look away and he felt trapped. "Casey, you're hurt."

He opened his mouth, but a sob broke out of his chest.

"Oh, Casey, Casey please let me—" She reached for him again, but he shoved her. As hard as he could, with every bit of strength he had left, he shoved her and tore off for the side entrance to the school. He heard her cry out and someone yelled after him and he was pretty sure he'd knocked her down. Pretty sure this was the worst moment in his whole life. And there had been a lot of bad ones.

He got himself to the boys' bathroom and hid in the corner stall, his feet curled upon the seat next to him so no one could see him by looking under the door.

Snot ran down across his lip and the tears stung the cuts on his cheeks and he hissed when he tried to wipe them off on the knees of his jeans. He was panting and crying and he couldn't get himself to stop. He unrolled tons of toilet paper and held it up to his nose, trying to stop the bleeding.

"Casey?"

It was Mr. Root, and Casey held his breath.

"I know you're in here."

The door to his stall rattled and he squeezed his eyes shut. "Casey," Mr. Root said. "Please, come out. Ms. Monroe said you're hurt."

The sob ripped through him. Did he hurt her when he'd pushed her over? Oh, God, he wanted to throw up.

"Buddy?"

"Go away!" he yelled.

In the end, Mr. Root got the janitor to take the hinges off the door and they came and got him.

* * *

Ty turned the corner into the school's office, ready to take his son apart.

Honest to God, what part of "you will be suspended" didn't the kid understand?

Ty had been fooled by this weekend, by their Sunday afternoon together. They'd had fun after church. They'd gone to Cora's and had fritters and then headed out to the river to throw stones. They went to go see the new aliens-and-robots movie and had popcorn and licorice for dinner.

The phone call from Vanessa never came up again.

He'd thought, stupidly maybe, that they'd turned some kind of corner. It had been fun. Happy. Easy.

And the very next day Casey gets suspended for fighting. And Ty just couldn't believe how angry he was. How . . . betrayed. How fucking at the end of his rope he was with this kid.

But then he caught sight of Casey slouched in the chairs outside Mr. Root's office and all the anger he had toward his kid for pulling him out of work, for fighting during school, for getting suspended, vanished.

Casey's head was tilted back and a cold pack wrapped in paper towel pressed to his nose. The neck of his white tee shirt was red with blood.

Ty had gotten the shit kicked out of him more than once.

But he wasn't prepared for the sight of his son's face.

The terrible squeeze around his heart, the push and pull of his guts, made him stop for a second in the doorway. Made him brace his hand against the door frame.

He's so little. So young.

All Casey had wanted from him was to take him out of those foster homes. To keep him safe.

Oh God, I'm failing him. I'm failing him so bad.

"Mr. Svenson," Colleen said, looking over the top of

her computer at him as if he had single-handedly ruined the delicate balance of her whole damn day.

Stirred into motion, he ignored Colleen and stepped right to Casey. He leaned over to try and see his son's face past the brown paper towel. To access the damage.

Casey saw him and closed his eyes with a moan.

Part defeat. Part fear. All grief.

"Casey," he breathed, reaching for the cold pack, but Casey turned away. When he reached again, Casey jerked away to sit on the chair sideways, his back to Ty, the small knobs of his spine pressed against his tee shirt.

"You okay?" Ty set his hand against his son's back, spread out his fingers, and covered all those knobs.

"Don't." Casey jerked away.

Mr. Root's office door opened behind him, and Ty turned, only to see a boy in the same shape as Casey and a very grim-faced mom behind him walking out of the office.

The mother stopped the boy beside Casey's chair and she gave her son a little nudge with a sharp elbow.

"I'm sorry, Casey," the boy said, not making eye contact.

Casey was silent for a long minute and Ty didn't nudge anything. He had no idea what had happened, but until he got an idea, he wasn't sure who owed whom an apology or if one should be accepted.

After what seemed like a good mental shake, the mother turned to Ty. "I'm Mary James, John's mother. I'm really very sorry. If Casey needs to go to the hospital for his nose, please let me—"

"Hospital?" Ty said. He turned Casey around in his chair, just picked him up and moved him, and Casey didn't fight it. He just let himself be manhandled and that was a terrible indication of how low Casey was, because there was no other time he would have stood for this.

Ty pulled his son's hand and the cold pack away from his face.

"Holy shit," Ty breathed, and John, the other kid, snorted.

His son's nose underneath the cold pack was swollen, red, and bruised. Blood was smeared all over his face. It looked broken.

"I'm so sorry," Mary whispered. "Really, I don't—"

"Someone needs to tell me what the hell happened, right now." He stood up, glaring at every adult in the room.

"Come on inside the office," Mr. Root said. "I'll explain."

Ty looked from Casey to the other kid, who had a split lip and a dark bruise forming under his chin. John. The kid's name was John and when he looked at Casey, he didn't look sorry. He looked mad, as though if there weren't any adults around he'd do it all again.

"Really," Mary said, and for a moment all the grim fell from her face and he saw a woman with her back against the wall. Her hands shook as she dug through her purse and her eyes were wet with tears. "Here's my number," she said and handed him her Mary Kay Representative business card. "It's just me, so you can reach me at those numbers and if you do need to go to the hospital just . . . let me know that he's okay."

Ty took the trembling card she held out to him. He wanted to be furious with her; he wanted to yell that she needed to manage her son better. She was just like him, though, a parent who was trying really hard. And screwing it up sometimes.

But he was still pissed, still scared, and all he could do was take the card and nod.

Mary force-marched her son out the door.

Ty looked down at his son, at that defeated bend to

his body, the blood splatter across his shirt. The broken nose.

"You okay?" he whispered. Casey didn't answer. "Son?"

"I'm fine."

"I'm going to talk to Mr. Root. I'll be right back."

Casey's ice-blue eyes twitched to him. Full of doubt and hope and fear and worry. Ty squeezed his shoulder and stepped into Mr. Root's office.

The door shut behind him and he sat down in the chair that Shelby had been sitting in the last time he was here. "What the hell happened?"

"Well." Mr. Root walked around his desk. "Your son won't say a word, so all we have are the stories told to us by John and Scott and Mr. Phillips and Ms. Monroe."

"Ms. Monroe?"

"She broke up the fight."

He stretched out his hand, trying to shake away the instinct to make fists. "Start at the beginning."

"Your son was playing by himself and Scott and John approached him. Casey tried to leave, but John grabbed his sweatshirt and tore the pocket. According to Scott, Casey just went berserk. He started punching John."

"Why?"

"No one knows."

"Of course they know."

Mr. Root nodded. "They aren't saying. In any case, Scott tried to pull Casey off of John but Casey kicked him."

"How did my son's nose get broken?"

"Mr. Phillips and Ms. Monroe said that when they found them, Scott was holding Casey down while John punched him."

Ty stood up. Those words—oh God, how they hurt. Someone held down his son and hurt him. This pain was searing, like trying to hold onto something that was too hot. He bent over, his hands braced on his knees.

Mr. Root leaned back from his desk and held up his hands. "Please. Mr. Svenson, let me finish."

"There's more?"

"When Ms. Monroe broke up the fight Casey ran away, but he shoved her, knocked her over—"

Oh God. "Is she okay?"

"A minor scrape. But when I found Casey, he was crying in the bathroom stall."

"Yeah, I can imagine. Because his nose was broken."

Mr. Root shook his head, seemingly uncertain. "He hasn't told us his side of the story. He hasn't defended himself, or accused John and Scott of anything. He's been silent."

He got where Mr. Root was going. "He's not really a silent kid."

"No. He's not. Most fifth graders who'd been held down and beaten would be pretty quick to tell their side of the story."

Ty rubbed his forehead. "Every time I come in here I have less clue what I'm doing."

"I know and I'm sorry." That Mr. Root sounded sincere was nearly the end of him. It was so much better when Mr. Root was the bad guy. When he was understanding, Ty had no place to put his ugly emotions. He just had to hold onto them.

"Is he suspended?"

"All three boys are. For the rest of the week."

Four days. Casey would just have to come to work with him.

"Next week, every morning before school I need to have all three of them in my office. I'm going to have some work for them to do."

"Together?"

"Supervised. They'll be supervised, but hopefully we

can get everyone past this. It's a small school, Mr. Svenson. And this kind of thing can be a cancer."

Ty nodded, his back teeth nearly cracking in his mouth he was grinding his jaw so hard.

"You should know, Scott told us all of this and he was very . . . very upset."

"Yeah, I'd imagine holding a kid down while your buddy smashes his face in would be upsetting."

Mr. Root said nothing, as if Ty's sarcasm was totally warranted. "Like I said, it's a small school, Mr. Svenson. A small town. Scott and John have been friends since kindergarten. John's parents have been going through a very ugly, very public divorce."

"Are you defending them?"

"No. I'm . . ." He shook his head. "I think I'm just trying to give you some context."

Fuck your context, he thought. "I'm not interested in gossip, Mr. Root."

"Fair enough."

"Can we go?"

Mr. Root nodded. "I can't . . . I can't tell you how sorry I am that this happened at our school. It should be a safe place."

"Yeah," he said, in total agreement. Casey didn't have a whole lot of safe places left. "Is Ms. Monroe in class?"

Mr. Root shook his head. "The teachers' lounge."

"Thanks."

Ty opened the door, and at the sight of his son's scuffed shoes and the torn pocket of his red hoodie on the floor in front of him, he was struck to the core by a moment of such painful, terrible doubt.

"Mr. Svenson," Mr. Root said.

"You can just call me Ty," he said, staring at that red hoodie.

"Ty. Try to get him to talk to you. To talk to anyone."

Ty looked over his shoulder, surprised by his change of heart regarding counseling. "I will," he said.

He just had no clue how.

"Let's go, son," he murmured. He put his hand under Casey's elbow to help him stand up, but Casey twitched away, doing it all on his own. Casey scooped his hoodie up from the floor and dumped the cold pack and the paper towels on Colleen's desk.

"Thank you," he murmured to her and walked out of the office. Ty could only follow.

Chapter 11

In the hallway, Casey was at the doors heading outside before Ty could catch up with him.

"Hold up, Casey. You know where the teachers' lounge is?"

Casey looked back, his blue eyes so clear in his red, swollen face. His nose was twice its normal size and the bruising was showing up under his eyes. He would have two shiners in the morning.

"Why do you want to go to the teachers' lounge?" he asked, so wary.

"Because we need to see if Ms. Monroe is okay."

Casey let the door close shut behind him and walked down the opposite way, through the hallways and the empty gym to a small set of stairs on the other side.

"Up there," he said.

"You're coming with me."

"Kids . . . kids aren't allowed."

"They are right now."

Ty went up first, because he understood the holy mystery that was the teachers' lounge to a fifth grader, but he heard Casey's footsteps behind him.

He opened the door at the top and found Shelby sitting at a round table with a man.

"You don't want a bandage?" the man was asking, pulling away the cold compress that she was holding to her cheek. The guy sat close, close enough that he was touching Shelby in about four different places, and surprisingly, Ty felt jealousy blast through him.

"It's a scrape," she said. She was flushed pink. "Hardly worth all this."

"Shelby," the guy breathed, looking at Shelby as though he wanted to wrap his arms around her, and Ty cleared his throat, shattering this little scene in front of him.

The guy jumped back and Shelby's wide brown eyes flew to his. At the sight of him she stood and looked behind him, where Casey was standing.

"Casey," she said. "Are you okay?"

Ty stepped sideways trying to get out of the way, but Casey kind of stepped with him. He was hiding behind him. Christ, this was all so strange.

Shelby glanced up at Ty and he shrugged, because he had no clue what was happening.

"Are you okay?" Casey asked, from behind him.

"I'm fine. It's just a scrape. See?" She came around the table and turned her face. She had a bright red scrape across her cheek. "Are *you* okay?" she asked. "When I saw—"

"I'm sorry I pushed you."

She stepped closer and when Casey shuffled back until he was almost backed into the corner, Shelby pressed a quick hand to her mouth. "Can you tell me what happened?"

Casey just turned and walked out the door. By the sound of his footsteps, he ran down the steps.

Ty met Shelby's eyes, and there was nothing either one of them could say that would dissipate this black cloud. "I'll talk to you later," he said, then jogged down the steps to catch up with his son.

Casey had slowed down and it was obvious his face hurt. Silently they left the school and got into the truck. Instead of heading through town toward the house, he headed back toward the interstate.

"Where are you going?" Casey asked.

"We need to get your nose checked out." He watched Casey lean sideways against the door. "Does it hurt?"

Casey nodded.

"You going to tell me what happened?"

"Mr. Root already did, didn't he?"

"I know you threw the first punch and I know that Scott held you down while John punched you."

"That's all," Casey said, his eyes shut.

"Why'd you throw the first punch?"

Casey didn't answer.

"Were they making fun of you?"

More silence.

"Casey?"

Nothing.

"Is this about your mom calling?"

"No!" The venom with which he spat the word would indicate otherwise.

"We can talk about it—"

"I don't want to."

He turned into the parking lot at the clinic and switched off the ignition.

"I'm sorry. I'm sorry she called. You don't have to ever talk to her if you don't want."

"I don't give a shit about her."

That was clearly a lie and Ty didn't know what to do about it. It sat between them, steaming and rotten. Casey cared about the call. He cared about all of it.

"When she calls, there's this recording saying that an inmate at the prison is calling. You have to accept the call before you even hear her voice."

"I . . . I don't want to hear her voice."

"Then you just hang up. If she calls again, we'll just hang up."

He stared at Casey, trying to gauge if his words gave him any comfort, but he was still curled around himself as if waiting for another punch.

The deep breath Ty took filled up his whole body, blew out his chest, cleared out his brain, and he decided he just had to be honest. There was no point in trying to protect Casey—he'd failed at every turn. This kid was doing it all himself. He'd been fighting his own battles . . . God, he couldn't imagine how long. How bad things must have been with Vanessa. And in those foster homes. That walk across the river. He handled all that shit himself.

There was no protecting this kid.

He had to just get into the trenches with him.

"I'm so scared, Casey," he breathed. "I'm so scared I'm screwing things up for you. You walked across that bridge." His words squeezed past the heavy rock of emotion in his throat. "You walked into that garage, and that was the fucking bravest thing I'd ever seen."

The American flag on the pole at the entrance to the clinic snapped and twisted in the wind against a stone-gray sky. It was ragged, that flag; the seams between the red and white stripes were splitting. Frayed.

"I've never done anything half that brave in my life and I just want to deserve that. Give you something that's worth the risk you took. I don't know if I'm ever going to figure out how to be your dad. Or if we're going to figure out how to be a family. But God . . . I just want to help."

He blinked back the hot tears behind his eyes and turned to face Casey, who was staring back at him. His blue eyes wide and bright and awful in that red, swollen face.

"I . . . I ah, I don't know if I ever told you this, but I moved in with my grandparents when I was thirteen." Of course he'd never told Casey this. He'd never told Casey anything about his life, scared that it would make him seem weak or that Casey would take one look at all the mistakes he'd made and follow in his footprints. He'd thought his parenting style would be to pretend he'd been a different person. But Casey had found his old footprints anyway and seemed pretty damned determined to follow him.

"My folks had been killed in a car accident," he continued. "And I know that sounds sad and it was, but it was kind of the best thing that ever happened to me. They weren't nice people. They weren't nice to each other or to me; we moved all the time because they couldn't keep it together to hold down jobs or pay rent. I don't know what would have happened to me if they hadn't died. Pop was the one who got me started with bikes, riding them, fixing them, refurbishing the old ones. About two weeks after I moved in with them, I'd gotten into all this trouble at school. A lot like the trouble you got into today. Some kids were mouthing off about my hand-me-down shoes and high-water pants and my secondhand backpack, and I just took a big swing at one of them. They ganged up on me and I got the crap kicked out of me."

He shot his son a wry look, but Casey remained silent. *So much like Pop,* Ty thought with no small amount of affection.

"Well, your mom was right about me: I was a troublemaker. And so the weekend after I got in all this trouble, Pop took me out to the garage and I thought he was going to beat the living tar out of me. Pop was huge and he had monster hands." He held up his own hands, remembering suddenly what it felt like when Pop's big hand landed on his shoulder. How comforting, how he'd thought Pop and those big, strong hands could fight back anything that would try to hurt him. Those hands made Ty feel safe—for the first time in his life.

Had Ty ever done that for Casey? Ever made him feel safe?

"It's what my dad would have done," Ty said. "But instead Pop had this old Royal Enfield and he said we were going to fix it. And I couldn't figure out how we could fix this thing. I mean you should have seen it." He nearly laughed at the memory. "It was rusted and old and dented and just looked like scrap to me. But Pop said, we fix it one piece at a time."

One piece at a time. He'd forgotten those words when it came to Casey. He'd tried so hard to wipe his past clear, wipe out all the trouble and all the problems that had driven Casey across the bridge with that address in his pocket. That had been his first mistake—Casey was never going to forget where he'd come from, just like Ty had never forgotten. He remembered it all, the very, very bad and the very, very good.

"Did you fix it?"

"No, actually. The motor was shot and we couldn't find the right parts, and eventually we just used the thing for scrap."

Casey burst out laughing and then groaned, holding his nose. "That was a terrible story."

"I guess it was." Ty couldn't help laughing either. He popped open his door. "Let's get your nose looked at."

Chapter 12

The end of the day was a relief. Shelby just wanted to go home, take a hot bath, and try to get hold of Ty to see how Casey was. It would be a very long time before she would forget the look on his face when he'd turned to face her in the school yard. Bloody and beaten, but wild and terrified.

And so sad.

And then in the teachers' lounge when he wouldn't look at her.

She couldn't stand the idea of him beating himself up that he'd hurt her.

The beautiful weather from the weekend had taken a turn, and while the sun was still clear and bright, the January chill was back in the air, so she zipped up her coat against the wind as she crossed the parking lot to her car.

"Shelby!"

She turned to find Joe Phillips running across the lot to meet her.

"Hey," he said, coming to a stop. His panting breaths fogged in the air. "I'm glad I caught you."

"Thanks again, Joe, for all your help today with the kids."

He waved it away, like he'd been doing all afternoon. "I'm glad I was the teacher closest to you when you yelled for help."

She smiled at him but the silence went on for too long, and she couldn't hold onto that smile forever.

"Well," she finally said. "I need to get—"

"This Friday some teachers are getting together down at The Pour House and I thought I'd see if you wanted to come?" His glance darted to her face and away, only to come creeping back.

She blinked, rocked back onto her heels. "The Pour House?"

"Yeah. Sean's got great barbecue now and there will be a bunch of us there, so you know . . ."

Not a date. Whether he was trying to make that clear for her sake or his, she wasn't sure, but she chafed at the reminder.

Calm down, Shelby, she told herself. *Not a date, but fun. And if there's anything you need in your life right now, it's fun.* The pressure had to be regulated before she went nuts the way she had with Ty.

Accusing him of following her to church?

Her crazy *had* been showing.

"Shelby?"

God, she was standing here thinking about Ty while talking to Joe.

"Maybe," she said. She needed to check with Deena, make sure she could come over to hang out with Mom.

"Friday, around seven?"

"Sounds great."

"Great!" he said with a big smile. "I'll email you with details."

She nodded, trying not to say "great" again. *We sound like idiots.* "Good night, Joe."

He jogged back toward the school and she got into her car. She started the ignition, but couldn't quite put the car into drive.

What a weird day, she thought. *A really weird day.*

*   *   *

Ty cleaned up the paper plates from the barbecue they'd picked up at The Pour House and brought home after the clinic. Casey hadn't eaten half of what he usually ate, so Ty wrapped up the half rack of ribs and put it in the fridge for later. Maybe after the Tylenol he'd taken kicked in, he'd get his appetite back. But for now, Casey had gone to his room with an ice pack and instructions to rest, like the doctor told him.

The doctor also said nothing had been broken and there wasn't a concussion, which had caused Ty to sag in his chair with relief.

But the relief had been momentary.

Casey still hadn't told him why he'd thrown the first punch.

"Why are you protecting them?" he'd asked.

"I'm not protecting them," he'd said, staring at the yellow barren fields as they drove back home.

Ty threw away the paper plates and headed out to the garage.

But the Velocette carburetor didn't hold his attention. The pieces spread out on his workbench were a puzzle he didn't care about at the moment. The puzzle of his son had apparently turned him off mysteries.

The Indian Chief, gleaming under the garage lights, was a problem solved. It had seen the best of Ty's attention, and it was obvious for some reason at this moment that it was time to let it go. He'd held onto the bike for long enough.

When he finished with a bike, he had a small group of collectors he emailed to gauge interest. Sometimes, no one was interested and he went to an online auction site, but if there was a lot of interest, he just set a time and a date for the sale himself. The bike went home with the highest offer. He had enough of a reputation that his group of buyers grew bigger after every auction, and at this point he had about seven men and three women he could email.

Ty went back into the house to find his laptop. It wasn't where he'd left it on the couch last night, or in the "office" where, quite frankly, it almost never was. It wasn't in his bedroom or the back porch, where Casey sometimes used it for homework.

He knocked on Casey's closed bedroom door.

"Come in," came his son's muffled voice.

Ty pushed open the door to see his son sitting cross-legged on his bed.

He should have a dog, he thought, for no other reason than that his double bed looked empty. As though a dog would fill up some of that space around the boy. Make him seem so much less alone.

I am barely managing what I have, he thought, immediately cooling on the idea.

The dark circles under his son's eyes looked worse in the weird green light from the computer screen in front of him.

"You're supposed to be icing your face," he said.

"I did; it was too cold."

"That's kind of the idea."

Casey didn't say anything. He sat hunched over the screen, his arms wrapped around his stomach.

"What are you watching?" he asked, stepping into the room, trying to be cool, because being overtly demanding and overtly concerned hadn't gotten him very far today.

Casey was, oddly enough, a neat freak, and there were no toys or books to kick out of the way as Ty made his way over to the bed. He wondered suddenly if that was a product of the foster system or if that was his nature.

"Nothing."

Ty looked down at the YouTube home page. "What's up, buddy?"

Casey flinched and Ty held himself still, unsure of what he'd said or done to cause the reaction. But Casey didn't explain. "Look, you can choose not to tell me, it's okay. I get that you want your privacy, but I think you'll feel better if you just get some of this stuff off your chest."

Casey turned miserable eyes toward him, swimming with worry and grief.

It was without a doubt the most emotion the boy had ever shown him, a true glimpse behind the I-don't-give-a-shit mask of the last few months.

Ty ran a hand over the footboard of the bed, his thumb stroking the cheap wood because his son wouldn't let Ty touch him and he wanted to—so badly, just give the kid a hug. He'd tried that once before a few weeks after they'd started counseling, when the overworked woman at DCFS had told him that Casey had missed out on all the normal affection that kids his age grew up with.

That hug had not gone well. Stiff and awkward. Fast. Not to be repeated.

"How about if I promise you won't be in trouble, whatever it is."

"I'm not scared of being in trouble."

"Then what *are* you scared of?"

Casey took a deep breath, opened his mouth, and the words just poured out.

"I punched John because he was saying awful stuff about Ms. Monroe. How last summer there was this TV show that came to Bishop and this guy . . . this like cookie guy, I don't know. He said some stuff about Ms. Monroe on the show."

"What kind of stuff?" Ty asked carefully, feeling like the ice he thought was solid beneath his feet was actually razor thin.

Casey shook his head, the tips of his ears glowing red hot.

"Case—"

"That she was a slut. That she . . . she sucked his dick."

Ty sat down hard on the edge of the bed. His muscles turned to water, his bones pudding. "That's why you punched him?"

"Yeah."

"Good for you, son."

Casey shot him a wan smile over his shoulder. "That's why I wouldn't tell anyone what happened."

"I totally understand." Ty put his hand around the back of Casey's neck and gave it a little squeeze. What he wanted to do was haul the kid into his arms, hide him from a world that was too damn much for both of them at the moment. "I'm proud of you."

"Well, that's why I hit him the first time. I don't know why I kept hitting him. Or why I kicked him. Sometimes . . . sometimes I just get so mad."

Pop used to have a dog, a mutt with some kind of crazy hunting instinct, and it would see a squirrel and just go so still. He'd turn himself into a dog statue.

That was Casey. A kid statue.

Ty tried to blow out a long breath as quietly as he could, so it didn't sound like a heavy sigh. "I understand that, too. You've had a few shitty breaks, kid; being mad makes sense. We just . . . maybe we just need to find you a way to deal with it instead of beating up kids in your class."

"I'm the one that got beat up."

"I don't know about that," Ty said. "I saw that John kid—you got in a few good punches." Casey smiled at that. "And two against one, that's not fair."

Casey stopped smiling and looked back at the screen. "I don't know why Scott would let John say that stuff about Ms. Monroe. She's so cool to him at the Art Barn, she like . . . she's just cool."

Ty winced and swore silently, unable to believe what he was about to say. "Apparently Scott and John have been friends for a long time. And Mr. Root said things aren't great in John's house."

"That makes it okay?"

"Absolutely not. It doesn't make it okay at all. But things don't happen without a reason, you know? Sometimes it helps to know the reason."

"John said it was all on YouTube. The whole thing with Ms. Monroe and that guy on the TV show."

Ty glanced at the YouTube home page on the computer. "Have you looked?"

Casey shook his head.

"Maybe it's best not to know," Ty said.

"Do you think it's true?"

"I don't think it's any of my business," he said. "And no matter what happened between her and this guy, no one ever says that kind of stuff about a person to other people. It's mean. It's rude. It's not . . ." *Oh Christ, is this really happening? Hasn't enough happened today?* "Look, when you get older and things start happening between you and girls—you don't brag to your friends about it. You don't make up shit about girls just to seem cool. A girl decides she likes you enough to do anything with you it's kind of a gift. And you treat it like that."

"I just can't believe anyone would say anything like that about her on TV."

"Me neither," he said. And if it was true? God, he just couldn't imagine. A woman like Shelby, who wore her privacy, her reputation like a suit of armor, what would the world thinking *that* about her do to her? Frankly it explained a lot of the hot/cold treatment she dished out.

Sometimes knowing the reason did help.

"I was going to send out some emails. Can I use the computer?"

"Yeah." Casey shoved it over with his toe. "I'm done."

"You know," Ty said, grabbing the laptop. "We've got an early morning tomorrow."

"But I'm suspended. I don't have school."

"Right. Which means you're going to work with me."

"What?"

His face would have been funny without all that bruising.

"Them's the breaks, kid. You're on my chain gang until you're back in school."

"You're working at Cora's, right? The deck? That won't be so bad."

"Fritters aren't part of the deal," he said, crossing the room with the laptop under his arm. "Ice your face and get some sleep."

Ty took the laptop into the living room and stretched out on the leather sectional with the computer in his lap. He emailed his potential buyers, then contacted his buddy the auctioneer who was licensed and worked for a case of beer and a tune-up on his Harley.

And then, his breath held, he went over to YouTube.

It wasn't his business. It wasn't. And a better man maybe would honor what he'd told his son and not look it up.

But he was Wyatt Svenson, and Shelby Monroe let him in just enough that he felt like it *was* his business.

So, with a mostly clear conscience, he typed *Shelby Monroe + TV show* into the search engine.

No results.

See, Ty thought, *there's your sign. Stop now.*

Instead he typed in *Bishop, Arkansas + TV Show*. The menu showed up with a list of segments for the morning show *America Today*. The first one said "Hilarious finale. Slut-shaming and small-town mayor implodes."

At first it was a slick piece about the Maybream Cookie Company moving its factory back to a small town in the States. Apparently, this was the finale and

America had given the highest number of votes to three towns: Bishop, a town in Michigan, and one in Alaska. After the slick promo, two anchors talked about the three towns and then introduced the live shot of Bishop.

Immediately, he noticed Shelby looking utterly terrorized. He recognized Cora, holding onto her and Monica. A dark-haired man and a blond guy were squared off in the center of the shot. The dark-haired guy was trying to get to Shelby, but the big blond wasn't letting him past.

"That's not what you said, Shelby," the dark-haired guy said, his face filled with ugly hate and fury. "When you were sucking my dick. When I was fucking you like an animal."

Ty gasped. He couldn't help it. It was worse than he'd even imagined. It was . . . it was as terrible as the pain on Shelby's face on the screen. She looked gutted. The big blond guy punched the asshole in the face, knocking him to the ground, and then, as if stunned that he'd done that, he turned to the camera with a blank expression.

"Vote Bishop," he said.

But in the corner of the shot he saw Shelby's face turn to stone and where other women would cry, she walked away. Dry-eyed. Back straight.

Christ, he thought, proud and horrified on every single level. *She's so damn tough.*

He played it again, figured out all the players. The blond guy was Jackson Davies, Bishop's former mayor. The dark-haired guy was Dean Jennings. And he watched everyone else's faces. Absorbed their shock and horror. Cora in particular looked like she wouldn't mind taking a swing at that man herself. He caught sight of Sean in the background, watching Shelby as she ran away, the look of helplessness on his face one he could totally sympathize with.

He turned off the computer and shoved it off his lap.

If he ever met Jackson Davies he was going to buy that man a beer. If his son were old enough he'd do the same thing for him. All the sideways looks he got from everyone when he said he was going out on a date with Shelby, he now understood them a little bit better.

They were just worried about their friend and he was a stranger. Perhaps a stranger that had seen this very YouTube clip and wanted to test his chances.

You won't tell anyone about this.

Oh God, remembering her words from that night just ruined him. But it also made him angry, because he was nothing like Dean Jennings and if he let her have her way, she wasn't going to give him the chance to prove that to her.

Suddenly, he had a lot he wanted to talk about with Shelby Monroe.

He found his phone on the kitchen counter and texted her.

Hey. You awake? All right?

A few seconds later she messaged back.

Fine. Doing some work in the barn. How is Casey?

We went to the clinic. No broken bones. No concussion. He'll be fine. Can I come over and talk to you real quick?

It took a little longer for her to write back and he imagined her staring down at the phone, the corner of her lip caught in her teeth.

Sure, she finally wrote back. *Come on back to the barn.*

Give me ten, he said.

He went up to Casey's room and found him playing video games.

"I iced," he said quickly. "I just finished."

"I need to go over and talk to Shelby."

"You're not going to tell her, are you?"

"I don't know," he said honestly. "I thought I would tell her some of it. Just so she understood. And frankly, someone should understand what a jerk that John kid is."

"I don't think that's a secret."

"Frankly, Casey, what you did—I would have done the exact same thing, if some guy said that about Shelby." He would have done worse. Thinking about Dean Jennings, his blood ran hot and thick with the need to teach him a lesson. "And she's really worried about you. I want to just tell her everything is okay. You want to come with me?" he asked, hoping Casey would say no, because there was another huge conversation he needed to have with her about how he wasn't Dean Jennings, and he wasn't going to humiliate her. Or hurt her. And if that was why she didn't want to date him, she was going to need a better reason.

But then he thought of Shelby's mother in church on Sunday.

Was that Alzheimer's? Was she the only one caring for her?

Shelby was dealing with a lot.

"Heck no." Casey was wide-eyed in horror.

"Fine. I won't be gone long."

Casey nodded and went back to shooting zombies in the head.

Ty changed his shirt and washed his face. Brushed the barbecue smell out of his breath.

And wondered what the hell he was getting into when he crossed the street.

Chapter 13

Shelby quickly ran a hand through her hair and put a little lip gloss on and then, sick of herself and not even sure of what she was doing, she wiped it off.

"Hello?"

Ty's voice in the barn sent a lick of flame through her blood.

She stepped out of her office and down the dark, narrow hallway into the bright sparkle of the Art Barn. Ty stood at the door in that denim jacket with the shearling collar and the cowboy boots. Tonight he wore dark denim that hugged his long legs.

What she'd been so quick to dismiss about him—his beauty, masculinity, the raw appeal of him—she now quite liked.

That man, that beautiful masculine creature right there. I had sex with him.

"Hey," she said.

She set down the construction paper she'd brought with her and began to sort it into five piles with one of each color. There was no reason for this, but it gave her something to do with her hands.

"How is Casey?"

"The nose isn't broken, but he's going to have a few shiners to brag about, so he's pretty excited about that."

She gave him a wry smile.

"Thank you," he said, approaching the table where she sat with one long step. "Thank you for stepping in when you did."

Her sorting paused on the pink paper. "I only wish I had gotten there sooner."

"Yeah," he said. "Me, too."

"Why did Casey start the fight?" she asked.

Ty's silence had a certain loaded quality to it.

"I understand if you don't want to tell me," she said when he didn't answer. "But chances are, whatever it was, it hasn't gone away, and in a week's time when they're back together they'll fight about it again."

"So why would telling you change anything?"

"Wow. Is it all teachers and schools you don't trust or just us?"

"I had my fair share of teachers who didn't care."

"I care, Wyatt. I care a lot." Her gaze tangled with his and she found it impossible to pull herself away. He wasn't just handsome, which lord knows he was. He was also . . . magnetic. He carried himself the way she imagined cowboys did, or outlaws. Men who were their own law, their own code. That kind of authority over one's life, over one's perspective—it was attractive.

Sexual.

That kind of authority . . . it dared her. It dared her to test it. Or try it. To taste it.

She had to look away. The events of the day had been trying to say the least, and she felt undone by it all. Worn down. Having sex with Ty would not fix that.

"I know you care," he said, his voice low, and for a moment she wasn't sure what he was talking about. *Oh God, right. Casey.*

"Everyone does. I know you didn't get the best impression of Mr. Root, but he's working uphill against budget problems and cuts to child mental health in the state and, since the closing of other area schools, a spike in enrollment. He's trying to do the best he can for all the kids."

"That doesn't mean Casey needs drugs."

She sat back against the chair. Ty was not a see-all-sides kind of guy, not when it came to his own; she understood that. "No. It doesn't. But whatever they were fighting about, the more the teachers know, the more they can help."

"John was talking about you."

"Me?" She sorted the yellows into each pile. And then the pinks. She was one short. "What about me?"

As soon as the question fell from her lips she knew the answer. There was only one thing people would say about her.

She lets men fuck her like an animal.

Her heart shriveled and her stomach froze for just a moment before hot blood flooded her whole body.

No one believes it, that's what Joe had said. And she'd believed him.

She looked up at Ty. Ty believed it. Ty believed it because she'd let him do it to her. Or, more honestly, she'd done it to him. She'd fucked him like an animal.

"What . . . what did he say?" she whispered.

"It doesn't matter."

Her laugh was a jagged mess. "To you maybe. It matters very much to me." John was her student. One of her many students, and if John was talking about her, there was no way she could go back into her job believing that all of them weren't talking about her.

"It was fifth-grade bullshit and . . . well, Casey handled it."

She shook her head, stunned by the machismo of such a stupid statement.

"Casey didn't handle it. He punched a kid. *I* handle it, Wyatt. Me. Every day." The chair she was sitting in screeched out behind her. "Every time someone looks at me twice. Every time I go into the grocery store and people pretend not to watch me through the produce section. Every time some stranger from out of town ap-

proaches me in Cora's wondering why I look so familiar. Every time someone looks at me like they *know*
me. No one knows me!"

She was standing. Yelling. Her skin burned and she
stepped away. Wishing she could just disappear. When
had she gotten this bad? This nearly out of control?

It was her father's congregation all over again.
Strangers believing some version of her that was far from
the whole truth. And it was terrifying to her, terrifying
that she would fight so hard to not be what they thought
of her, just to be perverse.

She was beginning to scare herself.

"Having sex with me doesn't mean you know me."

"You don't know me either," he shot back, revealing
his own anger. "And clearly you didn't want to."

I'm sorry, she wanted to say. *I'm sorry I acted that
way. I'm sorry I don't know how to be sexual and
human and kind all at the same time. I am sorry my
father ruined me and my mother couldn't quite save me
and all I have left for people are these broken pieces.*

"But," he said with a small smile that somehow
smoothed so many of her jagged edges, only because it
revealed his own. "But you helped me with my kid.
And . . . and I saw you at church. I met your mom." It
was an arrow through her. His gaze. His words—they
pierced her skin, slid through muscle and bone. It was
true, she could pretend otherwise because she'd kept
her dress on while they had sex, because she didn't go
out to eat with him. But every time he looked at her she
had the sense that he saw her—and all those things
she buried. "And . . . and I think maybe I know more
about you than you'd like. Because you sure as hell
know more about me than I'd like."

"I'm sorry," she said, because she felt like she should.
But he only laughed and shrugged.

"Can't do anything about that now." He glanced

around, and she was reminded of one of the stray dogs on this street. One summer when she'd kept all the doors open trying to get a cross breeze, this skinny, nearly feral dog had wandered into her dining room. It didn't growl or lunge or try to bite, it looked around like it just couldn't believe it had wandered into such a place.

Ty looked the same way.

"You have any more of that bourbon?"

She nodded and went back to her office to grab it. Back at the table she put down the mugs and Ty took the bottle from her, pulled the cork out with his teeth—which was such a weirdly attractive thing to do—and poured two shots in the mugs.

"Can I ask you something?"

"Sure," she said, taking a sip of her bourbon.

"Why did you have sex with me?"

She choked on the bourbon.

"Because . . ." *Your leather bracelets, your hair, your beauty, your easiness. I want all of that.* "I wanted to feel something."

"What was it that you wanted to feel?" he asked, sounding like he really wanted to know. Like it wasn't just a ridiculous thing to say.

"Powerful. Powerful and out of control and . . . alive."

"You made me feel that way," he said. "The other night."

She felt as if the tide had come in and parts of her were just washed away by his words. And he was still talking, revealing bits of himself, but somehow even more of her.

And she wanted to fight it. Pack up the mugs and the bourbon and shoo him out the door like that stray dog. But she couldn't. Her body would not obey her scared impulses.

"I understand why you were scared that I might tell

someone what happened. And I get it why you didn't want to go out. I can't imagine what it must be like to have people whispering behind their hands. I get it."

"Thank you," she whispered.

"But I want to feel that way again." The sound of his mug hitting the table made her jerk. "There are things in my life I'd like to forget about for a few hours, and maybe you feel the same way?"

Oh God. She did. So badly, she did.

He stepped a little closer. "I'd like to feel good. Alive. And I'd like to make you feel that way."

He was a breath away, a tiny step, and she was riveted to the floor, unable to move. It was as if he'd opened up her head, read her dirty secrets.

"Do you want that?" he whispered.

She nodded.

His eyes blazed and he took the mug from her suddenly limp fingers before she dropped it.

"Tell me," he breathed.

"I want it."

He laughed. "What?"

"I want you to make me feel good. I want to make you feel good."

"Oh, sweetheart. That's the nicest thing anyone has ever said to me."

She reached up to pull apart the snaps of his coat, but he stopped her. "I was naked last time," he said. Under her skin she shivered. "You this time."

She shook her head and he stepped away.

"Wait—"

"I want you, Shelby. I really do. And I can play any kind of game you want, but it's got to be an equal thing."

There had to be rules. She couldn't just let everything go. She'd tried that. So desperate to feel something, so desperate to be connected, she'd let Dean dictate every-thing. She couldn't let that happen again.

"Trust me," he murmured. "I won't hurt you."

"What if I hurt *you*?" In her life, no pleasure came without pain. Everything was a double-edged sword.

"I'll take it."

I'll take it. I'll take the pain. Who said that? Who offered that in return for sex?

And why am I so turned on by it?

She didn't think about it, gave herself no time to second-guess. She pulled her sweater over her head, and the tee shirt went with it. And she stood there in her bra and yoga pants. It was so pedestrian, so everyday, and yet he looked at her as if she were riding out of the waves in a clamshell.

She wanted to scoff at him, wound him, so he'd really see her. Her belly and the frayed strap to her second-oldest bra and her anger . . . the anger she tried so hard to keep at manageable levels. But it bubbled and spit and overwhelmed her.

But then she realized he really did see her, and the bra and her belly—it didn't matter to him.

"I'm angry," she said, for no good reason.

"Tell me about it."

"No. I'm . . ." She shook her head, her hands clenched into fists.

Knowledge coalesced on his face and he nodded once. "Take off your pants."

"Ty—"

"Do it."

The tone of his voice was hard, a brick wall she would not be able to get around. A hard wall she could only heave herself against until she was exhausted by the ef-fort.

Her lust unwound in her chest; like a giant sleeping jungle cat it woke up and took over, colored everything.

Changed her perspective on herself. Her second-best bra.

In a blink she had her pants and underwear off and she stood in her Art Barn naked but for a bra and socks.

Ty still wore his jacket, but sweat trickled from his hairline down the side of his face, across the stubble of his cheeks.

"Go over to the couch," he said. "The velvet one."

She walked away, aware that Ty, who was gorgeous, was staring at her very average ass, and she resisted the urge to put her hands behind her, covering herself. As she walked she heard the snaps of his jacket opening and the thud as the heavy coat hit the floor. She imagined him taking off his shirt, dropping it on the floor. His belt, his pants. He would toe off his boots and shuck down his underwear and then . . . at last . . . cover all of her bare skin with his.

She'd never had sex like that. Two people fully naked. That was sad, suddenly. To be her age and have only had frenzied and half-dressed sex in the back of cars or in dorm rooms or apartments shared with girlfriends.

But that was how she had liked it; the clothes seemed to remind her that she had parts of herself that were better hidden.

Nudity was something she didn't entirely know what to do with.

At the couch she turned to face him, surprised to see him—except for the coat in a heap on the other side of the room—fully dressed. Relieved, actually, to see him fully dressed.

"Turn around," he murmured, his eyes trailing over her breasts, across her shoulders. Down over her hated belly.

She lifted a hand to cover her stomach, the rolls there.

"Don't," he whispered. "I told you to turn around."

The command, the blush rolling up from his neck, they

were powerful convincers, and she turned away from him, facing the couch.

"Get on your knees," he whispered. "Hold onto the back."

Her heart pounded between her legs as she did what he told her to do. Now, she heard the snap of his shirt buttons being popped, the rustle of clothes falling off his body, and she looked over her shoulder at him, stunned anew by the rough, masculine beauty of him. The heavy muscles in his chest, across his arms, the narrow waist.

Chest hair that she could imagine against the tender skin of her back.

A low sound rolled out of her throat and their eyes met over her shoulder and she couldn't control any part of her reaction to him.

"Hurry," she breathed.

"Be quiet."

Oh, she sighed, turning to water. *Oh, he knows what I want.* She turned, putting her forehead against the back of the couch, unable to stop her restless hips, her restless body.

The couch creaked as he put one knee between hers. The rough scrape of his jeans against the inside of her knee sent sparks over her skin, from her knee to between her legs, where she was hot and wet and *waiting.*

A long moment passed without another touch, and impatient, she shifted back against him, pressing her ass against his body, feeling that he'd unzipped his pants and put a condom on over a very hard erection.

Moaning, she hung her head.

His heavy hand landed on her ass, not hard enough to hurt, but hard enough that she had to bite her lip from crying out.

"You ready?" It was just that hand against her ass

and the denim against her knee. The memory of his erection in latex. He didn't touch her anywhere else.

"Yes."

His knuckles brushed her as he positioned himself, and suddenly anxious and needy and desperate, she reached back to grab his thigh.

He stopped. The tip of his cock pressed against her.

"Don't move," he told her. "Both hands on the back of the couch."

She slapped her hand back on the couch.

The longer he waited the more desperate she became, and she arched her back, trying to ease him in by degrees. *Something,* she thought, *just give me something.*

"Don't. Move."

He spanked her again and she had to lock her arms to keep from falling onto the couch.

"Fine," she muttered. "Just . . . hurry."

His laughter flowed over her spine, sending gooseflesh across her skin. "Like this?" Without warning, he slammed into her.

She screamed, bracing one hand against the tissue-paper flowers so she wouldn't go headfirst into them. Again. And then again. The couch rocked as her body opened itself up to all the pleasure she could take.

He curved his hands over her shoulders and found some leverage as he fucked her relentlessly.

"Yes," she whispered, her breasts mashed against the back of the couch as he covered her, rocking into her, tip to root, over and over again as if measuring her from the inside, cataloging the depths of her pleasure, the scales to which he could make it grow.

"Yes. Yes. Yes," she whispered, feeling tears build in her eyes. Tears because it was all falling away, because without having to humble herself or compromise she was getting exactly what she wanted.

He lifted her torso, his hands sliding from her shoulders to her breasts. He was not gentle and it was exactly right. His big hands cupped her, the calluses on his fingers were crazy-making, and she stroked him, shifted her hips forward and back, squeezing him between her legs.

"You . . ." he breathed in her ear before he bit her neck. "I want to fuck you everywhere."

"Yes." She wanted that, too. She wanted everything.

He lifted her again, this time her whole body, and he spun, sitting on the couch so she sat, impaled in his lap, her back to his front.

He arranged her boneless legs so they were on the outside of his, splayed open. Both of them reached down between her legs. His fingers finding her clit, hers finding him where he was pushed so hard inside of her.

Both of them groaned, curling against each other, finding a thousand ways to touch, each one better than the last.

"Stop," he said.

"No." She shook her head, her fingers mapping the outline of his sac.

He pinched her clit and a lightning bolt sizzled through her. Her hands flew back against the couch as she felt like she was leaving earth. Leaving her body.

He moved her legs again, this time inside of his, and he tilted her up and forward. "Fuck me."

Breathless, on the edge of what felt like the orgasm to end all orgasms, she put her feet on the floor and began a slow undulation against him.

"Yes, oh, God," he groaned, catching her hips in his hands, squeezing her in a way that made her feel like she was torturing him. Which was perfect. Which added an element to her pleasure that she'd never felt before.

Her hair had come loose and she shook it out of the way so she could look over her shoulder at him. He was perfect. His muscles flexing, his skin red, his eyes trained on her body. He had his lower lip caught between his teeth like he was a man on the rack.

Very suddenly, it just wasn't enough.

She stood so quickly, he didn't stop her, and then she pulled him down onto the floor with her, on the rug that was abrasive and rough against her naked skin, but she didn't care. There was nothing in this world that she cared about more than his body covering hers.

He slid back inside and she lifted her legs around his hips. He rested on his bent elbows, his cheek pressed against her hair.

"You ready?" he breathed into her ear.

She nodded.

It was wild. Hard and fast and nearly punishing. Both of them straining against each other. They ended up on the other side of the rug, her head hitting the opposite couch. He was groaning in her ear, telling her how hot she was, how perfect, how good she felt, how he didn't want to leave her, and she was speechless against the growing painful tension in her body. She put one hand overhead to stop them from slamming into the couch and the other she slid between their bodies, her fingers knowing just where to touch herself.

"Yes," he hissed, easing himself up onto his knees. "Show me how you do it."

So she did, her face turned into her arm; she made herself come while he watched. It took nothing. Three hard, fast touches and it was over, she was up and over the wave, falling breathless and different, on the other side.

"So beautiful," he whispered when she was done, panting, sweating, and shaking.

"You," she gasped, and he needed no other invitation. He braced himself over her and pounded into her until he, too, tensed, his face locked down, his eyes squeezed shut. She touched one of the rigid muscles in his arms, traced the vein standing out against his skin from the inside of his elbow up to his shoulder.

He had a tattoo there. A motorcycle thing.

He was primal and wrong in about a million ways—but in this he was unbelievably perfect. He roared and growled and shook, and she wrapped her arms around him, clutching his easy wildness to her chest.

Finished, he hung his head against her chest, kissing her left breast and then her right one before pulling himself out of her body.

The haze and fog of desire was slowly dissipating and she felt very keenly the rug burn on her shoulders. The wet ache between her legs.

It's so messy, she thought. *And awkward.*

The aftermath of really good sex was everything she hated.

"You okay?" he asked.

She nodded and sat up, fighting the wince.

"Your back," he breathed.

She had a hard time reconciling the kind, worried expression on his face with the man who'd smacked her ass and fucked her across the carpet.

"It's fine," she said, patting his shoulder. Bones creaking, she stood up and her knee popped. *Oh, that wasn't sexy.* She felt his eyes on her as she walked across the room to put on her clothes. On the way back she grabbed his shirt and handed it to him. He'd taken off the condom and pulled up his pants.

He was watching her with a wary smile, as if he just wasn't sure what she was going to do. "You're not very good at this, are you?" he asked.

"I thought I did all right," she said, gesturing toward the rug and the couch as if it were the wrestling mat they'd just battled upon.

"No." He stood. "At *that*," he jerked his thumb behind him, "you're amazing. The undisputed champ."

Well, didn't that just wreck her.

"The after part. You've got a shitty dismount."

The hoot of her laugh was a surprise to both of them.

"I suppose you're right," she admitted with some difficulty. "I don't . . . I don't really know what to do. Or say."

"Well, let's start with a drink." He walked across the room to their mugs and the bourbon. He splashed some into both and walked back over to her. "Here." He handed her the mug and sat down on the leather couch.

She sat across from him on the velvet one.

"Okay." He stretched out his long, lean body, still without a shirt, and that was all right with her all of a sudden. "I'll start." He lifted his mug toward her. "Thank you very, very much for that." He took a sip, his eyes twinkling over the mug at her.

"Thank you," she said, doing the same. "That was—"

"Awesome?" It was perhaps a terrible time to be thinking this, but the way he grinned at her, she saw Casey. For a boy who didn't look much like his father, there were moments of similarity that could leave no question about DNA. That grin was something they shared.

"It was awesome," she agreed, and then because he'd been so sure in handling this, so capable and somehow knowing, she mustered up her courage and beat back the black shadows of her doubt and terrible persistent self-denial. "And exactly what I needed." She met his eyes, feeling a strange and terrible gratitude to this near-stranger. "Exactly."

He nodded graciously, and then the grin was back and he left his couch to come to hers.

Leaning over her, surrounding her with the scent of

sex and sweat and him, he pressed a warm closed-mouth kiss to her forehead, her cheek, and then, tipping her face up, he kissed her lips.

For the first time tonight he kissed her lips and she gasped with the pleasure of it, the chapped dry lips against hers, the wet slide of his tongue, the spicy taste of his mouth.

He leaned back again, just as her body was warming up under his attention. Like clay that had to be handled before it could be used. She felt malleable to his touch.

He flopped back to the other end of the couch and had another sip of his bourbon. Belatedly, she realized she had hers, and embarrassed by how quickly she was turned on by his touch, and disappointed that that wet, messy kiss wasn't going to go anywhere, she took a big gulp.

Chapter 14

He needed a second. It was hard to admit but he was showing his age, and after sex like that . . . he needed a cooldown. A few laps around the track at a slower pace. She looked all tousled and fucked and gorgeous, everything they'd done to each other written large in her dilated eyes, her messy hair, the blush to her skin—and he just needed a second.

"What are you going to do with Casey this week?" She curled her body in tight until she was just a little ball in the corner of her couch. He wanted to pick her up and put her in his lap, smooth out her hair. Kiss her collarbones, the down-sloping curve of her shoulder.

Maybe he wouldn't need as much of a cooldown as he'd thought.

"He'll come to work with me," he said. "We're finishing up Cora's patio."

"How did you end up being a carpenter and a mechanic?" she asked. "That's where Casey found you, right? Your grandfather's garage?"

The fact that she remembered lit a small match in a very dark place inside of him. "I've always been good with my hands." He waggled his eyebrows at her and she laughed, which had been his intention. He reached out and grabbed her foot. "You're so far away."

She scooted closer, halfway across the couch, and he pulled her stiff and awkward body closer. Until she had her legs across his lap and she was leaning sideways against the back of the couch, chewing on the edge of her thumbnail before catching herself.

There was no part of her that looked comfortable, as if she was enjoying this, and he wondered if maybe they shouldn't just leave things at filthy sex on the floor. But their lives were already brushing up against each other in a dozen places and, well, he didn't want to leave it at filthy sex on the floor.

He liked her.

Liked her awkwardness and her seriousness. He liked what she hid behind them. Suddenly, he wanted to see her smile. Hear that hooting laugh again.

He ran a thumb across the bottom of her bare foot, but she didn't even twitch. Of course, Shelby Monroe wasn't ticklish.

"Tell me about your grandfather's shop."

"Mostly we worked on motorcycles. Pop was one of the best in the business; he had customers from all over the country."

As if she knew what he wasn't saying, she brushed her hand over his tattoo, the stylized Indian 4 motorcycle on his shoulder, a brief, fleeting touch that he wanted to grab onto.

"When did he die?"

"Years ago." He shook his head, surprised by the catch in his throat. But that was what great sex did, it just laid him out flat and emotions walked right over him. "All this stuff with Casey, though, makes me miss him. Makes me wish he were here so I could ask him what I'm supposed to do with the kid."

"He would know the answer to that?"

"I moved in with my grandparents when I was thirteen. My parents died in a car wreck and I was wild. Totally wild."

"So, what did your pop do with you?"

"Well, for one thing he had Nana. And she was a

hugger. A total lover—she just smothered me with the kind of affection I'd never had. That helped."

Shelby laughed and he reached out to touch her fingers, the top knuckles, the half-moons at the base of her ravaged nails. She had competent hands. No rings. No nail polish. Just her. She spread her fingers out wide, giving him more room to play.

"Kids should have affection," she said, her eyes trained on the small dance of his fingers over hers.

He imagined her as a child. So serious and tidy, her hair in pigtails.

"Did you?" he asked, hoping that serious, tidy girl was smothered in love.

But she pulled her hands away and looked up at him with an overly bright smile. *Uh-oh,* he thought. *I guess that's a no on the affection question.*

"Well," she said, "if you need help with Casey this week, I have after-school programs on Monday and Wednesday and a birthday party on Friday."

He wanted to pull her hands back into his, get back to that quiet place between them that had felt so good, but that moment had passed. She was sharp and bristly again, and because he was perverse and loved a puzzle, he suddenly wanted to fuck her back into relaxing.

"I approve of the reasons he fought, but I don't think I need to reward him with more art classes."

"Oh, no," she said with a devilish little half-smile. "The classes are for toddlers—I was going to make him work."

Warmth surged through him. "I like the way you think, Shelby."

She buried her face in her mug, the blush rising up her neck. Oh man, she just killed him with all her conflicting pieces.

He took her feet into his lap and when she stiffened he

gave her the chance to move, but after a moment she relaxed just slightly, just enough to seem like a yes.

"Can I ask you something?" He applied pressure with his thumb against the bottom of her foot and she melted.

"Anything if you keep doing that."

"That Dean guy . . ."

"Why'd I do it?"

"You wanted to have sex. Seems pretty straightforward to me."

She blinked at him, like an owl facing moonlight for the first time.

"I suppose for some people it is."

"Not for you?"

"No." She pulled her feet away from his lap. "Not for me."

He stared at her, his lap feeling cold, his hands empty without her to touch.

"I have a reputation in town."

"As what?"

"As a teacher. A good person."

"And wanting to have sex makes you bad?"

"Don't oversimplify something you know nothing about. I don't imagine the world knowing you let someone fuck you like an animal ever damaged your reputation?"

He laughed in the face of her ire. "Are you calling me a slut?"

"No. I'm just saying . . ." He could see the moment on her face when she realized how little she knew him. The brief flicker of alarm that flashed across her face. "Well, maybe I am. I have no idea. Are you?"

"Nope. I'm dangerously monogamous. No matter how toxic or poisonous the relationship, I tend to go down with the ship." He thought of Vanessa, begging her to marry him. "You?"

"I've never really had a ship to go down with. Though I imagine I would."

"You haven't had a serious relationship?"

"In college, I did. I moved back home afterward and I dated the guy long-distance, but it got complicated and, well, there just wasn't anyone in town interested in dating me."

"Were there people you were interested in dating?"

"Sure."

"And you didn't ask?"

"Again, you're oversimplifying things."

He tugged her leg back into his lap. "I think you like making things more complicated." He thought, quite seriously, that she was encased inside her reputation. Rusted over with who the world thought she should be.

"Who was he?"

"Who was who?" she asked, distracted by his fingers between her toes.

"The man you wanted to date?"

"A guy named Joe. A teacher."

"And he hasn't asked you out? Why?"

"I think because I'm the kind of woman men don't think about dating. They think of me as a sister and a friend. Not someone they want to have sex with."

"*I* want to have sex with you."

"And that works out very well for me."

He ran a hand up the leg of her pants, squeezing the firm muscle of her calf.

"I thought . . ." she said, all loose and unwound by his touch and the sex and the bourbon. He loved this gooey center of her, a woman with her edges softened, her defenses down. This version of her was just for him. Just for the guy who got through her guarded gates. "After the whole thing with Dean that maybe . . . maybe he . . . maybe everyone in town would think differently and someone would ask me out."

"You're kidding."

"No." She laughed, rightfully embarrassed. "I know, I should just have the guts to do it myself, but every time . . . I don't know. The rejection doesn't seem worth the risk."

"So did men come knocking?"

"No one believed Dean. At least that's what they say to my face. I'm not sure what they whisper behind my back. But the town line is no one believes I would ever do that."

"Are you upset that your reputation is intact? Or upset that it's not in ruins?"

"Both. A little."

Nothing was ever easy with this woman. At least she was consistent in that way.

"Can I ask you another question?"

"You're really chatty tonight."

"Well, considering how much you know about me, I think it's only fair I know a few things about you if we're going to continue."

"Continue what?"

He smiled. Honestly, he couldn't help it; she was so damn easy. "Fucking each other like animals."

That got the hoot laugh. "Sure," she said. "Ask away."

"Your mom."

The words weren't even out of his mouth before she was pulling not just her legs away, but her whole body. Her entire being was suddenly somewhere else.

"What about her?" she said, so stiff and absent he was utterly disarmed. How did she do that? How was she here and then gone from one minute to the next?

"Is she okay?"

Her lip curled with something angry, and if she were any other woman he would brace himself for some kind of viciousness.

I'm angry, that's what she'd said earlier, and he saw very clearly that she was.

And then that, too, vanished, her face once again schooled into calm and quiet lines. He wondered where she put that anger. Was there some pit she tossed it all into, all those things she tried not to feel?

He imagined at some point that pit would swallow her whole.

"Alzheimer's," she finally said.

"Do you have help?"

"I do."

"Do you have enough?"

"We're fine. Mom and I . . . have always been fine. Just us."

"Are you—"

"I don't want to talk about my mother." She shifted on the sagging blue couch as if to stand but he pulled her back into his arms. Bourbon sloshed over her legs and she resisted him, pulling away.

"Calm down," he said. "Just sit here for a second."

"I don't want to."

He shifted her back against him so she was leaning against his chest, her ass nestled up against his growing erection. As what she was sitting on finally registered, she stopped pulling away and he dropped his arms.

"I don't want to fight," he whispered.

"Me neither. But there are some things—"

I don't want to talk about. Things that hurt. Things I deal with on my own.

She didn't have to say the words, they were right there, strung like lights between them.

"I get it. I have some things, too."

He felt her laugh. "Now I want to know what they are."

For some stupid reason his heart soared at her words. At her interest. Even if it was just callous curiosity, she was sitting on his dick, warm and heavy and beautiful, and they were just getting started. With everything.

She leaned back against him and he lifted her hair out of the way so he could kiss her neck. Her cheek, the pink shell curve of her ear. Slowly, she circled her hips against him, and he brought his hands up over her breasts. She was round and soft in his palms and he wanted very suddenly to see her.

"Take off your shirt," he whispered. She leaned forward, and he hissed as the pressure on his cock got serious. Within seconds she'd whipped off her sweater and tee shirt. She shifted as if to lean back against him, but he undid the closure to her bra right between her shoulder blades. The straps fell away, revealing red marks where the elastic had bit into her skin.

Must suck, this part of being a woman, he thought, touching each mark with his thumb. She was beautiful from behind. The muscles in her back shifted under pristine pale skin, and he ran his hand down her spine, his fingers spread wide to touch as much of her as he could.

But then she leaned back him and he looked down her chest at her breasts.

"Ah, honey," he sighed. "Look at you."

Immediately she put her hands over her breasts. "They're—"

"Beautiful." As if to prove it to her, he lifted them reverently into his hands. They were big and soft and full and his hands were not nearly big enough, but he gave it his best shot. The pink nipples were buried in his palms, the blue veins stood out against her skin, and suddenly, he needed more.

He shifted her back onto the couch and spread himself out over her, lifting those breasts so he could kiss. Lick. Suck.

"Oh my God," she breathed, and he sucked harder,

feeling her grow wild under him, her legs shifting, her hips arching hard against him. She spread herself out a little so he fell right into the deep vee between her legs and they both gasped. Her nipple popped from his mouth and he looked down at her while at the same time thrusting hard and high against her.

Her eyes went wide, her mouth fell open.

Bingo.

"You like that," he whispered.

She nodded, and to his delight her hands went under his shirt, ripping it off his body. He shrugged himself out of the sleeves and the shirt fell to the floor. His skin felt feverish from the inside. His whole body felt too hot. Her skin under his hands was cool.

He sucked on her flesh while he set a steady rhythm between her legs.

"Get a condom," she whispered.

"I only brought one."

"What?"

He laughed against her breast, licking her nipple. "I did just come over to talk. Don't worry." He bit her, holding the hard pink flesh of her nipple between his teeth with just enough force. "I'm going to make you come."

"Like—" Her breath broke as he thrust against her again. He couldn't feel her clit though the clothes, but the way she reacted, the jerk and jolt of her limbs, indicated he was in the right spot.

"Like this."

He curled one hand over the arm of the sofa, burying his hips against her, giving her hard, fast friction until she began to tense against him. Her hands in fists in his hair.

"Come on," he breathed, licking the arched line of her neck, and as if she'd just been waiting for the go-ahead, she bucked hard against him, a long, low moan coming from her throat. He held himself against her until her hands dropped from his hair to his waist, pushing him away.

He sat back, aware she was probably sensitive. He sure as hell was. The front of his jeans were damp, from her, maybe from him.

"Did you . . . ?" she asked, tucking her hair behind her ears.

Really, the most he could do was shake his head. He was so close, so nearly a mess.

She slipped to the floor between his knees and within breaths she had his pants undone and his cock out in her fist. Her lips slipped over him and his head fell back against the couch in ecstatic relief.

Shelby Monroe was not like any woman he'd ever known. And he didn't know what that meant for him.

But he wanted to find out.

Chapter 15

Casey woke up with a start, his face throbbing in the blackness. His heart hammering in his throat.

What was that sound?

Moonlight fell in a big checkerboard across his bed and he sat up, blinking.

CRASH!

The sound came from outside. The dog, he guessed. The dog that had been sniffing around the garbage.

After Dad left to talk to Shelby, Casey had put his leftover ribs outside on the trash can hoping to lure the skinny gray dog back because it had been a few days since he'd seen it.

He scrambled up to his knees and looked out his window, which had a view over the garbage and the fields in back. The dog, skinnier than ever, was there, standing next to the spill of trash from the overturned garbage can.

Before running downstairs, he glanced at the digital clock by his bed. 2:10.

Ty's door was open and he was snoring on his bed. Ty slept like he was dead. At first Casey had been scared; the only people he ever saw sleep like that were the drunk guys that sometimes hung out with his mom. But Ty always woke up when Casey shook him and he never smelled like booze, and Ty never hit Casey.

All good things in Casey's book.

He crept down the steps, avoiding the creaks and the rug, which bunched up on the second stair. From the

fridge he grabbed some cheese and leftover potato salad.
He had no idea if dogs liked potato salad, but he figured
it couldn't hurt.

As quietly as he could manage, he slipped out the
back door, making sure the storm door didn't bang shut
and scare away the dog. But as soon as he stepped past
the grill and onto the grass, the dog must have smelled
him or something, because it looked up, one of the ribs
sticking out of its mouth.

Casey stopped, one foot on the cement pad, one foot
in the wet grass. Behind the dog was the field of tall
weeds that he wondered if Ty was ever going to tell him
to mow. That seemed like the kind of thing dads were
supposed to do. Make their kids mow the lawn.

But so far, all Ty really made him do was go to his
room.

The dog watched him for a long moment and Casey
stood very still, he barely breathed, and finally the dog
went back to eating, but its ears were up and it kept one
eye on Casey.

Very slowly, Casey just sat down on the lip of the cement. The dog lurched as if to run, but when Casey
didn't move anymore, it seemed to relax again.

It was hard to say what kind of dog it used to be, because now it was just a sack of bones. But it was big and
its fur was short and one of its ears was torn and it was
covered in bloody, crusty cuts, as though it had gotten
through some barbed wire.

The dog was back at the leftover ribs like it was in a
race to gulp them down.

"What's your name?" Casey whispered. The dog
must not have heard him because it didn't even lift an
ear. Casey tried to remember some dog names. "Snoopy?
Rover? Jones?"

The dog picked up another bone between its teeth
and began tearing the meat off.

Not Snoopy. Definitely not Snoopy.

He refused to call the dog anything but its name. He'd spent the last six months being called *Buddy* by various cops and social workers, counselors and intake personnel. All people who didn't know his real name, so they used the generic catchall, "Buddy."

As if they were friends. As if they knew what his life was all about.

He hated it.

He really hated it when Ty called him that.

"Scuzz?" He kind of hoped the dog's name was Scuzz. Scuzz was a good name for a tough, ugly dog. That would be awesome. "Is that it? Are you Scuzz?"

But no sign of recognition from the dog.

Casey took a piece of cheese and threw it into the grass between them. The dog looked up, its super snout twitching, but it ignored the cheese.

"You don't like cheese?" Casey whispered and opened the container of potato salad. He could hold out the open container and hope the dog came to him, but in the book he read about a guy who got a hurt wolf to let him help it, the guy made a trail of food, luring the animal closer until he could pet it.

He needed a trail. A lure.

He wondered how to do this, and then he just scooped up some potato salad with his finger and flung it toward the dog.

It splattered against the garbage cans, hitting the dog on the ear. The dog jumped and ran away.

Great, Casey thought, watching the dog disappear into the tall grass behind the house. *Just great.*

In the moonlight, everything looked super creepy and still. Like those scenes in horror movies just before the evil ax dude came out of the bushes to kill everyone.

Out of the corner of his eye he saw some movement and he turned, hoping it was the dog coming back, but it wasn't. It was farther out in the field . . . something moving out there in the grass. Something white. Something tall.

Holy shit, it's a ghost!

He stood up, dropping the potato salad and the cheese.

Honest to God, it was floating. There was something white floating out there in the grass.

He peed. A little bit he peed in his sweatpants.

Slowly, he backed up toward the house, his mouth open to scream for help, but only a sucking whisper sound came out.

The ghost thing turned, walking closer.

"Ty!" the sound was a high-pitched whine in the back of his throat. "Ty!"

But then . . . the ghost started to look like a woman. Which was still super weird and scary. And then he realized it was Ms. Monroe's mom. Walking through the grass in her nightgown in the middle of the night.

He didn't even think about it, he just took off past the overturned garbage cans into the tall grass.

"Mrs. Monroe?" he called out when he got closer, and the woman stopped. Her hair was down around her shoulders and it was silver in the moonlight.

She looked super old. Like . . . really old.

"Mrs. Monroe?" he asked again and she turned. She looked worried, and his stomach cramped with its own worry.

But this was a little old lady freaking out in her nightgown in the middle of the night; he couldn't pull up the bridges.

"Are you okay?" he asked.

"I lost my keys."

"Out here?"

"No." She looked across the field to the houses on the other street.

"In one of those houses?"

"I think so, yes." She looked at him, her eyes sharp for a moment. "What are you doing up?"

"There was a dog." She nodded as if that made sense, and maybe it did to her. There were a lot of strays out here. "The gray one, have you seen it?"

"He got caught in barbed wire."

"I thought so, too. Do you know its name?"

"They don't have names. None of them do out here. You shouldn't feed him. He's probably dangerous."

Casey didn't think so, but he kept his mouth shut. "Do you . . . you need some help?"

"Finding my keys?"

He nodded.

She shook her head and he looked down to see she was wearing rain boots, the big, serious kind. That was good, he thought. As if that one normal thing sort of made all the rest of the crazy parts of this seem okay. *She has shoes, so it's totally cool that she's walking around in the middle of the night looking for her keys in a field.*

Maybe he'd just go in and wake up Ty and tell him about this. That seemed the right thing to do. Sometimes adults did weird things, and normally he had a pretty good idea of when it was just an adult being weird and when he should hide in his room, and this felt kind of dangerous.

"I think maybe . . ." She looked over at the houses behind her. In the tall grass he could see her path, the broken weeds, the dew all wiped away. He realized her nightgown was probably soaked. "I think I've made a mistake."

"No," he lied. "It's all cool."

She smiled at him, but her eyes were sad. "You're a good boy, Casey."

"You remember my name?"

"We just met on Sunday. At church."

"Yeah, but you're walking around in the middle of the night in your nightgown. Looking for keys."

She nodded, her hands running down the front of her old-lady nightgown. "I suppose that would seem strange."

"A little."

That made her smile, which made him smile, because he was a terrible island.

"Don't tell my daughter," she whispered. "Please."

Oh man. Shit. Keeping this a secret was a bad idea; he understood that. Was totally aware of that. But she was asking and she looked so embarrassed. And sad. And sometimes life was really awful and you had to do some strange shit just to cope. He had a drawer full of little things that he'd stolen from school and the Art Barn and Cora's and The Pour House. Little pieces of garbage that most people wouldn't miss. That was what he told himself, anyway, when he felt bad about that drawer, that he was collecting the inconsequential things, the forgotten things, the stuff people left behind.

The stuff like him.

So, Mrs. Monroe was walking around in her nightgown?

He could totally relate.

"All right," he said. "I won't tell. But you have to go home."

"I know."

"Do you know where you're going?"

She laughed, as if that were a totally ridiculous question. Just because she was wandering around other people's houses looking for keys didn't mean she was totally crazy. "I'm fine. You should go to bed," she said. "It's chilly out. You'll catch cold."

She seemed a little obsessive about colds, but maybe

that was just an old-person thing. He didn't know any old people. Maybe all of this was normal.

Yeah. Let's go with that.

It probably was totally normal, he realized, feeling a giant weight roll off his back. This whole forgetful thing she seemed to be doing—Ty did it sometimes; walked into a room and said, "Why did I come in here?"

Casey took a deep breath and let it out. This was not all that scary or weird. It was just different.

"You won't tell?" she said.

"Nah, Mrs. Monroe, we're good."

She nodded at him, as if a deal had been made, and then walked away, the bottom of her white nightgown all muddy and grass-stained. But she wasn't walking toward home, she was heading out to the highway.

"Wrong way, Mrs. Monroe."

"I know where my house is."

He pointed across the field at the farmhouse, dark in the dark night.

She changed direction and he watched, trailing after her until he saw her get into her house, and then he turned around and walked back home only to find the dog eating all the cheese and potato salad he'd dropped.

But when he caught sight of Casey the dog vanished. A gray ghost into the purple shadows, as if it had never really been there at all.

Taking Casey to work with him on Tuesday morning did not start well.

"Let me use the saw."

"No way, Casey. You've got to earn using power tools."

"You don't trust me?"

"Not really."

Casey muttered under his breath and slunk back to his job measuring lumber.

Was he supposed to say he did trust the kid and then watch when he cut off his hand because he wasn't paying attention?

Fatherhood was not easy.

"I didn't know you could do this stuff," Casey said, pulling the lip of the retractable tape measure over the edge of the board and then making a mark with his pencil on the wood. "You worked in that motorcycle shop when I found you."

"It's good to be able to do lots of things," Ty said and lowered the arm of the chop saw, the whirr of the blade through the wood a quick whine and then over.

"What do you think you're going to do when you get older?" he asked. Casey didn't answer right away and Ty looked over his shoulder to see him, sitting back, fiddling with the tape measure, pulling out a foot and letting it skitter back.

"You really want to know?"

"Of course," Ty said, surprised.

"You won't make fun of me?"

"Oh my God, Case—no."

"Mom sometimes made fun of me. She said it was stupid and—"

Ty held up his hand. "I am not Mom." Internally he braced for something someone like Vanessa would find laughable. She had a pretty narrow view of the world— men were men, women were women, and anything outside of that was an object of derision. A dancer, maybe. The circus?

"An animal trainer for movies."

"A . . . what?"

"You know in movies, when there's a dog and it does tricks and stuff."

"Yeah. I know."

"I want to do that."

Oh Christ, would this kid ever stop wrecking him? "We should get you a dog."

Casey blinked wide eyes at him. "Really?"

"Yeah. You should have a dog. You can start by training him."

For a second Ty didn't understand what was happening on Casey's face. There was grief and excitement and confusion and worry.

"Case—"

"That would be awesome. Mom always said we moved around too much to get a dog."

"Well, we're sticking around, at least for a while."

Casey's face fell into panic. "We're moving?"

"No!" How the hell did he construe that? "I'm just saying, even if we move it's okay to have a dog."

"I don't want to move."

"We're not. Seriously, Casey. Forget I said anything." Ty sighed. "We'll head down to the shelter in Masonville, see what they got."

"That would be awesome." Casey pushed his hair out of his eyes and smiled at Ty's chin, not quite looking at him. But also not looking at a spot three feet away from him either, so progress.

A car door slammed behind them and they both turned to see Brody climbing out of his truck.

"Who is that guy?" Casey breathed.

"My boss."

"He's a scary dude."

"Not really. Well, not once you get to know him."

In a glance Brody took in Ty and Casey, but whatever reaction he had to seeing Casey on the work site on a Tuesday morning was hidden behind his glasses.

"Are you going to be in trouble?" Casey asked.

"No." Though it seemed unlikely Brody would be entirely cool with an eleven-year-old here slowing things down on the arbor to nearly a crawl.

He reached into his pocket and pulled out a ten-dollar bill. "Go get Brody and me some coffee."

"Can I get a fritter?"

"No."

"Ty," he whined.

"Get."

Casey left and Ty turned to Brody, who was putting on his tool belt.

"I take it that's your son?" Brody asked.

"Yeah."

"He looks like you."

That took Ty aback. "You think? I keep seeing his mom. The red hair, I guess."

"Nah, he's you. You can tell. There's no school today?"

Ty rubbed his hand over the back of his head. Ty had enough in savings that if Brody fired him he'd be all right for a while. But then he got that old fire up his spine, that if Casey was suspended and Ty got fired, maybe this was the signal to ditch Bishop and find a fresh start somewhere else. Casey wanted to stay, but they could find a house and a school he liked somewhere else. Maybe Florida. Living by a beach would probably make Casey happy.

"Casey got suspended." Brody just watched him and Ty found himself babbling in the silence. "It was a fight. The wrong thing for the right reason."

"I know those kinds of fights," Brody said. "My brother used to run his mouth off and I was the one to back it up."

That came as zero surprise to Ty.

"He's out for the rest of the week."

Ty waited for a reaction, but Brody was still silent. Maybe he didn't understand the ramifications of that.

"He's got nowhere else to go, so he's going to have to hang out with me. He's working pretty hard. It's going to slow me down some, but it shouldn't be too bad. But if this is a problem, and trust me I get it, maybe we should just shake hands and call it—"

"It's fine, Ty. Stuff happens, no worries."

"Still, I know it's inconvenient."

Brody took off his sunglasses and polished the lenses with his shirt.

"Ashley is real big on community. You know what that means?"

"No."

"Yeah, me neither. But I think it means, it's okay, Ty. You. Your kid being here. It's all okay. I've never been a boss before."

It was a relief. The fire in his spine was hard to sustain, especially now with Casey. "Really?"

Brody smiled—well, as much as he ever did, which meant he gave the impression of smiling without actually moving his face. "That's a surprise?"

"Yeah, you just seem kind of like a guy people follow."

"I suppose I have the Marines to thank for that." Ty had the impression that it was more than military training, but he kept his mouth shut. "Anyway, you do good work, Ty. I'm glad you work for me and having your son here is just fine. Stop worrying."

"Thanks, man," Ty said, relieved and slightly embarrassed. Behind him there was the sound of a car pulling up, and grateful to end the conversation he turned expecting Sean or maybe Ashley, but it was a Bishop Police cruiser and two cops stepped out of it, adjusting their duty belts and sunglasses.

"Wyatt Svenson?" one of them asked.

Ty jerked in surprise. "I'm him."

"I'm Officer Jenkins," the bigger of the two said and

he nodded toward his partner, a compact black man. "This is Officer Debreau."

"What can I do for you?" he asked, taking off his gloves and tucking them in his back pocket. The two men fanned out in a move Ty had seen a million times. Jenkins faced him, one foot up on the sidewalk, while Debreau took a look around, taking in the arbor and the tools. Brody came to stand behind him.

"There were some break-ins in a few houses out by you guys," Jenkins said. "And we're checking with some neighbors to see if they might have seen or heard anything last night."

Ty shook his head, caught for a moment in the memory of Shelby. Of her heat and her softness and her wildness. "What time?"

"After midnight, before four a.m., best we can tell."

"I was asleep at midnight. Didn't hear a thing. Was there anything stolen?"

"No. Just messed with."

"Messed with?" he asked. "Who breaks into houses and just messes with stuff?"

"Kids," Officer Debreau piped up. "You know where your son was during those hours?"

From his head to his feet and all the way through, he just bristled with a sudden and all-consuming anger.

"Why are you asking?" he said through his teeth.

"Just covering the bases," Jenkins said, but Debreau lifted his sunglasses away from his face, revealing hard eyes.

"Your son's been in trouble at school. Fighting."

"Three kids were suspended for that. You talking to the other parents?"

"They live on the other side of town."

"Right, and Bishop is so big there's no way they could get over to my neighborhood between the hours of midnight and four a.m."

"Do you have a problem, sir?" Debreau asked, his hands on his belt. "Because you could answer these questions down at the station."

"Max," Brody said, his voice a quiet menace.

"Stay out of this, Brody," Jenkins stepped in.

Twelve years ago, after Pop died and Ty just fell apart, he would have been the guy who had to be taken down to the station. The guy who wouldn't quit pushing until someone pushed him back hard enough so he could feel it. Feel something.

But he had Casey to think about.

"He was asleep. In his bed. The whole night."

"Are you sure?"

"Of course I'm sure!"

Debreau backed away, his raised hands a gesture that told Ty that he shouldn't get all worked up over nothing, a gesture that made him see red.

"If you hear of anything, or see anything, please let us know. We don't want messing around to escalate into something more dangerous," Jenkins said, and the two cops got back in their car and drove away.

Ty watched them go, and finally, when their taillights were no longer visible, he turned to Brody. "That your idea of community?" he asked.

"I'm so sorry, man," Brody whispered.

"Yeah, me, too."

Tuesday night, without looking at the screen Shelby picked up her ringing cell phone, her attention focused instead on the agenda for the Chamber of Commerce meeting next week.

"Hello?" she said, making a note to bring up the slowdown in City Hall to get permits. She had the high school art show in two months and so far no word on permits.

"Shelby?" Ty's voice made her stop. It made all the hair on her body stand on end. She felt blood vessels dilating inside her.

Him, her body whispered. *I want him.*

"Ty. How are you?" There was no way to keep the warmth out of her voice. The pleasure she felt just hearing his name, and she wondered what was wrong with her that that was her instinct—to deny herself and him.

"Good."

She glanced up at the wall clock in the living room. Eight p.m. She was working in the house tonight because Mom had seemed very agitated, and even being in the barn felt too far away. "How are you?" he asked, his voice pitched low and quiet, and she tried to imagine him in his home and realized she'd never seen it. That seemed very not right.

For two people who had shown each other so much, they were total strangers in the practical sense.

"Fine. Just doing some Chamber of Commerce paperwork," she said. "What's up?"

"Well, I'm not sure if the cops came and talked to you—"

"Cops? About what?"

"Apparently there've been some break-ins around us, and I just wanted to check in and make sure you're okay."

"Was anything stolen? Were people hurt?"

"No. The cops think it's kids, because things were just messed with."

"Were you broken into?"

"No. You?"

"No!" At least not that she could tell; if things had just been messed with it would be nearly impossible to surmise a difference in her home from the mess they lived in on a regular basis.

"Well, lock your doors tonight," Ty said.

She laughed. "I'm not sure any of these doors have ever been locked."

"Country girl," Ty murmured, "you need to take care of yourself."

The silence between them seemed to pound with unsaid things and she stood up from her chair and walked through the house, locking doors, checking windows.

"Make sure you lock *your* doors, city boy," she said, climbing the stairs. Mom was in her room, sorting through a box of keys. She could steal away a few moments.

"Have you always lived in Bishop?" Ty asked, and she paused on the steps, surprised by the question.

"I went to school in Savannah, Georgia," she said. "I spent five years there before moving back to Bishop."

"You don't think of leaving?"

"Oh," she laughed. "I think of leaving all the time. I can't remember the last time I had a vacation. But I don't dream of staying away. This is home."

"Home." He said the word like it was a surprise.

"You are unfamiliar with the idea?" she asked, and his rough chuckle warmed her from the inside.

"My parents moved around a lot. There *was* no home with them. But Nana and Pop had a big house on a bunch of land outside Ellicott City. That was home for a long time."

"But you left it?"

"I blew it, actually. Started getting in trouble after Pop died. Nana kicked me out of the house, I was with Casey's mom and running with her friends, and I just woke up one morning and knew I had to get out of there."

"That's when you went to St. Louis?"

"Man, I love that you remember everything."

The tenderness in his voice was like the touch of his hand on her spine; it was like a thread slowly stitching them together in the dark of their separate houses. Pulling around her, reaching across the distance to wrap around him.

The quiet huff of his breath through the phone made her warm, made her blood beat hard.

She knew so little of intimacy. So little—but this was it, she was sure of it.

It was shocking to realize that she did remember everything he'd ever told her, that all the things he'd said and done in the handful of times they'd been together had been cataloged somewhere deep in her brain.

"I remembered," she said, feeling as if she were admitting something important.

"I was in St. Louis for two years, and I got bored and moved on."

"To where?" she asked, imagining him loading up his bike, those cuffs around his wrists, riding off into a sunset somewhere.

"Everywhere," he said. "Texas, Utah, Missouri, Illinois for a while. Until Nana had her first heart attack and I headed back to West Memphis and Pop's shop and tried staying put for a while."

"You don't like it?" she asked. "Staying put?"

"It's not easy, but I'm trying."

"All that moving around sounds lonely."

"I had friends," he said, almost defensively.

"Friends are good." She sounded far more coy than she'd intended.

Again she heard that dark laugh of his that reminded her of how he seemed to know what her body wanted better than she did. "Speaking of good, do you want to—"

"Yes," she said, without hesitation, knowing exactly what he was going to ask. "But I can't. Mom is restless and I don't want to leave her alone in the house."

"I understand."

"I just . . . I don't have a nurse here all the time," she

said. "It's just been the two of us for so long, I'm not sure if it's such a good idea to introduce someone new. If that might cause more problems." She laughed. "I have no idea why I'm telling you this."

But she knew. She did. Intimacy. That thread in the darkness.

"Sometimes it's just nice to talk."

"Yes," she whispered, though it wasn't usually for her. But their relationship or friendship, or whatever it was, was miles outside of her "usual." "It is."

She stepped into her bedroom and shut the door, pressing her forehead against the wood. She was at loose ends again, doubting herself, feeling alone with her mistakes and decisions, and everything inside of her believed he had the power to settle the worst of her fears, her frayed edges.

"Where are you?" she whispered.

"My bedroom. You?"

"My bedroom."

There was a pause and then the purr of his laughter. "Is this where I ask you what you're wearing?"

She'd never done this before, but again she reached deep into the dark place where she buried all of those things she wanted—all those secret, shameful desires that never, ever seemed to scare him away—and pulled them out for him. For her.

"This is when I tell you how much I like your cock."

"Oh Jesus," he sighed and she heard rustling, the muted scrape of a zipper, and she bit her lip as pleasure poured through her. "How . . . how do you like it?"

She lay down on the bed in the dark of her bedroom and despite the distance between them, the stretch of road and the dark lawns, the cold plastic of her phone in her hand, she felt as if he were right there, his hands on her body.

Chapter 16

"Who is coming over?" Casey asked, pushing the second grocery cart up to the back of the truck.

"Just some friends." Ty piled the cases of beer and bags of chips and the shrimp into the back of the truck. He stacked things strategically, hoping he could keep stuff from sliding around. The loaves of bread and bottles of wine would have to go inside the cab.

"Ms. Monroe?"

Ty paused, his hands on the bottles of white wine. He'd thought about asking Shelby, but truthfully, he wasn't sure how that would go over. The people coming in tonight were from different parts of his old life. Friends he'd worked construction with in St. Louis. A few rich investment bankers who'd been buying his bikes since the first online auction. One of Pop's old mechanics, and some of the guys from the Outlaws who had left the club after he did. Some of them had splintered off and done other things like him, some had joined other clubs, but all of them were about as far away from Shelby Monroe as the moon.

"No. Shelby won't be there. Why?"

"This is just a lot of stuff. A lot." Casey was looking at the cases of beer.

"It's a party."

"I thought you were auctioning off the Indian Chief."

"I am, but first I just thought I'd have a party for some of the people who come by to bid. Does that bother you?"

"No." Casey shook his head, but it was obvious he was lying. He was pale under his freckles. "It's fine."

"Casey, it's just a party. Nothing will get out of hand—"

"I said it's fine, Ty. Whatever."

Casey stomped around to the passenger side of the truck and Ty guessed that was the end of the conversation.

There was a lot of work to do before the guys started showing up around seven. Cliff the auctioneer was coming at nine. Ty had polished up the bike last night after another phone call with Shelby. Christ, that woman. She was no end of surprising. Twice he'd called her over the week, just to check up on her, see how she was doing, and twice he'd ended up with his hands down his pants listening to her gasp and groan her way through an orgasm.

The impulse to call her, to hear her voice, was getting larger every day and Ty wasn't very good at ignoring his impulses.

"Hey," he said, digging his phone out of his back pocket and handing it over to Casey. "Call Ms. Monroe and ask her to come on over tonight."

"Yeah?" Casey lit up like a Fourth of July firework.

"Yeah."

Fuck it, he thought. He wanted to see her and whatever was happening between them, she might as well experience this part of his life. Maybe she'd like it. Maybe she'd sit down with some of these men and women, look past the surface tattoos and hair and leathers and attitude, and see what he saw—good guys who'd found a place in the world that accepted them for who they were. Trouble and all.

"It's her answering machine," Casey whispered.

"Leave her a message. Tell her to come by at eight and she should be hungry."

"Hey, uh . . . Ms. Monroe. This is Casey. From school. And . . . you know . . . across the street." Ty smiled at his son. "Anyway, it looks like we're having a party and Ty says you should come. At eight and you should be hungry. You can bring your mom. See you." Casey ended the call.

"Her mom?"

"Yeah." Casey shrugged and settled against the door with Ty's phone. The familiar Plants vs. Zombies song filled the cab. "Why not?"

He could think of a couple of big reasons why not, but he said nothing.

"Your room clean?" Ty asked, turning the corner onto the old highway heading out to their house.

"Why?"

"People might spend the night."

"In my room?" Casey cried.

"Yeah, you can bunk in with me."

"I'm not sleeping with you just because your friends get so drunk they can't drive home."

They pulled into the driveway and Ty turned off the truck. Casey made a move to jump out of the car, but Ty stopped him. "Tell me, Casey, what's bothering you about this?"

"Nothing." Casey hurled himself out of the truck and headed into the house, leaving Ty to unpack the truck.

Ty was going to chalk up Casey's attitude to . . . attitude. To the fact that they'd been together 24/7 for a few days and both of them needed to just blow off some steam. He hoped Jimmy and his wife brought their kids so Casey would have someone he could hang with.

He ran through the house making sure things were clean. He got out Nana's big pot and set it on the stove full of water. Potatoes were chopped. Onions and corn. The shrimp was already peeled, so he kept that in the fridge. He put big buckets of ice outside and dumped the beers inside to get cold. He wedged a few bottles of white wine in there as well.

Ah . . . what the hell, he thought, and took his phone out of his pocket and called Shelby himself.

"Hey," he said to her machine. "Not sure if you got Casey's message, but we're having a party over here tonight. It's casual. Lots of food and drink. It's . . ." He stopped and then just decided to hell with it, he wasn't interested in playing games by seeming less involved than he was, because he was totally involved with Shelby. "I'd love to see you."

Shaking his head at himself, he hung up and got back to work.

Outside he cleaned up the garbage that one of the wild dogs or a pack of raccoons kept getting into; honest to God, he was going to have to put bungee locks on these cans. From the front of the house he heard the roar of twin cam engines and he felt a leap of excitement.

He circled the house just as Jimmy and Rita pulled in on a Harley Dyna Super Glide.

"Hey man," Ty said, stepping forward to shake Jimmy's hand. Jimmy had been one of Pop's mechanics for a few years before he got married and moved to Indianapolis. Now he was a pastor. The head of the Bikers for Jesus, Indianapolis chapter.

He was also the most badass motherfucker Ty had ever known. And he looked it. Heavy leather, some of it studded. Heavy ink, some of it left over from his Hells Angels and prison days; heavy facial hair, including a long Fu Manchu. But if you could look past all that and get to the man's eyes, you saw everything that mattered.

"My brother!" Jimmy yelled, pulling Ty into his arms, slapping his back. "So good to see you, Ty. It's been too long."

"Obviously," Ty laughed, reaching forward to help Rita off the back of the bike. "When did *this* happen?"

Rita, normally thin as a rail, looked like she'd swallowed a beach ball. "About six months ago," she answered, kissing Ty's cheek. "And you're not supposed to notice."

"I'm not sure that's possible," he laughed. "Congrats. I had no idea you guys were going for more kids."

"Neither did we," Rita said with a wry smile. Her dark hair was pulled back in a ponytail, and while always beautiful, she looked tired.

"God works in mysterious ways," Jimmy said.

"Not when you forget to wear a condom." Rita scowled at her husband but he only smiled and kissed her cheek, his hand curving over her belly.

"Let's get you something cold to drink," Ty said.

"And food! This baby is hungry."

"Well, we've got food and cold drinks—come on back."

"Where's your son?" Rita asked, her arm tucked in Ty's elbow. "I haven't seen him since he was little."

He stopped in his tracks. "When did you meet Casey?"

"Shit," Rita breathed, and she and her husband shared a telling look.

"You let the cat out of the bag," Jimmy said. "You better finish it."

"Yeah, you better," Ty agreed, stunned by the knowledge that Jimmy and Rita had met Casey before and not bothered to tell him when he'd called Jimmy with the news about the boy.

"My brother got involved with the Outlaws," Rita said with a big sigh, her hand flattening over her belly. "Jimmy and me were in Memphis trying to convince him to come stay with us in Indianapolis, to get himself cleaned up. Out of trouble. We were at a party and Vanessa had Casey there. He was probably five. Six. We didn't know he was yours. Had no idea. Until you called to tell us everything that happened with Vanessa and the custody stuff, and we figured it out."

"We didn't tell you about seeing him at the party," Jimmy said. "We figured you already had to be feeling terrible and had enough reasons to be pissed off at Vanessa and didn't need to know she was hauling her kid around to some pretty fucked-up scenes."

Great. No wonder Casey was having problems with the idea of this kind of party. Guilt that he hadn't been there, that he hadn't been able to protect his son from that situation, bit deep into his chest and he had to tip back his head in order to get a breath.

"You got nothing to feel guilty about," Jimmy said, reading Ty so well, because that was what the man was genius at. "Nothing."

"But—"

"You didn't know." Jimmy put a hand on Ty's shoulder. "And if you had, it would have been a different story."

"That's what I feel guilty about. If I had just known. If I had reached out to Vanessa at some point during those years. If I'd stayed put in Memphis and given her a chance to find me. I could have stopped Casey from seeing . . ." He stopped, having been down this road a thousand times. He hadn't known about his son and that was the end of it. Beating himself up over how things would have been different didn't do anyone any good.

"I'm sorry, Ty. I really am," Rita said. "We weren't going to say anything but I had to open my big mouth."

"No. It's fine. I'm glad you told me."

"How are things working out between you and Casey?" Rita asked.

"Other than Casey being suspended from school for fighting—great."

"Fighting?" she asked.

"Wrong thing for the right reason," he said. "Trust me. But it's actually going pretty good. He's got a teacher he really likes and is doing some art classes with her on the side."

"Our Oscar likes art," Rita said. "He gets bullied at school a little, and the teacher says art helps him."

"Breaks my heart what that kid can draw," Jimmy said.

"I feel like everything Casey does breaks my heart."

"Welcome to parenthood."

Rita plopped down on the couch and put her feet up while Jimmy and Ty went out to the garage and looked at the bike. "Oh, man, she's beautiful," Jimmy said, running his fingers through the fringe on the seat. "I don't think I have the bones to buy her, though."

"I think Gordon is coming up from New Orleans," Ty said.

Jimmy blew out a breath. "Then I definitely won't."

Gordon McNeill was a classic collector with a deep pocket. When he was involved in the auction there was a good chance that no one would outbid him. Bad news for Jimmy. Good news for Ty.

"How are you guys settling in out here in the sticks?"

Ty blew out a breath. "I feel like maybe it was too much all at once, you know. Not for Casey, he's digging it. But maybe . . . for me. Being a dad, figuring out school and teachers, and then being away from friends and trying to figure out how to just stay put, you know. It's like every time we hit a bump I get this itch to just pick Casey up and start over."

"That boy needs some stability."

"I know. That's what I keep telling myself. Hey." Ty smacked Jimmy's shoulder, changing the subject. "It's good to see you. I've forgotten how nice it is to have friends around."

"Well, you'll have some friends here tonight. I've called some of the old boys and told them to meet us here."

Ty opened his eyes wide, thinking about beer and food and just how many old boys Jimmy was talking about. "Calm down, Ty," Jimmy laughed, slapping him on the shoulder. "Five guys and their ladies, tops."

The door from the house into the garage opened and Casey stood there in one of his oversized tee shirts and baggy jeans, looking so old and so little all at the same time.

"Well, there's the little man," Jimmy said, pushing his shades up onto his face.

"Hey, Casey, this is my friend Jimmy."

Casey nodded at Jimmy, watching the old biker out of the corner of his eyes.

"We met once a long time ago," Jimmy said. "You might not remember."

"At a party, right?" Casey asked.

Jimmy and Ty shared a quick surprised look. "Yeah."

"You played cards with me," Casey said, staring at his feet and at Jimmy in turns.

"That's right. Go Fish."

"You cheated."

"I can't believe you remember that!" Jimmy laughed, but when Casey raised his eyes to Ty's he felt a jolt through his chest, like getting kicked off a bike going forty miles an hour. Casey remembered that party. He probably remembered every party Vanessa took him to that he shouldn't have been at. He remembered because he'd been scared. Because even if everyone at that party had been as decent as Jimmy, it didn't matter—Vanessa never helped him feel safe.

"There's a woman asleep on the couch," Casey said.

"That's Rita. She does that," Jimmy said. "She's pretty tired these days."

Casey nodded and then stepped backward as if to head back inside, and in a heartbeat Ty knew what to do. He could tell Casey that no one here would hurt him, that no one would be out of control and that he was safe with Ty, or he could show Casey that he understood. And that even though he was a kid, this was his house, too, and Ty could respect that.

Pop used to say, *I could tell you or I could show you.*

"We're not doing the auction here," he said.

"What?" Jimmy asked.

"Yeah. There's a great bar and barbecue place in town; they've got a big lot. We'll do it there."

"Really?" Casey asked, looking as if a weight had been rolled off his back.

"Yep. You can stay here if you like or come with us— your choice."

"I'll stay."

"I imagine Rita might want to stay, too. That all right with you?" Jimmy asked. "She'll sleep and then wake up and eat every chip you've got in the house."

Casey smiled quickly. "We've got a lot."

"She'll dig that."

"I'll call my people, you call yours, and we'll meet at The Pour House on Main Street," Ty said to Jimmy.

Casey went back inside and Jimmy started laughing. "Man," he said. "You're a natural."

"I'm glad you think so, because I have no idea what I'm doing."

Shelby was a little drunk. Just a little. Just slightly more than she liked to be in public. Being drunk in the Art Barn with Ty was one thing, but here at The Pour House

surrounded by teachers she worked with it seemed . . .
unwise. In fact, the whole thing seemed a little unwise.

Deena had come over to be with Mom, but she still felt
as though leaving was a bad idea. It had been a rough
week. Which was why, frankly, she'd needed to get out
and blow off some steam.

Apparently she wasn't alone. All the other teachers
were hammered. Just plain blotto.

But what was really making her nervous was that what
she'd wanted from Joe Phillips seemed to be happening
now. Right now.

He was sitting so close to her at the tables that Maureen Jones, the kindergarten teacher, had pushed together that his knee kept brushing up against hers. And
instead of delicious, instead of wonderful, it felt awful.

Because she couldn't stop thinking about Ty.

And not in an *I'm betraying this man I have no actual
commitment to* kind of way. In the way that she couldn't
stop wishing that it was Ty's leg brushing against hers.
That it was Ty going to the bar to get her more white
wine spritzers.

"Another?" he asked, stretching his arm across the
back of her chair in a gesture so . . . date-like, so overtly
masculine, that she actually cringed away from it. Which
was hilarious and slightly troubling when she thought
about the overtly masculine things she liked from Ty.

There were times she had the real sense of herself as a
lie, a dual personality.

"No," she said. "I'm fine."

"You having a good time?" he asked, lifting his beer
glass to his mouth. Across the table Mrs. Jordal was
laughing at something Maureen was telling her, and both
of them set their glasses down so hard that the drinks
sloshed out of them.

"I am," she said. "Though it's a little weird to see
everyone so loose like this."

"They do it once a month."

"Why haven't I ever been asked?" She'd had no idea that she cared until the question was out of her mouth. He blinked in reaction, probably astonished that she'd asked. She had a habit of asking the things no one ever asked.

"I don't think anyone thought you would want to come."

"Why?"

He laughed. "You know your reputation, Ms. Monroe." He leaned in close, his voice pitched somewhere between teasing and seductive, and she was so shocked she could only stare at the bubbles fizzing in her wineglass. This was happening. She wasn't imagining it. He'd invited her here to hit on her. To flirt. For a woman who hadn't had a date in years, or a lover almost ever, there were now two men interested in her.

She didn't know how to handle this. What did other women do? Well, they probably didn't put down their glass and go running home to their mother, like she was planning. Nor did they run off to the bathroom just to break the sudden tension.

"What is my reputation?" She leaned away from him, but was turning toward him at the same time.

"Prim." His glasses had slid down on his nose and they were slightly cockeyed, a sweet disheveled man. "Proper."

"I'm not," she said, suddenly and oddly angry. "No one ever sees that, though."

"I'll see whatever you want me to."

But you didn't, she thought. *And I know part of that is my fault, because I'm cowardly and odd. And perhaps not unlike some kind of tin woman, frozen from the years of inattention. Rusted over by a childhood warped with fear and worship. But for years I've been waiting and you never saw me.*

Outside there was the far-off roar of motorcycles getting louder, one of those clubs, perhaps, that followed the Mississippi River. Sometimes, on beautiful mornings, there would be a dozen bikes outside Cora's as the riders grabbed coffee and eggs on their way through town.

The sound made her think of Ty.

Ty, who saw her, or wanted to see her because of what she showed him. And when she showed him more he wasn't scared of it. The more she showed him, the more he seemed to want.

She grabbed her purse, slung over the back of her chair. "I think I should go home."

"Really?" He looked astonished. After years he'd finally worked up the courage to come on to her and she was leaving.

Served him right. Or her right. She didn't know anymore; she just knew she wanted to leave.

"You shouldn't drive," Joe said, reaching into his pocket for his keys. She put a hand to his arm, because she could. Because thoughts of Ty somehow freed up some of her rusty joints and made her feel more human.

"Well, neither should you. I can walk."

Joe said something, but it was drowned out by the roar of the motorcycles getting very close indeed and then stopping all together. Shelby glanced behind the bar, where Sean shared a look with Jim, his weekend bartender.

The front door opened and as if she'd summoned him, as if all the things she'd grown so used to denying herself—all the big and small pleasures, the guilty ones and the innocent ones, the ones rated X and the far more pedestrian—had coalesced into living, breathing flesh, Wyatt Svenson walked into The Pour House.

The sight of him, in his shearling jacket and cowboy

boots, his blond hair loose for once and falling in thick, waves down to his shoulders, made her stand up.

And Wyatt, catching the movement from the corner of his eye, shot one look over at her and then did a quick double take. And for a moment, made crystal and slow and delicious by three white wine spritzers, suspiciously low on spritzer, he smiled at her. He stopped walking and grinned as if he was just so damn happy to see her.

And then Joe grabbed her hand, coming to his feet beside her. "Let me walk you home."

Ty glanced at Joe and then back at her face and because she was a terrible tin woman, because she'd never, ever in her life been in this situation, because she didn't entirely know what exactly this situation was, she could not hide her guilt.

Ty's sweet smile fled and he walked quickly back to the bar.

Chapter 17

What the hell! Ty thought, more gutted than he'd really thought possible. Because what were they, really, but people having sex with each other?

But he'd called her. His son had called her. And he really wanted to see her tonight, share this side of his life with her.

And she'd clearly been here, and judging by the way that thin guy with the glasses—the same guy who'd been in the teachers' lounge with her, tending to her scrapes—grabbed her hand, it seemed like they were here together.

"Hey, man," Sean said from behind the bar. "What can I get you?"

"Look, I've had a little change of plans. I was going to auction off a bike at my house tonight—"

"Auction what now?"

Ty shook his head, realizing Sean, realizing no one in town, knew what he really did. How he actually made his money. "There are going to be about . . . twenty bikers in here in about fifteen minutes. I'm hoping I can auction off a refurbished bike in your parking lot."

"Ah . . . what?"

Ty threw his credit card on the bar, very aware that he couldn't vouch for every man and woman coming in those doors. "Food, drink, damages—charge everything to this."

"Damages?" Sean asked, holding the Visa card in his fingers.

The door to the bar opened and a steady stream of people came in. Some friends, some strangers. Some bad-ass motherfuckers in beat-up cuts with badges. Gordon and his wife walked in wearing their top-of-the-line Italian leathers.

Men, women. All outsiders in this place.

"Ty," Sean said. "What the hell is this?"

Ty turned. Sean wasn't angry; he had dollar signs in his eyes, and Ty had his full attention. "I refurbish old motorcycles and about once a year I auction one off. I was going to do it at my house but I can't. So I am hoping I can auction off my bike in your parking lot."

Tom and John Kavanaugh from St. Louis came by, said hi, and ordered drinks.

"Are you still serving food?" John asked, always so polite. During the school year he taught English at a charter school. In the summer he tore down condemned buildings in the city for Tommy.

"Ah, yeah, here." Sean handed him a menu.

"We need like twenty of these." John lifted the plastic menu and scanned the beer tabs. "And a few pitchers of the Sweet Georgia Brown on tap."

"Right. We're on it," Sean said, giving Ty a sharp look.

The brothers left with beers and menus.

"How many people you expecting?" Sean asked.

"Twenty."

"All of them are going to eat and drink?"

"Yes. A lot."

"Christ, man, this is crazy." Sean nodded as Jim Gensler started to work like a man possessed, pulling beers and pouring shots. "But you could have told me. This is more business than I get in a week and I'd like to do it right."

Ty hadn't thought of that. Sean had just started serving food and the business had picked up from nearly nothing. "Fair enough. You want me to help?"

"No. I want you to make sure there are no damages. I'll call in Cora and Brody. Now what's going on with the auction?"

Ty explained how it worked and Sean shook his head.

"You can't do it past ten," Sean said. "My patio closes at ten because of a noise ordinance and it wouldn't be a big deal, but Mrs. Phillips on the corner has the cops on speed dial and any noise on my patio past ten gets the cops called."

"I didn't think you had the permits yet."

"I don't. Which is why I don't like it when the cops come."

"All right, I'll do my best."

Sean laughed. "This is either going to be awesome or a total disaster."

"You got that right," Ty agreed.

Sean grabbed his phone and ducked out of the way. Ty turned, only to be brought up short by Shelby standing next to him.

"Hi," she said, her level gaze unflinching.

She doesn't have anything to flinch over, he told himself. But he wasn't buying reason. Not at the moment. He wanted to kiss her. In front of that guy with the glasses and all the people in this bar, he wanted to bend her over his arm, over the bar, and mark her.

Own her.

"Shelby," he said.

"What's happening here?"

"I'm auctioning off my bike."

"Your bike?"

"The Chief." She was blank. No one knew. "I refurbish old bikes and auction them off."

"Refurbish?"

"Am I not speaking English?" He was being mean and he liked it.

Her eyes narrowed at his tone. "That's what you were doing the first night I came over to your house?"

"You were happy enough fucking a carpenter?" He pitched his voice low so no one heard, but still she went pale, glancing around to see if people were watching.

Yeah, can't have anyone know, he thought.

"That's not fair."

He shrugged, because he could give a shit about fair.

Jim handed him a Shiner Bock and Ty took a long drink. "What are you doing here, Shelby?"

She blushed red, giving herself away. "It's a work thing."

"And the guy?"

She glanced over there as if she were unsure, but he could tell she was stalling for time. Trying to figure out what to say. *You don't care,* he told himself. *You don't. You had sex two times.* Well, four times if you counted the phone sex. And since it had been so insanely hot, he decided to count it.

But he liked her and moreover, he trusted her. He'd trusted her more than anyone since Nana and Pop died.

"Just someone from work."

He laughed and took another drink. More than half the bottle was gone. This could be a very bad idea.

"You don't have to lie. You don't owe me anything," he told her, more rough than he needed to be. More hurtful than was his nature. "We don't owe each other shit."

"That's—" She blinked and blinked again. Apparently this was Shelby flustered. *Interesting.* "That's not true."

"Then who is the guy?"

"It's Joe."

He remembered immediately, because he remembered everything she'd ever told him. Every look she'd ever given him. "Joe. The guy you'd like to date?"

Ty leaned back against the bar and looked across the room at Joe. Nice-looking guy, unassuming. Smart. All in all the kind of guy he would have thought a woman like Shelby belonged with.

If he hadn't fucked Shelby. If he didn't want to do it again. If he didn't know how she tasted and felt and what she liked. If he didn't know who she was underneath that façade she wore, he'd think Joe there was exactly the right guy for her.

But he'd seen behind the façade, and that guy . . . she'd chew that guy up in a heartbeat.

But if that was who she wanted, he wasn't going to stand in the way.

"Yes, I did want that."

"Well, good luck with that." He toasted her with his half beer and headed over to the other side of the bar with his friends.

If it hurt, he ignored the pain. Because if there was one thing he knew how to do, it was leave.

Shelby didn't leave. Despite being all but dismissed by Ty, she couldn't leave. All the other teachers were gone, except for the new first-grade teacher and Joe, who had attached himself to her side, claiming he wouldn't be much of a friend if he left her here with strangers.

After trying to get Ty's attention for the last half hour she'd decided enough was enough. She wouldn't sit here waiting for him to glance at her, waiting for him to give her a chance to explain. He clearly wasn't in the listening mood.

And what the hell do I have to explain? she thought,

but knew that was just false indignation. She'd seen his face when he saw her, the happiness he'd been unable to hide, and she'd seen it vanish the second Joe grabbed her hand.

"Hey, Shelby?" It was Cora, her brown skin bright and shiny from her work in the kitchen. She smiled once, before her features settled back into seriously angry lines. "My stupid boyfriend—"

"I heard that," Sean said, walking by with a tray full of drinks.

Cora rolled her eyes. "Sean hired teenage girls to be waitresses and none of them are interested in showing up this late on a Friday. Is there any chance we can get your help?"

"Waiting tables?" she asked.

"No. Actually, we're just going to throw some stuff up buffet style, but even with Ashley helping, we're going to need a few more hands."

"Absolutely," she said, suddenly excited to have a reason to stay. Suddenly thrilled to be given something to do besides sit here and pretend she wasn't waiting for a man to pay attention to her.

Thrilled to have a way to be a part of this, off the sidelines and right in the heart of it.

She turned to tell Joe what she was doing, but he was asleep, his head against the wall.

"Joe." She gave him a shake and he woke up, his hands reaching for his glasses.

"What?" he asked, glancing around at the party happening around him. "Oh, God, I passed out, didn't I?"

"You did," she said with a smile. "You should walk on home. I'm going to help Cora in the kitchen."

He yawned so big she heard his jaw crack. "You are probably right," he said. "You sure you're okay?"

"I'm fine," she told him, growing annoyed with his chivalry.

"I'll call you," he said as he stood, and she nodded, because this wasn't exactly the place to discuss future dates with him or with Ty. He leaned over as if to give her a quick kiss on the cheek, but she ducked backward so quickly she ran into the chair she'd been sitting in.

His eyes flared and his cheeks burned.

"Good night, Joe," she said with some finality, and he finally left.

She turned to follow Cora into the kitchen, but her attention was snagged on Ty. On the golden, shiny beauty of him across the room, surrounded by people she didn't know.

He was watching her. His blue eyes searing as if they were alone in the Art Barn and she was taking off her shirt for him.

"Shelb?" Cora said. "You coming?"

"Yes," she said, jerking herself free from his gaze. "I'm coming."

The twenty people Ty had been expecting were actually nearly thirty. The break in the cold weather had brought a few more than he'd anticipated. He'd been worried that the thirty people on top of Sean's usual Friday night crowd might be too much for the small bar and restaurant, but Sean had called in reinforcements and Brody and Ashley, Cora and Shelby were all pitching in.

All of his worlds were colliding, and he'd stopped drinking after that first beer. If he hadn't, he might have given in to the temptation to grab Shelby every time she walked by, one of those white aprons around her waist, carrying dirty plates of food back to the kitchen.

He chafed at the thought of her doing this work. At all of them doing this work. Not because it was bad work, but because he didn't have the first idea what to do with his gratitude.

"You ready to do this?" Cliff Hines, his buddy the auctioneer, asked. Cliff glanced down at his old fake Rolex, which he kept trying to tell people was real. "We're coming up on eleven."

"That late? Crap." Ty whistled to get everyone's attention and the room quickly went silent.

"Let's get this started," he said. "Head on out to the parking lot."

The crowd filed out, leaving behind a few regulars.

Sean and Brody and Jim, behind the bar, all took a giant breath and then started working on dishes and clearing out the empties buckets.

Ty went out the back and rode the Chief around to the front, where the streetlight created a big golden pool that showed his bike off pretty nicely.

"You guys know the drill," Cliff said and then began reading—at super speeds—from the card Ty gave him. "Up for auction tonight we have a 1942 Indian Chief. The odometer has 7,100 miles on it. Matching frame and motor numbers. A 74ci engine, foot clutch, three-speed tank side shifter. Six-volt battery system, stainless steel exhausts—"

"Just start with the bidding!" Bruce Olep, a former Outlaw from Memphis who got out of the club just after Ty left, yelled out. "So Gordo can take it and we can get back to drinking."

"We'll start the bidding at twenty thousand dollars," Cliff said.

The bidding was fast and furious. The booze helped, and Gordon from New Orleans didn't let anyone get too far ahead of him. Ty expected twenty-seven thousand, but they blew past that pretty quick.

"We have thirty, do I hear thirty-one?" Cliff looked over the assembled crowd, but no one so much as twitched. "Bidding stands at thirty thousand dollars.

Going once. Going twice. Sold to Gordon McNeill for thirty thousand dollars."

There was a smattering of applause and whistles, and of course a few grumbles as the guys Gordon outbid headed back into the bar.

"It's a beautiful bike," Gordon said, shaking Ty's hand.

"I know you'll take good care of her," Ty said.

Thirty thousand was the most he'd ever made on a bike. Ever.

And he knew that wouldn't settle in for a while, distracted as he was by the sight of Shelby inside the bar. He should be sick with pride, crowing with accomplishment, but he was just pissed off.

"What are you working on now?" Gordon asked.

Ty started telling the older man about the Velocette just as police sirens broke through the silent night.

Shelby leaned back against the counter, feeling like every muscle in her body had been worked to exhaustion. But the adrenaline of it all still hummed through her. "That was fun," she said. "I never thought working in a kitchen would be so exciting. It's all so fast."

They still had some food out on the buffet. Cornbread and beans. But they were out of ribs. Out of chicken. Out of wings. The thirty people Ty brought in had been like locusts, eating their way through everything Sean had in his fridge. Including the coleslaw.

"Ah, another one gets the bug," Cora laughed, pulling off her barbecue-sauce-splattered white apron and setting it on the counter. Shelby did the same. "Well, let me introduce you to the finest aspect of the restaurant business. The after-service cocktail."

A drink sounded good, and Shelby followed Cora out

of the kitchen into the bar, which was silent for the moment as the auction went on outside. Through the big garage doors in the eating area, they could hear the auctioneer describing the bike.

She didn't know anything about motorcycles, but the bike outside underneath the streetlight was a beautiful piece of machinery. Of art. And it looked as if it had been created and handled with love.

"You worried about the noise ordinance?" Brody asked. Sean checked his watch.

"They're not that loud," he said, though he was clearly worried. "And if he works fast, maybe Mrs. Phillips won't have time to even get to the phone."

Sean leaned over the bar to tilt up Cora's face and press a long, sweet kiss on his girlfriend's lips. "You are amazing," he whispered to her. "Amazing."

"I am," Cora laughed. "And you owe me your very finest Old Fashioned."

"Whatever the lady wants," Sean said, clearly hopped up on the energy of a good night. "And you?" he asked Shelby, putting out napkins in front of them. "Better get it quick before the hordes come back."

"I'll have an Old Fashioned, too," she said.

"Make it three," Ashley said, coming around the bar to sit with a heavy sigh on the empty stool next to Shelby. "But make mine a Sprite." Ashley put her hand to her stomach, and Cora caught her eye, raising an eyebrow.

Sean turned to line up the drinks, singing under his breath to the Taylor Swift song on the sound system.

"Crap, why does Jim keep moving the private stock?" Sean said.

"So you don't use it!" Jim yelled from the corner of the room, where he was bussing empty beer bottles and pitchers from the empty tables. "It's in the office."

Sean skipped back to the office. Brody went to change a keg in the basement.

"There something you need to be telling us?" Cora whispered to Ashley, who seemed to be glowing red hot.

Ashley shook her head, all flushed and pink and twinkly. "It's still super early."

Was this code? Shelby wondered.

"But you think?" Cora asked.

Ashley bit her lip and nodded.

"Oh my God!" Cora squealed and Ashley shushed her. "We don't want Sean to know yet," she whispered.

" 'Course not—that man can't keep a secret to save his life," Cora quickly agreed, but she leaned over to squeeze Ashley's hands. "So excited for you, honey."

"What is going on?" Shelby asked. Granted, she'd been drunk earlier and was now buzzing on adrenaline, and any moment she was going to be exhausted, but she could not, for the life of her, figure out what they were talking about. Whatever secret decoder ring other girls got in their first box of tampons, Shelby had missed out on.

"Brody and I are going to have a baby," Ashley whispered just as Sean came back into the bar.

"Oh my God," Shelby breathed, delight for her friend filling her. Cora shushed her and Shelby grabbed Ashley's hands under the bar, squeezing them.

A few people came back into the bar just as Sean pushed two Old Fashioneds and a Sprite toward the three women.

They lifted their glasses in thanks and all took sips. The drink was strong and sweet and Shelby took a big swig of it, feeling celebratory and grateful and sad all at the same time. Grateful for her friends, for this community that she was a part of. That a wonderful couple like Ashley and Brody were starting a family. That they could pull off an event like this without warning for a man none of them knew very well.

But the thought that she might not get to know Ty any better was a sad one. Repellant, even.

She had to convince him that she wanted nothing to do with Joe.

That she only wanted Ty.

"To Bishop," she said, drawing surprised glances from everyone, just as police cars pulled up outside.

Chapter 18

Crap. The noise ordinance. Ty had hoped they'd gotten in under the wire, but apparently not. Most of the crowd had gone back inside the bar, so it was just him, Gordon, and Cliff the auctioneer still out on the asphalt. But soon word got out that there were cops in front and a small group of men and women stood at the door watching.

Some of the guys inside the bar had a long and complicated relationship with law enforcement, and after a couple of drinks that relationship got pretty volatile. The last thing this night needed was anything volatile.

Ty turned to face the cruiser just as the two officers stepped out.

Jenkins and Debreau, who'd given him the gears the other day at Cora's.

Great. Just great.

"We meet again?" Jenkins said without much of a smile.

"Sorry if we got too loud," Ty said, trying to cut off the good cop/bad cop routine before it got started. "Sean warned me about the ordinance, but I lost track of time."

"The neighbors called," Jenkins said. Again the officers split up, Jenkins coming to stand in front of him, Debreau strolling around to check out the bike behind him.

Sean and Brody came out, followed by Ashley, Cora, and Shelby. "Hey, sorry, guys," Sean said, jogging out to the curb where they all stood. "The time kind of got away from us."

"That's the fifth complaint this month, Sean. You said you'd stick to the ordinance," Jenkins said. "We're going to have to start fining you."

"It's my fault," Ty said, trying to keep Sean from getting in trouble. After all the guy had done for him tonight, it seemed the least he could do was handle the flack from the neighbors. "Honestly, mine. If anyone needs to be fined it's me."

"What's going on here?" Debreau asked. Ty turned to face the cop, who was crouched down looking at the bike.

"I'm auctioning off the bike," Ty explained.

"It's a nice bike," Debreau said, standing upright again. His knees popping. "Where'd you get it?"

Ty crossed his arms over his chest. "Bought it in pieces mostly."

"Yeah?" Debreau shifted his belt, getting comfortable with his foot up on the curb. "Like on those TV shows?"

"Sure." Lying was easier than explaining how all those Learning Channel shows did was make things look easy and fast when they were in fact the opposite.

"So you fix this kind of stuff up and then auction it?"

"Yes." He glanced over at Brody. Shelby stood beside him, soaking all of this in. The gold of the streetlight washed over her, gilding her hair in sparkles.

Debreau whistled, forcing Ty's attention away. "You do good work. Real good work. I've got my dad's old Harley growing rust in my garage. Maybe you want to take a look at it?"

"I don't take clients."

"Why not?"

Ty shrugged. *Because I don't like working for assholes like you,* he thought, and though he didn't say it,

Debreau clearly got the point. He sniffed and stiffened and got back to remembering he was some badass small-town cop on a power trip.

"You got the permits for this auction?" Debreau asked.

"Permits? What do I need a permit for?" Sean asked.

"I have a license," Cliff spoke up, reaching into his wallet. "And the sale is private—"

"This area here is still public property," Debreau said, pointing to the blacktop that Sean was planning on making patio space. "Your zoning hasn't been approved yet, has it, Sean?"

"Are you kidding me, Max?" Sean asked, his hands on his hips. "You know I filled out the paperwork. We're just waiting for everything to go through. It's not my fault City Hall works on a skeleton staff."

Debreau shrugged. "You need permits for this sort of thing, Sean."

"Look, I'll go into City Hall tomorrow and take care of everything." Ty tried to placate everyone. "I'll pay fines or fees or whatever you need me to do."

"I'm afraid it doesn't work retroactively." Jenkins pulled out his ticket book. "Sean, I'm going to have to write you a ticket for the noise and the auction."

Sean started swearing but Brody put a hand on his brother's shoulder, calming him down. Jenkins handed the ticket to Sean, who wouldn't take it, so Brody did.

"Your son here tonight?" Debreau asked.

"My son?" Ty jerked backward at the question, the sudden change of subject. "No. I didn't bring him to a bar."

"You got someone watching him?"

"A friend."

"A friend like these guys?" He pointed toward the bikers in the doorway.

"Jesus, man," Ty breathed. "What is your problem?"

Debreau stepped forward, but suddenly there was Shelby. Shelby smelling of barbecue and bourbon, with a halo of sparkles in her hair.

"We appreciate you coming out," Shelby said, calm and level, a bucket of water on a growing fire. "The Chamber of Commerce is going to be looking into the issues with permits, and we'll set up a better system so this doesn't happen anymore."

"That's a good idea, Ms. Monroe," Debreau said, backing off, but those sharp brown eyes didn't leave Ty's. "Why don't you see what you can do about keeping these people out of trouble tonight."

"No one is getting in trouble," she said. "I promise."

Jenkins and Debreau stepped back into their cruiser and after a moment pulled away from the curb and headed back out into the night and whatever passed for crime in Bishop, Arkansas.

"Thank you, Shelby," Sean said, and Cora and Brody all chorused their thanks. Ty just looked at her.

"You keep stepping in," he said, amazed and irritated all at the same time. He wanted to cup his hand around her neck, pull her in close to him, rest his weary and tired body against hers. Work out the giant mixed bag of emotions that had been dogging him all night with her. In her.

Hell. He wanted to celebrate with her. Put his arm around her. Kiss her in front of her friends and his. Thank her for being a part of this night; whether she was doing it for him or for Sean didn't matter.

She was here. She'd stayed.

But he couldn't forget the look on her face when that Joe guy grabbed her hand.

"Holy shit!" Sean yelled, looking at the tickets. "That's half of what we made tonight!"

"Look, guys," Ty said, shaking free of his Shelby thoughts. "I'll pay the tickets."

"No," Sean grumbled. "I agreed to do this. It's my fault."

"Sean." Ty stepped closer to the guy, surprised that he was being so noble about the whole thing. "Do you know how much I made on the auction tonight?"

"It doesn't matter," Sean said.

"Thirty grand." Sean blinked. Shelby's mouth fell open. "Give me the tickets. I'll pay them."

Sean handed them over and Ty shoved them in his pocket. "I'm sorry things ended the way they did here," he said. "But I really appreciate the way you accommodated us. On the fly like that, too. You did a great job." He glanced at all of the people standing behind Sean. Brody, Cora, Shelby, and Ashley. "All of you. I know you chipped in to help Sean, but it was a big deal for me. And I really appreciate it."

"Don't be sorry," Sean said, sticking out his hand, and Ty shook it. "It was an amazing night. And you know if this is something you do a lot of, we can work something out. A collaborative thing." He turned to Shelby. "Can you imagine the draw we'd get for the Okra Festival if we had one of his bikes to auction off?"

"It's not something I do a lot of," Ty said, ending the conversation. "And I'm not for hire."

"Thirty thousand dollars?" Sean asked, totally ignoring him. "In what, like four minutes? And this crowd? With advertising, we'd have double, probably triple!"

"It took me a year to build the bike, Sean. It's not like it was easy money."

"The Chamber of Commerce can take care of the permits," Shelby said. "If you joined—"

"I'm not interested in the Chamber of Commerce," he said, a little too quickly. A little too roughly. She paled slightly but didn't back down.

"That's too bad," she said. "Because you could be a real asset."

"Asset?" He hadn't been an asset. Ever. "To what?"

Shelby and Cora exchanged a quick glance. Brody wrapped his fingers around Ashley's. A small raft of community around him.

"To us," Sean said. "Bishop."

Ty laughed. "You're kidding."

"No," Shelby said. "We're not."

"Look, guys, I'm not interested in a Chamber of Commerce or helping this community. I appreciate what you've done tonight, but I'm going to head home and check on my kid. Sean, I'll take care of the tickets and come back tomorrow to settle up the bill."

Ty went back inside to say goodbye to the people who were still left. Jimmy said he'd be following him home in a little bit, but he was finishing up a conversation with one of the locals, who had turned himself into a mess over his ex, and Jimmy was being a kind ear.

Ty made a quick circle of the bar, making sure the guys who'd had too much to drink had a way home that didn't involve them getting behind the wheel. He shook hands with Sean and Brody once more and then made his way out to his truck, which Jimmy had parked around the corner on another dark street.

And there, leaning against the driver's side door, was Shelby.

She heard the crunch of his boots over the asphalt and pushed herself away from the truck.

"What are you doing?" he asked, his face in hard lines that only reinforced the misgivings that this had not been her best idea.

He needed a chance to cool down; she should have waited until tomorrow. But no, she'd ignored the reasonable voice. For the first time in her life she ignored the reasonable voice. It was highly uncomfortable.

"I'm hoping for a ride home." She lifted her chin, braving it out.

He glanced around at the shadows of the street. "You don't have your car?"

Her breath stalled in her chest. He was not going to make this easy. "I do."

"You drunk?"

She shook her head.

"Where's Joe?"

"He went home."

The streetlight slashed across his face, shadowing his lips, illuminating his eyes, cutting him into pieces so she could not be sure of the whole of him. He reached past her and unlocked her door.

"Get in," he said, holding open the door for her. She climbed into the cold cab and he shut the door behind her. She watched as he walked across the front of the truck and wondered how this had happened. How this wild man had stepped so thoroughly into her life. And how it seemed he wanted to be there. What in her narrow and rigid world could possibly be keeping him?

He climbed in on the driver's side and shut the door behind him, but didn't start the truck. Their breath fogged slightly in the cold air; the shadows made everything stark.

And clear.

She didn't want Joe. Not even a little.

"Ty—"

With one hand he reached over and cupped the back of her neck, pulling her toward him, and she went. She coiled and sprung and launched herself at him. His lips met hers in a bruising kiss that barely held onto civility. On her knees beside him she buried her fingers in his hair, feeling the shape of his head in her palms.

His hand slid over her hips, grabbing her ass with

force. With intent. His fingers slipped down between her legs, pressing hard where she wanted him most.

"Ty—"

"Don't talk."

Fine. Yes. Like that. Exactly like that. She put a hand against his jeans, the faded spots where the buttons of his fly had worn into the denim. He was hard under those buttons. Hard for her.

She shifted her weight, sitting back against her knees, trapping his hand between her legs. She rocked against him, using his fingers to push her higher. Make her wilder. Quickly she undid the buttons of his fly, finding the heat of his flesh beneath layers of clothing.

She was dying. Dying for him, so empty inside it was all she felt. Vacant and blank and waiting. For him.

Somehow he got his hand free from the trap between her legs and he put it in her hair, pulling out the rubber band, tangling his fingers until it stung. She gasped, tilting her head back to alleviate the sting.

His other hand cupped her throat, her chin, pulling her face down to his. Looking into his eyes, she wrapped her hand around his dick. Jacking it slowly up and down its length while his eyes burned into hers.

They didn't kiss. Open-mouthed, they breathed into one another. Eyes locked, bodies inside coats, and clothing straining toward the other.

"I want to have sex," she whispered.

"No condom." He took her lower lip between his teeth and she cried out in pleasure and pain. Between her legs, her arousal pounded, and she had to have him inside of her. In any way.

Scooching backward, she eased down into the foot well, her body over his leg, and she took him into her mouth. Sucking him so hard and so fast his hands flew back against the seat, as if to keep himself steady.

"Oh God. Shelby," he moaned, his hips pushing up

against her, and she eased off. She found a rhythm, hard and fast, and then slow and teasing.

His laughter had an edge that sent her blood sizzling through her. With one hand, he grabbed her and pulled her back up onto the bench seat. She pulled away from him, about to ask what he was doing, but he stopped her with a hand at her chin.

"Keep going," he breathed.

She arranged herself as best she could on her stomach and he reached his hand down the back of her pants, finding her where she was empty and aching and wet. His fingers stabbed into her and she arched backward against him.

It was messy and fast and frantic, but soon she was shuddering against the worn nap of the bench seat, breaking into a thousand dark pieces. A thousand dark and wanton and needy pieces. And then he was, too, holding her head in his hands, arching against her, moaning her name as he came.

In the silence of after, she pulled away slowly. Her mouth, then her face. She got to her knees very carefully, because she felt in some ways like she'd been broken and put together with an unreliable hand.

As she moved, his hand slipped away from her and she felt the scrape of his calluses and blisters against the tender skin of her hips, caught between her skin and the fabric of her jeans. She twitched, then shifted, wanting to keep him there. His large palm, warm and firm against her flesh.

His hand could stay there forever. In fact, the two of them could move into this truck and never leave. Pizza could be delivered. They could just have sex and live in this moment without anything but them—no reputations, no sons in trouble, no mothers slipping farther and farther from shore.

Just them. And the sex that turned her inside out.

He squeezed her cheek as if he understood that, but still he pulled away, and then there was nothing to do but sit up, wipe her mouth, and try to make sense of what had happened. Of what this was between them.

The windows were foggy; the air, chilly only ten minutes ago, was now humid, smelling of bodies and sex. And part of her was thrilled to find herself here, as if she'd been waiting for just this sort of invitation to be opened to her, while the other part of her was astonished that she wanted this.

Wild, nearly out-of-control sex in a car with a man whose anger toward her was something she felt in the air. Like a coming storm.

She pushed her hair away from her face and found him watching her. His lush lips red, as if he'd been biting them, and she reached out to touch them.

But he caught her fingers in his hand.

"I don't share."

She blinked, curling her fingers against his.

"Did you hear me, Shelby? I don't share."

"What a ridiculous thing to say."

"If you want to date Joe, you don't get to fuck me."

"Is that what you think I'm doing?"

"I have no clue what you're doing."

"I don't want to date Joe."

He began to do up the buttons of his jeans, lifting his hips to tuck himself back into his boxers. She watched as his pink flesh, slick with her saliva, disappeared.

"I only want you." The words were a surprise. To both of them. His hand stilled on his pants and she held her breath, feeling like she'd just changed the game between them. Shoved them into unfamiliar territory. All the guards they wore, the masks and personas, fell away, and she felt suddenly more naked in this moment than she had with him ever.

"Then what were you doing with him?"

"I was finding out that I don't want to date him. For a lot of years I thought he was exactly what I wanted. But he's not." She thought of how Ty never got scared. He met her head-on, every single time, with his own damage in tow. "You are."

And then his fingers shifted against hers and he twined their hands together. "Yeah?"

"Yeah."

Despite having long hair her entire life she'd never quite mastered the toss, but somehow she managed to get it done so she could look him in the eye.

His smile was of a different variety. It wasn't cheeky or cocky. It wasn't sexy or a barely veiled threat. It was an invitation to a place deeper inside of him, past the sex and the shared weight of the heavy loads they carried in their lives.

It was a glimpse of who he was and what he wanted.

And part of her reared up in fear. In panicked fear.

She didn't know how to be the kind of person people let in like that. She didn't know how to be close to someone in that way.

It was as if all the wants and desires she'd suppressed, the anger and fear created in her by her father, her inadequacy and her awkwardness, were too heavy and she couldn't carry them with her, couldn't get them through this door that he was opening for her, and so she was stuck, marooned on an island of her own baggage.

I can't get there, she thought. *That place you are showing me. That secret side of yourself. I can't reach it.*

"I only want you, too," he said.

She pushed herself back up on her knees and then sat down properly, blood rushing back into her feet, which had fallen asleep the way she'd been crouching.

"Shelby?" He touched her face and she nearly flinched away. "Shelby, look at me."

"Ty—"

"Look. At. Me." His voice was firm but soft, and as she lifted her eyes to his, her attention got snagged on his smile. "You think I don't see you?" he asked. "I do. I see you."

She wanted to ask him what he meant, or maybe make a joke, but she couldn't. Because she knew exactly what he meant. He saw her marooned on that baggage.

"We're two people." His fingers touched her face, the edges of her lips, where if she smiled more she might have wrinkles. Lips she never thought about until he touched them. "Two people who just want each other. Who like each other. It's not a big deal. It's nothing to be scared of."

But it is, she wanted to say. Because it had been years since she'd started a relationship with a man. Years. And those early relationships hadn't exactly been giant victories. They'd been mostly cold, slightly awkward affairs with men she wanted very little from. Men there was never any fear would try to get more from her.

Men who would never claim to see her. Men she'd never give that opportunity to.

"Shelby?"

"Okay." She pulled her face away but he didn't let go, and his fingers bit into her cheeks as she continued to try and dodge his gaze. He wouldn't let her. So finally she looked up at him, feeling defiant and wrecked at the same time.

"Don't be scared," he whispered, his beautiful lips curved in a soft smile. "I'm not Dean. I'm not going to hurt you."

Oh, you stupid man. I'm not scared of being hurt. It's my sharp edges that will slice you open. You are the one that will regret this. Keep your secret self, keep your softness and your vulnerability. Don't show it to me, because I will inevitably hurt you.

"You're nothing like Dean," she said. "You're not like any person I've ever known."

"Yeah?" He laughed. "Because I only take you to the

finest places?" He glanced around the truck and she smiled, the tension inside of her cracking.

"I like how you take me," she whispered.

His eyes narrowed at her words and she felt his desire; the surge of it in his body crashed over his boundaries and onto her.

"It's you." He whispered kisses across her lips. "It's you who takes me. Every time."

She melted against him. The hard stones of her doubts and worries became inconsequential when he touched her.

Maybe it will all be okay, she thought. *Maybe this time, it will be fine.*

A knock on the window sent her scrambling back, her hands on her lips as if she could hide the proof of the kiss.

It was one of the men from the bar. The man with tattoos on his neck and across his knuckles, with the long beard and mustache.

A sound embarrassingly like a squeak came out of her throat.

Ty smiled, swearing under his breath, and unrolled the window.

"Hey, Jimmy."

"Sorry, man, I didn't mean—" Jimmy's eyes darted over to Shelby, who tried to fade into the shadows. "Sorry."

"It's fine," Ty said, keeping his hand over Shelby's. "What's up?"

"John poured Tommy into their truck and took off and I was hoping for a ride back to your place."

"Hop in."

Jimmy ran around the back of the truck to the passenger side and Shelby scooched over to the middle of the bench seat, pulling her purse onto her lap, trying to take up as little space as possible.

"Thanks, man," Jimmy said, slamming shut the passenger door. He was big, but he turned himself against the door, making sure there was distance between him and her. Which was nice. "I'm sorry if I was interrupting."

"You weren't." Ty glanced down at Shelby and then started the truck, easing them off the curb and onto the road. "Shelby, I'd like you to meet one of my oldest friends, Jimmy. Jimmy, this is Shelby. She's the teacher I was telling you about."

Shelby glanced sideways at Ty for a second, slightly alarmed that he'd been talking about her.

"You're the one working with Casey," Jimmy said, holding out his hand. "Ty says you're doing great things for the kid."

"Well, he's the kind of kid you want to do things for," she said, slipping her hand into the biker's giant paw. "Nice to meet you."

"You, too. This is a pretty great town you've stumbled onto, Ty. Good people."

Ty drove through the square toward the highway out to his house. "It was a good night, wasn't it?"

"Thirty thousand?" Jimmy whistled. "I'll say."

Ty laughed and rubbed his hand through his hair. "Yeah, that was something."

"Sucks the cops had to come and write those tickets," Jimmy said.

"No shit," Ty agreed.

"You should think about the Chamber of Commerce," Shelby said.

He shook his head. "Shelby, I'm not a business. I refurbish old bikes in my garage. It takes me a year to do one. It's not like I'm ready to open a shop."

"What about a garage?" Jimmy asked. "I mean, it's good you found steady work, but you're not a carpenter."

"You're not?" she asked.

"I am for what Brody needs," he assured her.

"You planning on doing that for the rest of your life?" Jimmy asked. "I'm sure you're a fine carpenter, and if that's what you want to do, great. But you loved Pop's shop—"

"I'm not planning anything past getting Casey back into school on Monday morning," Ty said as they pulled into his driveway.

Across the street, Shelby's house was dark, the illumination from the kitchen windows in the back falling onto the rose skeletons. She imagined Mom and Deena back there working on the photo album. She'd called to say she'd be late, but her phone had run out of charge hours ago. And she very suddenly had that sneaky suspicion that she'd been gone too long. That something might have happened and Deena hadn't been able to reach her.

Deena would have called The Pour House, she tried to reassure herself. *She knew where I was.*

But what if Sean had been too busy behind the bar to answer?

That internal panic button was well and truly pressed, and she felt the need to get home and make sure everything was fine.

Jimmy opened the passenger door and slipped out. Shelby followed, spilling from the warm truck into the cold night. "I better go check on Rita," Jimmy said.

"I'm going to walk Shelby home," Ty said. "I'll be back in a minute."

"Nice meeting you, Shelby," Jimmy said, his eyes twinkling. "It's about time Ty here started punching above his weight."

"Go!" Ty laughed, taking a fake swing at Jimmy. "Make sure your wife and my kid haven't eaten everything in the house."

Shelby started across the street. "Was that a crack about my weight?" she asked.

"No. God no." He grabbed her arm and they stood in the middle of the highway, in the dark between street-lights, staring at each other. "It was a crack about how much better than me you are."

She blinked. *What a ridiculous idea!* "I'm not."

"You are. Trust me." He put his arm around her shoulders and set them back in motion, walking in tandem, their hips brushing. She was awkward at it, never having walked with a man's arm over her shoulder, forcing her to change her stride and compensate for his. It was harder than it looked. "But I think I can handle it."

"Do you want to open a garage?" she asked.

He shook his head. "Jimmy's been on a follow-your-bliss thing ever since he became a minister."

"He's a minister?" She didn't even pretend to hide her shock.

"Look at you, judging a book by the cover. I didn't think teachers were supposed to do that," he teased, and surprisingly she loved it. No one ever teased her. People always treated her so seriously. Ty didn't treat her like anyone she'd ever known. It was addicting. Spectacular.

"Is being a mechanic your bliss?"

"I don't know." He wasn't lying, but he wasn't quite telling the truth. She knew this trick. Every fifth grader started the school year somehow knowing the trick: to downplay what they wanted. To make their desires seem less than they were in fear of ridicule. In fear of failure.

"Everyone in town has to go to Marietta to get their cars fixed," she said, nudging him toward his bliss, if that's what it was. "A garage in town would be amazing—"

"Whoa, whoa," he held up his hands. "Stop, Shelby,

honestly. I've kind of got my hands full right now. I'm not thinking of anything past getting Casey back in school and out of trouble. Starting a shop, opening a business, that takes time—"

"I know what it takes," she said and his eyes met hers, solemn and still in the shadows.

"I don't know if I have it in me," he told her. Obviously he wasn't just talking about time. Or Casey. He doubted himself. His abilities. "Pop's garage was established. The customers built-in. He had good guys working for him. Accountants and stuff. I don't know if I can do that by myself."

"You're not by yourself," she whispered. The words seemed to implode the silence of the night.

He groaned, leaning in to kiss her.

"It's what the Chamber of Commerce is for," she said against his lips. And after a moment they both broke into laughter.

"You say the sweetest things." Again with the teasing, and it felt like a different kind of affection. Another kind of touch. The kind of intimacy that it was all right to flaunt in front of other people, but still tied them together in that secret lovely way.

"Think about it, Ty. If it's what you want, I will help you."

He touched her nose, the top of her lip. Her bottom lip and then the edge of her collarbone, just above her shirt. "I'm so glad—" he breathed, and then stopped.

"What?"

Instead of answering her, he leaned down and pressed a sweet, soft kiss to her lips. A kiss unlike any other that they'd shared. It was unsettling, like being tipped just a little off balance.

Behind her, she heard the kitchen door open.

"Shelby?" Deena said.

"I'm here," Shelby said, pushing away from the kiss

and the shadows she and Ty were standing in, and stood in the light pouring from the back door.

"I'm sorry," Deena said, her eyes drifting over her head to where Ty stood. "I don't mean to interrupt. But there's been an accident . . ."

Reality, like a brick, settled back onto her chest, bringing her right into balance, and she took off at a run for the back porch.

Chapter 19

"She's fine," Deena said quickly as Shelby charged up the back steps. "There was a lot of blood. But she's fine."

"Blood?"

Evie sat at the kitchen table, surrounded by dishtowels soaked in blood, her face and hands covered in raw, red scrapes and scratches. On her forehead there was a white bandage.

"Mom!" she cried.

Evie's face was blank, her eyes empty. She looked at Shelby as if she were a stranger.

Shelby gasped, a giant sinkhole opening up in her chest, swallowing her heart. They'd told her, the books, the doctors, the online support groups; they'd told her it would happen, that at some point her mother would look at her and not recognize her.

They'd said there was no preparation that would make it okay, that would lessen the burn and sting of it. It was simply the predatory nature of the disease.

"Mom? It's me, Shelby."

Evie blinked, then glanced down at her hands, the bloody towels on the table.

"What happened?" she whispered.

Shelby swallowed back the sharp lump in her throat. *I don't know. I wasn't here.*

"You tried to pull up those rosebushes, Evie," Deena said, squeezing past Shelby, who was rooted in the doorway. Belatedly, Shelby realized that Deena had her fair share of scratches, seeing a long red scrape across her neck. "I went upstairs for a second to go to the bathroom, and when I came out, I couldn't find her in the house. I tried the Art Barn and some of the other buildings. By the time I found her she'd already dug up three of the plants."

"How did she hit her head?"

"She wouldn't leave, so I grabbed her hand trying to lead her out of the bushes, but she jerked back, tripped, and hit her head on the side of the house."

"Shelby!" Mom's voice was high and panicked. "Who is that woman? Why is she here?"

"It's Deena, Mom."

"Where is my husband. Where—"

"It's okay." Shelby stepped across the kitchen to her mother, who shrank away at her approach. Flinched from her outstretched arms. Her neck and face were raw with scratches, one of which had caught the thin skin near her eye and still oozed red blood.

"Where is my husband?" she cried again. "I don't understand what's happening."

"Mom—" Shelby sat down on the banquette, sliding across the old pink vinyl toward Evie, who trembled and shook, trying to escape out the other side. Shelby forced herself to stop, to not try to get any closer. Inside she was explosions of emotion, giant nuclear blasts of fear and worry, but she held herself very still. Forced herself to be calm. "Mom. You're safe. I'm your daughter, Shelby. This is Deena, your friend—"

"I don't have any friends!"

This was painfully true, not that she could do anything about it. Or knew how to change their natures. Friends were luxuries they'd never had for a dozen reasons.

"Mom, you're safe. It's okay. Everything is okay."

Mom's breath shuddered in her throat and after a moment she allowed Shelby to put a hand over hers. Her skin was like velvet and paper under Shelby's fingers. So fragile. So thin.

"I tried to call," Deena said. "But—"

"My phone ran out of charge," Shelby whispered.

"Don't," Deena said, reading the guilt in her face. "If it was an emergency I could have called The Pour House. I knew where you were. We've got this handled; I just wanted to give you a heads-up, not make you come home."

"Do you want a ride to the hospital?" It was Ty in the doorway, his hands shoved in the pockets of his shearling coat.

Shelby had forgotten he was there.

Forgotten all about him.

How odd he seemed there in the doorway. How terribly out of place in this house of old photographs and fading memory. Of friendless women.

He was too bright, too big. Too alive. There was no room for him here. What she and Ty had . . . it didn't come into this house.

She shook her head, denying him. Denying his help and anything he would offer her past the sex they could have in secret.

"Let me help, Shelby." His voice and eyes steadily sending her the message that he saw her. All of her.

"Get out of my house," Mom spat. Startled, Shelby turned to find her mother seething, her eyes narrowed. She picked up the bloody dishtowels and began flinging them at the door. She managed to get her hand on a teacup and it crashed against the doorjamb a foot from Ty's head.

"Mom!" She tried to catch her hands, to stop her from hurling the teapot, the first-aid kit, and the scissors, but they were all flung at Ty.

"Get! Get out. I've told you a hundred times, get out of my house. We don't want you here anymore. You're mean, Thomas. You hate her. You hate her because she's better than you and you can't stand it. You don't deserve her. You don't deserve either of us."

Oh good God, the world was just too much tonight. Just too much.

"Shelby," he said, still in the doorway, leaning down to pick up the things Mom had thrown.

"Please, Ty," she whispered, trying to stop her mother from throwing anything else at him. "Please go."

"Shelby—"

"Get out!" She and her mother both yelled it.

She knew he would stay and fight, try and help, if she gave him any indication that she wanted that, needed that. So she gave him none. She looked at him as blankly as her mother had looked at her.

And after another moment, he left, closing the door behind him.

Saturday morning after Jimmy and Rita took off back to Indianapolis, Ty loaded Casey into the truck and they went over to The Pour House to settle the bill.

The combination of saying goodbye to his friends and the lingering unease from that scene in Shelby's kitchen last night sat heavily on his shoulders, and he couldn't quite shake the sense that she was pulling away. That despite how much he wanted to try and help, she wouldn't take it.

Her years of carrying her burdens on her own had left her not just unwilling, but unable to share the load.

"It doesn't look open," Casey said, looking at all the bar's dark windows. Ty ran out to check. The doors were locked, and when he peered through the windows he saw the stools still up on the bar. Chairs still up on the tables.

He took a shot and much to Casey's delight, drove to Cora's.

The bell chimed as he and Casey walked in the front door and as he'd witnessed a couple dozen times, half the place glanced over to see who it was coming in. A few people lifted their hands in welcome and Ty did the same.

"Why is everyone looking at us?" Casey whispered, shrinking a little closer to Ty.

"'Cause we're beautiful," Ty joked. Casey gaped at him, and Ty laughed, jabbing him in the side with his elbow. "They're looking because a bell rang, that's all."

"Ty!" It was Sean calling him from the booth he shared with Brody.

Ty gave Casey a little nudge forward and they crossed the restaurant, which was filled to the rafters with the incredible smells of Cora's kitchen.

"Heaven probably smells like this," Casey said, and Ty totally agreed.

"Hey man!" Sean said, scooting over to make room like it was a foregone conclusion that Ty and Casey would just sit.

Maybe it is, Ty thought. *Maybe you just need to get used to the fact that these guys are your friends. And they're good friends.*

"How are you guys this morning?" Brody asked.

"Good." Casey sat down next to Brody. Over the course of the last week of working together Casey had warmed up to Brody, and the two exchanged a very cool and elaborate fist bump. It had worked out last week, between bringing Casey to work and his helping out at the Art Barn in the afternoons—they'd managed

to survive suspension. Now, they had to make sure it
didn't happen again.

"Who else is here?" Casey asked, looking down at
the plate of half-eaten toast in front of him.

"Ashley," Brody said. "She just went to the bathroom."

"I went by the bar to settle the bill," Ty said to Sean.

"Ty," Sean said, digging back into his jalapeño om-
elette. "It's ten a.m. on a Saturday."

"I know, but I didn't want to leave it hanging for too
long."

Sean laughed. "Well, I think you can leave it hanging
until after breakfast."

"Anything happen after I left?" Ty was braced for
news of a fight.

"No. Broke up pretty quick, actually. I think one of
the boys from St. Louis stayed with the new first-grade
teacher, which means The Pour House has had its first
stranger-to-local hookup. I feel like I've arrived."

Cora came by with a pot of coffee and a menu. "Hello,
boys," she said, giving Casey a special grin. "You here
to finish up my arbor?" she asked, and Casey shook his
head.

"I go back to school on Monday," he said.

"Well, I suppose that's all right," she teased. "You
want some breakfast?"

"I can't believe you're here working," Ty told Cora.
"You must be beat after last night."

"Actually, I just got here," she said. "Sean and I slept
in and my staff opened the place."

"And look," Sean said. "It didn't burn down."

"I know," she agreed. "One of these days we might
actually get to take a vacation."

The two of them made like lovebirds, and Brody
nudged Casey and rolled his eyes. Casey pretended to
put his finger down his throat and gag.

"Now," Cora said. "You want some breakfast?"

"We just ate, actually," Ty said at the same time Casey piped up. "Pecan pancakes."

"All right," Ty said, not interested in fighting the tide. He turned over his mug. "Pecan pancakes, and I'll take some coffee."

"You know some folks have been asking about you this morning," she said, pouring coffee into his mug.

"Me?" he asked, alarm bells ringing.

"It's gotten around that there was a guy in town who fixed up old motorcycles. Sounds like half the town has one in their garage." She watched him through the steam billowing up around his coffee cup.

"Who has been telling people?" Ty asked. The auction was less than twelve hours ago. News doesn't usually travel *that* fast.

"Me," Sean said.

"Me, too," Cora said.

"I've kept my mouth shut," Brody said. "I don't want my carpenter to open up a garage while I've got all this work."

"I'm not opening a garage," Ty said.

Ashley came out from the back hallway leading to the bathrooms. She had her hands tucked into the sleeves of her navy sweatshirt and her freckles stood out harshly against her pale face.

Brody gave Casey a nudge and scooted out of the booth.

"You all right?" Brody whispered, rubbing his hand down her back.

"I'm going to head home," she said with a wan smile. "You can stay."

There wasn't even a question. He grabbed their coats from the hooks by the booth, threw some money on the table, and off they went.

"Why are you smiling?" Sean asked Cora, who was

leaning back against the booth, watching them go with a grin on her face.

"Because love is a wonderful thing," she answered. "I'll be back with your pancakes."

Casey asked for Sean's phone and he handed it over, and within seconds the theme song to Plants vs. Zombies was blaring. Casey quickly turned it down, and Ty was struck with the sudden need to touch his son. To hug him.

And he didn't know how to get from where they were to where he wanted them to go.

Sitting here in this booth, with these people, after what they'd done last night and the way they treated his son . . . it felt right.

He still wasn't sure if leaving Memphis was a mistake, but coming here certainly wasn't. And how those two things existed in tandem he had no idea, but there it was.

This place, these people—they were good for Casey. And maybe they'd be good for him, too.

"Hey, so what's happening with you and Shelby?" Sean asked.

Casey's head sprung up from the phone.

Ty shot Sean a death stare.

"Sorry," Sean whispered.

Casey glanced from Ty to Sean. "What's going on?"

"It's complicated."

"No, it's not." Casey said, putting down the phone. "That's just what adults say when they don't want to tell kids about something."

Sean snorted.

"You know," Ty said to Sean, "I was just starting to like you."

"Ty!" Casey cried, and Ty realized that this was very serious for the kid.

"I like Shelby," he said, honestly. "A lot."

"Does she like you?"

"I think so, yes. Does that bother you?"

"Bothers *me*," Sean joked, but Ty ignored him.

"Casey?" he asked again.

"You shouldn't hurt her," Casey said, looking back down at the phone. His finger pressing against the plastic that surrounded it.

"Why do you think I would?"

Casey's eyes shifted from Ty to Sean and then back to Ty. "Because that's what adults do, right? When they like someone?"

Oh, God. That's what love looked like in Casey's world. Like fighting and doors slamming and crying. Love was ugly for Casey.

"Not all adults," Sean said quietly. "I would never hurt Cora. Brody would never hurt Ashley."

The corner of Casey's lips shifted. "He'd probably kill anyone that hurt Ashley."

"This is true," Sean said.

"I won't hurt Shelby," Ty said, though he couldn't guarantee that she wouldn't hurt *him*. In fact, the more he thought of last night, and the moat she had dug around herself, the more inevitable it seemed.

Casey didn't look up, so Ty leaned over and put his hand over the phone. His fingers brushed Casey's and he jerked them away. *Right,* he thought, *that's how far away we are from a father/son hug.*

"Did you hear me?" Ty asked, and Casey's blue eyes held a thousand questions. A thousand doubts. "I won't hurt her."

Or you.

Love should be beautiful. Love should be quiet and full of grace and kindness, and Ty didn't know how to show that to Casey the way that Pop and Nana had shown him. Maybe he could bank on Sean and Cora,

Ashley and Brody to do that. To show both of them what love between adults looked like.

He half-expected the kid to make a flip comment, some kind of joke, but instead he nodded, as if he understood all the things Ty was trying to say. And then he slid the phone out from under Ty's hand, without ever touching him, and was soon back to killing zombies with weaponized cartoon plants.

"Excuse me." An older man and woman stood at his elbow beside the table. There was something about the guy that reminded him of Pop. Maybe it was the dark blue work pants he wore, or the chambray shirt rolled exactly to his elbow. "You the fella that fixes motorcycles?"

"I ah . . . I guess I am. I mean, I don't have a garage or anything . . ."

"My husband has a problem," the woman said, getting to the point. "He's got a collection of bikes that he always says he's going to fix up, but all they do is sit in our shed rusting."

Ty perked up. This was how he found parts for his rebuilds, old guys like this with a shed full of rusted machines.

"Are you selling them?" he asked.

The old man looked doubtful, but his wife nodded emphatically.

"There's two I'd like to keep," the man said quickly, before his wife could go cleaning out his shed. "I'll pay you to work on them with the parts from the others and whatever cash makes up the difference."

Ty nodded. "I'll come and look at them."

With a shaky hand the old man wrote his name, Otto Turner, and phone number on a napkin, and they made a plan to speak later in the week.

Before Casey was done with his pancakes, another guy came by asking questions about his Harley's clutch, and Ty found himself inviting the guy to bring it around to the house so he could take a look at it. And as Sean and Ty and Casey were standing to leave, a woman stopped by and asked if he worked on cars, too, since she thought the mechanic in Marietta was scamming her because she was a woman and didn't know anything about cylindrical belts.

"That's because no car has that," Ty said. "He's making it up."

"And charging me three hundred dollars," she said, nearly in tears, and it was the tears that did it.

"Can you get it to my house?" he asked, and the woman nodded. "Get it there today and I can have a look at it tonight."

She left, grateful and smiling, and he could feel Sean beside him laughing.

"Not in business, huh?"

When Casey had walked into Pop's shop, Ty's world had tilted with certain inevitability. And he felt the world tilt again in a way that told him he couldn't avoid this. He couldn't pretend any longer. If this was home—and his son seemed to want it to be—then it was time to put down roots.

It was time to grow up.

"When does this damn Chamber of Commerce meet?" he asked. "Because I'm going to need some help."

Gravel crunched and pinged under her car's tires as Shelby rolled to a stop in front of the old Del Monte factory her mother used to run.

The chain-link gate was topped with barbed wire and another layer of razor wire on top of that. Chain the size of Shelby's arm locked the doors together with three different padlocks. But next to the gate, a section at the bottom of the fence had been rolled back to make a hole a person could squeeze through.

Before the *America Today* show and the Maybream contest, this factory had been abandoned, but it remained remarkably undamaged. There hadn't been a lot of graffiti, and the windows had been untouched.

But after the fiasco with the live taping and the factory going to that town in Alaska, the building had taken the brunt of the town's anger.

The windows gaped, rimmed with shards of broken glass. Graffiti covered the stone and brick walls. Beer cans and litter blew across the old loading dock.

Shelby had always loved the fact that the old factory never looked abandoned. It had seemed as if it were just waiting for work to resume, patiently sitting here on the south side of town for its chance to once again be useful. To bring back jobs and save the town's economy.

Now it looked abandoned.

It looked uncared for and unwanted.

There was no more pretending.

In Evie's lap was a pile of Kleenex she'd torn to confetti, creating a bird's nest of anxiety. Mom had kept it together in the doctor's office, but Shelby knew when her mother was faking it, when she was pretending to understand what was going on. Evie had spent most of the Saturday morning emergency appointment struggling through the questions.

Faking the answers.

"What happened to your head, Ms. Monroe?" Dr. Lohmann had asked.

"An accident," Evie had answered, feeling for the bandage as if the answer might be there. But Shelby knew she'd forgotten all about the bandage. About digging up the rosebushes despite the puffy and no doubt painful scratches all over her exposed skin. "I'm fine, though, Doctor. Totally fine. How is your wife?"

Dr. Lohmann wasn't married, but he'd smiled and held the light up to check her pupils.

You can't pretend anymore, he'd told Shelby. *You can't stubborn it out anymore. The disease is winning and it's time to change the way you live.*

"What are we doing here?" Evie asked, blinking through the windshield at the factory.

Shelby didn't have an answer to that. She didn't have answers for anything. She had a file full of the names of nurses Dr. Lohmann could recommend for in-home care. And an ache deep in the pit of her stomach, where all of her fear lived. Her worry.

They'd left the doctor's office and she'd driven them here, to the south side of town on the far side of the river to the abandoned factory. This factory for so many years was who her mother was—it had been what she was good at. The part of Evie that Shelby's father could not crush.

On autopilot she'd driven here, or maybe her subconscious had made the choice, coming to this place that had been a source of strength for her mother. For them both.

Because they would need strength for what was coming. And right now, she had none.

Inside her purse in the backseat, her phone dinged. Another text message received.

Ty, she thought. He'd texted her twice, once last night and then again this morning, and she'd texted back brief replies, that her mother was fine. That she was fine. That she appreciated his worry, but they were okay.

Truthfully, she wasn't sure if she'd ever been farther from okay. Last night had been awful. Her mother, agitated and upset and probably in pain, had wandered the house all night and Shelby had been too scared to sleep.

Instead she made a pot of coffee and remembered the

first time she'd logged onto one of the Alzheimer caregiver chat rooms and read what people had posted. Adult children, exhausted and at their wits' end, locking their parents in their rooms. Tying bells to their ankles. Drugging them to sleep.

Five years ago, when Evie had been diagnosed, Shelby couldn't even fathom doing that to her mother. She'd thought, stupidly, innocently, that she would be so much better than those people she'd been convinced were mistreating their parents.

Last night at the worst of her mother's confusion and aggression and wandering, she'd considered all of those things.

And today she felt sick with guilt. Crushed by her own inadequacy.

She wanted Ty. She wanted to see him, rest her head on his shoulder, let his touch take away some of this dread and guilt and worry that skittered under her skin.

That was the pressure valve. She wanted to see him, touch him, so that she wouldn't have to think. So that she wouldn't have to deal with finding a nurse, convincing her mother to accept another person in their home. Accepting that person herself.

But she couldn't avoid this any longer. Her mother was deteriorating past the point that Shelby could care for her herself. Past the point that she could fool anyone that she was doing an okay job.

And Ty had allowed her a few weeks to forget, but now it was time to remember. It was time to get back to her reality, difficult as it was.

"Mom, we need to talk."

"About the factory? Because I know our numbers are down, but I've made some changes to the—"

"It's not about the factory."

"I can't lay anyone else off. We're running on a skeleton crew."

"Mom. We're going to have to bring someone into our house. A nurse. To care for you."

Mom was silent, and the tall weeds growing through the cracks in the asphalt and between the stones of the drive were laid nearly flat by the wind. Sturdy weeds leveled.

She felt an acute sympathy.

"We need help," she breathed.

"With what?"

Shelby's laugh was barren of joy. "With everything."

"Nonsense. We've never needed help before. I can run the factory just fine—"

"I know, but now we do. And I need you to understand that. I need you to understand that and to say it's okay. To say I did my best. That it's all right that I can't do it on my own." Her voice cracked and she closed her burning eyes.

I need you to say that you love me anyway. That you love me despite all the ways I was to blame in how Dad treated you. That despite all the ways I have let you down, my love for you has evened the scales at least a little.

Can you tell me that?

Mom, please tell me that it's okay.

Dust and stones pinged off the car and the dust swirled in tornadoes and cyclones around them, obliterating the rusty gates of the factory. The dark broken windows stared down at them like a thousand glittering eyes.

"Did we eat?" Mom asked.

Shelby sagged against the steering wheel.

"We had lunch an hour ago."

"I'm hungry."

Shelby dug through her purse and handed her a bag of crackers. Evie took them, worried the edge of the plastic ziplock, but didn't eat any of them.

"Did we eat?" Mom asked.

Shelby hadn't expected anything different. Not really. She wiped her eyes and started the car.

I have to do it myself, she thought. Trying to muster up the wherewithal to not only understand that she had to be her own comfort, her own counsel, but that she had to not *need* anything from her mother anymore. She had to separate the relationship in her memories from the relationship now; otherwise she would only be hurt.

Shelby put the car in reverse and left behind the ruins of the factory. Not bothering to look back.

Chapter 20

Casey stared out the windshield at the school. It was Monday morning and the playground was empty. School looked weird with no one around it.

Ty turned off the truck, and the silence was so thick Casey found it hard to breathe. Outside his window the sky was white-blue like ice.

Here comes the father-type-person-and-son chat.

"You know you can go in there and get in trouble again."

Well, Casey thought, looking at Ty, who was leaning forward, resting his crossed arms on the steering wheel. *That's a different tactic.*

"You can get into it with John again. You can piss off teachers, you can refuse to do whatever it is Mr. Root thinks you should do. Hell, you can take a swing at Mr. Root." Ty rubbed a hand over his face. He'd been acting weird since Friday night. Distracted. But not in his usual way. He seemed sad.

"You can do all that stuff, Casey. And you'll get suspended. And I'll ground you, and we'll manage, but . . . nothing will ever change." Ty looked right at Casey. Like *right* at him, and Casey felt hunted by that look. He stuck a finger through the tiny hole in the knee of his jeans, making the hole bigger on purpose, but Ty didn't say anything. "Or you can choose. You can choose to not do those things. You can ignore John if he tries to get in your face. You can listen to the rest of your teachers like you listen to Ms. Monroe. You can always get in trouble or . . . you can try and stop." He popped open the driver's side door and cold air washed into the cab of the truck. "I wish you'd stop, Casey. For us. So we can catch a break."

Ty didn't wait for Casey to say anything, he just got out of the truck, and Casey had no choice but to follow, feeling like his stomach had been hollowed out.

Inside the office, Scott was sitting in one of the two chairs outside Mr. Root's door. When Casey and Ty walked in Scott snapped up in his seat, watching them as they crossed the room.

"Have a seat," Ty said, and Casey slumped down in the chair next to Scott while Ty went in and talked to Mr. Root.

The second hand on the clock over Colleen's desk seemed like the loudest sound in the world. A minute thundered by and they didn't say anything. In the silence, Casey imagined using his foot to kick all the shit off the front of Colleen's desk. Those stupid bobble-head figurines. The Roll Tide flag. The pen jar. He wanted to shatter that jar. Watch those pens go flying.

"How was your suspension?" Scott asked. Casey turned sideways, ignoring him.

If he kicked hard enough he could put a dent in the front of that desk. He could get a couple of kicks in before someone came and stopped him.

"John's mom moved back with his grandparents. He's not in school anymore."

Well, that was awesome news, but he still didn't say anything.

Colleen had changed the poster over the coffeepot. It was a picture of two cats, big gray fluffy ones with long whiskers that pulled their faces down so they looked like they were frowning.

We are not amused. That's what the poster said.

Casey could rip that stupid poster off the walls. That

poster and the fire drill instructions. Like they even needed instructions.

If there's a fire, run. Every idiot knows that.

"I'm so sorry," Scott whispered. "I'm so sorry I held you down and let John hit you like that. I'm—" His voice broke, and Scott swiveled away so they almost sat back to back. Casey looked over his shoulder to stare at the back of Scott's head. "I feel really bad."

"Yeah? What about what John said about Ms. Monroe? Because that's the stuff you should feel bad about."

Scott swiveled back around. "Did you look on You-Tube?"

Casey shook his head. What Ty said that night made sense to him, and he didn't really want to look. He liked thinking about Mrs. Monroe the way that he did. "I'm not going to. It's not my business." Scott looked surprised by that and Casey felt very suddenly grown up. Very suddenly *better* than Scott. "He shouldn't have talked about her that way."

"I guess you're right."

"I'm totally right."

They were silent again, but Casey didn't feel like kicking a dent in the desk anymore. Or tearing down the posters.

"What do you think Mr. Root is going to have us do?" Casey asked.

"Clean the fold-up chairs under the stage in the gym."

"Really?"

"It's what he always has kids do when they come back from suspension."

"That doesn't seem so bad."

"There's like a ton of chewed-up gum stuck to the bottom of them. You have to pry it off with a screwdriver."

Well, that was gross.

"What did you do all week?" Casey asked.

"Went to my grandma's. What'd you do?"

"Worked at Cora's with Ty."

Scott's eyes went wide. "That's cool."

It was.

He'd learned how to do shit. And Ty had treated him pretty good. And Cora gave him free fritters when Ty wasn't looking and Brody showed him how to use the power tools.

It had been about the best week of his life.

And then on Friday, Ty had called off the party with all the scary biker guys and Casey and Rita sat up late and watched all the Iron Man movies back to back. And on Sunday they ate about a gazillion fritters after church. And even church wasn't so bad. There had been a bell choir there, and when they played, he could feel those bells ringing in his chest.

But Shelby and her mom hadn't been at church, and that kind of bummed Casey out. Ty was bummed out, too; that was obvious. Casey suggested they get some fritters to take to Shelby and her mom, and Ty had looked at him like he was the smartest guy in the world.

"Isn't Ty your dad?" Scott asked.

"Yeah."

"Why don't you call him that?"

I don't know anymore.

And right then Casey decided he would try. He'd pull up the bridges and he'd be an island, and he would try to stay out of trouble.

To give them a chance.

Friday night Ty walked across the highway to Shelby's house. He tried the barn first but the door was locked, so he jogged up the cracked cement steps to Shelby's back door, unsure if he was doing the right thing but sure that he couldn't take another day of not seeing her. Another day of her brief answers to his texts.

The rosebushes Evie had yanked out of the ground were still lying there like dead soldiers, and Ty took a second to pull them by their root balls into a pile. He'd come over later with a paper bag and clean up the rest.

Casey said Shelby hadn't been at school all week. And she'd sent out an email on Saturday morning that all the classes in the Art Barn had been cancelled for the week. Whatever was happening inside this house, it was big. Big enough to knock the most competent woman he knew off her stride.

He knocked carefully on the back door, and within seconds, Shelby was there opening the screen.

She looked like she hadn't slept since last Friday night, or eaten. Or seen daylight.

She was pallid and messy. And his stomach pulled up hard at the sight of her so undone.

"Ty," she breathed, and for just a moment he rested in the warmth of the fact that she missed him, too. Whatever else was going on, she missed him. It was obvious. Everything about her screamed that.

"Hey," he whispered. "I just wanted to check on you. Everything okay?"

"We're . . ." She glanced backward, her face reflecting for the briefest moment a terrible grief. "We're doing okay."

"Liar," he said without any heat.

Her lips pursed in a tight smile, an acknowledgment that he was right but she wouldn't go any further.

"We missed you at church on Sunday," he said.

"I . . . I got the fritters," she said. "On the steps? I'm assuming those were from you?"

"Casey's idea, but I'll take credit." *I'll take credit if it means you'll hug me*, he wanted to say. *I'll take credit if*

you bend just slightly and let me help you shoulder
some of this load you're carrying.

"Casey said you weren't at school this week."

"I took the week off to interview some nurses to move in."

"Wow. That's a big step." He remembered that night on the phone, her misgivings about having someone in the house, how it might make her mother worse.

"I should have done it weeks ago, but I didn't." The sound of voices trickled out of the house behind her and Shelby glanced over her shoulder. "Deena just arrived so I could take care of some paperwork and some Art Barn stuff. I'm sorry I had to cancel classes at the barn, but I just have to get someone permanent in here."

"How is your mom handling it?"

She took a deep breath and he could tell that she was about to lie. She was about to say "fine" when nothing was fine.

"Baby," he breathed and cupped her neck in his hand, and for a moment she pulled away, she resisted what he was offering, but he held on. "You don't have to do this alone."

Her laughter splintered and he could feel the tension in her bones. Under her skin. She was razor wire and unrest. She was dark sharp knives and billowing red clouds. She was full of awful.

"Shelby?"

When she looked at him, he saw a version of the woman he'd seen before—the night she came and yelled at him for working on his bike too late, and the night of their date, with that red mark on her cheek and all the heartbreak in the world in her eyes—she was that woman, pushed to the ugliest extreme.

"You're going to break, honey. You're going to crack if you don't—"

She fell into him, against him. Gratefully, his body

caught hers. His hands, as if simply waiting for the chance, curled around her back, her waist.

It was a hug. Long, long overdue, and he was just settling into it, hanging his head against that perfect place on her shoulder, squeezing her into his body so not even air came between them, but then she pulled back and grabbed his hand, leading him off the porch, across the lawn toward the barn.

"Shelby, wait."

"I don't . . ." She shook her hand in front of her chest as if she were trying to shake something off and her manic energy was a cloud around her. Impenetrable and real. "I don't know what to do, Ty. I just want to forget for a minute. That's all. That's what you promised, remember? You promised to make me feel good."

"God, that's all I want to do, baby. But this is bad medicine for you right now." Even he could see that.

"Don't say no," she begged. "Please."

He couldn't stand to have her beg, not for this. Not for something he wanted so badly he was nearly hard at the thought of her in that barn. Of what they did to each other in that barn. He let her pull him toward the dark building and watched as she unlocked it with a key she'd pulled from the pocket in the hooded sweatshirt she wore.

Inside, in the gloom of the Art Barn, she pulled him into her strong arms and he went without a fight, because it had been a week since he'd seen her. A week since he'd touched her. And it felt like years.

Kissing her, he walked her backward toward the couches, navigating the small tables and the shelf in the middle of the room.

If there was a voice in his head telling him to slow down, he couldn't hear it.

He'd missed her. Missed her more than usual because he'd been sure that this weeklong silence was her way of breaking it off with him, and he was so damn relieved to have her back in his arms, her body tight against his.

Her skin was cold but her mouth was wet and he sunk deeper into the contradiction of her, held harder to the sublime paradox of her. They hit the back of the leather couch and he toppled them over, controlling their fall, so she landed carefully on her back and he braced himself above her.

Moonlight slipped through the high windows and they lay in cool light and thick shadow. The entire world reduced to black and white.

He sat back on his knees between her legs and slowly pulled off her running shoes, dropping them on the carpet. Her yoga pants followed, the dark cotton of her underwear. She reached up to pull at his belt, but he stopped her.

"Let me take care of you," he said.

"I don't want that."

"Oh, honey. I think you need it."

"Don't," she snapped. "Don't tell me what I need."

She wanted to work out her anger with him. That was all she wanted him for, and funny, the last time they were in this barn he had been totally on board with that. Completely happy being a simple tool to fix her complex desire.

But now it felt off.

Because he wanted more.

Because he wanted to be more than just an angry fuck.

In the truck, after the party, he'd told her that the two of them wanting each other wasn't something to be scared of. That whatever was happening between them wasn't a big deal, but then he saw her mother not remember who Shelby was. He saw Shelby broken wide open over the guilt and pain of her mother's accident and he'd been ruined.

At that moment Ty wanting Shelby had become profoundly a big deal, because he wanted to help her. He wanted more than just this nasty amazing sex in the barn, he wanted more than the freedom of her body. He wanted her to see him as more than a simple tool.

I'm falling in love with her.

"Are you saying no?" she asked, and he could see her closing up, shutting down, reaching for her things on the floor.

If he let her go he knew it would be over, and he could hardly blame her because he had fucking signed up for this. It wasn't her fault he wanted more.

But he wanted more right now.

So he could deny her and be pushed back out of her life.

Or he could soak up this anger of hers, pull out the poison, and see what lay underneath.

"Spread your legs," he said, and she stilled. For a heartbeat no one moved, and then, very slowly she spread her legs, just a little. Just enough that he could see the pink of her. He slipped one finger from the hem of her tee shirt, which had ridden up to her ribs, across the soft, giving flesh of her belly and down, slowly, through the soft curls covering her until he found her warm, damp skin.

She sucked in a quick breath as if she'd been touched by something cold. She wasn't ready for sex. Not at all. Not her body or her head. She was a mess of mixed signals and crossed wires. Anger and grief made her think she wanted some kind of release, but her body wasn't agreeing with that.

I will do this for you, he thought, breathing soft kisses against the skin of her stomach, feeling against his lips the muscles trembling under the skin. *Because that's what you want and I can't say no to you. But I won't do this again.*

He slipped to his knees on the floor beside the couch and put his hands on her hips, lifting her, shifting her until she was positioned just the way he wanted. In front of him, with one leg beside his arm, the other resting over his shoulder.

From the corner of his eye he watched her pull her shirt down over her belly—hiding her body from him, proving that she was so far away from the moment, light-years away from being turned on enough that she didn't care about whatever imperfections she imagined she had.

You're beautiful, he breathed against the inside of her thigh because if he said it aloud she would deny it and pull farther from him.

So he would show her. He would show her everything he felt that she was so scared of.

Roughly, because he knew she liked that, he pulled her down, closer to the edge of the couch, closer to his mouth so that when he exhaled, he could see her curls move. He could see the ripple of goose bumps over the skin of her thigh.

Open-mouthed he kissed each thigh, he licked the muscle and tendon that connected her legs to her body, bit the soft and trembling rise of her belly. He waited until she was panting, until she was lifting her body up to his mouth, giving herself to his care, and finally, with his callused and grease-stained thumbs, he spread her open for his eyes.

He touched her with the tip of his tongue. Just the edge of his flesh against hers, and she sighed as if the relief were amazing. He could taste her and the salty-sweet beginning of her excitement. Slowly, he lapped at her, finding the soft spots, the hidden places, the hard knot of her clitoris. He circled it once, twice, until she jerked against him as if he were touching her with a hot wire. He eased off, found the beautiful, tender entrance to her body, and paid homage.

She was moaning now, her fingers dancing over his shoulder, up into his hair.

He loved that. Loved her fingers in his hair, and he quickly pulled out the rubber band that kept his hair back, and as if she'd been waiting for that, she pulled it into her fists, yanking at the small hairs, the sharp sensation rocketing along his nerve endings.

Blood flooded his cock.

He laid the flat of his tongue along her clitoris, pressing hard against it, and slipped one finger inside of her. There she was wet. There she was ready. She pushed down against him, using his fingers, his tongue, for her pleasure.

"Tell me you have a condom," she breathed. And he laughed. After Friday night he'd put one in his wallet, because he wanted to be prepared, because he didn't want to miss another opportunity to be deep inside of her when she came, shuddering and crying.

He reached into his back pocket and pulled out his wallet, setting it on her stomach, his mouth still busy between her legs. She found the condom and tore it open with her teeth. Oh God he loved that and he rewarded her with another finger, which sent one of her arms out wide against the leather cushions. A flush climbing up her neck, across her chest.

He replaced his tongue with his thumb, rolling the hard kernel of her clit, and reached for the condom.

"Undo my pants," he said, and the words weren't even out of his mouth before she'd lifted herself forward and gone to work on his belt, the buttons of his jeans. Her cool hand slid around the base of his cock and he groaned.

"Hurry," she said.

He put the condom on with shaking fingers and then

rose up on his knees. He grabbed the back of the couch with one hand and her knee with the other and pressed slowly into her. Inch by hot, wet inch.

"Fuck, Shelby. So—"

"Good."

He looked down at her, caught the glimmer of her eyes and held them as he slid deep into her, then pulled up her knee and slid even deeper. He felt like he was right under her breastbone. Right next to her heart. And staring into her eyes he knew she felt it, too.

He wanted to believe no one had ever had her like this. Ever.

Because he'd never been had like this. Ever. All the way. And it wasn't just sex, it was everything. Every single fucking thing about her.

She closed her eyes, breaking the contact.

"Look at me," he growled.

"Ty—"

He stopped moving. "Look at me."

Her eyes when they opened were furious. She knew what he was doing and it was cheap, but he didn't care. He'd use whatever means necessary to make himself important to her. To tie them together even if only for a few minutes.

He cupped her cheek, his fingers pulling at the fine hair at her temple, and the words, the words he knew he shouldn't say, that were so new he had no business thinking about saying them, rose to his lips, and as if she knew—and hell, if she felt half as connected to him as he did to her, she totally knew—she closed her eyes and turned her head, burying her face against her arm.

"Just . . . fuck me, Ty," she breathed.

Right. Not love. Not even close.

So he did what she asked, because he was such a simple tool, helpless against her complexity.

Chapter 21

Shelby carefully pulled her pants on. She glanced around the shadows for her underwear but couldn't find it. Tomorrow morning she'd come in and get it before the Saturday classes.

Then she remembered she'd cancelled the classes for the week.

Then the rest of it, like an avalanche, settled back down around her.

She hadn't slept more than four hours a night all week.

Mom was confused. Angry.

Every candidate she'd interviewed had seemed terrible. And she didn't know if their righteousness was real or a product of her guilt. The woman today, Melody— she'd seemed okay, but Shelby was beginning to doubt her own judgment. Was she the right woman by merit or because Shelby was at the end of her rope?

She swallowed the small moan in the back of her throat and put her face in her hands.

"Shelby?" Ty asked, from where he sat on the carpet. "What can I do?"

"You just did it." She tried to make it a joke, but it wasn't funny.

"Your mom?"

"We're coping." That was all she could say, a bland half-truth that didn't come close to the ugly reality. *We are falling to pieces, more and more every day.*

"Is there . . . is there anyone else who can help you? Sisters, brother, aunts, uncles?"

"It's just us. Just Mom and me."

"A nursing home?"

Her ponytail had come loose, and when she spun her head to look at him, she was glaring at him through long strands of hair. But he got the point and lifted his hands as if she'd pulled a gun on him.

"All right," he murmured. "No nursing homes."

She couldn't imagine this house without her mother. Couldn't imagine being able to breathe in it if she weren't there.

"Where's your dad?" he asked.

The silence was so thick and so heavy she could hold it in her hands, watch it drip onto the floor. He'd fucked the anger out of her, but now she was left with nothing. And half the time it was the anger that kept her moving.

And that man, her father, seemed more and more like the poison at the root of her life. Nothing she ever did was untouched by him.

"He died. My first year of college. That's who she thought you were the other night. When she told you to leave." He sat on the floor, on the rug in nearly pristine condition rolled up and left on her front porch like a child at an orphanage.

Suddenly, she thought that of all the things that had washed up here on her property, Ty was somehow the most amazing. The most surprising. He came as one thing and had turned into another. Actually, he'd turned into a dozen other kinds of things. He kept multiplying when she wasn't looking, growing more important. More useful. More endlessly . . . necessary.

"Was she talking about you?" he asked, quietly. "The girl he didn't deserve."

"I'd imagine she was. Though he really didn't deserve either of us."

His silence was a very specific question, a very clear demand for more, and she knew in her heart she should stand up and go, put an end to this thing building between them because she would never be able to be what he needed, but . . . she couldn't.

Her inner stores of strength and wherewithal had been used up this week and she was beyond empty. But still she tried, because being alone was so much easier than being with someone else. She pulled her legs together as if to stand up, but that was as far as she got.

She opened her mouth to tell him he should go, to tell him actually to leave, but instead she told him everything else. As if the story had just been waiting for a weak moment to get out.

"In college I took this psych class and when we got to the part about narcissism, it was like my head exploded. That was my father. Right there in the textbook. On the page. And not just a little bit. My dad was a narcissist with a god complex. He didn't see anything that wasn't a reflection of him. He was a preacher of this bullshit faith he cooked up, opened a church down along the south highway, a tent really. And he got every alcoholic, every addict, every wife-beating husband who wanted to believe he could change, he could be saved, and my father just . . . he just lied to them. He told them what they wanted to hear and they ate it up. They ate it up until they got drunk again. Or high again. Or beat their wives and kids again and then they'd come back to Dad, hat in hand, tears in their eyes, and beg forgiveness and Dad would give it to them. He'd absolve them of their sins and take their money."

"How did he and your mom meet?" Ty asked.

"He sought her out. She was older, awkward, I think, around men." She glanced over at Ty ready to joke "like mother, like daughter," but Ty was staring at her so earnestly, soaking up all she had to say, that the joke died on her lips.

That's right, she thought, *he doesn't see me that way.* The reminder was a painful tender sting.

"But she owned this farmhouse and she had a good job at the factory and was really well-respected in town, and he needed someone who would foot the bill for this church and someone who could make it seem legitimate and someone he could fool into thinking he loved her."

"You don't think he loved you?"

"I was seven, standing at the county carnival handing out fliers for one of my dad's revivals, and I saw all these families . . . all these happy families. Dads with kids on their shoulders, moms taking pictures, kids puking up cotton candy after a ride, their moms stroking their heads, and I realized Dad was never going to love me like other kids were loved. That he was different and he'd made me different. He'd messed me up in some way and I hated him. So, I dumped all the fliers in the garbage and just wandered the fair all night. Dad found the fliers, and when we got home he—" She hadn't thought of that night for so long, a horrible bloody thing she'd buried.

Ty made a low sound in his chest as if he could see the memory, the way the belt had smacked between her shoulder blades, over her arms.

"Well . . . it was bad. But because I hated him so much, he lost all power over me. He could hit me, he could force me to pray all night long, he could haul me up in front of his bullshit congregation and make up lies about my sinner's heart—but he couldn't even get close to hurting me. I was so far away, so locked down, he couldn't even get close."

Her nasal passages burned and she wiped her hand under her nose, tucked her knees up to her chest, feeling the sting between her legs from Ty. From them together. "And it felt so good for a while to have all that power."

"I'm sure," Ty said. "I used to dream of having some kind of power over my parents. When they would fight, I used to wish I mattered enough to make them stop. But I never did. No matter how good I was or how bad, it didn't matter. They were locked up in their own hell and I was never a part of it."

"I'm so sorry," she told him. Her measly spirit eased open, grateful for the chance to be kind. To offer him a share of the comfort he offered her. "I'm so sorry you had to go through that. And I'm so glad you had your pop and Nana to show you that there was another way to live. I'm glad you're that person for Casey. You're doing so well with him."

"I wouldn't go that far." She glanced away from the gleam of his smile. "Did your mom do that for you? Show you another way to live?"

"She loved me. Really loved me. And she tried to be a buffer, to teach me how to be useful, that no matter what he said I had tremendous worth. She just never seemed to be able to believe that about herself."

"Did she ever try to leave?"

"I think there was a time when if it hadn't been for me she would have left. But after that night when I was seven . . . she didn't stand a chance."

"What are you talking about?"

Oh, this was her darkest shame. Something she'd never told anyone. Never had the courage to share. "The angrier I got at my father, the more I hated him, the more he turned on my mom. She was like this open nerve for him. Everything he did made her jump and when I wouldn't react to him the way he wanted, he just . . ." She remembered all of it with a knife-sharp clarity—all of the terribleness her father would smear all over Mom, because Shelby was impervious.

"Hit her?"

She shrugged. What were a few slaps, really, com-
pared to the rest of it? "The worst was the way he would
just grind her into dust. Make her feel like nothing.
He'd pile on abuse after abuse, looking me right in the
eye, wanting me to know that this was my fault. I'd
gotten asked to Homecoming by a friend of mine and
Mom and I bought this dress, this beautiful blue se-
quined, ruffled dress, and I knew I was beautiful in it.
And Dad tried to hurt me. He called me horrible names,
said things no father should say to his daughter, but I
just stared at him. Dry-eyed and hateful. And I thought,
'I win!' But then he turned to Mom and told her he was
embarrassed to have his congregation see him married
to such an old woman. A woman who didn't take care
of herself. Who dressed like a man and did a man's job.
He just . . . *crushed* her, right in front of me. And all her
internal light, it just vanished."

In a heartbeat he was beside her, his hands at her
back, and she flinched away from his touch. "Shelby, it
wasn't your fault."

She laughed at him, because what a stupid thing to
say. What a hope-riddled, naive thing to say. "Don't
laugh," he demanded. "Don't brush me off, Shelby. He
was a sick man and your mom—"

"Was a victim, probably before she met him, but it
doesn't change anything, Ty. It doesn't change that I let
it happen, that I grew up knowing what he would do if
I didn't bend, just a little, just enough to keep her safe,
and I still didn't do it. Tell me who was worse. Him?
That sick man, or me?"

Tired of this conversation, the weight on her shoulders shifted enough that she stood. "My dad told me I
was unlovable, that I was cold and unnatural. And that
no one—*no one*—would want me. Not really. And maybe
he was right, or maybe he just made me so scared that

I would never try to test that. Never find someone who would fight through the distance I put around myself. But what he really taught me was that I'm not capable of loving anyone."

"That's not true." He stood up, too, and she stepped away, out of the reach of his heat. His hands. She wanted no part of him touching her. Couldn't bear it. "Look at the Art Barn, and what you're doing for your mom. You can't tell me that's not love."

"If I loved her . . . loved her like you're supposed to love someone, I would have stopped letting my father abuse her. I would have stopped creating reasons for him to hurt her. I would have found one way to get us out of this house instead of finding a thousand ways to infuriate him."

"You were a kid—"

"You're only seeing what you want to see, Ty." Braving the warmth of him, the ruining pleasure of his touch, she stepped right up to him, close enough that his beautiful face was all she saw and her face was all he saw. "I will still fuck you, Ty. You and only you. And I'll help you forget the things you want to forget as long as you keep doing the same for me, but I'm warning you, don't love me," she told him. "Because I will never love you back."

She left him there, in the gloom of her Art Barn, where his touch more times than she could count now had calibrated her, made her able to live in her own skin again. In this world that she'd made.

She left him there alone, because in the end, that was better for him than being with her.

"Bullshit."

She dropped the door handle and turned. "What?"

Slowly, he straightened his clothes, shaking out his pants before buttoning them up, strapping on his belt. "I call bullshit."

Was this a joke? His attempt at being funny?

"Everything you just told me, it's awful. Honest to God, Shelby, if your father was alive I'd find him and—" He stopped, but there was no question what he'd do. The thwarted violence rolled off of him and it made her both nervous and delighted.

The man was long dead, the wounds he'd inflicted scabbed over, but never had anyone sought justice for what her father had done.

It's because you never told anyone. Those well-meaning teachers, the social workers and friends' parents. You never let anyone in. She knew that was true, but there was more to Ty's anger, more to his coiled muscles and hard jaw, and she didn't want to fully address it.

He's falling for you, a voice whispered in her head. A young-and-terrified-and-hopeful-all-at-once voice that almost never had the nerve to speak up.

But she shut that voice out, because if it was true, if he was really falling for her, she would have to end it. No more anger sex in the barn, no more recalibrating touches, no more of the way he watched her—seeing something in her that wasn't there, but seemed like it would be nice if it were.

"But it's still bullshit."

"That's not funny, Ty."

"I know. After my pop died, I ran for years. Picked up and moved every single time things got hard. Or boring. I bailed on everyone and everything for almost seven years. I thought that's who I was, and despite everything my grandparents showed me I decided to live the way my parents did. Rootless, no ties, not needing anyone and not letting anyone need me. And then Nana got sick and Casey showed up—" He cleared his throat, his emotions sitting so close to the surface of his face she could see them. She clasped her fingers together so she didn't touch him. So she didn't reach out and try to ease some of his pain. It was exhausting feeling so much for this man. The sympathy and the grief and the affection and the anger—she was not made to hold so much. She was brittle and small; she did not expand.

She only broke.

"I can't believe I'm having this conversation with two people twice in the same week, but you can make a choice now, Shelby. You're not that girl anymore. You've locked yourself up in that house thinking you're repaying a debt you owe your mom, but you don't have to live in suspended animation."

"I haven't locked myself up."

He shot her a cut-the-crap look.

"It's not that easy," she said, knowing he was right but so was she, and nothing was as simple as just making a choice.

"I know. It's really fucking hard. But my son walked across state lines to go looking for a new life, a new way of being. He shed all the garbage Vanessa piled on him and tried to get something better. You can do the same thing."

She couldn't speak. Couldn't speak for all her shocked outrage that he would try to marginalize this.

Ty glanced over his shoulder at the couches, as if what they'd done there were still visible. Their bodies, see-through and ghostly, still locked together. "I want something better, too. I deserve something better."

When he looked back at her, she took a step away, nearly put a hand to her throat. The intensity and grief on his face, the resolve directed toward her, was something she'd never seen from him. Never seen from anyone.

"I'm no one's dirty secret. And I won't be yours anymore."

"You're not a dirty secret." She was lying, they both knew it, and his hands scraped his hair from his face, tucking it behind his ears. She couldn't look at those hands without wanting them on her. Without remembering and imagining and wanting.

But that was all she could give him. And she wanted it to be private. Secret. Not because she was ashamed of him, or thought less of him, but because her entire life she had kept the things she wanted very small and very secret—so her father could not touch them.

Hot shame flooded her.

"Then let me take you out to dinner."

"When?" She laughed, because her schedule was tied to this house and everything going on inside of it and there hadn't been time to even shower lately.

"Tomorrow. Next week. Whenever you can do it."

The words weren't even completely out of his mouth and she was shaking her head, denying him. Denying the idea.

"You've got time to have sex with me in the Art Barn, but not to have dinner?"

She was frozen in silence.

"I know you've got a lot on your plate, Shelby. And I'm not going to push, but I want to help. More than fucking you until you can live in your skin again. I want more. And I'm willing to wait, to be here when you're ready."

I'll never be ready, she thought. *I will never be able to give you what you want. I am not made for that.*

If she said that, he wouldn't hear her, would try to find some way to change the way she saw herself, as if perception were the only problem.

"Ty, I'm a mess. My life is a mess, this . . . you can't want any part of this."

"Your life is a mess?" He sat back. "Have we met? I'm Ty, I just found out I had an eleven-year-old son five months ago."

She didn't laugh. If she laughed she was afraid she

would cry. Ty stepped closer, a sweet smile on his face. "I like your mess, Shelby. I like *you*. You've helped me so much, and I just want to return the favor. But with my clothes on." He ducked his head to look into her eyes and she looked right back, forced herself to meet those smiling blue depths.

"You want something I don't have to give," she told him, her voice burning through her chest.

"I think you do."

"Why?"

"Faith, baby," he breathed over her lips. "I have faith."

He touched her cheek as he walked by, a glancing touch more suggestion than reality. "I have to get back to Casey," he said. "You have my number. The offer for dinner stands—any day, any time." And then he was gone.

And the barn was cold and empty. A giant shell she rattled around in.

He'd been trying to give her hope, and she appreciated that, but all he'd done was prove her point.

If this was about faith, then it was over before it even started.

Faith had been beaten out of her years ago.

Chapter 22

It took nearly two weeks for Ty's hope to be extinguished. Two weeks of really believing that Shelby was going to call. That underneath the fear and the guilt she was capable of seeing what was right in front of her.

Namely him, with his heart in his hand.

But after two weeks without word, two weeks without seeing her at church, two weeks of unreturned texts and messages, even he was able to see the writing on the wall.

He'd taken a gamble and lost.

And it fucking hurt.

And he was pissed.

And sad. Sad for her that she was so locked down behind the walls she'd created as a kid.

And sad for himself that she didn't think he was worth breaking down those walls.

All day, every day he walked around as if there were something lodged in his chest that he couldn't get rid of. He worked hard, tearing out the ceiling in the kitchen at the old mansion in the center of town called The Big House, and then he went to town on the floor with a sledgehammer, working until sweat soaked through his shirt and jeans.

He tried distraction, but Casey didn't want to go fishing after school; instead he wanted to hang out with the friends he'd made at school and at the Art Barn.

Ty was glad down to his bones that Casey had found some friends, but the empty house made his loneliness worse.

Thank God for Otto Turner and his shed full of bikes. Or as Ty was calling it, Otto Turner's Shed of Wonder.

He'd been going there every day after work and picking up a few more parts. A few more bikes.

Otto had a serious thing for old BMW bikes. And there was a nearly intact R52. A 1921 Victoria that used the BMW engine—that's the one Otto wanted refurbished, which would be the oldest bike Ty had ever rebuilt and a total pleasure to work on.

There was a military 16h Norton. A few Hondas in pieces. An old Ducati café racer that nearly made him weep. A sweet little SL70 that with a little work could be auctioned off at that Okra Festival thing that Sean had been talking about the other day. Maybe he could donate the money to the elementary school and they could get an art therapist on staff or something.

Ty had left most of the intact bikes at Otto's, instead moving some of the parts Otto had collected over the years. Including some rare BMW clutches that Ty had told Otto he would sell on his behalf.

In the back of that shed there were also a few bicycles—including an older Trek mountain bike Ty thought would fit Casey. Ty could clean it up for his birthday, with new tires. New paint. Casey would love it.

But not even this was enough to cheer him up.

Friday after school, Casey had gone with Ty to the Turners' house to pick up a load, but Ty had been so crabby that as soon as he rolled to a stop in their driveway the kid was gone. Ty couldn't blame him.

He didn't even want to hang out with himself.

His silent phone felt like a lead weight in his pocket and he stupidly kept checking, as if he'd missed the bing of a message coming in. The house across the street was both too close and impossibly far away. And he couldn't stop staring at it, hoping to catch a glimpse of Shelby coming and going from her car or the Art Barn, which was totally making him feel like a stalker.

I'm going to have to move, he thought, *just so I can get on with my damn life.*

Once all the parts were inside the garage, he fought the urge to take a hammer to both his phone and his own head and decided instead to get to work selling the clutches.

Inside he looked around for his laptop so he could email Tom Kavanaugh, who would buy some of the parts. But again, the laptop wasn't in the living room. Or the kitchen. Or the non-office office.

"Casey!" he bellowed. "Where is the damn laptop?"

He headed upstairs to Casey's room, which was empty, and the usually tidy desk was covered in a science project he was working on for school. Ty, still looking for his computer, dug through the papers and the papier-mâché planets that were supposed to turn into a solar system.

"Casey!" He opened the top drawer of the dresser, but there were only pens and papers and a broken iPod.

He opened the second and third; still no computer.

The last drawer was heavy. He yanked it out too hard and the drawer fell out on the floor.

"Ty!" Casey cried, coming into the doorway. "Don't open that!"

But it was too late. The drawer was open and Ty was looking down at . . . what, he wasn't sure.

Junk. Well, not all of it. There was a pack of cigarettes. A magazine with a mailing label from the doctor's office where Ty got Casey's school physical done. A coffee mug from Cora's. A bunch of . . . art stuff. A ton of art stuff, really. A crystal from Shelby's chandelier, a clay figurine. One of the tissue-paper flowers from the flower wall in the Art Barn. A shitload of art supplies. Little stuffed animals, batteries still in packages. Candy wrappers. A handful of pens that said "Welcome to Bishop."

"What is this stuff?"

"Nothing. Junk."

Casey rushed in as if to grab the stuff but Ty picked up a crystal tumbler; *The Peabody* was etched on the bottom of it, and Casey stopped in his tracks.

"This isn't junk." He picked up a ball cap that said *The Pour House* on it.

As much as he didn't want to believe the story this stuff was telling him, he couldn't ignore it when it stared him right in the face.

His skin buzzed with some strange version of panic. *This can't be happening. It can't.*

Where did you get this? was a useless question.

"Are you stealing this stuff?"

Casey stood in the doorway, breathing hard. Every muscle coiled to bolt. His silence more than enough answer.

"Why?"

Casey shrugged and Ty felt his temper, restrained by shock, flare.

"Really, you're just going to stand there and shrug?" he demanded, pulling out the stuff from the Art Barn and dumping it on the floor. It was a giant pile. He picked the stupid flower up in his hands and stepped toward Casey.

"Why would you steal from Ms. Monroe?" Ty demanded.

"I don't know."

"That's bullshit, Casey!" Ty yelled, and Casey flinched backward in the doorway. His arm lifted to block the punch he must have thought Ty was going to throw.

Oh. Oh God. Ty reared back, tripped over the drawer, and fell back against the desk.

Slowly, Casey lowered his arm, but he didn't look at Ty. Their breathing sawed through the silence of the room.

"Sit down," Ty said.

Casey shook his head and irritation spiked through Ty hard, making him clench his jaw against a thousand ill-advised words.

Handle this like Pop, he thought. *Not like your ass-hole father.*

"I swear to God, I'm not going to hit you, buddy—"

"Don't call me buddy!" Casey yelled, red-faced and small, from nearly behind the door.

Ty blinked, stunned. "What?"

"I hate it when you call me buddy. All the cops and the social workers and foster parents, they called me buddy because they couldn't remember my name. You should know my name."

Tears were flooding Casey's eyes and Ty was flat-footed and empty with shock. Too much was happening and he couldn't keep up.

"I do. Of course I know your name. I . . . I didn't know it bothered you. If I'd known, I never would have said it. Why didn't you tell me?"

Casey shook his head and a heavy damp silence settled in the room, extinguishing Ty's temper. *It's only been five months,* he reminded himself.

"We have to talk about this drawer, Casey," he said.

"It's nothing. Junk I found." Everything about his son was boarded up hard against him and Ty could not for the life of him see his way in. Between Shelby and now Casey, he'd never felt more alone. More ill-equipped.

Ty closed his eyes for a moment. He sat down on the edge of the desk, unsure if he was ever going to get back up again.

How do I get this kid to let me in? Before he gets thrown in jail. Or expelled from school.

"It makes it better," Casey whispered.

Ty lifted his head. Opened his eyes. "Makes what better?"

"When things are bad." Casey shook his head, watching Ty from the corner of his eyes like a wary animal. "Can we just forget it? I'll take all the stuff back and apologize but can we just forget it? I haven't taken anything for a long time."

"No. No, Casey, I'm not going to forget it. I'm not supposed to." When Ty stepped forward, Casey stepped back. So Ty sat down on the edge of the bed, making sure he kept that space Casey liked around himself.

He'd sort of thought they'd gotten their groove. Things weren't perfect, but they were better, and finding this pile of stolen junk in his kid's room was sort of like opening up a floor and finding all the support beams had been destroyed by rot. He wasn't angry anymore but he was worried. And impossibly sad.

Casey stood still in the doorway, staring at that spot three feet in front of him.

Ah, fuck it. Ty stood, got right in that spot, and forced his son to look at him. He didn't touch him, but by standing there, he forced Casey to look him right in the eye.

Casey looked up at him, as if surprised to see him.

That's right, Casey, no more running.

"Okay, listen. You've got a meeting with that art therapist that Shelby recommended. It's a month away and you can tell me now and we can talk about it. Or you can tell her. But I really wish you'd tell me. I thought we were doing better. I thought . . . I don't know, Casey, I thought you were happier."

"That's why I take the stuff," Casey said. "Because I was happy and it felt so weird at first and taking things made it feel better. Normal. You know?"

You know? God. No. I don't know. How am I supposed to know that?

But it started to make sense. What kind of practice did Casey have for being happy? What kind of framework to understand it? To understand that it wasn't going to go away.

His normal was being worried and scared, and stealing stuff probably made him feel that way.

"Yeah," he breathed. "I guess I do know. How long since you've stolen anything?"

"The first day of being suspended."

"That's not that long ago."

Casey shrugged.

"Why'd you stop?"

"I don't know," Casey said to Ty's knees. "I guess I just got used to being happy."

Oh, Christ would this kid ever stop wrecking him?

"I'm glad you're happy," Ty said. "Really glad."

"Are you?" Casey wrapped his fist in the hem of his shirt. "Happy, I mean?"

Ty blinked. "Of course."

Casey shot him a wholly adult cut-the-crap look.

"Look, Casey, with you. With us—I'm totally happy. I really am. I won't lie. Being a dad so suddenly like that, it was weird at first and I wasn't sure I could do it, but lately . . . lately it's been great." It wasn't a lie. No part of this was a lie and it felt so good to tell him.

"Then why have you been so grumpy? Is it Ms. Monroe?" he asked. "I mean, she's been kind of crabby, too, lately. At school and stuff."

"She's got a lot going on, Casey. Her mom isn't well and she needs someone with her a lot of the time."

"We could help her though," Casey said, and Ty just felt the ground open up under him and he grabbed onto his son for support. His shoulder and then the back of his head and then, though the kid was stiff and awkward, Ty pulled him into his arms. Held him as tight as he could.

"You're such a good kid, Casey," Ty whispered into his red hair. "I'm so proud to be your dad."

Casey let Ty hug him. It wasn't a reciprocal thing at all and after Ty realized that his son wasn't going to hug him back or even relax into it, he let him go. It was better than that first hug, months ago, but they had some work to do.

"Now," Ty said, forcing himself to be cheery. Forcing himself not to cry for the bittersweet pain of love and parenthood. "What are we going to do about this stuff?"

"Forget about it?" Casey asked hopefully.

"Fat chance."

He and Casey gathered up the stolen things. They threw away the junk, separated the stuff that needed to be returned, and got out in the truck to return the stolen items to the various businesses and people Casey had stolen them from.

"This is going to be terrible," Casey said.

"Yep," Ty agreed, pulling to a stop in front of Cora's.

"Do I really—"

"Yep."

Casey sighed and popped open the door, and Ty couldn't hold it in anymore. "I love you."

Casey didn't say anything. He just wrapped his hands around the plastic handles of the bag full of Cora's dishware and started to hop out of the truck.

Did you hear me? Ty wanted to ask, feeling like somehow saying those words had cleared out part of him. Created a hole that needed if not filling, then at least acknowledgment. But he knew Casey had heard him.

Maybe saying that had been too fast. Kind of like his big ultimatum to Shelby two weeks ago—he'd ruined everything by rushing in. Forcing things that didn't need to be forced.

And maybe it was unfair to expect more from Casey than what the kid could give.

God, he thought, feeling small. *I suck at this.*

Casey jumped out of the truck and when he turned to shut the door, Ty saw that he was smiling.

Smiling wasn't actually the right word. The kid beamed at super-high wattage. His freckles glowed, his eyes gleamed. He was a diamond polished to a high shine.

I did that, thought Ty, astounded by the transformation. This version of his son without the weight of his past, without fear or doubt, secure for just a few moments that he was safe and he was loved—he was beautiful.

Casey went inside the café and Ty imagined what Shelby would be like without being checked by her past. Shrouded in her fear, encased in her doubt.

How bright she would shine if she would just let herself be loved.

Shelby's house had changed. All the plates with the chips, the rose curtains, the blue carpet with the holes where she'd dropped the candle during Hurricane Katrina when the power had gone out, they were the same.

But the house was different.

Having Melody, the nurse, here every day changed . . . everything.

It wasn't just a weight off her back; it was as if she could lift her head, look around, and breathe for the first time in at least a year.

But all she saw when she looked around was how far she had let herself and her mother slip.

The boxes in the hallways. The living room overrun with photographs and albums. Mom's bedroom was a mess of clothing and shoes and discarded jewelry. Yes, things were in stacks, but she had to walk around the stacks to get to the bathroom. The laundry room. Mom's bed.

Her own room, which she'd kept notoriously tidy since she was a girl, now had stacks of homework and Art Barn projects that would normally be in the barn, but because of the last week with Mom, she'd been doing them in the house.

Saturday morning, as she walked out of the bathroom the hem of her robe caught the edge of one of the stacked boxes, and three boxes and a bag balanced on top fell to the floor, yarn, knitting needles, and pattern books spilling across the blue carpet.

That's it, she thought, and she decided to take the boxes to the Art Barn and maybe start a knitting class in partnership with Ashley's senior citizen programs.

But behind the boxes were more boxes. Inexplicably two of Mom's nightgowns, the hems covered in mud and leaves. Beneath that, old files from the church.

Shelby stepped into the kitchen, where Melody, in her no-nonsense scrubs, was standing at the counter. She had thought this would be awful, having a person in their house. But Melody was so . . . needed. Shelby's gratitude for her presence diminished any awkwardness and when she reached for the coffeepot, she gave the woman a warm smile.

"You getting any sleep?" Melody asked, putting Mom's pills into the pill case on the counter.

"Ah, she finally settled down around two a.m. last night," Shelby said.

"Are you staying up that late every night?"

Shelby took a deep breath, about to lie, but then decided there was no point. "I didn't use to. But with the routine being changed, I've been worried that she might wander."

"Has she?"

"I lock the doors at night."

"You know she can work a lock," Melody said with a smile.

"She doesn't leave the house," Shelby said with confidence that she didn't totally feel. "I'm going to clear out some of the stuff in the hallways."

"I think that's a good idea," Melody said, her features carefully revealing nothing.

"It's pretty bad, isn't it?" Shelby surprised herself by asking, by seeking this woman's opinion.

Melody smiled and shrugged. "I've seen worse."

"I'm not sure I have," she laughed.

It was as if visors had been lifted and the old cupboards, the placemats that had sat on that table nearly every day for most of her life—it all seemed so ridiculous. She'd been caught in the amber of the past by her mother's illness.

"Alzheimer's can swallow a lot," Melody said. "It's hard not to let it swallow you, too."

Oh, God, wasn't that the truth. She felt swallowed. Disturbingly missing from this house. Nothing ruled in this house except the past and Mom's illness.

The barn was where she lived, where she put her heart and her soul. She thought of Ty and the way he'd made her feel in that barn and how she'd liked it. Not just the sex, but the freedom of doing what she wanted, of saying what she wanted.

Being who she was.

She was still keeping the secret of herself from her father, from a man who'd been dead for years, and the thought was terrible. But the habit was painfully, deeply ingrained.

Ty's texts and messages still sat on her phone, small reminders not just of the pleasure she'd felt, but of the pain. The pain she'd somehow convinced herself was

her due. She didn't know how to deal with that, its in-
tricacies far beyond her.

But the state of the house she could fix.

She put down her coffee cup and went upstairs to
grab the boxes, bringing them down one by one to sit by
the back door.

Mom stood in the doorway, tearing a Kleenex into
shreds, asking two, three times in a row where Shelby
was putting them, but then Melody stepped in with
Mom's coat and an invitation for a walk.

"Show me where the old church was," Melody said,
and Mom brightened up, switched directions, and Shelby
could have wept with gratitude.

Outside the day was cold but clear. The sky the kind
of blue that seared her eyes, and she had to squint
against the sun. She took two boxes of yarn out to the
barn, setting them in the back with the rest of the stuff
she wasn't entirely sure what to do with. When she
stepped back outside she found Ty and Casey standing
at her back door.

After the initial heat blast the sight of Ty wearing his
jeans and boots and those cuffs around his wrists
caused under her skin, she realized both Ty and Casey
stood there like men who had bad news.

"Hi," she said, brushing her long bangs out of her
eyes. She needed a haircut about a month ago but had
not found the time, and had just managed to stop herself from cutting her own hair.

A woman could live like a hoarder and not realize it,
but she had to have some standards.

"Shelby," Ty said, his lips curving for just a moment
into a smile that sent her heart racing.

And because she could, because things had changed
just enough inside her head and her life, she smiled back
at him. And because she had this beautiful, painful insight into him she saw what her smile did, the way it

rocked him back, the way it pleased him somehow, deep inside.

He cleared his throat, turned his face away, controlled his reaction into something far less personal. Far less interested.

Unfairly, she felt robbed by his reaction, but then she had not talked to him in two weeks. He'd changed the rules between them and she'd rejected him.

"What are you guys doing?" she asked.

Ty gave Casey a little nudge and he stepped forward with a small box. "I'm returning this stuff to you."

Confused, she took the box, held it with one arm, and looked through the strange bits of things in it. She lifted her hand, the crystal from the chandelier she thought she'd lost hanging from her finger. That was weird.

"How did you get all this?" she asked and as the question left her mouth, she somehow knew what he was going to say.

"I stole it from you," he whispered. "I'm really sorry."

"Why?"

Casey glanced back at Ty, who after a moment answered, "It's complicated. But we're dealing with it." Ty gave Casey another bump with his elbow.

"Is there anything I can do for you?" Casey asked, his eyes on his shoes. "To make it up to you. I can mow lawns or . . . I don't know? Work. I'm already doing dishes at Cora's all day on Sunday, so I can't work for you then."

She could see that Ty was expecting her to say no. To say that she was fine. He already had his face schooled into understanding and slightly indifferent lines and the words were actually on her tongue, because for so long, since she was seven years old, she'd been turning aside help. Turning aside interest.

And it had gotten her nowhere.

She was well aware that no one outside of Cathy and

Deena and now Melody, people who understood Mom's illness, had been inside the house in years. And that to the average eye the state of the house was shocking.

But she was done pretending everything was fine.

That she was happy.

That she could do all of this without help.

"I'd love some help," she said. Casey frowned, Ty blinked, and she found herself smiling. Smiling for no good reason, and that felt like the best reason of all.

The house was clean but in shambles; there was no pretending otherwise. Walking into the kitchen and through the hall, Ty saw about twenty different things that needed to be done. Some for aesthetics, some for safety, some just to make Shelby's life easier.

And he wanted to offer his help, but he'd been shot down before. And no matter how . . . different she seemed right now, he found himself unable to trust that the change was toward him and not just the relief of having someone caring for her mother and some help cleaning out the boxes that lined the living room and the stairs leading up to the second floor.

"Wow, Ms. Monroe," Casey said. "You got a lot of stuff."

"Too much, Casey." She pointed to some boxes already stacked by the door. "You can take those to the barn."

Casey grabbed them and headed out the back door, leaving Ty alone with Shelby for the first time in two weeks.

"Ty, you don't have to help me with this stuff—"

"You need help, don't you?"

"But—" *We broke up. Or whatever.*

"Just show me what needs doing, Shelby."

Oh, God, wasn't that just the sterling silver truth of

this man. He would help her even after she'd rejected him. His friend Jimmy had it all wrong: it was Ty who was so much better than she, not the other way around.

"You can follow me," Shelby said, taking the creaking carpeted steps up to the second floor. A week ago, two, Ty wouldn't have even pretended not to stare at her ass. Now he watched the progress of his boots over the faded flowers of the rug.

"Where's your mom?" he asked into the prickly silence between them.

"Melody has her out for a walk. Watching me get rid of the boxes was making her anxious." Ty came up behind her and she glanced at him over her shoulder, her eyes bright. Her cheeks flushed.

Ty curled his hands into fists and looked everywhere but at her.

It was floor-to-ceiling boxes along one side of the hallway. Through one bedroom door he could see a bed stacked high with clothes. Shoes lined up along the side of the bed.

"It's something, isn't it?" she asked, and he looked down to find her watching him, that lip tucked up under her tooth. "I can't believe I let it get this bad."

"Then let's get this stuff out of here," he said.

She began to sort through the boxes, making two piles.

"Why was Casey stealing?" she asked.

"I'm not totally sure." He showed her a box of yarn and she pointed toward the bigger pile. "But I think it's because he didn't know how to be happy. He felt like he had to ruin it a little so he could trust it."

Shelby's implacable, rock-solid gaze made his heart stop, but he felt every inch between them as if it were a mile. He wished she would touch him. Hug him. He could really use a hug. It had been kind of a big few days. "That's kind of amazing."

"Yeah. He says he hasn't taken anything for a while now because he's gotten used to being happy. We have an appointment in a month with that therapist you recommended."

"That's great!"

He nodded, trying not to smile too hard or too much at her, trying desperately to seem casual, but he sucked at it. Because he wanted to talk to her, tell her that Casey had let himself be hugged. That Ty had told the boy he loved him and Casey hadn't sneered or run. That the two of them were slowly figuring it out, one giant mistake at a time.

"It is. I think he has a lot to talk about and maybe he's finally in a place where he can actually talk."

"How about you?" she asked.

"I set up an appointment for myself. I figure I can use all the help I can get." She was smiling at him like she was proud, like he was dear to her, and he couldn't stand it.

This woman didn't answer your calls, your texts for two weeks. She made it very clear she wanted nothing more from you than sex.

The self-inflicted reminder was bitter, and suddenly he had to get out of there. "You want me to take these out to the barn?" he asked, pointing to one of the piles she'd sorted.

She stacked three superlight boxes filled with yarn and handed them to him. He made sure his hands were nowhere near hers as he took them, but for a moment she didn't let go.

Her head was bowed as if she were reading the label, but she still didn't let him have the boxes.

"Why?" she whispered.

"Why what?"

"Why do you want more? What have I shown you that you want more of?" Her gaze flickered to his and then away. But in the moment he saw the beginning. The start of her knocking down the walls to let him in.

"Everything," he said simply. "I want more of everything."

"The sex—"

"Of course. But you mean more to me than the sex we've had, Shelby. I want more of your fierce heart and your secret smiles. Your loyalty and decency. I want to make you laugh until you hoot. I want to help you shoulder some of the load you've got because you've helped shoulder some of mine. I want to find out what you think and how you feel. I want to put you on the back of my bike and go for a ride. Lie down in a bed with you. I want to argue about what to watch on TV and . . . I want everything. Everything you have to give to a person, I want to be the man who gets it."

"I don't know how."

"Me neither."

She shot him a skeptical look and he smiled, happy just to have her eyes on him. Happy just to have her attention. "Everything with you is brand new," he said.

"I'm probably going to be terrible at it. I will be. I know it. I can be . . . I can be so cold. So awful."

"I don't think you're awful."

"You will. You will, trust me. And you'll regret ever wanting more because I have no idea how to give anyone more."

She thought her father had made her angry, and he had, but under it all she was scared. Scared that he was right. And that she would be alone.

"We'll go slow," he told her. "For both of us."

"Slow? We haven't done anything slow."

"We'll start with dinner. Sunday night, my house. I'll cook."

"You can cook?"

"See all the things we don't know about each other?"

She smiled at his joke and he felt the engine of his heart kick over. This was happening. It was really happening.

"What about Casey?"

"My son and I have kept enough secrets from each other, Shelby. If you and I are a thing, he's got to know about it. If we're in, we're all in."

She let go of the box only to cup his face in her hands. She pressed her lips to his, softly. Sweetly. She tasted of coffee and toothpaste, and if faith had a flavor, it was there, too.

Chapter 23

It was difficult making dinner while getting heckled by the peanut gallery. But it was fun. And kept his mind off the butterflies in his stomach. Never in his life had he had butterflies. He was a man, for crying out loud. Men didn't get butterflies.

But the butterflies were relentless. So were the sweaty palms.

"Who eats salad?" Casey asked, tearing lettuce leaves and putting them in a bowl.

"Girls do." Ty seasoned the last of the steaks and set the plate aside before opening up the bag of shrimp he had in the sink.

"Why do you make all this food for Ms. Monroe, but not for us?"

Ty didn't have time to get into the things men do for women, making Caesar salad being about the least of them. "You're eating it tonight, aren't you?"

"I'm not eating the salad, that's for sure."

"Sure you are. You need some vegetables in your life." The fact that salad was such a rare thing in their house and Casey was making such a stink about it would indicate he should have more than just a passing glance at a carrot.

"Don't be lame."

"Even if I tried, I couldn't be lame."

Casey began to list all the ways Ty was lame when the doorbell gonged through the house.

"Ohhhhh," Casey said, grinning at Ty. "It's your girl-friend."

Ty snapped the dishtowel over his shoulder at his son and quickly washed his hands before racing down the hallway to beat him to the door. He gave Casey a shove and he detoured off into the living room and the TV. So much for his help with dinner.

But when he opened the door, it wasn't Shelby. It was Officer Jenkins.

Crap, he thought. The day was going so well, too.

"Hello," Ty said, not sounding at all nice. "What's going on?"

"Well, the Cornells around the block were broken into again last night."

Ty leaned against the door. "Anyone hurt?"

"No. But things have escalated. Their kitchen was torn apart."

"Stuff was stolen?"

"Their keys. The keys to their house, the car. Her mom's house across town. Darryl works as a janitor at the high school and the keys to the school are missing."

"Shit, that's no good."

"Right. So, I'm here to see if you know anything. Have you heard anything in the last few days?"

"No. We've been keeping our doors locked."

"What about your son?"

Ty stood up from the doorway. "What about him?"

"This is a small town, Mr. Svenson. And this didn't start happening until you showed up."

Fuck you, you small-minded dick.

"Ty?"

Ty turned to find Casey standing in the hallway. They'd gotten the kid a haircut after church and that flop of red hair no longer fell over his face. And his boy was revealed. All the fragile tenderness of his youth on display. Ty wondered, when in the last few weeks had all the boy's hard edges been worn down? How did he miss seeing that?

"What's going on?" Casey asked.

"There have been some break-ins in this area," Jenkins said, leaning slightly to see around Ty's shoulder. "And last night some things were stolen. I just wanted to ask if you know anything about that."

"I don't know anything about that," Casey said with a shrug, but he was watching Ty and that bottom drawer full of stuff was right there between them.

Ty found himself trying to remember if he'd seen keys in that drawer.

But the second that thought took root, he pulled it out. His son said he hadn't stolen anything in weeks. Ty had to believe him. If they were going to stand a chance, Ty just had to trust his kid right now.

"Casey says he doesn't know anything," Ty said, filling the door frame so Jenkins couldn't ask Casey any more questions. "And I don't either."

Jenkins looked at him hard, but Ty looked at him right back. "If you want to ask us more questions, you're going to have to have a reason." And a warrant.

"Call me if you hear anything," Jenkins said, handing Ty a card. Ty slipped it in his back pocket.

"I will."

Ty shut the door, watching Jenkins through the fragile cream lace of the curtain he didn't pick out, would never have picked out in this house that felt like a stranger's.

"You believe me?" Casey asked, and Ty nodded.

And then he tore down the curtain. The sound of the threads tearing off the small curtain rod a satisfying answer to the itching sense of unease crawling over his body.

"What are you doing?" Casey breathed.

"We're not old women," he said. "We don't need lace curtains in our home."

"Does that mean I can get rid of the ones in the kitchen?"

"Yep." The boy's face lit up and he raced down the hallway.

Please, he thought, watching him go and biting his tongue. *Please don't know anything about those keys. Please don't prove my faith wrong.*

There was a quiet knock on the door and he turned to see Shelby there, unobstructed by lace. She lifted her hand in a wave—more shy than he'd ever seen her.

She was also wearing lipstick.

His heart chugged up into his throat and he opened the door with a smile on his face. Keys, break-ins, Officer Jenkins all forgotten.

"Hi," she said, handing him a pie box. Her nerves practically rolled off of her. "I didn't make that."

He laughed. "That's okay." He pulled her in for a kiss. She didn't resist but she didn't fall into him, either.

"I'm nervous," she whispered against his lips.

"I couldn't tell."

Her laughter was a sweet-smelling gust over his lips.

"Ms. Monroe!" Shelby jumped back, but Ty turned more slowly, keeping his hand on Shelby's back.

"Hi, Casey," she said.

"We're tearing down the curtains!" Casey held up the lace curtains from the kitchen. "Wanna help?"

"Go ahead," Ty said. "I need to finish dinner."

"Go ahead and vandalize your house?"

"It's our home, isn't it?" He felt like an explorer planting a flag in foreign soil. He didn't know what was going to come, what would be revealed, but he was here and he was going to stay.

"I guess so," she said with that bright, revealing smile. As she walked past he patted her butt, because he figured maybe he could. Because he wanted to. Because this moment really could only be improved upon by touching this special woman's butt as she walked by.

But then she glanced back and winked at him and then . . . then his life was complete.

Crap. Like double crap. Like all the crap in the whole world.

Casey walked the length of the field, pushing down the tall grasses as he went. He'd had this kind of half-baked idea that he'd track Mrs. Monroe, that he'd find her footsteps from when she'd crossed the field before and just follow her.

But it was too dark and he couldn't find any footprints, so he just kept walking back and forth across the field behind his house hoping he would miraculously run into her.

He hadn't seen her out here for the last few nights, so he wasn't sure when she stole those keys Officer Jenkins had been talking about.

But there was no doubt that it was her.

And he'd been about to tell Ty about it, but things were so cool between them now. Even after he found that drawer full of stuff Casey had stolen. And tonight, with Shelby . . . she told him he could call her Shelby when they weren't at school, and that was awesome. The whole night was freaking awesome.

Mom hadn't called again.

School was going better.

Scott was a pretty cool guy when he wasn't with John.

And Ty said that he loved him.

He shook his head, because the thought did weird things to him. Made his head buzz. Mom always said she loved Casey, but Casey wasn't stupid. What his mom felt for him wasn't love. But Ty . . . that was different.

Yep, life was pretty good.

Except Shelby's mom was breaking into houses stealing keys and he was the only one who knew about it and he'd made the old lady a promise, and now, if he told someone he wasn't sure if she would get in trouble.

Kind of seemed like she had enough bad stuff going on. Did they send crazy old ladies to jail?

So Casey's plan was to catch Mrs. Monroe and tell her she couldn't do this stuff anymore. That the cops were on to her. That if she did it again he was going to have to tell his dad.

He liked the sound of all of that. It sounded very adult.

There was rustling behind him and Casey whirled toward the sound.

"Mrs. Monroe!"

But it wasn't Mrs. Monroe. It was Scuzz, the dog. Looking skinnier than ever.

"Hey!" Casey whispered. The last few weeks he'd kind of forgotten about Scuzz, but when he came out here tonight, he'd grabbed some of the leftover dinner steak Ty had sliced up all fancy and shoved it in his pocket.

Casey threw the dog a strip of steak and Scuzz snapped it out of the air with his long white teeth.

"We still haven't figured out your name yet, have we?" Casey asked. "George?"

Scuzz stepped closer and Ty tossed him another piece of steak.

"Charlie? Rex?" Scuzz kept coming closer, which was weird. Casey threw him another piece of meat. "Buddy?"

His ears perked up at that and the dog cocked its head.

"Buddy?" Casey asked.

The dog whined.

"You've got to be kidding me. Really? Can I just keep calling you Scuzz? It's a much better name."

Scuzz lowered his muzzle to the ground and started to growl, deep and low in his throat.

All the hair on the back of Casey's neck went up. In school the other day they'd talked about the fight-or-flight instinct, and Casey was now experiencing some serious flight instinct. He suddenly remembered all the times a grown-up had told him not to get too close to these dogs. That they were vicious.

"Hey. Don't get mad. I've got lots of steak." Casey pulled all the steak out of his pocket and threw it at the dog, while at the same time slowly backing up.

But Scuzz ignored the meat, his eyes fixed over Casey's shoulders.

Dimly, he heard bells. Not like the bell choir at church, but little tinkling Christmas bells.

I'm totally losing my mind.

But the bells were getting louder and coming from behind him. He turned in time to see Mrs. Monroe coming through the tall weeds in her nightgown and rain galoshes but with a belt of bells around her waist.

"Mrs. Monroe, what are you doing with those bells?" he asked, but she wasn't watching him. She was looking at Scuzz. And Scuzz barked.

"Hey," Casey said. "You're kind of freaking Scuzz out, so maybe—"

But then she grabbed him, yanked him by the arm, and for such an old lady she was strong and he fell, shoulder first, onto the rocky ground and pain exploded across the shoulder he'd landed on. Hot sweat burned across his forehead and then cold, and the whole world swam for a second.

When he got his breath back, he rolled over and sat up. His arm hung at a weird angle off his body and he gagged at the sight of it, limp and gross.

Scuzz growled again and slowly advanced on Mrs. Monroe, who was standing very still.

Oh God. Oh God this was bad. He reached for some of the steak he'd thrown, wincing as the pain blasted in his shoulder. The edges of his vision went black for a second but he shook it off, picking up the dirty meat with leaves and yuck on it and tossing it at the dog, but it didn't notice.

"Hey!" he yelled. "Over here, Scuzz!"

"Casey! Don't!" she cried. But when she looked over at him, it was as if Scuzz was waiting for just that moment and he jumped on her, knocking her into the bushes.

Heart pounding in his throat, Casey scrambled to his feet and ran over.

Scuzz was standing on her chest, his teeth clamped onto her arm. She was crying and screaming, pushing the dog away, but he stayed on her chest, snarling and snapping as if trying to get to her throat.

Casey yelled and kicked at the dog, but it only worked harder to kill Mrs. Monroe. And she was getting weaker, her screams turning to sobs, her arms barely holding him off.

There was blood everywhere, the arm of her night-gown going totally red.

He spun around in a circle, kicking over the beaten-down grass and weeds looking for a big rock and finally finding one. He picked it up with one hand and threw it as hard as he could. It hit Scuzz in the back, knocking him off Mrs. Monroe. Sobbing, Casey found another and another, throwing pebbles and weeds and anything he could get his hands on until Scuzz yelped and took off running.

He waited a second, breathing hard, lights flashing at the edges of his eyes.

Don't pass out, he told himself and managed to listen. But just barely. *Don't do it.*

Scuzz didn't come back and he crawled on his knees

and one hand, his other arm hanging down from his body like it was broken, though he couldn't feel it anymore. He couldn't feel anything.

Mrs. Monroe lay still in the grass, her bloody arm cradled against her chest. She was staring up at the sky, blinking, her mouth opening and shutting.

"Are you okay?" he asked. "Mrs. Monroe?" He reached out to touch her but didn't know where. Or how, without hurting her.

And then a bubble—red with blood—popped on her lips.

In his dream, Ty was making out with Shelby in the cab of Pop's old truck and they were out by the river where he and Casey had gone fishing that first weekend. And she was warm and moaning in his arms and then she wasn't. And then she was back, but it was a version of her made entirely of static.

"Dad!"

Ty ignored the kid calling for his father and kept kissing Shelby until she wasn't static anymore, until she was sweet and real.

"Dad!"

Christ, he wished that Dad would answer the kid. It was kind of ruining his mood.

"Dad! Help! Please, I need your help!"

Ty snapped himself out of the dream.

I'm a dad.

And then he heard the frantic thump and stomp of someone coming up the stairs.

"Dad!" It was Casey, sobbing and freaking out, and Ty tore from the bed, racing to meet him in the hallway outside his room.

"What?" Ty asked. Panic was a white-out blizzard in his head and he couldn't make sense of what he was seeing. The way Casey was holding his arm, the blood and dirt and tears on his face.

"Help me," Casey sobbed, and the white-out vanished and the world was in crystal focus.

"Where are you bleeding?" He sat his son down on the top step and searched over his body for the wound. One of his shoulders was dislocated, but nothing seemed to have broken the skin.

"It's not me," Casey whimpered, pushing Ty's hands away with his one good arm. "It's Mrs. Monroe—"

"Shelby?"

Casey shook his head. "Her mom. In the field behind the house—she's been bitten by a dog." Casey's face shattered, his body rocking with sobs. "It's so bad, Dad. It's really, really bad."

"Stay right here," he said. "I'm calling an ambulance."

Ty ran down the stairs, grabbed his phone from the charger in the kitchen, shoved his feet into his boots, and was out into the field looking for Shelby's mother and calling an ambulance at the same time.

He found a trail in the tall weeds, and he followed the broken plants forever it seemed.

Finally, he found her.

Still. Quiet. Her white nightgown saturated with blood. Her hands, bloody and raw, clutched over her chest as if praying.

Shelby came running into the hospital wearing slippers and a robe, her face awash with terror. Ty stood up from the plastic seat by the window where he'd been holding his vigil, waiting for her. Waiting for word on Mrs. Monroe. For Casey to wake up after the doctor had set his shoulder.

It had been an hour since he was awakened from that dream. An hour and a lifetime.

"Hey, hey, it's okay, baby." In front of the reception desk he caught Shelby's elbows in his hands, but she shook away from him—on purpose or not, he couldn't tell. She was manic. Shaking so bad it was amazing that she'd been able to drive.

"Where is she?"

"Surgery."

She sagged and he grabbed her arms again, thinking to hold her, to help her into a chair, but she pulled away again, this time clearly on purpose, choosing instead to stand up on her own wobbly legs.

Oh honey, don't do this.

"I told them you were on the way, that you'd be with me. If there are any updates they know where to find you," he said, trying to answer every question as it appeared on her face, in the way she held herself. "Everything that can be done is being done."

"Tell me what happened."

"Your mom was bit by one of the strays. A fractured arm, broken rib, and a punctured lung."

Shelby gasped, her hand at her throat, like there just wasn't enough air. Ty knew the feeling.

"What . . . what was she even doing out there?"

"Apparently . . ." Ty let out a long, slow breath; he was exhausted and scared and running on fumes, and maybe because he'd found out about all of this only an hour ago it still seemed unreal. "Apparently your mom was the one walking into people's houses. She stole some keys the other night."

"No way." Shelby shook her head. "That's ridiculous. Mom doesn't wander."

"Casey saw her."

"Casey?"

"He says he saw her three different times."

"He saw her and didn't say anything?"

Ty nodded. The truth shocking to him, the ramifications of it devastating to all of them. All they could do was try to sort through this. Hopefully together.

"That's a little convenient, isn't it?" she asked and he knew where she was going with this, only because he'd thought the very ugly thought himself. But it didn't change the raw smack of it; her lack of faith in Casey hurt him. "He's been stealing stuff all over town since he's been here, but now he claims it's my mother breaking into people's houses?"

"I know it's hard to believe—"

"It's impossible to believe."

"Then what was your mother doing out in the field tonight?"

"I don't—" She stopped, pressed her shaking fingers to her lips.

"Casey says she had bells on her waist. A belt of bells."

"Melody." Shelby breathed. "Melody must have done that." She turned away, her shoulders painfully rigid under the worn fleece of her robe. He put a hand on her shoulder, felt the ice-cold skin of her neck against his fingers before she shrugged away.

His hope that she would walk into the hospital and fall into his arms and they could survive this night together, leaning on each other, had been the height of foolishness.

She hadn't had time to get used to him walking beside her; her instinct would be to go it alone, and that sucked. For both of them.

"Why didn't he tell anyone?" she asked. "He sees an old woman wandering around in the middle of the night and doesn't say anything?"

"He said he promised her he wouldn't tell. That he always made sure she got home safe—"

"That doesn't make it okay!" she snapped, and he

stepped back. "It's winter, Ty. What if she got lost? What if he wasn't there to get her back to her house? What if she wandered onto the highway? He needed to tell someone!"

"He knows that."

"Does he? Does he really?"

"Listen, my son is terrified and hurt and feels terrible already—heaping more blame on him isn't going to help."

"Someone has to take the blame!" she cried. "Someone—"

She reeled back as if Ty had punched her, and he saw her thought process flicker across her face in shades of guilt and shame. She was the only one to blame.

"Don't, babe. Don't do this to yourself. It was a shitty accident." He reached out to touch her, but she flinched away and he stood there with his arms, never so useless before, at his sides.

"I'm sorry," she breathed. "What I said about Casey—"

"It's okay."

Dry-eyed, she stared right at him. "No. It's not."

"Excuse me? Wyatt Svenson?" A nurse in pink scrubs approached them. "Your son is awake and asking for you."

Ty glanced back at Shelby and that self-contained universe of hers that had seemed so appealing, like a puzzle he couldn't wait to figure out and experience from the inside—he saw the reality of it.

The cold reality of it.

No one got on the inside.

And he could stand here and take the time to melt her, to make her see that she didn't have to shoulder the blame for all of this, but his son was asking for him.

That date of theirs, her faith—it was a product of sunny weather. It was easy to open yourself up to the good times, but opening yourself up to the bad? A totally different story, and she clearly didn't have the guts for that.

"I thought I could break down all your doors," he told her. "I could break your locks and force my way in, but you'll always find more, won't you? Something bad will happen in our lives and I'll be right back on the outside looking for a way in."

Nearly imperceptibly, she nodded.

His heart, under the too bright lights, shattered against the flecked linoleum floor, right at her feet.

"I'm going to go." He jerked his thumb back down the hall toward his son's room.

"That's for the best," she told him.

And they both knew he would be going on without her.

Any illusions that she had been doing all right, that despite her failings, on the average her care for her mother had been good—they were all shattered like the windows at the factory. Watching Ty walk away, leaving her alone with all of those things, big and small, that she'd done wrong, she wanted to melt into the linoleum.

She wanted to just stop.

But instead, after a few moments she followed Ty's footsteps to Casey's room and stood just outside of it, listening to the quiet hum of the nurse's voice. The rough reply of Ty's.

Casey was silent.

Shelby understood that her instincts right now were wrong. That she was living out the programming her father had given her when she was too young to understand. Too young to know that he was sick.

Despite knowing all that, she stood outside Casey's hospital room and knew that this was her fault. The boy in there. Her mother in surgery. Ty's barely contained anger and grief. It was all her fault.

Because for a little bit, she'd been happy.

The nurse stepped out of Casey's room, giving her a quick, understanding smile. It was a marvel, that smile, in all that it managed to convey. Sympathy, a willingness to help, a certain businesslike distance—all of that at the same time.

Shelby wasn't sure she could hold all those feelings in her body—all those opposing forces.

Taking a breath, determined to do at least one thing right, she knocked lightly on the cracked door. Ty turned to look over his shoulder, saw her, and stood up, blocking her view of the bed. The room was dark, the curtains pulled against the windows, the lamp over the bed on the lowest setting.

"Yeah?" he asked, almost as if she were a stranger. As if in the walk from reception to here he'd shed all his knowledge of her like a skin.

That's my fault, too, she thought, gathering up his indifference, his disdain, and adding it to the pile of all that was her due.

"I'd like to talk to him."

Ty stepped closer, dropped his voice.

"Not if you're going to make him feel bad."

She swallowed back the razor wire of emotion scraping her throat. "I won't. I promise."

Ty watched her for a second and then shook his head. "I swear to God, I don't know what to do with you, Shelby."

"I know. But please, let me put his mind to rest that this isn't his fault."

Ty waited a second and she really believed he was going to say no. That was what other parents would have done after the things she'd said. But Ty wasn't like other parents. Wasn't like other people, and he seemed to have this tremendous capacity to understand that second chances were a divine right, so he stepped aside, letting her in.

Casey looked tiny on the bed. A little boat in a sea of white. His red hair a sharp contrast to the white sheets and the paleness of his face.

"Hey," she said, trying to sound as if she weren't simply a bag of broken pieces. "How are you feeling?"

His big blue eyes filled with tears, his chin creased and wobbled.

"Oh Casey," she breathed, and she reached for his arm but it was bandaged and in pain, so she clutched the metal bed railing instead. Its cold reality a terrible substitute for human touch.

"Your mom?"

"She's going to be fine, Casey. Just fine. Don't worry."

"She saved me. Scuzz was going to bite me but she pulled me out of the way."

"Did she?" she breathed, trying to smile. "That's good."

"I'm so sorry. I'm so—"

"Listen to me," she said, leaning forward and using her best firm teacher voice. "It's okay. Everything is going to be okay. You didn't understand what was happening. And there were adults around who should have been taking better care. This is not your fault."

"It feels like it is."

"That's because you are a great kid." Finally, unable to resist the compulsion, she allowed herself to touch him. Funny how after the few weeks with Ty she'd gotten so used to touching. To the quiet stroke of fingers through hair. The press of a palm against another person's palm. She'd thought after that she'd understood incremental relief—but she hadn't.

Now she did, when it was too late. The soft touch of a loved one letting you know you are not alone, no matter how bad it is—that was relief.

So she stroked back Casey's hair, touched his sweet face, and watched some of the strain vanish from around his eyes, the load unburden his thin shoulders.

"Shhh," she whispered, and on impulse she leaned over to kiss his forehead.

His eyelids fluttered shut and she realized that in all the ways she knew children, all the hundreds of hours she'd spent with them, she'd never seen one fall asleep. It was beautiful. That kind of trust was really quite a special thing, and she felt better for having seen it.

Her choice to be a teacher was rooted entirely in the fact that the children passed through her life. They did not stop for long. She could love them and help them, but the relationship was not forever. It was safe.

She realized now what nonsense that was. Another tool to keep herself alone.

She stood up and found Ty standing by the doorway in the shadows left by the bedside lamp. He wore flannel pajama pants and the black Henley he'd worn at their dinner. They'd made out on the couch, deep, long, wet kisses until it had been time for her to go home, and she'd slid her hands under that Henley in an effort to touch as much of him as she could.

I am a hoarder at heart, she thought, *and I should have taken more of you when I had the chance.*

Tears sparkled in his eyes.

That box where she hid all the things she wanted disintegrated at the sight of those tears, and she ran at that open door inside of him that he'd shown her a few days ago, the door she'd been unable to get to with all of her baggage. "I'm so sorry. Please give me . . . give me another chance."

"Another chance at what?"

"Us. You, me, and Casey—" She was dizzy. It felt like

she was floating outside of her body and she reached out to touch him, to ground herself, but he pushed her hand away.

"You're desperate," he whispered. "Scared—"

"Yes. I am. I always have been. Except when I'm with you. When I'm with you it's like I'm the person I'm supposed to be and I want that. I want you, Ty. I want to try. Please let me try."

"Try?" He laughed, but then it turned into a groan as he rubbed his hands over his face. "Try what?"

Try what? She felt panicked, hysterical laughter build in her throat. *Try loving you. Try being loved. Try an honest, healthy family.*

"Try to let you in," she whispered.

Never in her life had she been so naked and aching, covered in the raw honesty of her failures and desires.

"What happens if it doesn't work out?" he asked. "What do I tell my son?"

I don't know, she wanted to scream. *I don't have answers to any of this. You were the one with the answers.*

"Where's your faith?" she whispered.

You destroyed it. He didn't even have to say it—it rolled off his body in choking waves.

Ty looked over her shoulder at his sleeping son. "We've already tried, haven't we? Again and again. I've got to take care of Casey."

Her breath was a moan and he flinched at the sound; the two of them already so broken and battered were only hurting each other more.

Leave, she told herself. *Leave before you make it worse.*

She pressed shaking fingers to her lips and then, because she was stupidly wearing a robe in the hospital, tightened the belt. Tightened the belt until it bit into her flesh through the tee shirt she wore, tightened her belt until the pain brought her back into her body.

"I'm going to go see if there's any word on my mother," she whispered.

"Good idea," he said, and stepped past her to be with his son.

Chapter 24

It was about nine a.m. when people started showing up. At first it was Cora and Sean with fritters and a thermos of coffee. And then it was Casey's friend Scott, from school, and his parents. They left some Percy Jackson books and a few games. Brody came in, his arm around Ashley, who looked green at the gills.

"You didn't have to come," Ty told his boss while Ashley and Casey played a game of war with the deck of cards she'd had in her purse.

"Of course we did," Brody said, squeezing Ty's hand as they shook.

"Have you seen Shelby?" he asked.

"Her mom is out of surgery but the door to her hospital room is closed," Ashley said, sweeping a pile of cards into her stack. "We didn't want to intrude."

Right, Ty thought. He tried not to be bothered by the thought of Shelby locking herself up tight in a room with all of her demons, but he couldn't stop himself.

Mr. Root came with flowers. Mrs. Jordal brought brownies and a book about how to draw superheroes. By two in the afternoon the nurse let them know they could leave after the doctor came by to give Casey one more checkup.

The room was stuffed with flowers and balloons and food. And despite the lingering effects of the painkillers, Casey was buzzing with a sugar rush.

Perhaps it was knowing that Casey was going to be fine and they'd be going home soon while Shelby and her mother were just beginning their stay, but Ty couldn't leave without seeing her. He had watched her with Casey, brushing the hair off his forehead, putting his fear to rest, and he'd realized once again what having a son meant.

I have to protect him. Protect him from all the things that would hurt him.

But that wasn't Shelby.

That was a smokescreen he'd thrown up to protect himself.

Ty gathered up some of the gifts and left Casey watching that actually pretty funny *Annoying Orange* show.

"Can you tell me what room Evie Monroe is in?" he asked.

The reception nurse, the happy recipient of some of Cora's fritters, obliged. "Second floor. Room 210."

His arms full of flowers and magazines and food, balloons trailing behind him, he walked up the flight of stairs to room 210. But when he turned down the hallway, he realized he shouldn't have bothered. Outside the shut door there were piles of food. Flowers. Books. Two thermoses of coffee. A few balloons that said "Get Well Soon" drifted on a draft.

He wondered if Shelby knew they were there. Or if she was just denying herself the gifts because that was what she was good at.

I want to try.

The memory of her face as she'd whispered that, the tears in her eyes, the total nudity with which she'd stood in front of him and begged for another chance—it shook him.

Because his odds weren't good with Shelby. The chances were high she'd crush him in some way and he didn't know how much tolerance he had left for that kind of pain.

But the chances were also high that she would love him. Save him, even. Drag him and Casey out of their

strange orbit of each other and into something closer.
Happier.

A family.

"Oh, Christ," he muttered. It seemed his faith was
not gone. It popped up like a ball held underwater and
then let go.

Maybe, in the end, she wouldn't be able to give him
what he needed. Maybe her try wasn't going to be enough,
but right now, he was going to be the guy that gave her
what she needed.

He sat down in the empty chair beside the rest of the
offerings. He'd wait as long as he could, and all he could
do was hope it was enough.

Mom had come out of the surgery. The surgeon, far too
young to actually have finished med school if you asked
Shelby, said she had come through it just fine. The lung
had been reinflated, the small wound there repaired.

"The real trouble was her arm. We have two screws
in there now, but she's going to need another surgery to
put in plates."

"Plates?" she breathed, because none of this was sink-
ing in. Her head was cloudy and slow. Everything seeped
into the haze and then disappeared.

"It was a compound fracture," he told her slowly.
"The ulna was shattered in two different places. But she
is going to come out of it."

Shelby nodded, Doogie Howser left, and she went
back to stroking the thin, see-through edge of the medical tape that was keeping her mother's IV in.

I'm sorry, she thought with every sweep of her thumb,
over tape and skin and the small hump of a blue-black
vein. *I'm so sorry.* The world faded away past the edge
of that tape and the litany in her head. Hours could
have passed.

"Ms. Monroe?" Shelby turned to find a woman poking her head through the door. She wore glasses and her long brown hair was in curls. She had the kind of face that instilled a certain relief. A kind of calm. And Shelby was not impervious to it.

"Yes."

"I'm Laurie, the social worker assigned to your mother's file."

Go away, she thought, out of a terrible lifelong habit. *We don't want you here.*

"I have some questions," Laurie said, sitting in a chair across from Mom's bed. It was a gray morning outside and the weak sunlight barely survived its fight through the glass. "Can you tell me what happened?"

"I wasn't there. She'd . . ." Shelby cleared her throat and attempted to sit up straight, having realized she was bent over the edge of the bed. "She'd wandered out into the fields behind the house across the street."

"Has she done that before?"

"Apparently that was at least the third time."

"How were you unaware? Most Alzheimer's patients don't return when they wander."

"The boy across the street brought her back home."

"But didn't tell you about it?"

She nodded her head, her thumb busy on the edge of the tape.

"Are you the primary caregiver?"

Shelby just opened her mouth and let it all out. Hiring the nurse. The house full of junk. The aggression and the sundowning. The cobbled-together schedule of care. A housekeeper instead of a nurse because she'd been too stubborn to admit they needed one.

"When was the last time you had a full night's sleep?"

Shelby shook her head. It had been a year. At least.

"You know, an injury like this, it generally speeds up

the decline. If she leaves the hospital, it is likely she won't be able to go to your home."

Shelby nodded, panic clawing at her throat.

"This is my fault, isn't it?" She looked up at Laurie, the social worker, with her clipboards and her sensible hair and her answers.

"Why do you think it is?"

She explained the nightgowns she'd found.

"I didn't even question them. I was just so happy to be emptying out the house, to have Mom on a walk somewhere else and a few minutes to put things back in order and I didn't—"

"That's quite a leap, Shelby. Not many people would be able to look at two nightgowns and surmise that Evie had been wandering outside of the house. Especially when the neighbor boy kept returning her."

"I should have had a night nurse, shouldn't I?" she asked. "I kept telling people I was fine. That we were fine. But we weren't. We haven't been fine in years and I just kept pretending—"

She stopped. Swallowed back the rest of her panic.

"Your mom already lives in the past," Laurie said. "She needs you to be in the present. It's not easy making these decisions, but you have a chance to be the daughter she needs now."

"You're recommending a nursing home—"

"No. I'm not recommending anything. I'm saying you need to see things clearly and be open."

"Open to what?"

"All the possibilities."

How? she wondered. *How does one do that?*

She thought of the nurse with her smile that said so much, of Ty with his capacity for risk and forgiveness. She thought of the kids she taught and their open, willing, loving hearts.

How did one live like that? How did someone get from where she was to where they were?

Laurie patted her shoulder and vanished.

Shelby's stomach growled and she checked her watch, astonished to find that it was afternoon. The daylight outside had only grown more and more gray.

Her knees creaked as she stood and her back protested as she tried to straighten herself up from her hunched position.

She wondered, as she walked over to the door, if a nurse might loan her some scrubs to wear and if the cafeteria would take an IOU, because after Ty called her with the news about her mother, she hadn't stopped to grab her purse, so she didn't have any money and she wasn't ready to head home to get those things just yet.

In the hallway she wasn't sure which way to go and she turned left, only to stumble to a halt at the sight of Ty in a chair outside her door.

Ty surrounded by balloons and flowers. Food. A coffee thermos. A stack of clothes from her house. Her purse.

It wasn't as if something burst inside of her. There wasn't a giant explosion of everything she'd ever wanted and denied herself. She didn't suddenly understand what it meant to be open.

But inside, that tiny voice she'd silenced far too many times whispered, *This. This is how you learn. This is where it begins.*

"Hey," Ty said, looking exhausted and beautiful and silly with a yellow Mylar balloon hitting him in the head, pushed by some unseen, barely felt current of air.

"You're here." That was stupid. A stupid thing to say, but she didn't care. He was here when she'd pushed him away. He was here when he knew all the ways that she might hurt him.

"I am."

"How is Casey?"

"We're leaving in a little bit. I just wanted—" He looked down at all the stuff around him. "Oh, hell, Shelby, I just wanted to be here."

She took a deep breath. Another. Deeper. More. Carefully, she took all those things from his lap and pushed them onto the chair beside him. Taking note of the fritters for later. And then when his lap was empty, his arms open, she set herself right down inside of them. It felt awkward, because she was still awkward—she had a lot of years to unlearn all the terrible lessons of her childhood—but it was right.

His body against hers. The hard thump of his heart against hers. The scrape of his morning beard against her cheek.

It was all right. Very right.

She curled her arms around his shoulders, pressed her face against his neck, and just let herself breathe. Breathe in the calm support of him. The beautiful, willing strength of him.

And she let herself feel better. Selfish, horribly painfully selfish, but true.

What was coming was bad; she knew that. This situation with her mother was only going to get worse, but she didn't want to lock Ty out anymore.

"I'm so sorry," she whispered.

"It's okay." His wide hands rubbed over her back, in long sweeps from her neck to the top of her hips. He was petting her and she loved it.

"It's not," she told him. She leaned back and looked him in the eyes, something she so rarely had the courage to do, and told him what was in her rapidly expanding heart. "People would say you deserve better. They'd be right."

"I don't give a shit what people say." He ran his hands over her hair, gathering it in his fists at the back of her neck. It hurt a little, like he needed all of her attention. "I want you. I want to try."

His beautiful face had grown so familiar to her over the past month, and when he smiled, creating wrinkles and lines around his mouth and eyes, she had to press her fingers against them. Confirming by touch what was too beautiful for her eyes to believe.

"I love you," she whispered.

He didn't say he loved her back and that was okay; she'd hurt him, and he was being careful and he had every right not to trust her yet. Not with his heart. Not with Casey.

But they would get there. In time. They would get there.

Chapter 25

The third Saturday of every month was theirs. And theirs alone.

It started at Cora's with fritters. And then they went out to Glen Home to see Mom. Shelby, with Ty's unwavering help, had kept Evie at home after she got out of the hospital for as long as she could. There were round-the-clock nurses that Evie had grown used to, but the stairs got too difficult. Ty modified the bathroom as best he could, but the shower was still too dangerous, and Shelby knew that before something awful happened, she had to make a decision. And the decision was Glen Home.

Shelby went there every day for lunch when Mom was at her best. Shelby, Ty, and Casey came every Sunday after church, and Casey would drop by a few other times after school when he could between piano lessons and his class at the Art Barn.

It wasn't great. The only one Mom always recognized was Casey, which was such a strange but beautiful turn in the disease. There were days Shelby felt destroyed by guilt that her mother was not living the end of her life in her home as she would have wanted, but Ty just pulled her into his lap and held her until she could bear it again.

But the third Saturday of every month, after taking

Mom some fritters, they drove up to West Memphis to Tilden Rodgers Park.

Shelby pulled into the parking area across from the pavilion and turned off the car. They could see her through the windshield, sitting at one of the picnic tables, her back in the pink jacket hunched against the cold wind. Her unbound red hair blowing in the sharp January wind.

On the table in front of her there was a wrapped package.

A birthday present.

Shelby nearly rolled her eyes at the gift. If that woman thought she could buy her way back into her son's affections, she didn't know her son.

"I'll be right here," Shelby said.

Casey, still staring at his mother, nodded. "I know."

"We can leave anytime," she said. "You don't have to stay the full half hour."

"You say that every time." He flashed her a quick grin and she took a breath. The first in what felt like fifteen miles. This was the fourth monthly visit between Casey and Vanessa. Ty took him to the first one, but that had been such a disaster that Shelby and Casey had decided it would be best if she went.

Casey had asked, actually. And Shelby had quickly agreed, her heart expanding with love.

"I mean it every time."

"She doesn't, you know, say anything mean. She mostly asks about school."

"Good," was all Shelby said, but she was thinking *she'd better not or I will be a million times worse than Ty would ever dream of being.*

Casey still didn't open the car door.

"Are you stalling because you don't want to see her?" she asked. "Because you don't have to—"

"No. No. It's fine. I better go." Casey popped open the door.

She wanted to pull him back, cover him with kisses, but he only allowed that when he was sick or about to go to bed, so instead she grabbed his hand and wrapped her fingers around his. "I love you."

"Shel-by," he groaned, but he was grinning, and she grinned back at him.

"Nothing you can do about it, Case. You just have to deal. Now go."

Casey got out of the car and she watched, holding her breath again. *God*, she really had to stop doing that; she was going to pass out one of these Saturdays.

Vanessa, when she saw him, stood up, and Shelby watched the woman's face through the windshield. She could not hide her pain, her regret, or her pleasure.

Shelby pulled some papers to grade out of her bag but barely glanced at the fifth-grade identity projects. Instead she watched Casey and marveled at the effect one kid's piece of art had had on all of their lives.

When the half hour was up, she put the papers away and honked the horn.

Casey waved at her and stood at the same time Vanessa did. Vanessa usually tried to hug Casey and he always stepped back out of her way, but this time she didn't even try. Maybe she was learning.

Casey got back into the car, smelling of cold and winter and the cigarettes Vanessa chain-smoked. He put the wrapped present in the backseat.

"You okay?" Shelby asked.

Casey nodded and she drove away from the park. Casey was customarily silent and she didn't push, but when they pulled out of the city and into the dark, empty fields of the country she put her hand on his head, her thumb feathering the hair over his ear, and he leaned into the touch.

Just a little.
Just enough.

"Sean!" Ty yelled, walking out of the back door of Shelby's house, carrying on his shoulder part of the kitchen cabinets. Inside, everyone was demolishing as fast as they could in the few hours that Shelby and Casey were gone.

But not Sean.

Sean was watching the twins, bundled up in their stroller, sleeping. He had wanted to take them out of the stroller, claiming it was too cold to leave them sleeping there, but Ashley had threatened to gut him—not joking, actually gut him—if he woke up Abby and Cole.

"Someone has to watch these guys!" Sean said. He pulled the stroller closer to the lawn chair he was sitting in. He tucked and retucked the blankets higher around their sleeping faces.

"Sean," Ashley said as she came out carrying part of the kitchen counter. "They're sleeping. When they wake up, trust me, we'll know about it. And if you wake them—"

"You'll gut me." Sean stood, but he couldn't look away from them. "But God, Ashley. They're so beautiful."

Ty threw his counter on the heap of scrap and then took Ashley's stuff. Cora and Brody came out, too, all carrying loads.

Shelby had been talking about remodeling the farmhouse for three months, she'd bought some kitchen magazines and the two of them had drawn up plans, but life was just so busy and things were pretty comfortable over at his place.

But it was something she wanted. Really wanted.

And so he was going to make it happen for her.

It would take a while—he was pretty busy, between working with Brody and the part-time garage he seemed to be running from his place—but he would see this done for her.

The phone in his pocket buzzed and he fished it out.

It was a text from Shelby: *On our way. Stopped for gas.*

Everyone okay?

Quiet but good.

The band that tightened around his chest every third Saturday of the month loosened and he took a deep breath. *Come to your house, don't go to mine.*

Why?

Surprise.

He grinned and put the phone back in his pocket.

"You should have some babies of your own," Brody said, slapping his brother's shoulder as he walked by.

"Hey now." Cora dropped smashed cabinetry on the junk pile. "Don't go putting ideas in his head."

"I've already got ideas." Sean grabbed Cora as she walked by and put a kiss on her lips.

A black SUV pulled into the driveway and before it had fully come to a stop, Gwen was out of the backseat.

"Hey!" she cried. "Are the twins here?"

"Do I ever go anywhere without the twins?" Ashley, who had survived a terrible pregnancy, asked her husband, and Brody pulled her in for a hug.

"Go out tonight," he said. "You and Monica and Cora. See if you can get Shelby to go, too. I've got the twins."

Ashley broke into tears. "Don't laugh," she said, her voice muffled in Brody's chest. "It's the hormones."

"It's you, babe," he breathed, walking her backward for some privacy.

Wonder Woman Monica came around from the passenger side just as Jackson Davies stepped out of the driver's side. She had a giant sparkling diamond on her left finger that Jackson had put there over Christmas, and there were plans in the works for a summer wedding at The Big House.

Which, to be honest, was giving Ty some similar ideas.

Ty liked Jackson. A lot. He seemed a little slick at first, but the guy was seriously devoted to Monica and to his sister. He was finishing up his law degree with plans to move back to Bishop. Monica's young adult book had come out last year to great reviews and success.

"Thanks for coming, guys!" Ty said, giving Monica a hug and shaking Jackson's hand.

"Sorry we're late. Gwen had a test in her last class." Jackson pulled a tool belt and some gloves out of the back of the truck. "Where do you need me?"

Another great thing about Jackson—the guy knew how to pitch in.

"We're taking down the kitchen," he said, and Jackson was gone.

"Where's Shelby?" Monica asked.

"She's still on her way back with Casey."

They started walking back to the house and Monica stopped him with a hand on his arm. "I don't know if anyone has said this to you, or if it can be said enough, but you are the best thing that's ever happened to her."

"It's the same for me," Ty said. Every once in a while, when he woke up in the middle of the night with his brain turned on and unable to turn back off, he wondered what would have happened to him and Casey if he hadn't picked this place to live. If it hadn't been Shelby teaching that art class.

Part of him liked to think that they would have made it. Somehow. Someway he and Casey would have been okay.

But the truth was probably very different.

He owed his world to Shelby Monroe.

Two hours later everyone heard the crunch of tires over gravel and they all stopped where they were in the living room, tearing up the pink-and-blue carpet.

"That's her?" Sean asked.

"That's her."

A ripple of excitement went through the room and Ty pulled off his gloves, shaking his head. "You guys are worse than Casey."

"Go get her!" Monica said. "I want to see her face when she sees what you've done."

Ty was walking down the back steps just as Casey and Shelby got out of the car.

A new routine had started since Shelby started taking Casey to see Vanessa and Ty didn't want to make too big a deal about it in case it stopped, but this new routine was everything to him. Everything he'd ever hoped he and Casey and Shelby would have.

"Hey, Casey," Ty said, searching his son's face for any signs of distress or grief. He was usually very quiet after seeing his mother, but after a day he seemed to snap back.

"Hey, Dad," Casey said, and then he walked straight into Ty's arms. Casey curled his arms around Ty's waist and hugged him. Hard. As if making up for every hug they didn't get in the eleven long years they didn't know each other.

Ty wrapped his arms around his boy and stared, his heart in his eyes, at the woman who made his family complete.

"Is that Monica and Jackson's car?" Shelby asked, pointing to the SUV.

"I tried to stall as long as I could," Casey said, stepping away, but the imprint of that hug lingered on Ty. His body, his heart, his soul—everything was made better by that hug.

"Stall me?" Shelby asked. Her smile these days was something to behold. If there was any doubt, any question that he made Shelby happy, the answer was in that smile.

She was easy, confident, loose. She was quick to hug and laugh and tease. With him and with Casey.

And when Ty got her alone in bed, or in the truck or in the Art Barn for old time's sake, there was no hesitation. No doubts. No anger. Nothing coming between them. She was as open a woman as ever lived and he'd never in his life felt so lucky or loved.

And those times she was quiet, when she needed to be alone, he gave her that distance. Because she always let him back in.

"What's going on?" she asked.

"Come on inside and see."

Casey ran on ahead and Ty could see him through the screen door making the rounds with their friends—high-fives and quick hugs, kisses for the twins, who were awake in their parents' arms, a shy, awkward wave at Gwen.

Ty held the door open for Shelby, who walked into her old kitchen and gasped. The purse over her arm fell to the floor.

"Surprise!" Cora cried, but Shelby wasn't smiling.

"What . . ." Shelby spun in a slow circle, her face totally unreadable. "What have you done?"

This was one of those times the self-contained universe of her had Ty fooled and his stomach fell to the wood floor they'd exposed when they pulled up the old linoleum. "We're starting the renovation," he said.

Oh shit, had he read this wrong? Was this the sort of thing that she said she wanted, but in reality she didn't really, and he'd totally screwed it up? "Are you mad?"

"You all came here to do this?" Shelby asked their

friends, who were all nodding and wincing at the same time.

"And you—?" She turned to Casey, who held up his hands and pointed at Ty.

"His idea. Be mad at him."

"Mad?" she breathed and put a hand back over her mouth. "I'm not—" She shook her head and launched herself into Ty's waiting and pretty relieved arms.

"I love you," she said, over and over.

"Oh honey," he said, burying his face in her hair. "I love you, too."

"Ooookay," Sean said. "Maybe we should take this little party over to The Pour House."

"No!" Shelby stood back, wiping her eyes, her cheeks pink and wet. "No. I want . . . I want to help. I want to do this, too."

Monica handed Shelby her gloves and Sean gave his to Casey, and Brody showed her how to pull up the carpet and use the crowbar on the floorboards.

She was relentless, systematic. Every once in a while her shoulders shook and Ty didn't know if she was sobbing or laughing. Slowly their friends filed out of the room, taking Casey with them back to his house, where Ty had food and drink waiting.

And then it was just the two of them, Ty and Shelby, tearing down the past, getting ready for the future.

A hot, addictive tale of passion and scandal
takes center stage in the next installment
of Molly O'Keefe's Boys of Bishop series

INDECENT PROPOSAL

In which a driven man who refuses
to be distracted
meets his match in a beautiful bartender
who just may change his life.

Available from Bantam Books

Read on for a sneak peek

Chapter 1

"Ken Doll is back."

Ryan Kaminski didn't have to look to see who Lindsey was talking about.

Ken Doll had been Lindsey's obsession for the last three nights.

"Yeah? What's he doing?" *Talking on his phone? Texting? Ignoring the rest of the world?* She did not understand why people came to a bar to stare at their phones and ignore people. Ryan scooped ice into the martini shaker, she poured in vermouth, the high-end vodka that cost about a week's worth of tips, and slid on the top before giving it all a good shake.

"He's not on his phone. Ken Doll looks sad," Lindsey added.

That made Ryan look over her shoulder at the handsome blond man at the far corner of the bar. For three nights he'd been coming in, working on two different phones. Making calls. Sending texts—never looking up. Never acknowledging that he was actually in a room full of people.

He ordered beer—Corona in a bottle. Tipped double the bill and usually left every night without saying anything more than; "Corona" and "thank you."

Ken Doll would be totally unremarkable—there were plenty of men at The Indigo Bar spending more time on their phones than actually talking to people and wearing beautiful tailor-made suits that clung just right to their bodies while they did it.

But they were not nearly as interesting as Ken Doll.

"God," Ryan muttered. "He's just so pretty."

"I know, right?"

Blond hair with a slight curl to it. Piercing blue eyes. Like they'd been computer enhanced, that's how blue they were. In the soft smooth plane of one cheek there was a dimple, she only saw it by accident when he smiled at a woman who asked to take the bar stool to his left the other day. But the real kicker, the show stopper— was how he moved, efficient and graceful, like there was simply no time to waste, because he was A Man Who Got Things Done.

Watching him unbutton his jacket before sitting down was a mission statement. A planted flag.

Gravitas.

That's what Ken Doll had that every other man in this bar was lacking.

But tonight he didn't have his phones out. He sat there, hands pressed down flat against the mahogany bar, raindrops caught in his blond hair. He was wearing a University of Georgia Bulldogs tee shirt under which his shoulders . . . oh, that slump, it told a very sad story indeed.

Ryan poured the martini into the chilled glass, took a twist off the fresh lemon behind the bar, and put the glass on a napkin before sliding the drink over to the woman who'd ordered it and collecting the twenty the woman had left on the bar.

"I want to ease Ken Doll's pain." Lindsey watched Ken Doll out of the corner of her eye while pulling a draft for one of the guys working the couches. "Like. Really."

Lindsey was well-suited to that task. The bar's uniform, short leather shorts, the fishnets and tall boots, took on a whole new level of sexy with her. She was a twenty-one-year-old party girl from the Bronx who could take care of herself and anyone else who wanted to have a good time.

Next to her Ryan felt old, way older than thirty-two. She felt old and crotchety and like she was only days away from yelling at kids to get off her lawn. Not that she had a lawn.

Ryan should just get out of the way and let Lindsey take care of Ken Doll.

But she didn't.

Once upon another lifetime she modeled and still did when she could get the work. When she couldn't she worked at an overpriced bar inside the very swanky Empire hotel in midtown Manhattan.

She knew all kinds of pretty.

But there was something about pretty and sad that got her antenna up.

"Switch sides with me," Lindsey said, referring to the neat down-the-middle line that split her side of the bar from Lindsey's. It was a Tuesday night, slow even by their standards, but that didn't mean it would stay that way.

"Nope."

"Come on," Lindsey pouted. "You hate the guys that come in here. He's wasted on you."

"This is true." Ryan had a fervent dislike for the posing and the posturing, the manicured and manscaped version of masculinity that walked into this bar. She hated the ego and the way the men watched her body—admittedly on display—but when she caught their eyes, no one was home. Or they were constantly looking past her for someone else.

For something better.

"But he's not like the other guys that come in here," Ryan said.

This was so true other people in the bar watched him

out of the corner of their eyes, as if they knew he was different than the rest of them. Or he was familiar and they just couldn't remember why.

She didn't want to ease Ken Doll's pain, at least not in the way that Lindsey did. But she'd been serving Ken Doll for three nights and she was dying to know his story. "And he's on my side. Sorry, Linds."

She tossed a black bar towel toward a scowling Lindsey and sauntered over to Ken Doll's corner. There was a weird energy rolling off him tonight and the air in this small part of the bar was electrified.

"The usual?" she asked, waiting for him to look up at her so she could smile.

He ran a hand through his blond hair, sending water droplets into the air.

"I'll have Scotch. Neat."

"Single malt?"

Finally, he looked up at her, and the distracted but polite distance she was used to seeing in his sky-blue eyes was replaced by a sizzling, terrible grief. Or anger. She couldn't be sure. Not that it mattered, really.

Because tonight Ken Doll burned.

"Whatever," he said, his voice low and broken. "Just bring me whatever."

She poured him Lagavulin and barely had the tumbler on the bar in front of him before he grabbed it and shot it back. "Another," he said.

Two more shots later, she brought him a glass of water and a menu.

"Thank you," he said, glancing at her through impossibly long eyelashes. But he pushed the menu away.

"My name is Ryan," she said. "Apparently I'll be the woman getting you drunk tonight."

His laughter was dry, like wind through November trees, but he didn't say anything.

"And your name?" she asked. "That's usually how it

works, in case you are unfamiliar. I tell you my name, you tell me yours—"

"Harri— Harry. You can all me Harry." His voice was laced with traces of the South, pecans and sweet tea.

She held out her hand and after a moment he shook it. "Nice to meet you, Harry," she said.

There were no calluses on that hand, which wasn't all that surprising in the land of his and hers manicures. But every time she shook a man's hand she thought of her Dad's big palms, the blisters and cuts, the thick calluses—a workingman's hands.

Harry's palms were smooth and supple but his grip was sure and strong and he didn't do anything skeevy— so points to him.

"You too, Ryan."

"Everything okay?" she asked.

He blew out a long breath, laughing a little at the end, like he just couldn't believe how everything around him had turned to shit. "Have you ever done everything in your power and not have it be good enough. And not just a little bit, but have everything you are capable of be not even close to enough?"

Every damn day, she thought.

"No idea," she joked, deadpan. "Ever since I was a girl I dreamt of making overpriced martinis for men who only stare at my chest."

It took him a second, the weighty stare of his checking to see if she was being serious or not, but finally he laughed. A weary humph that made her feel just a little victorious.

"Well, it's a first for me."

"It's no fun is it?"

He shook his head, the muscles of his shoulders flexing under his shirt, like he was about to twitch out of his skin. Empathy, something she very rarely felt at work, swarmed her.

"I'm—" he trailed off, his hands on the bar curled into fists.

"Angry?" she supplied, watching his knuckles grow white.

He nodded slowly. "And sad. Mostly . . . sad."

Inside, deep inside, a penny dropped and the complicated mechanism of her desire—of her elusive and rarely seen *want*—was engaged.

Well, shit, she thought. *Maybe I will be easing his pain after all.*

Later, she brought him the chicken and waffles, because while he'd slowed down on the Lagavulin, he hadn't stopped.

"I didn't order this," he said, looking down at their signature dish, guaranteed to soak up the alcohol in his stomach while making him thirsty enough for more.

"Comes with the Scotch."

"Speaking of which." He held up his tumbler. At least, he'd switched to Scotch and water.

"It's raining out?" she asked, setting the refilled tumbler back down in front of him.

"Yeah . . . I stepped out to get some air and it's cats and dogs out there."

Cats and Dogs? She thought, swallowing her smile. *That's just adorable.*

Rain could go either way for business, and Lord knows she needed the money of a good night, but she was content at this quiet end of her bar.

"This is kind of you," he said, contemplating the food.

"Well, you seem like a nice guy."

"Really? I've barely said two words to you."

"I have a sixth sense about these things and those two words were serious and well-meaning."

"Serious and well-meaning is exactly me," he cocked his head, watching her from beneath long lashes. "Or a pet dog, I can't be sure."

She laughed, happy to see he was getting into the spirit of the banter. "I have never had a well-meaning dog in my life. Thieves and layabouts, all of them."

"I had one. As a kid. Daisey. She meant well."

Oh God, he was walking down old dead dog memory lane.

"You are just all kinds of sad tonight, aren't you?"

He spun his glass in a slow circle. "I guess so."

"You know," she said, "where I grew up there was this bar called The Sunset right down the street. A real dive bar. Guys went in after their shifts on Friday and didn't come out until Sunday afternoon. Well, they got this new daytime bartender. A real soft touch. She fell for every hard-luck story that sat down in the corner. And then word got out that Ben Polecka came in there crying after his wife left and the bartender gave him free beers all afternoon. Soon, everyone was going in there pretending to cry to get free beer. And my sister, always a bit of an entrepreneur, decides she and I should go stand outside the bar and charge guys five dollars to kick them in the balls. You know, as a kind of guarantee of real tears."

He laughed, which of course had been the idea, but it still came as a bit of a surprise.

"How much money did you make?"

"Five bucks," she shrugged. "We were out there for like three hours and finally Bruce Dinkle took pity on us."

"That was his real name?"

"Yep."

"And Bruce Dinkle paid you to kick him in the balls?"

"He did. We bought some ice cream, and it felt like we were on top of the world."

His laughter faded and then the smile vanished and the weight of the world was rolled back up on his shoulders.

"Okay," she leaned against the bar and crossed her arms over her chest, well aware that her breasts nearly spilled from the vest she wore, but Harry's eye didn't wander. They stayed glued to hers as if he didn't even see the body beneath her chin. "You sad sack. Tell me. Who is your best not good enough for? A wife?"

"No wife."

"Girlfriend?"

He shook his head and she would be lying if she didn't say she was relieved.

"A boss?"

"I've never had a boss."

No boss? What planet was this guy from?

"Then who, my friend, is making you feel this way?"

"Why?" He smiled at her, looser than he'd been, but not yet totally unwound. The guy could hold his booze, she'd give him that. "You going to give them a talking to?"

"I just might."

"What would you say?"

"I would probably say, listen—" she paused, waiting for him to fill in the blank.

He shook his head, that blond hair gleaming red and then blue under the lights. "I'm afraid it's . . . complicated."

Gary, her manager, across the bar glanced over, and Ryan reached for some unprepped garnishes under the bar and made a good show of stripping mint leaves off the stem for their mojitos. "Give me the gist. You don't have to spill state secrets, but you might feel better getting some of this off your chest."

"You an expert on that, too?"

"I'm a bartender, Harry. I am an expert on lots of things." She chucked the mint stem into the trash under the bar. "Lay your burdens down, my friend."

"It's my sister. She's in trouble."

"Ah, oddly enough, this is a subject in which I have plenty of experience."

"You have a sister who gets in trouble?"

"I *am* the sister who gets in trouble." Something buzzed up the back of her neck. A warning to shut her mouth and walk on, perhaps send Lindsey over. But she ignored it, despite having gotten so much better at heeding those internal warnings. She grabbed more mint just so she'd have something to do with her hands.

"So, is she in big trouble or little trouble? Like if one is dating a jerk and ten is living on the streets, where does she fall?"

"She isn't even on that spectrum." Something in his voice made her realize the jokes were soon to be offensive. That there was no part of this he was going to find funny. And funny was a huge part of her armor. And without her armor she was just vulnerable and sympathetic—two things that had gotten her in more than her fair share of trouble.

Leave, she thought, *switch sides with Lindsey. Forget about Sad Ken Doll.*

But that was impossible. His anger and grief were magnetic.

She put down the mint.

"I'm so sorry, Harry," she told him sincerely.

"It's fine." His smile revealed the dimple, and for a moment she was distracted enough not to realize he was lying. But she had been a bartender for over a decade and she could smell a lie a mile away. And whatever the situation was with his sister—it was far from fine.

"That's what you've been working on for the last few days. With the phones? Trying to help your sister?"

"I couldn't stare at the walls of my room anymore. All day, every day trying—"

He sighed, pushed away the plate with the half-eaten chicken on it. For a moment Ryan thought he was going to walk out, he was coiled, poised to just vanish.

And that would be for the best, she thought. For her. Maybe for him. Because the last thing he probably needed was a sister in trouble and a hangover in the morning. And the last thing she needed was this compassion, this empathy and curiosity, the rusted guts of her desire—making her decisions for her.

But then he relaxed back into his chair. Back into the moment with her.

She exhaled the breath she hadn't totally realized she'd been holding.

"Not that it has done much good. I don't know if I'm going to be able to help her."

There was an invisible barrier down the middle of the bar. This one and every other upscale bar in the five boroughs. The barrier was well-documented in The Indigo Bar employee handbook, but also in her own rule book; no fraternizing with the drinkers. A lesson she'd learned twice the hard way.

But she shoved her fist right through that barrier and put her hand over his. To her surprise he grabbed her fingers, held them tight in his like a lifeline he was terribly in need of.

"She's . . . she's my baby sister. And she hasn't needed anything from me in so long, and now . . . now that she does, now that she really needs me, I might not be able to help her. It's killing me."

Everything, the empathy and the desire and the shock of his touch, twisted and turned inside of her, making her ache. Making her wish there wasn't a bar between them, that she could wrap her arms around him properly.

She squeezed his hand instead. "Do you have any family?" she asked. "Someone else who can help you?"

"I am heading home tomorrow morning to talk to them." His tone indicated that this was a bad, bad thing.

"They won't be able to help?"

"Help or hurt, it could go either way."

She stood there, silently bearing witness to his grief. Letting him grip her hand so hard the knuckles rubbed up against each other.

"It's so crazy and my mother . . . Mother is not going to handle this well. She's never approved of my sister and this is going to put her right over the edge." He shot her a wry look and then sighed. "The one bright spot is, I think I know a guy who can help."

"That's good," she said.

"Well, there is a decent chance that he will laugh in my face and tell me to go fuck myself. And then . . ." he hung his head, wiping his hand across his face. "Oh God, then I have no idea what I'm going to do."

Screw the barrier. Screw her rule book. Screw the rest of the bar, she lifted her hand from his grip and touched his cheek, the perfect bone structure of his jaw. The fine scruff of his beard felt good against her palm.

The man needed some sympathy. Some human connection. He'd been wrestling with what seemed like a nightmare for the last three days. And she . . . maybe she, who lived behind a solid glass wall of rules created by shitty past experience, could use a little human connection, too.

"He won't," she said. "You'll convince him."

He turned his face and whispered, "How do you know that?" into her hand.

The sensation of his breath between her fingers sizzled up her arm, across her chest, settling in her belly, where it smoldered and burned.

"Because I'm a little sister, too. And my big brother

would tear down the world to help me. That's what big brothers do."

She smiled into his bloodshot blue eyes when he opened them.

The air crackled around them, the power of all the desperate grief and anger he was throwing off turned to something else entirely.

She felt the touch of his gaze across her face. Her lips and eyes, the cheekbones that had earned her quite a bit of money. Her hair pulled back in a high ponytail and falling over her shoulders like a luxurious cape.

What he saw wasn't really her. It was a quirk of genetics, a lucky break in the womb. To have her mother's nose and her father's eyes. Her grandmother's bone structure and her grandfather's outrageous thick shiny hair.

It was just what she looked like. The tools she used to make a living.

And it had taken her years of destroying nearly every relationship that ever meant anything to realize that.

"You're the most beautiful woman I've ever seen."

She pulled her hands free of his. The moment of intense connection between them was fading to something slightly more manageable. Attraction and appeal. A rare camaraderie, but at least she wasn't ready to crawl over the bar into his lap.

"That's the Scotch talking."

"Give me some credit. It's not just your looks, Ryan. You're lovely." For no good reason, that made her flustered, made her feel stupid for reaching across the barrier.

The rules were in place for a reason after all.

"Ryan!" Lindsey said. "A little help?"

Ryan turned to see Lindsey inundated with gray-suited Wall Street types so she gave Harry a quick smile over her shoulder and headed over to help Lindsey.

"Getting a little cozy over there, aren't you?" Lindsey asked, her eyes twinkling. She was a good sport, Lindsey. As long as someone had the chance to get lucky she was happy.

"He's a nice guy."

"They always are. But listen," she jerked his chin across the bar where their manager was talking to a few of the regulars in the corner. "Gary's watching you, so just be careful. He fired Will last month for going home with that crazy bitch from Sak's."

As if he heard, Gary looked over. Gary was a nice enough guy, but the rules were pretty ironclad and he could lose his job for ignoring them.

The rush at the bar lasted a good hour and finally around ten p.m. slowed down to a trickle. Lindsey sent out another martini, a watermelon margarita, and three more Coronas and checked her watch. "It's cutting time," she said.

"You've been here since three," Ryan said, because the first one in was usually the first one to go home unless they were working a double. She set dirty glassware under the bar in the gray bins and then handed them to Sam, who was heading back to the kitchen.

"Grab me some lemons, would you? And more mint and more thyme. Thanks."

Sam, a notorious flirt, winked at her, taking the bins with him.

"Yeah, but I don't have a hot guy at the end of the bar waiting for me," Lindsey said.

Ryan looked over her shoulder where Harry sat, looking at his phone, nursing a Corona, the chicken and waffles forgotten at his elbow.

"I don't—"

"Ugh, denial is so boring," Lindsey said, grabbing two more pint glasses and starting the intricate pour and wait system for Guinness. "Get into my back pocket."

Ryan reached into the tight pocket of Lindsey's shorts, pulled out two sticks of gum, a twenty-dollar bill, and a condom.

"Go," Lindsey said. "Stock my garnishes and then take Sad Ken Doll someplace and cheer him up."

It had been a long time since Ryan had gone home with a guy. Picking up at a bar was for other women, younger women. Women who hadn't been burned quite as effectively as she had.

There was also the small matter of losing her job if management found out.

But like every job, there were ways around management, if a woman wanted it bad enough.

She glanced back at Harry and caught him staring at her.

His eyes flared and the bar fell away again, the whole world disappeared. He had some kind of magical power when he really looked at her, a way of making her feel like the only woman on the planet. And hundreds of lesser men had tried and never even came close to doing that. Of engaging the rusted and old machine of her desire.

This man did it in a look.

A sudden breathlessness seized her, and the fifteen minutes she had left on her shift was too much. The time it would take her to get up to his room was too much. The fact that he—serious and well-meaning— might not take her up on what she was going to offer, was a reality she had no interest in.

She wanted him, his scruffy face, the burning anger in his eyes, the beautiful symmetry of his body, the delicious humanity of his grief.

Without a second thought she slipped the condom in her pocket.

"Thanks Linds," she said.

"No problem." She wiggled her butt while Ryan tucked the twenty back in her pocket.

An asshole at the bar whistled.

"Oh, you wish, buddy," Lindsey said.

"Hey," the guy said, leaning across the bar toward Ryan. "You look really familiar to me."

"Because you were in here last week."

"No . . . my friend," he jerked his thumb over his shoulder, vaguely referencing one of the other guys in suits with manicured hands behind him. "He says you were the Lips Girl like fifteen years ago. Is that true? Can you do the thing? The slogan—"

"Your friend is wrong," she lied and dismissed the guy by turning her back on him. There were bigger things on her horizon than trying to put a shine on ancient history.

Ryan walked over to Harry and picked up his plate of half-eaten dinner.

"No wife?" she asked. "No girlfriend? No woman waiting at home for you? Don't bother lying, I'll be able to tell."

He shook his head.

"Are you gay?"

That made him smile and again she felt that little spike of pleasure. Of a job well done. "I'm not gay and no one is waiting for me, Ryan."

"Are you staying at the hotel?" she asked.

His burning blue eyes met hers, and there was no confusion, he knew what she was asking.

"I am."

"I'm getting off in about fifteen minutes."

Harry stood, a new urgency in his movement. He tossed several bills on the bar, but she pushed them back at him.

"It's on me," she said. "The Sister in Trouble special."

By the shocked and blank look on his face it was obvious no one ever joked with him and she wondered if he had any friends. Why a man like him in what seemed to be the worst three days of his life showed up alone at her bar.

But when he did laugh it was a good one. Full-throated and deep, the kind of laugh that made other people smile. But not Manager Gary, who walked by giving Ryan a serious warning glare.

She took Harry's plate and stepped away.

"Room 534," he said.

She nodded once, the number tucked away.

"Ryan?" He said.

"Yes?"

"Hurry."